MURDER
OF A
MOVIE STAR

A POSIE PARKER MYSTERY #5

L. B. HATHAWAY

WHITEHAVEN

WHITEHAVEN MAN PRESS

First published in Great Britain in 2017
by Whitehaven Man Press

A CIP catalogue record for this book is available
from the British Library.

ISBN (e-book:) 978-0-9955694-0-9
ISBN (paperback:) 978-0-9955694-1-6

For Heidi

Also by L.B. Hathaway

The Posie Parker Mystery Series

… and more to come.

Prologue

The girl was lying in the tiny, dim dressing room, flopped over her chair.

She was face-down, dangling, a blonde and plaited wig covering her whole head. Her arms hung, flailing. She looked like she had drowned and been pulled from the sea.

The movie star had obviously been dead for some time.

'Have a good look around, Posie, but don't touch anything,' said Chief Inspector Lovelace to Posie Parker, Private Detective, in a muted whisper. They stood on the edge of the doorway to the room.

'Tell me what you think. I'd never met Miss Hanro, but you met her only yesterday. I'll keep this pack of bloodhounds at bay.'

He indicated with a flick of the thumb behind him to where the Scotland Yard Forensics team, headed up by Mr Maguire, were getting ready to do their thing.

It was very early in the morning, not yet eight o'clock, but it was boiling hot already.

Dr Poots, the Police Pathologist, was standing outside in the glass corridor, looking considerably put out. Posie tried to avoid his gaze but she caught the furious scowl on his square doglike face and he brandished his grim black bag at her like a threat.

Posie forced herself to concentrate.

Something was wrong here. Horribly so. Personally, she felt dreadful: she had been entrusted with protecting this girl's life, and she had failed. But that wasn't what was wrong: it was more than that.

She had a strong sense of the presence of evil in the small dressing room. Posie could almost sniff at it, along with the horrible and unglamorous stink of death.

'Go on, she's not exactly going to bite, is she? Step in further.'

Posie walked further into the room. It looked exactly the same as yesterday when she had sat here chatting away to the movie star Silvia Hanro, when her friend Dolly, Lady Cardigeon, had sat drinking champagne and smoking her usual purple cocktail cigarettes. There was the same mess of cosmetics on the desk; the same pitcher of water on the low nest of tables; the same spray of red orchids in a vase, giving off their sickly-sweet smell. Her eyes took in the small ice-box in the corner of the room, and Posie shuddered and quickly looked away.

Silvia Hanro was wearing the same emerald-green kimono Posie had seen her in yesterday out on the lawn. A plain glass was turned over near the girl's outstretched hand, but it was impossible to say if anything had been in it, as the intense heat in the room had dried up anything there might have been. There were certainly no stains visible on the small, bright carpet.

'No obvious cause of death, sir,' said Posie, circling the body. 'No stab marks, or shot wounds visible from here. But of course, I'm not allowed to turn her over, am I?'

The Chief Inspector shook his head.

'Something feels odd here, though,' he said, scowling.

'It does, sir. I don't like it.'

And then Posie saw it. A gold thick band wrapped around the movie star's left-hand ring finger. But it wasn't a ring made of precious gold. It was made of tin foil.

'Oh!' she exclaimed.

And then Posie saw something else. Just beneath the kimono. A flash of colour. 'Hold your horses!' she gasped.

'This is worse than we thought.'

* * * *

24 HOURS EARLIER

PART ONE

(Wednesday 25th July, 1923)

One

'What on earth is *that* horrible thing?'

Lady Cardigeon, or, as she would always be known to Posie Parker, plain old Dolly Price, had just picked up a great grey scraggle of wool, out of which two very large knitting needles protruded at funny angles.

'It's a jumper, you noddle,' said Posie Parker sourly, wiping the sweat from her brow.

It was very hot and stuffy up in the Grape Street Bureau, Posie's Detective Agency in Bloomsbury, London. The clock was striking one o'clock, and Posie was hungry for lunch. To make matters worse, it was the hottest summer on record, and every sticky minute felt like an eternity.

'I'm trying to knit it for Alaric's birthday in two weeks' time. I wanted to replace his favourite jumper which I ruined last New Year. The trouble is, I'm not having much luck with the pattern. I keep getting lost. I never was much good at knitting, if truth be told.'

'You don't say!' Dolly said glibly, bending her shorn bleached-white head over the mess of wool. She started to unpick quite a bit, her slight, small hands moving furiously, her bare feet propped up on a wheel of a great double Silver Cross pram.

'I'd stick to solving mysteries if I were you, lovey. Much

easier. Besides, it's the middle of July! Why on earth are you makin' him such a heavy knitted monstrosity? Shall we get a cab and nip over to Harrods and buy somethin' suitable instead? Some little thing he can actually *wear*, I mean? Or did you want him to die of heatstroke?'

Dolly threw a quick, inquisitive glance over at her friend.

'What's happenin' with you two, anyhow? Still gettin' married?'

Posie scowled and stared momentarily at the large pink stone which glittered on her left-hand ring finger as if to check it was still there. In truth she didn't know the answer to Dolly's unwelcome question and it gnawed at her. She was in a fragile mood and the day had started badly.

Posie had woken from a bad dream in which Alaric had been trying to break some bad news to her, and the sense of foreboding which the dream had carried had been hard to shake off. She kept trying to forget the image of Alaric, leaning over her, trying to wake her, then disappearing in the haze of the dream. But she couldn't forget his ominous words:

'*Look, darling, there's something I need to tell you. Quite urgently.*'

'*Bad news? It must be. What is it?*'

Having woken up, Posie had then dressed in a particularly vibrant shade of yellow, as if to cheer herself up, and had regretted it ever since. In fact, the colour was giving her a headache. To make matters worse, on her way into work she had heard the cheery trills of the still-popular song, 'The Wedding Glide', blaring out of a small café and this had soured her mood even more.

Dolly carried on, less certainly now:

'I know we haven't seen each other in an age, but I thought you were goin' to be havin' a quick wedding earlier this year, but you haven't mentioned it lately. All okay, is it, lovey?'

Posie winced. 'Everything's *fine*. But it's rather difficult to get married when one of you is never in the country. Alaric's been in Morocco for the last two months, he's coming back for his birthday. I can't really say anything else on the subject, so please don't push me. You're right: let's nip out, shall we?'

Secretly she was rather relieved that time had been called on what had turned out to be rather a frustrating project and she grabbed at her vivid yellow cloche hat and her beloved old carpet bag, which didn't match, but who gave a hang?

Dolly and Posie had just started to manoeuvre the giant black pram towards the stairway to carry it downstairs when right at that very moment the twins, the Honourable Ladies Bunny and Trixie Cardigeon, decided to wake up and simultaneously exercise their one-year-old vocal chords. To great effect.

'Oh, lawks!' Dolly said, staring at the twins wide-eyed. 'They've only just been fed. What little horrors! What on earth do I do now?'

'No idea,' Posie said unhelpfully. 'Should I pick one of them up? Would that help?'

Dolly shrugged her tiny shoulders unenthusiastically and looked like she might burst into tears herself.

'My gosh! Why the blazes did you send those paid nannies away, Dolly? Where are they now? Killing time over in Covent Garden, shopping?'

'I don't like them,' Dolly harrumphed, struggling with the unwieldy pram. 'They're new, and I know they snoop. Rufus says they're the best of the best, but I feel like I'm bein' spied upon. This weighs a ton! How are we goin' to manage?'

'Exactly. We could be doing with those women now. We only got it up here with their help. It's a four-woman job. I never saw arms like theirs before! More navvy than nanny, if you ask me. Oh, golly!'

9

Dolly's little daughters were getting louder and louder by the second and were by now very red in the face. Posie thought disloyally that they were most unattractive-looking, even though they were dressed in the height of current baby fashion. In fact, although she forbore to mention it to Dolly, at that very moment they looked a good deal like their grandfather, the Earl of Cardigeon, whose resemblance to an angry toad was most striking.

Just then, and as luck would have it, Len Irving, Posie's partner in the Detective Agency at Grape Street, came up the stairs carrying a huge industrial metal fan. He took one look at the two women and came bounding up.

'What's wrong with the two of you?' he said, rolling his eyes heavenwards, grabbing the pram and wheeling it backwards and forwards on the tiny blue-carpeted landing. The babies immediately stopped crying.

'They want *movement*. Works with our Alfred every night. Sometimes I put him in the pram and wheel him up and down the streets of Leytonstone to get him to sleep.'

'You don't feel like lookin' after them for me, do you?' implored Dolly, her painted eyes widening in desperation. Even Len could see that tears were not far off.

'Where are you two off to, then?' said Len placidly, raising an eyebrow. 'And for how long?'

'We'll be quick,' said Posie certainly. 'One hour, maximum.'

It was true: they could make Knightsbridge and back in an hour. Just.

'Can you manage in the office with the babies? Without Prudence, I mean?'

Prudence Smythe, their first-class secretary, was away on her annual summer holidays in Ramsgate with her mother for two weeks, and they had hired a temporary secretary called Tess who seemed barely able to take the very few telephone calls which came through. Posie had already given up on the girl.

"Course I can manage!' Len was a shadower, and known for being excellent at his job: he worked for several lawyers, trailing errant husbands, and occasionally wives, trying to get hold of photographic evidence of extra-marital hanky-panky in order to bring divorce proceedings. It was grubby work, but lucrative.

Len laughed aloud. 'Your timing's perfect: I'm enjoying all of my clients being out of town in this heat. Come next week, I'm going to be rushed off my feet. Don't know how I'll cope, actually.'

Posie shuffled Dolly quickly off down the stairs, giving Len a backwards look laden with meaning.

'Thank you. It's very important,' she assured him.

'It always is!' replied Len ruefully.

* * * *

As they emerged out onto Grape Street both Posie and Dolly gasped at the heat.

The pavement was almost melting beneath their feet and the dry grit from the London plane trees danced in the hot air. Despite the shade of the little street, no-one was about. Not even for a cigarette. It was just too hot. The whole month of July had been swelteringly hot, and filled with sudden thunderstorms, the like of which no-one had ever seen before.

The childish euphoria they had felt at running away from Len and the babies evaporated instantly in the heat. Even the man selling sherbert and water from a small cart on the corner had packed up for the day. Even the beggars had found somewhere cooler to sit.

'Golly. It's yonks since we had a summer like this one,' muttered Posie, wiping the sweat from her brow with the end of her bright lemon-coloured linen jacket sleeve. Most of her clothes these days were made by the House of Harlow, the best designers in town, and today was no exception. The clothes were ridiculously expensive but they normally felt wonderful. Today, however, she felt like an over-large, over-dressed canary. Posie took a small bottle of Parma Violet perfume from her bag and squirted herself with it liberally.

'Last time it was this hot I think I was still in Norfolk. Living with my father. So that would make it...'

'Nineteen fifteen!' chipped in Dolly triumphantly. They had reached the junction with Shaftesbury Avenue and were waiting on the corner for a motor taxi, scanning the main road hopefully. But the street was empty, and there was only one rag-and-bone man riding listlessly up and down on his cart, led by a thirsty-looking horse. They started to walk up the empty street in the direction of Oxford Street.

'How come you remember the year so clearly, Dolly?'

Dolly's face brightened. 'Can't forget it, lovey. It was the year I went out to nurse in the war, in France. And lawks, were we fryin' up here in town beforehand. It was hot right up to September. We used to go and sit and watch the movies at the cinema, on an endless loop, just to stay cool. I must have seen Mark Paris in the same film at least twenty times. Not that I'm complainin' of course: the man was the nearest thing to God that the cinema had. The best of the best.'

Dolly lit a purple cocktail cigarette and inhaled deeply. 'Just like this, it was. But worse, as there were Zeppelin raids goin' on. Why, did you know, I was nearly killed when a Zeppelin landed on Red Lion Square, at the Dolphin pub, not far from here, just a few days before I left town...'

'No, I don't think I knew that. My gosh, that must have been awful for you.'

Dolly flicked the ash from her cigarette absent-mindedly,

staying silent, lost in her memories. She resumed quietly:

'All of us nurses who had been called up were glad to get the summons to Folkestone and get right out of London. So we all enjoyed the sea breeze for a day or two before boarding the boat out. I'll never forget the thousands of men lined up all along the Road of Remembrance, gettin' sunburn as they waited for a passage. Poor devils. Blimey! A lifetime ago! Those were the days…'

Posie raised an eyebrow and stole a sideways glance at her friend. She had never heard Dolly speak about her time in the Great War with anything other than sadness and horror; certainly not as a time to hark back to.

Posie was a bit worried about Dolly: she hadn't seemed quite her colourful self since the arrival of the twins the year before. She often seemed unhappy. Dazed. As if all the light had gone out of her.

Come to think of it, Posie realised that Dolly looked like she was wasting away, which was rotten news, as she had been tiny – just a slip of a thing – to begin with. Her clothes were positively hanging off her. But Posie forced herself to stay quiet, biding her time, waiting for the right moment to speak.

Dolly had turned up on Posie's office doorstep in the morning, unannounced, a great gaggle of babies and nannies in tow. And while Posie had been delighted to see her friend – this *was* the quiet summer season after all, when sensible people got the blazes out of town – the random visit was entirely out of character nowadays. In fact, Posie hadn't seen her friend in weeks and weeks: Dolly's town diary was usually chock-a-block with the important social engagements which went hand-in-glove with the gargantuan task of being Lady Cardigeon.

Dolly came to a sudden stop.

'This is hopeless. Not a cab in sight. And we can't very well go and catch the bus. The Number 10 will take *forever* to get us to Knightsbridge, let alone there and back in an hour. Shall we turn tail and go and rescue Len? *Not* that I want to, believe me. There are so many things I'd love to do with you, believe me. I bet you haven't even seen Betty Balfour's latest film, *Love, Life and Laughter*, have you?'

Posie shook her head.

'All of London are talkin' about it and it's jolly good. A scream, in fact. I'd happily see it again. Another time, perhaps...'

'Hang on a minute, don't let's give up. We still have nearly a whole precious hour to ourselves. Let's do something else, something *nice*.'

But before she could suggest something else to do, Posie got that familiar creeping pin-prickly sensation which usually meant that someone was behind her, watching her.

Unnerved, she turned quickly, and, sure enough, she saw that the two huge nannies employed by her old friend Rufus, Lord Cardigeon, were sitting side by side, squeezed tightly together on a small green wooden bench on the dusty street outside Caspari's, the famous Italian ice cream parlour.

They were both staring at Dolly with sneering faces, obviously mid-gossip about her. Each was firmly gripping a large pink ice cream cone as if for dear life, their faces disapproving beneath their smart unfashionable burgundy hats. Like naughty children who had been caught out, both big women coloured bright red under Posie's unwavering gaze.

Fortunately Dolly hadn't noticed the two women sitting behind her, and was ferreting about inside a huge and very expensive-looking lilac handbag for a lipstick. It would be a shockingly dark mauve, Posie knew. All of Dolly's clothes were dark purple today and she was never anything less than immaculately colour-coordinated.

Wretched nannies, Posie thought to herself. *Are they making poor Dolly's life miserable?*

Is that the problem?

She felt like sticking her tongue out at them and have done with it. So what if Dolly was unconventional and a bit madcap? They must be being paid a fortune by Rufus and could surely set aside their conventional tastes for a bit…

'I say,' Posie said, steering Dolly away from the direction of the ice cream parlour and hurrying her towards Soho. 'Let's have lunch.'

'Oh, lovey. I don't know. I'm not hungry; it's just so blimmin' hot.'

'Fishcakes,' Posie said decisively. 'Is there anything better in the world than fishcakes? Kettner's does the best in town, on Romilly Street. It's only a ten minute-walk from here at most. My treat.'

Dolly's elfin face cracked into a wide grin, won around at last. 'Oh, go on then. If you insist.'

And Dolly took Posie's arm and they swung off together jauntily, a bit like when they had first met; almost as if they didn't have a care in the world. But on the short walk through the tarry-melty smells of the Soho streets Posie felt that something still wasn't quite right. Even though the nannies had been left far behind.

It was a niggling feeling. It was strange, but she still couldn't shake off the feeling that someone was watching them. Or perhaps *following* them. Posie turned around several times, eventually annoying Dolly.

'What is it?'

'I swear to goodness that we're being followed. Twice now I've turned around and a lad with dark hair, just a wee slip of a thing really, has darted into an alleyway or doorway to avoid being seen by me. It's hard to follow someone in a heatwave without being seen; there are none of the usual crowds or stalls or tourists around to hide among. He's quite good, actually. Looks like he has the makings of a professional. A stringer, they call them, in the trade.'

Dolly rolled her elaborately-painted eyes heavenwards.

She spun around somewhat theatrically and scanned the unusually empty street. Kettner's was straight up ahead of them.

'You're obsessed, Posie. I know it's a quiet patch for you just now but you don't need to invent things. Now we've got Oliver Twist hot on our heels. And why would a poor wee mite want to follow *us*, might I ask?'

'There he is again!' exclaimed Posie half under her breath, moving around quickly and whisking off her summer hat to get a better view.

A horrible thought entered her mind.

'I say, does Rufus have any enemies at the moment? Is there any likelihood of you being kidnapped? Tell me, is he concerned about such a thing?'

Dolly was just making some disparaging remark about Posie being utterly, utterly paranoid when a flash of inspiration hit Posie. *The nannies! No wonder they were such great hulking beasts. Rufus must have employed them specially to protect his wife and daughters.*

Posie's brain was working overtime: perhaps the nannies weren't nannies at all, but hired bodyguards?

Perhaps they weren't even women.

After all, those voluminous burgundy capes and dresses could hide pretty much anything. And like complete idiots Posie and Dolly had left them behind.

But why on earth hadn't Rufus kept her up to date? Posie felt an uncharacteristic stab of anger towards her old pal: he knew that Posie could handle danger much better than most people, but it was far better to be forewarned about such things.

But before she could make much sense of the jumbled muddle of her thoughts, the dark-haired boy Posie had thought was following them, the stringer, had run on ahead of them into Romilly Street, making some sort of elaborate hand signal to some unseen person or persons.

'Up here, guvnor!' the lad shouted out in a hoarse voice. 'They're over here!'

Suddenly a motor engine was heard. Posie stopped in her tracks on the pavement. Her blood froze and she grabbed at Dolly's arm.

'What the blazes?'

Out of nowhere a sleek dark green Ford motor car with a gold crest emblazoned on the side drew up quietly alongside them and then cut the motor. It coasted along a bit and then parked a couple of feet away, up ahead of them. The stringer ran to the green car without a backwards glance at Posie or Dolly and jumped into the front seat.

Even Dolly was looking a bit worried by now.

Both women stared at the car in total silence. The silhouette of a hatless black-haired man sitting waiting inside the car was visible through the back window. The man didn't get out of the car though. It was most odd.

'Who is that man, Dolly?' hissed Posie. 'Have you seen him before?'

Dolly just shook her head miserably and Posie's heart pounded with dread, but she felt a sickening sort of inevitability about the whole thing, too.

So this was it, then. Not fishcakes for lunch, just a good old kidnapping instead.

They stood, like idiots, rooted to the spot, and before Posie had had a chance to decide what to do, there was a sudden loud CLICK as the car door opened and the man's face in profile was seen for a split-second as he moved to get out, and there was a sudden white blur.

* * * *

Two

Posie tried to put her arm out to protect her friend and instinctively made as if to cover her, but she almost collapsed with shock when Dolly pushed her firmly aside and went bounding up to the car.

'Lovey! What you doin' here?'

The white-clad man was out of the car and had stretched out his arms to Dolly. As he gave Dolly an over-the-top kiss it seemed to Posie that there was something quite familiar about him. And then the man turned to Posie and she saw him fully for the first time.

'Oh! My!' she muttered under her breath.

Decidedly, he was gorgeous. Jaw-droppingly gorgeous.

He was tall and muscular, late thirties, very dark. He could have been Italian, perhaps. Spanish, even. He was quite possibly the most handsome man Posie had ever clapped eyes on, and he seemed to glisten in the heat like an apparition, glossy all over.

In an instant Posie took in his perfect pearly cream teeth; his thickly Brylcreemed black hair, cresting like thick waves over his head; his white tennis clothes. An immaculate white linen jumper was knotted in front and thrown over his shoulders, mock-casually. He didn't seem bothered by the heat at all, not like Posie, who was sweating profusely.

Was he even real?

'Forgive the intrusion, Miss Parker.'

She felt herself drawn towards the man, stepping almost involuntarily forwards, fascinated, thankful for her cloud of perfume. The man didn't introduce himself. As if Posie should know him. He just raised a perfectly-coiffed black eyebrow, as if he found the whole meeting very funny.

'We called at your office but you were out; you'd just left. So my wee boy found you and followed you – he's good at that – and kept me abreast of your whereabouts. I was sent to collect you, Miss Parker. I've come on behalf of someone who believes themselves to be in danger. You'll be paid well. But I can't speak out here in the open. You'll just have to come with me in the car, now. It's very hush-hush: I was under strict instructions not even to telephone you, in case someone overheard. I had to come in person.'

His voice when he spoke was fine and deep. And was that a Scottish burr just beneath the smoothed-over English surface?

'Step this way, please.'

'Oh?'

And then reality kicked in.

Posie didn't trust this man: just what on earth was going on with his over-the-top dramatic entrance and the stringer on their tail?

How on earth did Dolly know him, *if* she knew him? Dolly was simply wonderful, but Posie felt that given her current state of mind she might not be the best judge of a person's character. Sure as bread was bread this man was a charmer through and through, and Posie had had enough of charmers to last her a lifetime. Len Irving, her business partner, sweet and useful though he was upon occasion, was one such charmer.

This might all just be a delaying tactic, a ruse, to get at Dolly. They had once both been kidnapped, and it hadn't ended well. Posie stared at the delicious-looking man through narrowed eyes, feeling the absence of the huge nannies keenly. She crossed her arms defensively.

'If you think you're here to steal off with Lady Cardigeon and put a price on her head you can think again. Besides, I've got a loaded gun in my pocket.'

The man started to laugh as if Posie had made a very good joke.

'Och! I didn't even know wee Dolly here was going to be with you, did I? It's *you* I've been sent for, Miss Parker. All strictly above board.'

'And who exactly are you? You haven't bothered to tell me.'

'Oh, Posie.' Dolly sighed, fanning herself with her hat. 'This isn't a kidnapper. Stop being so cross today, will you? This is Robbie Fontaine, the famous actor! Surely you recognise him? Don't you *ever* go to the movies?'

Posie stayed silent. Dolly was alight with excitement.

'I met Robbie at an actors' Charity Gala at the Savoy Hotel a few months ago, together with Miss Hanro. Robbie is Sunstar Films' most famous movie star. Well, together with Silvia Hanro, that is – you do know *her*, don't you? – she's his girlfriend, not to mention the most beautiful girl in the world. They're British cinema's golden couple; have been since the end of the war. Everyone knows *that*!'

Posie wanted to die with embarrassment. She felt her face flushing red, blazing in the heat. 'Oh. Oh, I see. Forgive my rudeness.'

In truth the name meant nothing to her; there seemed no end of movie stars these days, staring out of magazines and billboards in a glossy blur. So many that it didn't seem worth bothering about, somehow. But Mr Fontaine's face *was* familiar. And she *had* heard of Silvia Hanro, but not for a while now. Hadn't she retired?

Dolly was right; Posie didn't go to the movies. She had been once, with Dolly. That had been yonks ago, and had proved decidedly unmemorable. Posie always seemed to have better things to do than sit in the pitch-dark, in a cinema, watching made-up stories. There was always so much to do outside, in the real world.

The glamorous world of theatre and film was Dolly's world, not Posie's, although Posie *had* actually met a movie star once before, Amory Laine, in the course of her work.

Dolly had worked for a while as a Wardrobe Mistress in a theatre in London's West End and thoroughly enjoyed it, but her real passion now was film, and she bought as many of the cinema magazines as she could lay her hands on. Her newly-acquired aristocratic title and status as Lady Cardigeon, not to mention the riches she had access to, had lent her the added bonus of being able to patronise and support various theatrical and film projects and hers was becoming a famously generous hand when it came to sponsorship. It didn't surprise Posie in the least to hear she had been to a Charity Gala for actors.

'Lady Cardigeon is quite correct: I'm afraid I don't see many movies, Mr Fontaine.'

The actor came right up close to Posie and took her arm in his, giving her a glimmery sort of smile. 'Well, then. You're missing out on something *very* special, I can assure you. Now, shall we go?'

She could smell his aftershave, a strong citrus wave which invaded her personal space like an invisible third person.

Posie shook her arm free as best she could, cross at his familiar manner. Up very close she thought Robbie Fontaine looked decidedly strange: he was a very orange colour, and Posie realised that it was probably stage make-up on his face which made him glisten as he did. He was also wearing the remnants of kohl pencil around his eyes, which made it look as if he had been crying.

And then something snapped in the man.

His charms not having had the desired effect, Robbie Fontaine lost his patience. His smile vanished. He checked a huge golden wristwatch pointedly and motioned towards the waiting car.

'I don't have much time, ladies. I need you to accompany me to Isleworth. To the Worton Hall Studios. I was told only to fetch you, Miss Parker, but I don't see why you shouldn't come along too, Dolly old girl. *If* you want to.'

'Isleworth?' protested Posie, as her heart sank at the thought of a long, hot journey. She stood her ground. 'But that's miles from here!'

'Not really,' replied the movie star snappishly. 'It's only a wee hour out of town. You'll see. For goodness' sake let's get a shuffle on now.'

He swung himself up into the green car again huffily and lit a fat cigar. Posie was privately outraged. Movie star or no movie star the man was out of line. She simply couldn't be star-struck, as Dolly so obviously was.

What exactly was so hush-hush?

She decided on the spur of the moment that she definitely wouldn't go.

'Come on, Posie!'

Quick as a flash, Dolly had jumped into the high back seat of the green Ford motor car beside Robbie, and was motioning excitedly for Posie to join her, patting the hard leather seat invitingly. Up close Posie saw the words 'Sunstar Films' emblazoned on the glossy green paintwork.

'I've never been to a real film studio before. And Isleworth is the best of the best. You know, Worton Hall Studios – it's Bertie Samuelson's place – a stately home hiding a film studio inside. Come on. Stop being in such a foul mood!'

Robbie Fontaine was getting distinctly irritable. He poked his head out. 'Please hurry, Miss Parker. I simply don't have all day to wait for you. I have filming commitments this afternoon.'

The green-uniformed driver up front sat still and unmoving, gloved hands clasped calmly on the steering wheel. The stringer sat in the front too, oblivious to everything, sucking a red lollipop and flicking through the pages of the *Beano*.

And then Posie was struck by Dolly's face, beaming out at her joyously through the window. Almost her old self again. There was no getting out of it. Dolly was determined to go to Isleworth.

'But what about the babies, Dolly?'

Posie saw her friend give a small moue of distaste.

'We can't just leave them with Len, Dolly. That's not fair. It'll take the whole afternoon, a jaunt there and back.'

'*What* babies?' asked Robbie Fontaine quickly, and Posie was amused to hear the note of panic rising in his voice. There was obviously no way out.

Posie sighed, defeated. 'Never mind. Just take us to Isleworth, then, Mr Fontaine. I'll meet your mysterious friend. But we must go via Caspari's ice cream parlour in Covent Garden. Urgently. You know where it is, driver?'

The man nodded. Posie was sure that the nannies would still be there. She got into the car.

And just a moment later they were pulling up at the corner of Shaftesbury Avenue, and sure enough, under the green-and-white striped awning of Caspari's, the nannies were sitting. Dolly went pale under her dark tan Maybelline foundation.

'Oh, lawks!'

The green Sunstar car parked just a few feet from the bench.

'I'll deal with this,' Posie told Robbie and Dolly. 'It won't take a second.'

Posie jumped out of the car. She felt like giving the nannies hell. It was true that she was still in a foul mood, probably something to do the heat, which she never dealt with very well. And Alaric…

The nannies caught sight of her and watched her approaching. They had both pursed their lips and crossed their arms, bracing themselves for an attack.

23

'I say, aren't you both supposed to be looking after the Cardigeon babies? I need you to go straight away to my office on Grape Street and resume your duties there. The Honourable twins are waiting for you.'

The larger of the two nannies scowled, righteous with indignation.

'I can't say it's any of your business, is it? We don't take orders from you, Miss Parker. Besides, we were dismissed from your *fine* establishment earlier by Lady Cardigeon herself. Told to go away and entertain ourselves for a few hours. Which is what we're doing.'

'So good day to you, Miss Parker,' cut in the other one in a final sort of tone, and buried her substantial nose in a penny magazine.

There seemed nothing to be done. Perhaps Posie should have been more conciliatory, after all? Or paid them off privately?

Just then Posie heard a rustle behind her and, caught off-guard, she turned to see Robbie Fontaine, smile back in place, bad mood seemingly gone, his good looks lit up by the bright sun filtered flatteringly through the green shady canopies of the trees overhead. He sauntered over, cigar raised extravagantly, every inch the movie star.

'My days!' one of the nannies exclaimed. 'Am I dreaming? Is that…'

Posie turned, half-shocked, half-fascinated, to watch the nannies.

They, unlike her, had obviously seen Robbie Fontaine in a film or two. Or more like four hundred. Their tongues were almost slack and their jaws were hanging open in surprise. Too late Posie saw that the penny magazine they had been sharing was actually a movie magazine, and Robbie Fontaine's face was plastered all over the front. The caption read '*IS MR FONTAINE THE EIGHTH WONDER OF THE WORLD?*'

She saw him make a courteous half-bow before he started to talk.

'I say, ladies. I have a bit of a wee problem which only you two can help with. Would you like that magazine signed? It would be my absolute pleasure. Now, I was just wondering…'

A charmer, Posie thought again to herself. *Nothing but a charmer*. But the world and its screaming babies had need of charmers such as Robbie Fontaine now and again.

That much at least was indisputable.

* * * *

Three

Isleworth was a small town in the countryside to the west of London, beyond Richmond. As they passed through it Posie caught glimpses of the glittering River Thames here and there, sparkling silver in the sunshine, and then some Georgian houses straggling along a small high street. Leaving the town behind again, she saw snatches of wide green fields through her half-closed eyelids.

Early in the ride, Posie had tried to get out of Robbie Fontaine just what all the fuss was about, pressing him for details of *why* exactly she was needed at the Worton Hall Studios. But he wouldn't answer a thing, just lighting another cigar and puffing on it intently.

'Strict instructions not to tell,' he said, tapping his nose in a confidential, irritating manner. And so Posie gave up.

Nevertheless, she had started to enjoy the ride as soon as central London was behind them, as the air was cooler and lighter and less gritty out here. They drove with the window protectors down. She hunkered down next to the door on the tough leather seat of the Sunstar car and pretended to doze. This was mainly because she wanted to drown out the sounds of Robbie Fontaine's voice which seemed to hold Dolly so enraptured. His conversation revolved only around himself.

He was still working his way through a well-used and boring series of Robbie Fontaine anecdotes when a smart shove in the ribs from Dolly told her they had arrived at the Worton Hall Studios.

'Pssst. Wake up, lovey. We're here.'

Posie opened her eyes. They were driving up a big gravel driveway, with neatly tended gardens on both sides. The driveway gave on to a perfectly manicured bubble of green lawn.

The driver pulled up in front of a lovely white-painted mansion house, square-built and three storeys high, a dolls' house sort of a place. A graceful white portico framed the red front door and on either side of the house square white extensions jutted outwards, giving it the impression of having arms.

The overall effect was of cool greenness in among the sizzling heat. Lawns extended outwards in all directions right up to a wire fence at the front, giving on to the main road. Oak trees and hawthorn bushes stood motionless with the lack of breeze. There was an impenetrable silence. Even the birds were too hot to sing. The white house was moored at the centre of this green paradise like a stately yacht.

'Welcome to Worton Hall Studios,' said Robbie Fontaine half-heartedly, pulling out what looked like a cheap notebook, much marked up, from the car's footwell. A film script, Posie supposed. She noted that he avoided giving her any eye contact.

'Of course, this is just the front of the place. The real studios stretch way, way back behind here. It's like a little town out there. We've been filming this current movie for three months, and most of Sunstar's films are made here. Now, Sidney, you get a shuffle on and run to my dressing room, and get me what I need.' He jerked his thumb at the stringer who jumped out of the car and sped away.

'And you, driver, you lose yourself too for a while. Go

and have a ciggie or something, will you? Leave these ladies alone.' The green-uniformed man frowned in the mirror and looked uncertain, but did as he was told, and sauntered away out of sight, taking the car key with him.

Robbie Fontaine got out, nodded towards Dolly, and indicated his script.

'I'm off too, Dolly old girl. I've got my next take to prepare for. It's a big scene. We're wrapping this film up tomorrow so it's got to be done well. Stay here in the car, will you, Miss Parker? Someone will come for you in just a minute or two.'

Posie lost her temper, a rare occurrence.

'*Someone?*' yelled Posie out of the window-hole at his retreating back, but Robbie Fontaine left them without a backwards glance.

Frustrated, Posie flung herself back on the seat, balling her fists up angrily. Even Dolly allowed a second of a scowl to flit across her elfin face before the eager, desperately-attentive look from before returned. She was busy drinking in the details of Worton Hall as if it was manna from heaven.

Ten minutes passed.

No-one came, and no-one was about. A smart blue-and-gold van labelled '*NATHAN'S COSTUMIERS*' drew up at one point, seeming like it was lost. It backed away again after a few minutes and rumbled off around the back of the house.

Posie kept checking her red-leather wristwatch, sticky in the heat. Something felt wrong: the quiet of the house was all wrong. Her paranoid brain kicked into action again.

Was this a kidnapping plot after all, despite the earlier reassurances, into which they had walked like prize idiots? Albeit a plot with a well-paid and famous movie star as the bait with which to lure them to Isleworth? And here they were; sitting ducks in a car without a key.

'Right, Dolly. Let's get out of here and try and get a train back to London,' Posie whispered softly.

'I'd drive but that man took the key. Probably on purpose. This stinks! It's fishy as hell. That man Fontaine is a prize rat. I bet he was paid a handsome wad of cash to come and get us out here with that half-baked story of his about a pal being in trouble! I know we're in danger for some reason. Gut instinct. I didn't like it from the start.'

Dolly gasped. Posie continued softly:

'But at this point I don't know if it's you or me who's the target. It could be you that's the prize, if a gang wants to extract money from Rufus. Or, it could be me, with my old pal Caspian della Rosa coming back for what he didn't get last New Years' Eve.'

Dolly looked shaken.

'Either way,' continued Posie firmly, 'we're not going to sit here waiting for *them* to come to us. Now, take your heels off, we'll have to run in our stockinged feet. On the count of three, we'll open the door and run, down the drive and out along the main road back to Isleworth. Ready, Dolly?'

'Hang on a minute, Po. We'll be okay here anyway. Even if we just sit here. Even if kidnappers *do* come for us.'

'How do you figure that out?'

'You've got a loaded gun. You said so. You can just aim and shoot at them, can't you?'

Posie sighed in exasperation. 'I was just blustering. Of course I haven't got a loaded gun. What sort of idiot goes around with one of those nowadays?'

Dolly stared blankly. 'Len? Rufus? Caspian della Rosa? Inspector Lovelace? Sergeants Binny and Rainbird? Take your pick.'

'Fine. Virtually everyone we know.' Posie frowned in exasperation. 'I take your point, Dolly, but unfortunately I don't happen to have a loaded gun with me now. Or ever. Right. Are you ready? On the count of three. Okay. THREE. TWO...'

Posie had taken off her heeled pumps and was slowly opening the heavy Ford's passenger door, checking the empty surroundings outside, her head minnowing backwards and forwards.

'ONE! *NOW...*'

'STOP! *Please* don't go anywhere, Miss Parker.'

Posie and Dolly jerked their heads around in surprise, their senses razor sharp, every nerve in their bodies on edge. The voice was low and sultry, and female, and there was a plummy, cut-glass edge to the vowels.

'I beg of you. I'll get in frightful trouble if you leave. Apparently we need you here. I'm sorry you had to wait so long. I know this looks unprofessional.'

A tall, strong-looking girl wearing a large straw hat pulled down low had climbed quickly up into the empty driver's seat. She was covered all over in a rough white muslin wrap, the material even reaching up around her head, covering most of her face. The effect was of a walking, talking Egyptian mummy. Or perhaps a beekeeper.

They both watched as the girl whisked off her hat and peeled down the muslin wraps. And then they both gasped aloud as the girl in the driver's seat looked at them first from the indicator mirror, then swung around in the seat so they could see her for real.

She glistened all over, just like Robbie Fontaine.

Her wide, splendid face was perfect. Her heavy fake-silver bob with its thick fringe which she wore like a close helmet, and her huge china-blue eyes were immediately recognisable to anyone in the land, even to Posie.

It was Silvia Hanro, the most famous movie star of them all. The most beautiful girl in the world.

'Oh! It's *you!*' breathed Posie and Dolly in unison, despite the fact that it was only Dolly who had met the actress before.

The girl smiled, and it was as if the sun had come out. She seemed used to such familiarity.

'Hello, Lady Cardigeon, and Miss Parker. A pleasure to meet you.' She stretched out a hand with strong, long fingers. It felt greasy, waxy to the touch.

'I know I look odd. I just can't take the hot sun right now, you see. What with this Leichner stage make-up all over my face and body, it will run right off me in great dollops, and I'll fry to a crisp in the process, just like a little pig in cooking oil.'

Posie immediately felt a thankful calm settle over her, mixed with a genuine curiosity at meeting such a star. She began to breathe normally again.

But she felt a prize idiot, too. She had shown a serious lack of judgement during the entire afternoon: what with her misplaced, ridiculous kidnapping theories which she had trotted out again and again. It was odd: usually her gut instinct was so good.

And then, as if things couldn't get stranger, a tall, lean, tatty-looking man in his early forties darted out of the main house. He opened the door on the passenger side of the car in an impatient manner and jumped in. In one hand the man clutched a megaphone, and in the other what Posie now recognised as a script.

Posie had no idea who he was, but Dolly obviously did, as her face had taken on the same adoring look as when she had been in Robbie Fontaine's company. The man turned abruptly towards them both.

'Miss Parker, how good of you to come. I'm Brian Langley, Producer and Director and owner of Sunstar Films.'

He nodded curtly but didn't extend a hand towards Dolly.

'I see you've brought along a wee pal of yours for company, eh? Or is she just your well-dressed secretary? I hope she can keep her mouth buttoned tight shut, whoever she is, for all her fancy clothes.'

He lit a Turkish cigarette and took a deep drag.

Brian Langley was hatless and he wore a crinkled white linen shirt and white flannel trousers. His face was crumpled into what looked like a permanent frown, his tiny eyes just pin-holes in a fraught, harried face. He had the look of a man who needs to shave at least twice a day, and even now a creeping fly-blue beard was spreading over his face. What could have been real handsomeness was rubbed away by tiredness and worry. Hostility buzzed from him like a force-field all of its own.

Posie opened her mouth to introduce Lady Cardigeon, but before she could do so Brian Langley had hurried on:

'I see you've already met my two brightest stars, eh? They pretty much *are* Sunstar Films, you know. I need to keep things that way. Especially since we've got a new film out which will hopefully make the country forget all about *Love, Life and Laughter*, and that darned Betty Balfour girl. Look, you need to help us out with a small problem. Got it?'

Posie simply nodded, narrowing her eyes, waiting for more information. Brian Langley obviously wasn't one for pleasantries. He reminded Posie of a particularly vicious crow that used to terrorise the garden of her father's Norfolk Rectory. The reign of terror had gone on for years.

Mr Langley turned to Silvia Hanro angrily and spoke in a still-audible whisper, as if Dolly and Posie weren't still sitting on the back seat.

'What sort of bally mess is this, Silvia? I gave specific instructions to Robbie to bring the woman detective straight to your dressing room for a briefing, not to leave her sitting out here for all and sundry to chat to. I emphasised that *complete secrecy* and confidentiality were key to this operation when he was sent to collect her. And here we are, sitting out here in cars! I can't think what's got into him. Idiot! Do *you* know?'

Silvia Hanro looked blankly back. But to Posie's mind there was something else there, too. Was it *fear*?

'No idea, Brian. I haven't seen him today. I only found out the lady detective was here because I happened to run into your driver, who'd been paid to leave them by Robbie!

He was having a cheeky ciggie over near my dressing room. He told me these good ladies were sitting waiting up front, so I came over. And that's when I sent a messenger to tell you to meet us out here.'

Silvia pulled out a car key. 'Care to start her up, Brian?'

'Don't be daft.'

Brian Langley turned again to the women in the back seat.

'I'll leave you in Miss Hanro's very capable hands. She'll explain. Just sort this mess out for us, will you, Miss Parker? Sooner the better, huh? Come and speak to me but only if you *really* have to, okay? I'm pushed for time as it is and every second I spend away from this film is a potential disaster.'

'I'm not quite sure I understand, sir. Can you tell me why I'm here?'

'No time. You'll get the gist of things in a minute. You're supposed to be a clever girl, aren't you? No need for me to hold your hand, then, is there? Just buzz around and ask sensible questions. But don't call in the police, okay? And don't reveal exactly who you are to anyone, either. Everything's got to be sorted by tomorrow afternoon. I think it should be pretty straightforward. There's a creepy chap – a stalker – involved. He might be behind this trouble.'

'A stalker? What sort of trouble?'

But Brian Langley just grabbed in his back pocket and brought out an expensive-looking leather money fob. He counted out ten crisp white pound notes and thrust them at Posie. A great deal of money. She took it warily.

'Silvia will explain. There'll be the same amount for you tomorrow if you sort this out. Okay?'

And before Posie could ask again *what* needed to be sorted, or explain that she usually didn't just take large wads of cash from clients, Brian Langley was off and out of the car. It all felt very illicit. She didn't like it one little bit.

Silvia Hanro looked up at them from the front mirror. She looked worried.

'What do you think of our divine Mr Langley, then?'

Posie grimaced. 'Lovely.'

'Isn't he just? He's the best Film Director and Producer this country has, and we all have to dance to his tune, but he has no manners whatsoever, and he also hasn't got a clue how to drive a car.'

She shook the car key. 'I was just teasing him, silly old sausage. But I bet one of you lovely ladies knows how to drive. Right?'

Posie nodded, feeling more comfortable than she had done for the last hour and a half; *this* was more her world. In fact, she had been toying with the idea of buying a car recently, only she had nowhere really to drive it to, and probably no-one to come with her, either.

Posie jumped out of the car and swapped places with Silvia Hanro, starting up the engine. Posie was a dab hand at driving: she had been an ambulance driver in the First World War on the Western Front and had had to coax an engine into life on even the coldest and dampest of mornings.

'We're good to go, Miss Hanro,' she called. 'Where to now?'

Posie yanked the handbrake off.

'Let's drive around the back way, to my dressing room,' said Silvia Hanro, 'and I'll explain everything when we get there.'

* * * *

Silvia Hanro spat in the eye-black and then applied her signature feline eye-flick carefully in the large oval mirror with its rainbow rim. But Posie noticed that her hands were shaking slightly as she drew on the line of thick kohl.

'I always do my own make-up,' Silvia said, gesturing to the messy tubes of paints and bottles littering the table in her dressing room on the set of *Henry the King*. Silvia then patted more orange goo all over her face from a pot saying 'LEICHNER STAGE MAKE-UP NUMBER ONE'.

There were no windows and the room smelt lingeringly of old pressed powder and damp books. A huge bouquet of vivid pink and red blooms over in the corner by the mirror gave off a heavy, almost funereal smell. The combined scents were cloying. Posie had noted how the tiny room sat among a jumble of others in the main house; dressing rooms and waiting rooms and props rooms all vying for space on crowded white-painted corridors which echoed constantly with the sound of shouting and running feet. Unlike its exterior, the inside of the house was the very opposite of calm. Posie felt quite claustrophobic.

'Why's it so dark in here, Miss Hanro?'

'Call me Silvia, please. I insist. It's because the set where we film is dark, like this; so the make-up has to be applied in the same light, to get the right effect.'

Silvia picked up a big white ruff off the floor and pinned it around her neck. She was wearing a rich red velvet gown covered in fake pearls and sequins, which must have been stifling.

'I dress myself, too, even though I have a paid dresser who comes with the place. I guard my privacy fiercely.'

'Don't blame you, lovey.' Dolly blew a perfect smoke ring up into the dark fug. 'You must get all sorts of nutters followin' you about.'

Dolly was in her element, sitting in a wicker chair with her legs pulled up beneath her, a large glass of chilled champagne in one hand, looking as if she had never left the world of actors and actresses behind her, not even for a day. Posie was willing to take a bet that Dolly hadn't been this happy in ages.

'That's why I can talk to you frankly in here. It's my sanctuary. As soon as we leave this dressing room anyone can hear anything, so just remember that.'

Posie nodded, hastily arranging her notepad and pen. She was waiting for the case details. There was no glass of champagne or cocktail cigarette for her. Hopefully just cold, hard facts.

Up close, Posie found Silvia Hanro impressive: she seemed very professional, despite whatever problem it was that she was encountering just now, and she was courteous and polite, which was the complete opposite of Amory Laine, the only other movie star Posie had met before. Posie noted how Silvia checked her watch constantly for fear of being late for Brian Langley.

Posie felt calmer now, partly because she had managed to track down a telephone booth in among the warren of corridors of Worton Hall. She had placed a call through to Grape Street where Len had answered breezily; reassuring Posie that all was well and that he had fed Mr Minks, Posie's Siamese cat who lived in the office.

He had reported that Trixie and Bunny Cardigeon had behaved beautifully for him, and were now safely off the premises, home-bound for Chelsea in the care of the two paid nannies.

Posie relayed the good news to Dolly, who had simply nodded, wide-eyed, as if the twins' welfare was a whole new concept to her.

Len had also told Posie that the office was very quiet, and that the temporary secretary, Tess, had reported no calls at all since the one which came through from Worton Hall Studios at coffee time, earlier that morning.

'What call was that, Len? I didn't hear anything about that?'

'Oh, I dunno, Posie.' She had heard Len sigh half-heartedly in the background and the sound of paper rustling; she could imagine him hot and bored back at

Grape Street and ferreting around on the secretary's desk for something to eat.

'Apparently the studio tried to call you about eleven o'clock, but it was an odd call: just a fella with a Scottish accent asking if you happened to be in today. When Tess said you *were* in, he hung up. She only knew it was Worton Hall Studios 'cos the Operator told her so when she connected the call.'

'You're sure?'

'Yep. I'd get the girl here to talk to you herself but I've sent her out to buy postage stamps; I'm trying to keep her busy with tasks she can't mess up. I do recall that she said the line was awful, full of hissings and beeps. Worse than usual, I mean.'

'I don't like the sound of that, Len. Can you arrange for a telephone engineer to come and check our office line? Today if possible. As soon as possible. Check we're not being bugged?'

'Seriously, Po?' Len had laughed easily. 'It's the height of summer. I bet neither love nor money will get an engineer out here before next week.'

'*Try*,' she had said angrily and slammed down the receiver.

She knew she was being overly cautious, but the line had been bugged in the past, with disastrous consequences. On her way out of the booth she had banged four-square into a man waiting to use the telephone. He had been queuing patiently behind the baize curtain with a clapperboard and a newspaper. Posie had an impression of height and a blur of bright white summer clothes and hat, but had been too embarrassed to stop and apologise properly.

Posie came back to the present with a sharp bump and cleared her throat in the smoky gloom of the dressing room.

'Forgive me, but *why* am I needed so urgently, Silvia?'

For a split-second Silvia's eyes were huge in the oval

mirror, like a horse about to bolt. And in them Posie saw real, raw, honest fear.

'Because my life has been threatened,' Silvia Hanro explained simply. She was fishing in a small drawer under the table of the dresser. She found what she was looking for and passed it over.

'I think it's real. Here, look at this.'

* * * *

Four

Posie took a small and shabby piece of lined paper in both her hands and unfolded it. She recognised it as paper torn from a script. In crude, coarse green ink a stark message stood out:

DEATH COMES FOR YOU TOMORROW.
THURSDAY 26TH JULY WILL BE YOUR LAST
GRAND ENTRANCE.
P.S. Do you think this is a joke?
Here's something to make you think about it.

'*This* is why I need you so urgently. I got it this morning, just before I started filming. It was in a sealed envelope along with my coffee, brought to me by Elaine. She's my so-called dresser, but she's more of a general dogsbody.'

'Nice,' said Posie, trying not to appear too shocked and passing it over for Dolly to inspect. She had dealt with blackmail cases before, but never death threats. She didn't like the look of it.

Dolly shivered dramatically. 'Oh, lovey,' she said with feeling, casting a sympathetic look over at Silvia. 'This is *horrible*.'

Posie picked up her pen again. She made a few notes in her pad.

'But is it serious, Silvia? Or is it someone's idea of a joke? Is it the first note you've received like this one? And why do you want *me* to come out here, rather than the regular police? I don't like the look of this at all. I can highly recommend a jolly good Chief Inspector at New Scotland Yard…'

'No, no,' Silvia said hurriedly, looking panicked. 'No police. Not yet anyway. I don't want them sniffing around here and all the newspaper journalists coming along hot on their heels. It's terrible timing: Brian Langley would kill me first himself!'

For a second she looked as if she would weep, then there was that strength, that resolve again.

'And no, it's not the first note. There have been two others. I received the first on Monday morning, and the other yesterday morning. They all came in the same envelopes and all said much the same thing. They were to the point: they all said I would die on Thursday 26th July. They gave me no directions, either; no ransom money to pay to get these people off my back.'

'Did you keep the envelopes?'

Silvia shook her head.

'Do you remember the postmark? Was it central London?'

'No. There was no postmark. I'm pretty certain that they were all hand delivered.'

'I see. But why did you only call me in *today*, if there have been other notes? Why not call me in on Monday or Tuesday? What changed? What changed since yesterday?'

A strange look settled briefly in Silvia's lovely eyes. Posie saw it and frowned. *Was it worry, or something else?* A cloud seemed to pass over the movie star's face.

'Oh, I suppose I'm scared because tomorrow seems so soon.'

'Really? Nothing changed? You're sure?' Posie was unconvinced by the reasoning, but Silvia's reflection looked back at her from the mirror, her mouth a grim line, the touch of bravado clinging about her. Posie changed tack:

'What's the significance of *tomorrow* in particular? And why did you say this is "terrible timing"?'

Silvia grimaced.

'We've been filming this huge film, *Henry the King*, for almost the last three months. It wraps up tomorrow. Thursday 26th July is our last day here. Truthfully, Brian Langley can only afford one more day in the studios; he's hired the place from its owner, Bertie Samuelson, for more than a year now, using it for a whole bunch of previous films, and it's costing him an arm and a leg. He can't go on renting the whole place for Sunstar Films alone.'

Posie scratched a note. 'I see. But that's good news to be finishing the film, surely? Hasn't filming gone well here?'

Silvia shrugged.

'Well, yes and no. I think it's gone well. But we've been filming under the shadow of knowing that this *has* to work out; there's no room for error. It's supposed to save Sunstar Films, to save our careers. We've all been putting in very, very long hours, through the night sometimes. *Henry* is a huge budget film and Brian Langley has spared no expense: he's got hundreds of extras here every day for the crowd scenes, costing a fortune, and beautiful costumes hired from Nathan's Costumiers which cost goodness only knows how much. It's not a comedy, but we're hoping it will do well. It *has* to do well.'

Silvia Hanro rose from her stool, placing a long blonde wig on her head and checking her reflection in the mirror, sashaying from side to side. Dolly had risen automatically, and was moving fluidly this way and that, unasked, smoothing the false hairpiece into position.

'The pressure was always on for this film to be a huge success: Brian's got a handful of financial backers who are expecting a big return on *Henry*, and he's put every last penny he has into the film himself.'

Silvia sighed. 'What with all the competition from Hollywood right now and with British films being so horribly unfashionable since the war, this was a chance to fly the flag and show the world just how good a British film could be. The financial backers are hoping that they can sell *Henry* in America, too. But if the film is a flop then rumour has it that Brian Langley will become bankrupt, and Sunstar Films will go the same way. Down the plughole.'

Posie raised her eyebrows dubiously. 'No wonder the man was so vile earlier, then. Or is he always like that?'

Silvia laughed. 'Oh, his bark is worse than his bite. Poor old darling Brian. He's rather a softie underneath. Do you know, he keeps hothouse flowers as a way of relaxing? Orchids. See those there? They're beautiful, aren't they? They're from him. He pays an oriental gardener just to tend the things. He lives very near here, you know. At Richmond. On the river.'

'Is there a *Mrs* Langley in the picture?'

'Oh, no.' Silvia shook her head. 'Brian only has time for movies, and movie stars. And sometimes for flowers.'

She grinned impishly for a second. 'He does have a Housekeeper. Cleeves, I think she's called. But she's about as glamorous as a pair of muddy Wellington boots, so he'd hardly bother with *her*.'

Posie lowered her pen, staring again at the green scrawl of the death threat. 'Is there anything else happening tomorrow which I should know about?'

Silvia looked bemused, as if Posie was asking something she ought to know the answer to. 'Do you mean the Wrap Party?'

Posie shrugged, feeling even more out of her depth. Dolly chimed in, trying to help. 'On the last day of filming there's always a final party, a "Wrap Party", to celebrate.'

Posie wrote it down. 'And where will that be?'

Silvia gestured around her. 'Oh, here of course. In the house and gardens. It will start with a lunch, around noon, and will go on all afternoon. You'll stay, please?'

'Will it be a big party, then?'

'You bet. Huge. All the financial backers will be here, and Bertie Samuelson, the owner of the place, will be here too. And all of the current stars who are on Brian Langley's pay-roll with Sunstar Films will be made to dance attendance, too, to add a bit of sparkle. In fact, I'll bet half of fashionable London will be out here in their finest frocks. It will be quite some party. They say that even Ivor Novello will come, but who knows? It's also the best opportunity for Brian to sell the film; so all the American and English cinema company representatives will be here, and Brian's hoping he'll be able to get them interested, even though they won't be able to see the final product for a couple of weeks.'

'Golly!'

Posie blew out her cheeks. This didn't sound good at all: a huge lunch party in a whopping great house, with film stars and important businessmen crawling all over the place, and umpteen opportunities for somebody to kill Silvia Hanro, if they really wanted to. With only Posie around for protection, and no police allowed.

Not good. Not good at all.

Posie chewed her pen-lid. Unless, after all, this turned out to be an empty threat, designed to spook the girl.

But Posie felt it went deeper than that. Unconsciously, Posie trailed her pen lightly over the words in the note which read '*YOUR LAST GRAND ENTRANCE*'.

'And let me guess: you and your boyfriend Robbie Fontaine will make some kind of big entrance with Brian Langley tomorrow lunchtime, to add that necessary "sparkle"?'

Silvia nodded, but Posie was already imagining the

scene at the party: it would be a prime opportunity for a public shooting. Posie shivered despite herself.

'And what about this "*P.S.*"?' she asked. 'Where the note says "*Here's something to make you think about it*"? What's that all about?'

'I was coming to that. It's not very nice, I'm afraid.'

'Oh? Go on. I'm quite a tough cookie, you know.'

'I got something with this third note. A token.'

'What was it?'

'It's disgusting. Depraved. It's why you got called in, really. Brian insisted.'

Silvia had crossed to the back of the room, and opened a small ice-box which Posie now saw was set up on a console table; a cocktail shaker and various glasses and liquors scattered around. Silvia opened the ice-box, withdrew something small and sashayed back. Whatever it was, was a couple of inches long, and wrapped in a silvery paper.

'Not squeamish, are you? Only I'm *not*, but this managed to make me throw up my breakfast.'

'Thank you for the warning.' Her heart beating, Posie took the object, unwrapped it and then promptly dropped it.

Dolly screamed.

It was a human finger.

****

Five

After they had had a chance to calm down, and Dolly had drunk a bit more champagne, Posie forced herself to think logically. She studied the severed digit.

It was grey and sad-looking, and there was a slip of gold foil in a makeshift ring around the severed end, which made it all seem worse, somehow.

It was obviously a woman's finger, a left-hand ring finger. Apart from the neat severance, there were no other marks or scars upon it. The nail was unpainted and short and clipped and neat.

'Golly.' Posie nodded, chewing her lip. 'I see this quite changes things. No wonder you're worried.'

'Exactly.'

'I think this finger looks like it's been frozen.'

'It has. It's been in my ice-box all day.'

'No. I mean it looks like it's been frozen a long time: weeks, months, more like.'

Dolly squealed. 'Does that make it in any way better, Posie?'

Posie shook her head. 'No. It's still awful. But it could mean things are different to how they seem just now: it hasn't been chopped off anyone alive, or a recently dead corpse. It's a prop, albeit a grisly one. Can you put this horrible thing back, please, Silvia? I guess you'd better hold on to it in there for now.'

The movie star did as she was asked and walked to the ice-box. She looked at Posie expectantly.

Posie's mind was scrabbling over this gruesome new detail. She longed for the calm reassuring tones of Chief Inspector Lovelace, or even, at a push, Len, who was good in bad situations, even if he was a charmer. 'Why do you want *me* to deal with this, anyway?'

'As I said, it was Brian Langley who called you here, actually. Not me. It was *his* idea.' Silvia splayed her hands apologetically.

'When I got the first of these notes I showed him and he shrugged it off. Well, when I went to see him earlier today with the third note, and the finger, he panicked: he couldn't bear the thought of losing one half of his wonder-duo, I suppose. He'd seen your advert in *The Lady* earlier this week. He thought discretion was vital. He insisted on not calling in the police, even *with* the finger in the equation. I agreed. And he'd heard good things about you. Thought you'd be able to have a good old snoop around Worton Hall and suss things out without asking awkward official questions, and try and find out who's behind this. You can just pretend to be an old school friend of mine, here for a jolly. Can't you?'

Dolly looked smug despite her pallor. 'Mr Langley chose well. Posie is the best detective in town,' she said loyally. She lit up another violet-coloured Sobranie. 'Posie's made such a good name for herself; solved *ever* so many cases.'

Silvia gave Posie a look of careless curiosity, taking in the pink sapphire.

She nodded.

'*I* had heard about you, too, of course. You're Alaric Boynton-Dale's girl, after all, aren't you? Bring him along to the party tomorrow, if he's free, that is. *Do* bring him. Won't you?'

'Well…actually…'

And there it was again. That unwelcome, cold whisper of unease which seemed to come, unbidden, at the very mention of Alaric: Posie's throat was constricted, and she thought she might choke, but before she could answer fully there was a knock at the door and a small, finely-boned, pale woman with unfashionably long frizzy hair held in place by a tortoiseshell clasp darted in, flooding the room with some welcome air.

'Twenty minutes to your next take, Miss Hanro. I'm just off to check on Mr Fontaine now. Do you need anything here?'

'Thank you, Elaine, but no. I'm just coming. Can you set up two extra chairs for my two friends here behind where Mr Langley is filming, please?'

The woman nodded timidly, hazel eyes anxious in an oval face, and hurried out, and then Silvia turned and looked at Posie and Dolly conspiratorially. She seemed to make up her mind about something.

'Talking of *men*, there's something important you should know. A secret. And I know I can trust you both with it. But it's seriously off record.' She indicated to Posie's notebook. 'If you don't mind?'

'Not in the least.' Posie put down her paper and her pen. Nothing could get much stranger.

'Robbie Fontaine is *not* my boyfriend. We loathe each other. I'm glad you think Robbie is a rat, Posie. And an idiot. I heard you talking in the car to Lady Cardigeon before you saw me. It's true: he is. He's both those things. Always was. Always will be.'

'*What?*' gasped Dolly, almost dropping her cigarette. 'My gosh! But the whole world thinks you two are a couple! You're very convincin'. You're always together at press events, and in interviews, and you always play opposite each other in your movies. Like this one. You have done for years, since the war… The nation is holding its breath for an engagement announcement any day now!'

47

Silvia rolled her eyes at the ceiling.

'They'll wait forever then. It's all show! All for the cameras. Pure acting. Robbie is plain old Glaswegian Robbie Doone; he has a wife called Sheila who he married fifteen years ago when he worked as a riveter at the Govan Dockyard. He was an amateur wrestler back then, too, winning prize fights in his local area, and going on to catch the eye of a talent scout for a film company. Robbie was always easy on the eye, even covered in bruises. Sheila was his manager's daughter, from way back in the early days. They were from the same world, you see. *Very* much lower class.'

So Silvia was a snob. But with those plummy vowels was it really so surprising? Posie found herself cooling just a little towards the girl; after all, one couldn't help where one was born. Posie smiled, but there wasn't as much warmth in it as before.

'And you? What was your world?'

Silvia laughed. 'Oh, I was always Silvia Hanro – that *is* my own name, surprisingly – but I'd also had a romantic life of my own before I was a movie star: a boyfriend from my early acting days, Tom.'

A look of brief pain passed over Silvia's face.

'You see, both Robbie and I agreed to leave the past behind us when we signed up with Brian Langley and Sunstar Films. Brian understood we would be cinema dynamite, together. We sell films as a couple, Robbie and I. And so the Robbie and Silvia show goes on and on. It has done for at least five years now.'

Posie tried to understand:

'And so Sheila and Tom had to disappear? Is that right?'

Silvia nodded. 'Except they didn't, of course. They're both still here: they were relegated to the shadows when we signed away our right to happiness with the people we loved. No-one knows who they are. But they're always present: just part of the scenery.'

'That must be tiring. Not to mention awkward for you. For you *all*,' said Posie sympathetically.

Silvia nodded briskly. 'That's the problem when you go plucking stars out of the gutter. First you have to brush off the dirt, and let me tell you, Robbie Fontaine definitely came from the dirt. Talk about a rough diamond...'

Posie frowned: the thought of Robbie Fontaine, glimmering and gorgeous, like an unwelcome spectre, rose in front of her eyes. 'But why did you send Mr Fontaine to collect me today, especially if you loathe him so much?'

The movie star cast a worried look over in the direction of the ice-box and shivered.

'*I* wasn't free this morning to come into central London, and neither was Brian, but Robbie wasn't due to film until now, you see. Brian told him to come and get you, not to call you. We might be movie stars and paid a small fortune, but we're creatures of Brian Langley, through and through: if he wants us to wait on tables, we do it; if he wants us to help him on the cutting-room floor, we do it; and if he wants us to dash around London collecting people, we do it. He paid for us and he gets his pound of flesh. I suppose that Brian thought if you simply *saw* Robbie you'd come running and do his bidding.'

Dolly laughed. 'He miscalculated there, then. Posie must be the only person in London not to recognise the "Eighth Wonder of the World"!'

Silvia smiled. 'Quite.' The actress checked her delicate silver wristwatch for the umpteenth time. She was slowly gathering her things together, including a big marked-up script.

But Posie was miles away, worried: all this talk of secrecy and discretion, and no phone calls to warn her, but Len had mentioned that a phone call *had* come through to Grape Street from Worton Hall Studios that morning. It had been a man with a Scottish accent, which meant that it was, in all probability, Robbie Fontaine who had made the call.

What had that been all about?

Something wasn't right and it nagged at her. Everything to do with Robbie Fontaine seemed wrong, somehow. Posie made a note to explore the business of the telephone call later. She turned and smiled, smoothly, professionally.

'Just quickly, who do *you* think wrote the notes?'

Silvia swallowed nervously. She was fanning herself with her script.

'I don't recognise the writing, if that's what you mean. And as for who might have written it, well…I think it could be Robbie. But there's a couple of others.'

'Sorry? *Robbie Fontaine?*'

Silvia nodded, her painted face flushed with anxiety. Or was it something else?

'I told you, we loathe one another. We're from opposite ends of life. And with me dead he'll be rid of me at last and free to be with Sheila, who's the love of his life, goodness only knows why. They can live together out in the open as man and wife then. I'm just an obstacle in his way. He's also insanely jealous of me; I'm the bigger movie star, and he hates it. He'd become even more famous with me dead.'

'NO!' exclaimed Dolly. 'I don't believe it! He'd be nothin' without you!'

Posie frowned. 'But why would Mr Fontaine choose to do this now? To kill you at a Wrap Party on a film which might be the highlight of his career? Why mess that up? Are you serious? You mentioned there were others?'

'I wouldn't rule him out. But you're right: the timing is odd. And, yes. There are others.'

'Go on.'

Silvia bit at her lip savagely. 'I have an estranged sister, Pamela. She hates me. We became estranged before the war; she was a suffragette and had got herself quite a name for her troublesome ways. Hated me because I didn't support her. It got worse when I became famous, of course. And last year she begged me for a sizeable amount of money.

Fifty pounds, twice over. She said if I didn't pay it, she'd go to the papers with stories of our past: she'd expose the truth about Robbie not being my real boyfriend. Explain about my boyfriend, Tom, from back in the old days. She said if I paid the money she'd leave me alone forever.'

'Blackmail?'

'Call it what you like. I paid it, twice, and I haven't heard from her since. I haven't seen her in years, and I have no idea even where she lives. I paid the amount directly into her Savings Account at the big Post Office on the Strand. As she told me to.'

'So perhaps she's run out of money and wants more?' said Dolly, her head cocked on one side like an inquisitive purple-painted robin. 'But why the finger? That's really horrible. It doesn't make sense, does it, Posie?'

Posie looked up from her notepad and shook her head. 'No, it doesn't. And it sounds as if you're more useful to your sister alive than dead. Unless Pamela benefits from your death? Does she get anything under your Will, Silvia? Do you even have a Will?'

Silvia nodded. 'Oh, yes. I made it a couple of years back. And no: Pamela gets nothing. Everything I have, every last bean goes to a children's charity.'

'Nothing for your boyfriend, Tom?'

Silvia shook her head. 'I've provided for him already, bought him a small flat a few months ago. That's enough. He doesn't expect more.'

'Who else could have written the notes? You said there were a *couple* of others…'

'I do have the obligatory stalker. A fan, really.'

Posie nodded, remembering Brian Langley mentioning the stalker to her. 'Go on.'

'He's very into the theatre and the cinema, but he's particularly interested in *me*. He's nice enough when I've met him for real, but he's quite odd. He's called Hector Mallow, and he manages to sneak in pretty often. He's done it for almost every movie I've worked on over the last few years. The truth is, security's a bit lax with Sunstar Films, and he either manages to disguise himself as a cameraman, or a runner, or, more often than not, as one of the extras. He's turned up several times these last few weeks on *Henry*. Often I'll turn around and he'll be right next to me, dressed as a sixteenth-century peasant and grinning away. It's quite maddening.'

'Goodness! How alarming. Can't they get rid of him?'

'Oh, they do. Security come and throw him out. But he always seems to come back. A few days later, there he is again. The trouble is, he's very good at disguising himself: he's a plain sort of man, in his mid-forties, I'd say. But every time I see him he manages to look slightly different. He's a bit of a chameleon.'

Posie nodded. She knew people, or one man in particular, her own 'stalker', Count Caspian della Rosa, who could be chameleon-like in his appearance. It was a deadly knack.

'Is he dangerous, this Hector Mallow? The sort of man to send stray body parts to those he adores?'

Silvia shrugged. 'Who knows? He's never threatened me before, he's just written letters over the years. And sent me photographs and postcards from his holidays. I think he thinks I care for him. Sometimes he turns up at my dressing room with flowers and chocolates.'

'Did you keep his postcards? Any writing from him?'

Silvia shook her head scornfully. 'Of course not. I don't keep anything from anyone. That way madness lies.'

'Can I keep this note? I presume you destroyed the others?'

Silvia nodded. 'Yes to both those questions.'

'And you don't know anything else about Hector Mallow? Where he lives? What he does with himself when he's not following you?'

'Goodness, no. Why would I? In any case, I feel his interest in me might be waning.'

'Oh?'

'There's another actress, a gorgeous young slip of a thing, called Meggie Albanesi. Hugely talented. You might have heard of her?'

'Oh, yes!' gushed Dolly quickly. 'She's quite *the thing* right now in town!'

But then Dolly realised her mistake, flushed red, and backtracked. 'I mean, apart from *you*, of course, Silvia. Meggie Albanesi is a *theatre* actress, anyway: not a full-blown movie star. She can't be compared to you at all. Absolutely not...'

'Don't worry,' Silvia said, smiling, but slightly tight-lipped. 'I'm not at all offended. There's room for lots of us in this game. Anyway, Brian is interested in signing Meggie to Sunstar, but she keeps saying "no". But he's insistent: he's trying to keep "in" with her, anyhow. And what he heard the other day was that Hector Mallow has been trailing around after Meggie; up to his usual tricks. It's quite possible he's switched his affections from me to her. Which is quite a relief, really.'

Silvia had her hand on the door handle of the dressing room. She looked around herself briefly. Posie and Dolly took their cue and stood. Posie kept her notebook out, and swallowed, not liking to ask her next question, but seeing it as a necessity. After all, the horrible statistic that ninety-five per cent of murderers were known to their victims, usually intimately so, demanded that she ask.

'I have to ask you this, Silvia, but is everything fine with your real boyfriend, Tom? No rows? No arguments? No reason he'd wish you out of the way himself? I'm sorry if this is indelicate...'

The star put her head back and laughed. 'No! You'll meet Tom. If you're in love with Alaric Boynton-Dale then you'll love Tom; he's a similar type. Same good rugged looks, same enigmatic expression.'

Posie frowned, hating the personal connection, for she

liked to keep her home life and her work life separate to a fault, but Silvia didn't notice, and just gushed on:

'He's movie star material.' She paused, her face twisted for a tiny second into a prism of acute pain. 'Well, sort of.'

She shrugged. 'Besides, we're madly in love. Have been for years. He benefits too out of this arrangement, you know. He has a job on the team and he's paid a monthly salary by Brian.'

'To keep his mouth shut?'

'Essentially. Yes.'

'And what about Brian Langley himself?' Posie asked innocently. 'Would *he* want you out of the way? He seems hot-headed enough.'

Not to mention horrible enough, somehow.

Silvia flashed Posie a look of absolute incredulity, as if Posie had just said something verging on the blasphemous.

'Gosh, no! Brian wouldn't wish me dead. What on earth might lead you to think that? Besides, *he* was the one who wanted you here. He'd hardly invite you here if he was the one orchestrating the whole thing, would he?'

'Oh, you'd be surprised what people do. A double bluff. I've come across it before. Besides, I'm just thinking things through.'

Posie explained: 'You see, Silvia, the motive in these things is usually one of two factors: love or money. So here I'd plump for the second: you mentioned Mr Langley might become bankrupt. I wondered if he might have some sort of insurance on your life, on behalf of Sunstar Films?'

'No idea. I doubt it.' The girl shook her head, but she was nervous, Posie could tell.

She's scared of him, thought Posie with sudden certainty. *Whatever she might say, she's scared of her own Producer. Something in her history and in his has made her frightened of him.*

But what? And is it relevant now?

Silvia shook her head firmly. 'Brian wouldn't want to

kill me. In fact, Robbie and I have just signed up to Sunstar for another three years. Besides, there's too much between Brian and I. A lot of water under the bridge.'

What kind of water? But Posie kept her thoughts to herself.

'I see.'

Posie stared at her notebook, at the hastily-scrawled points. She had forgotten to ask perhaps the most important thing. She stood with her pen poised.

'Tell me: who knows about these notes, Silvia? Who *exactly*? Is it known generally? Has it become set gossip yet?'

'Just the inner circle: me, obviously, and Brian, and Tom. Oh, and Robbie and his wife, Sheila. Oh, and Bertie Samuelson, the owner of this place. Brian thought it best to keep him up to date, in case drastic measures had to be taken at any point.'

'That's it? You don't think your dresser read the notes and talked about them to others? Or that Robbie Fontaine or his wife would blab about it?'

'No. We're a tight ship here, Posie. We all know too much about each other to gossip. It's dangerous for us all. Besides, Brian made us swear on our lives and our pay packets not to speak. Robbie and Sheila need money like nothing else; they wouldn't risk it being cut off. And Elaine's a little nobody but she's not a snoop. No way.'

Posie nodded and tucked away her notepad in her carpet bag. She spied a half-eaten, twice-melted bar of Fry's 'Five Boys' chocolate lurking in its depths and she grabbed at it. As if on cue, her stomach groaned.

It was almost three o'clock and she still hadn't eaten lunch.

Silvia fixed her muslin wraps in place again, so that only her eyes were visible, and pulled a bright green kimono over the top of everything. She signalled to the door.

'Remember, out there we can't talk. So if you need to

ask me something it will have to be later, in private. Is that okay? In the meantime, Posie, you're to keep your eyes and ears peeled in the studio, watching people, observing. And covering my back, too. If necessary.'

No mean feat, then, Posie thought to herself ruefully.

'It sounds more like surveillance than detection to me, Silvia,' she protested quietly. 'I really think you need police cover. This finger business is really macabre. One lady detective on her own is simply not going to cut it, I'm afraid. I'm good, but I'm not *that* good. This is your life at stake here.'

'I'm sure you'll do just fine.' Silvia nodded in a convincing fashion. 'And anything is better than nothing, isn't it?'

Posie just about stopped herself from rolling her eyes in exasperation. A practical detail occurred to her.

'Oh, one last thing! If I'm an old school friend of yours I need to know where we went to school, don't I? In case anyone asks. You never know.'

'Of course. I was at Wycombe Abbey.'

Ironically, Posie hadn't actually been to school; she had been tutored at home in the Norfolk Rectory by a succession of prim governesses after her mother had left them all in the lurch by walking out one Christmas and never coming back. Amazingly, Posie had got herself quite a good education in the end, mainly by piggybacking off the holiday lessons of her hugely clever brother, Richard. But this wasn't the first time she had been asked to pretend to be a school friend, and she betted it wouldn't be the last time, either.

'Thank you.' But something about the name of the school was ringing a bell in Posie's mind. Her puzzled look obviously gave her away.

'Yes.' Silvia smiled, as if happy to make a connection. 'You realised! I was at school with Alaric's sister.'

'Oh.'

'Well, Violet was younger than me, of course. But we

ran with the same crowd. I remember *him* though, Alaric, coming to Prize Days and Sports Days and so on. A real golden boy. Everyone had a bit of a mad pash on him. Even then. You know what little girls are like... Quite some family, aren't they? Small world, isn't it?'

There was that horrid flicker of fear again. Posie smiled tightly. 'Mnnn. Isn't it?'

'Shall we go?'

Posie couldn't shake off her anxious mood. But secretly she was cheered on by the thought that Chief Inspector Lovelace was just a telephone call away. She was also cheered by the fact that today was the 25th July, not the 26th, and the writer of the notes had seemed peculiarly concerned about being very specific about the date.

'I haven't actually said I'll take this case on, you know,' she muttered in a low undertone to Dolly as they followed Silvia out of the dressing room. 'I don't like this. She isn't telling me everything and that's a bad start. I also feel she resents my presence here, too. There are so many layers of deception involved.'

'Of course there are layers of deception! She's an actress, darlin'!' hissed Dolly. 'But she needs you! What she isn't sayin' is that she's pushin' thirty, and she's almost bein' pushed out of the limelight. There are loads of other actresses muscling in on her crown, and she's just about clingin' on for dear life. And Betty Balfour and Meggie Albanesi are just the half of it! She needs to make it to that Wrap Party tomorrow, Posie. Alive.'

'I quite see that. But it's not my problem, is it?' Posie muttered. 'In fact, I've half a mind to leave now.'

''Course you won't, lovey!' Dolly beamed. She seemed to have recovered her earlier cheer, finger or no severed finger.

'You'd be daft to go. And stop hangin' on to that huff. This is the most fun we've had in ages!'

* * * *

Six

They emerged squinting out into the bright daylight of the glass-filled corridor. Out here Silvia Hanro seemed completely unreal. Posie tried not to stare too much.

Several glass doors were set in matching pairs along the corridor, leading onto a small paved terrace outside, and then onto a scrubby grass-covered lawn the size of about eight tennis courts, what must once have been formal gardens. It was now an outdoor workshop packed tightly with at least one hundred people, all busy working in the relentless sunshine.

They passed through one of the double glass doors and Silvia stopped on the terrace to put up a small purple Japanese silk parasol. When she spoke it came out muffled through the wraps:

'Golly! This heat is sweltering. It's not far. We're heading up there. To the dark studio.'

Silvia gestured ahead of them to where a cinder path led towards two large temporary-looking buildings with triangular roofs. To the left stretched fields of wheat and what looked like an old, dark farmhouse nestled on the crest of a hill, and away to the right stretched grassy fields and rows and rows of greenhouses for growing vegetables.

On the lawn the noise was immense and Posie

remembered what Robbie Fontaine had said about Worton Hall Studios being like a small town. But it felt more like a busy dockyard: cloth-capped carpenters were clustered in islands across the grass, sawing vast timbers into pieces, shouting at each other, and yet more men in blue cambric overalls were busy painting stiff sheets of canvas stage scenery, their faces covered in sweat and dust and daubs of bright paint. A couple of black horses, big as shire horses, were tethered together on the cinder path in a bit of shade cast from a yew tree, waiting patiently, their cart being loaded up with what looked like just-finished stage scenery, huge and cumbersome.

'My gosh! This is quite some operation! No wonder it's so expensive,' Posie muttered to herself, squinting against the harsh sun, despite her hat drawn well-down over her eyes.

There was a sudden hush and all eyes were immediately riveted on Silvia Hanro, whose white coverings and dash of purple parasol stood out ridiculously. Silvia, being big and tall and powerfully built, took large strides, despite the wraps, covering the ground easily.

Posie automatically stepped back behind the girl, not wanting to be noticed and hating the feeling of so many eyes upon her. Yet again she wished she had worn black or brown today, not bright yellow: it was hardly the colour to stay unobtrusive in. Dolly trotted along happily with Silvia, almost running at her side to keep up, either oblivious to the looks or enjoying the attention.

To the left of the lawn, under a small white marquee, a mixed crowd of men and women of all ages hung around listlessly in the heat, sipping tin cups of tea. They all stared over, too. Silvia jabbed her parasol in their direction.

'The extras have been filming all morning, so they're having a break just now.'

Picking their way through the groups of people took some doing, and required full attention, and it wasn't until they had reached the cinder path and the welcome shade of the trees that Posie realised they had acquired quite a little band of followers in their wake.

The pale frizzy-haired woman from the dressing room, Elaine, was looking harried, carrying a big pile of what could have been velvet curtains in her arms. She was clipping along as fast as she could on what looked like eminently unsuitable shoes for a dresser to wear. They were very high, and bright orange. Elaine couldn't match Silvia's stride though, and trailed quite a long way behind the star.

The boy from earlier, Sidney, the stringer, was also just behind Posie, much closer, swinging a bag of marbles in one hand and carrying a chalk slate. He was whistling:

'In and out the dusty bluebells, in and out the dusty bluebells. Who will be my master?'

And it was very annoying.

'Good grief!' Posie turned and scowled, just about to tell him to be quiet.

But someone else got in first.

'Put a sock in it, will you, Sidney? I for one would like a spot of peace and quiet before Langley's onslaught.'

Out of the blue, a tall man with a razor-short blonde haircut drew alongside Posie on her left-hand side. He was wearing blue sunglasses and dressed in what looked like crumpled cricket whites.

The boy immediately stopped whistling and looked cowed.

The man was like some kind of Norse God, a mythical Loki, tanned and fair and with strong, muscular, oiled arms. He smelt strongly of yew and pine trees and mint, and something else, unplaceable; burnt toffee, perhaps, or toast kept on the fire a moment too long.

The man was obviously some kind of crew member and he carried a huge crescent-shaped silver lamp in his arms, with a straw boater hat balanced on top. He radiated presence. Posie found herself taking tiny greedy glimpses at his lovely aquiline-nosed profile.

Silvia turned around a few times from up ahead, saw the Norse God next to Posie, but walked on breezily, not acknowledging him. He overtook their group after a bit and dashed on ahead, disappearing into the doorway of the left-hand building of the pair of studios.

'Here we are, then,' said Silvia, half-turning again and indicating in the direction the man had disappeared. 'The dark studio.'

Up close, the 'dark studio' was a flimsy corrugated-iron affair like an airport hangar. A huge chalked-up blackboard outside the building read:

FILMING: HENRY THE KING.
Leads: (1) Miss S. Hanro &
(2) Mr R. Fontaine

No alcohol on set at the
request of Management.

As they passed inside the vast hangar the darkness hit them, and it took a few seconds for their eyes to adjust to the new, strange light. Posie saw that Dolly was staring around at this strange new world: the immense space with scatterings of wooden stage-scenery; intensely bright lights far over in a corner on the left where they seemed to be heading, where a group of people with cameras and make-up trays and clipboards were thronging, all shouting and clamouring in a mad rush. But it was cool in the dark studio, at least. Thank goodness.

Cooler than they had been used to for days.

Silvia walked on assuredly like a stately galleon. All around her, people were keeping their distance, but dipping and bowing to her in acknowledgement, as if royalty were passing by.

'GET A MOVE ON, MISS HANRO! WE HAVEN'T GOT ALL DAY!'

Brian Langley's voice, gritty and shrill at the same time, called out across the studio in a booming fashion and Silvia moved towards the busy arc of light in the corner, where Posie saw that a sort of stage had been set up, brightly lit on all sides by about thirty of the same strange crescent-shaped lamps she had seen the blonde man carrying. A bank of perhaps twenty white-clad men with cameras and tripods were waiting around the stage like shadows, loitering, their cigarettes glowing like will-o'-the-wisps in the darkness.

Brian Langley appeared out of the gloom, furious, a megaphone in his hands. All eyes in the crowd of people swivelled round towards Silvia, who was shedding her green gown and her pale muslin wraps like a snake shedding its skin in summertime. Brian Langley tapped his wristwatch in an accusing fashion.

'You're two minutes late and what with your wretched mysterious appointment this morning we're all running well behind schedule.'

He scowled critically at his leading lady who was now de-mummified. 'You look like you've been dragged through a hedge backwards, Miss Hanro.'

It was true. The blonde wig was looking decidedly wild now, and despite her best efforts to protect the thick make-up from the heat, Silvia's black eye kohl was smeared over her nose and the thick orange foundation was looking patchy.

'What do I pay that dresser for? Isn't that wretch able to keep you looking as you should?'

Brian Langley was obviously losing his temper, and Elaine had materialised out of the darkness with a frozen expression on her fine-boned face.

'Oh, it's not as bad as all that, surely? Elaine can't help the Leichner dripping, can she?' Silvia Hanro laughed.

Still Elaine didn't move, just stood rooted to the spot. She was obviously terrified of Brian Langley. Posie felt a stab of pity for her, regardless of the inappropriate orange shoes.

Meanwhile, quick as a flash, Dolly had thrown off her violet gloves, whisked out of somewhere a tin of Vaseline White Petroleum Jelly and a clean handkerchief and was ministering to Silvia Hanro with lightning speed. Silvia Hanro just stood, letting Dolly fix her up. Within a few seconds everything was good as new.

Brian Langley swallowed down his rage and stared at Dolly.

'I don't know who you are, Missie,' he said, taking a pencil from behind his ear, 'but you obviously know your stuff. Shame it's pretty much the last day of filming, otherwise you'd have had a job here. Tell you what, you keep on like that, and I might look to hire you in the future. You keep Miss Hanro looking good this afternoon and you can go and claim a day's wages in cash over with Reggie, my secretary. You'll get the same pay as he doles out to the extras. Six-thirty sharp at the upstairs office. Okay?'

He scribbled something on the back of his notepad, ripped it off and thrust it at Dolly, who took the chit and beamed.

'Thank you, Mr Langley,' she simpered.

Posie blew out her cheeks, incredulous.

What would Rufus say? Not to mention the fact that it was most likely illegal to pay a married woman for working on a film set; the wretched marriage bar was a blight on almost every profession by now.

But thoughts as to the appropriateness or inappropriateness of Dolly becoming a working woman again for the afternoon flew out of the window as she caught the tail-end of Brian Langley's next diatribe.

'Yes. That's much better. You look much more like Anne Boleyn now.'

Posie gasped. She was stunned at the historical inaccuracy of the thing.

Anne Boleyn!

Silvia Hanro who looked like a strapping blonde Valkyrie in real life was playing petite, dark, foxy-faced Anne Boleyn, Henry the Eighth's femme-fatale of a second wife!

How ludicrous!

Posie was just about to say *Anne Boleyn wasn't a blonde* when she suddenly saw Robbie Fontaine, done up to the nines in rich jewelled velvets and a glittering crown, come prowling down from the stage; his dark eyes roving around, his glimmery smile already fixed in place.

'Good grief!' Posie exhaled slowly, incredulous.

Robbie Fontaine looked nothing like a Henry the Eighth should do, with his neat dark looks and his tall, muscular build, rather than the porcine ginger giant he was attempting to play, but before she could think on it anymore, Robbie Fontaine came over and made a big show of kissing Silvia on the mouth, as if they were lovers who couldn't get enough of each other. Many pairs of eyes swivelled their way. There were several titters.

It was the first time Posie had seen them together.

'Darling, you look too, too adorable. I love you so much,' Silvia simpered.

You had to admit, they made a good go of looking like a couple in love. Several of the cameramen were snickering and tut-tutting, but in a good-humoured way, as if they saw such shenanigans often. Posie remembered that Silvia had called the performances both on and off camera as the 'Robbie and Silvia show', and Posie saw now that that seemed a fairly accurate description.

'ON SET! ON SET! NOW!' roared Brian Langley, raking through his thick hair, holding up his watch. Within seconds everyone had scarpered and the place became silent and even darker than before. People had run off into their positions, leaving Posie and Dolly standing there like idiots, quite alone.

Posie strained her eyes through the bank of shadows of cameramen up ahead. She scowled. *Where were they supposed to sit?*

Apparently she needed to watch and observe and, if necessary, protect. Hadn't Silvia asked for some chairs to be provided?

As if on cue, Elaine the dresser materialised again and Posie and Dolly found themselves being gently guided through the darkness towards the very first row of chairs and tripods set right next to the stage, with a good view, as if at the theatre.

'Sorry to keep you waiting,' the little woman whispered, indicating towards where three canvas camping chairs were drawn up.

'Do sit down. Make yourselves comfortable, ladies. I'm afraid I didn't catch your names – school friends of Miss Hanro – isn't that right? Would you like an afternoon tea? Or more champagne?'

Posie collapsed into one of the uncomfortable chairs, but the sound of a tea cheered her up no end. 'Oh yes, please, Elaine. Tea sounds good.'

'Would you like fancy buns, or plain? They're all made onsite, by the cook. They're very good.'

'The lot, please.'

'Right you are.'

'STOP THAT BALLY WHISPERING ON THE FRONT ROW!' screamed Mr Langley. 'Lights all okay? Action!'

And Silvia shook out her blonde, historically-inaccurate wig and made her entrance. Posie sat watching, half-amused, half-annoyed.

She turned to Elaine, who was still hovering nearby, hands fluttering at her mouth. Was it her imagination or was Elaine staring at Robbie Fontaine, transfixed, a look of adoration on her face? So she was just another of the nation's womenfolk who had fallen for Robbie Fontaine's charms.

'What is this scene?' Posie butted into the girl's reverie.

'It's the execution,' Elaine whispered. 'The one where they use the guillotine. It's very dramatic.'

'*WHAT*?' hissed Posie, more to herself than at anyone in particular. 'Anne Boleyn was beheaded, but the guillotine wasn't invented yet for another two hundred years! Goodness me! What a lot of tosh! What about accuracy?'

'Oh lovey, do be quiet,' said Dolly in hushed tones.

'It's the movies, darlin'. When it's this fabulous who cares a jot about accuracy?'

* * * *

Seven

For an hour Posie ate iced halfpenny buns and drank strong China tea out of a tin mug. She was also watching the stage, peering into the light from the darkness, but it struck her there was little to observe.

Brian Langley was simply making Silvia Hanro act out the same scene over and over again: forcing her to cast a sort of dramatic, over-the-top look of repentance towards Robbie Fontaine, all while being pinioned down to the fake guillotine.

'AGAIN! TAKE SIXTEEN! ACT THIS TIME! COME ON! It's all about the eyes! Work your magic, Miss Hanro.'

Brian Langley was timing the footage as well as trying to direct the scene in general; holding his watch outstretched in his hand and meticulously checking that the film reels were being run at the same speed. He shouted frequently at his cameramen. It was dull, tedious work and Posie didn't blame him for being angry most of the time. It looked dashed difficult and it made her feel irritable to even think about it.

Posie shifted in her chair. She was bored, and the heat from all the lights and their strange carbon stink were making her hot.

Dolly meanwhile was riveted, sat on the edge of her seat and dashing up and down to the stage to fix make-up as and when Brian Langley called her, much like an overactive ball-boy on the tennis courts.

Her eyes having adjusted to the strange working conditions, Posie now knew who were the key members of Brian Langley's little filming crew. In a way it was like watching a cuckoo-clock do its little performance in slow motion: the same people darting forwards again and again, the same regular, repeated movements; the same haughty shuffle onto the stage by Robbie Fontaine, again and again, always from the left-hand side. It was relentless. And hardly glamorous.

She checked her wristwatch as best she could in the darkness.

Four o'clock.

Posie had had enough. She couldn't get her notebook out here, so she mentally ticked through the people Silvia Hanro suspected of having written the death threats: the co-star, Robbie Fontaine; the sister, Pamela; the fan, Hector Mallow. Added to these were Posie's additional suspects, Brian Langley and Tom, the boyfriend.

Of all of these suspected people only two were in the studio right now, and it was ludicrous to think that either of Robbie Fontaine or Brian Langley were in a position to strike down their leading lady under the gaze of an entire film crew.

If ever.

Robbie Fontaine was distasteful, for sure, but Posie was willing to bet her life on the fact that he wasn't a killer. And unless Brian Langley was the perpetrator of the notes, there was precious little to investigate here.

Posie needed to look at the other suspects, or else come up with her own theory as to who was behind the threats. And there was hardly any time left before tomorrow's Wrap Party. She was horribly unprepared, and sitting here wasn't helping.

Posie knew that she needed to prowl around. She promised herself just one more hour at Worton Hall, to see what else she could find out before digging deeper.

She started to rise to her feet, watching Dolly over on the stage, dabbing and primping. Posie knew she'd never catch her eye to tell her she was leaving, and knew still further that she'd never prise Dolly away from what looked to be the time of her life.

'Excuse me, Miss Parker, isn't it?'

Posie collapsed back down into her canvas seat again in a sprawling ungainly fashion as the blonde Norse God sat down right next to her on her left-hand side. He stared straight ahead at the setup front, not turning her way in the slightest. The lights reflected brightly in his blue sunglasses. But a smile was playing through his voice:

'We haven't been formally introduced yet, and it looks like you're about to leave. It's a bit of a maze getting out of here. Shall I be your guide?'

She could just about make out his sharp profile in the pitch-black; she could smell his pine scent and the burnt sugar. She felt an awkward thrill of excitement tingle up her spine.

'Erm, yes. Well, that would be very kind, I must say. Thank you.'

'My pleasure. I'm Tom, by the way. Tom Moran. Assistant to the Under-Director at Sunstar Films.'

'Tom?'

Tom, Silvia Hanro's boyfriend?

It must be.

Posie remembered Silvia's description of the man: the rugged good looks, the enigmatic expression. It all fitted. And there was more than a whiff of Alaric about the man, too. It was true.

Posie felt a strange sinking feeling quickly envelop her.

'Yep. *That* Tom.' There was that tone of a smile in the smooth, deep voice again. 'Now, grab your things and follow me. But I must warn you of something.'

'Oh?'

'When we hit the light, the *natural* light, over past the door to this studio, you're going to see something which might make you want to scream. I beg you not to, for my sake.'

'Okay.' Posie nodded, intrigued. But before she could ask anything else she saw that Tom had sprung to his feet and was already beginning to move off. In his white clothes he was faintly luminous through the darkness. She followed, hot on his heels, away from the artificial light. At the exit, Tom walked straight through and Posie stepped outside into the July sunshine which immediately made her eyes squint. The man had disappeared.

'Here I am, Miss Parker.'

Posie turned and saw that Tom was standing beside the big blackboard, obscured by layers of smoke from a just-lit cigarette.

'Takes some getting used to, that lighting inside, doesn't it?'

'It does. I couldn't make out much at first. I can quite see why you chaps all wear white.'

Tom laughed. 'We don't have to, but it does make things slightly easier. But the lights themselves play havoc with the eyes, even if they are better than they were before the war. Those old lights, Klieg lights they were called, were a dreadful blue colour and they could almost burn right through a fella's retinas if you looked at them a second too long. You'd be seeing them when you closed your eyes for bed twelve hours later. We called it "Klieg eye".'

The cigarette smoke suddenly cleared, and then the penny dropped. Posie saw at once what Tom had meant about seeing something which might make her scream.

Tom Moran was missing half his face.

* * * *

70

Posie found herself accepting a smoke which Tom offered from a dark blue packet. Despite the fact that she hardly ever smoked.

'The war, I take it, Mr Moran?' she said, inhaling, trying not to look shocked or disgusted, and trying not to stare too much. She understood now the reason for Tom's strange manner earlier, the way he always stared straight ahead, and the reason Silvia Hanro had called him movie star material – *almost*. It explained the tiny second of pain which had crossed Silvia's face when she spoke about her boyfriend.

Tom Moran had obviously once been ridiculously, out-of-this-world gorgeous.

But now, on his left-hand side, where an eyebrow and an eye should be, a flesh-coloured patch had been stuck into place by way of a covering under the blue glasses. The left side of his nose and the cheek below the patch and the chin beneath were burnt quite away. The parts of skin which were left looked dry and sore and blazed a vivid red, and the rest was covered in gauze. His lips were a mass of criss-crossed pale scars.

'Pretty, isn't it?'

'Shrapnel?'

Tom nodded.

'Yep. I was at Ypres at the end of July 1917, unfortunately. I was left for dead on the first day of the battle. Ended up in a flipping great bog-hole and by the time the stretcher-bearers found me three days later it was too late to save my face. But I was one of the lucky ones. I should have died out there. Everyone else in my division did.'

Tom lit another cigarette and smiled. It was a curious smile, joyful on the one side and pulled-down and sad, like a ghoulish clown on the other side.

'To your credit, Miss Parker, you don't seem shocked.'

'I couldn't be, Mr Moran. I've seen far worse, unfortunately. I was an ambulance driver out on the

Western Front up until Christmas 1917. I'm afraid that faces such as yours were my daily bread and butter for a while there. More's the pity.'

Tom raised his good eyebrow. 'Ah? Well. That explains it, then. Plucky girl. I don't know many men who could stomach that sort of work. I try to warn people about it in advance; the reactions I've had have been pretty extreme, you see. Even out and about, on the streets of London, where you'd think people would see all manner of poor souls still floating around from the war. But the stares I get, well, you'd think I'd wished it upon myself. Like I actually *want* to look like a freak.'

Posie nodded. 'People are cruel when they're scared of the unknown, Mr Moran. Not that it excuses them in the slightest. I also have friends who have been disfigured, and they say the same as you.'

Posie was thinking in particular of Alaric's best friend, Major Hugo Marchpane, a flying ace from the Great War who had been shot down in flames on what would turn out to be his last ever plane journey; he had been badly burned, and although he tried to pretend he didn't care, especially now that he had a very important job as a high-ranking Government Official, he often complained about the way people stared at him in the post-Great War world. Even in the corridors of Westminster.

Tom shrugged. 'It's ironic, that's all: it wasn't the war to end all wars, everyone knows that now. Trouble is, people don't like being reminded about it now we're into the roaring, blazing 1920s. Most people just want to have fun, and even if they can't, they want to *forget*. They force themselves to forget, by any means necessary. Cocaine, usually. It's easy enough. But people like me are the walking, talking, revolting reminders of that war from a lifetime ago. We don't just go away.'

'It's bad luck, for sure.'

That lopsided smile again. 'Yes. It most definitely is. But

listen to me rattling on. *I* need to help *you*. Not the other way around. You looked like you weren't enjoying yourself much in there. Brian briefed me on your visit; told me to assist you however I could. So where do you need to get to now?'

Posie had got out her notebook again and gave it a brief glance. 'Could you take me to see Reggie – I think that's his name – the secretary? I heard Brian Langley mention him earlier. Is he out here?'

'Yes. Reggie Jones. Somewhere about, keeping the extras all in check.'

Tom thrust on his straw boater and they set off across the grass and the cinder path in the direction of the small white marquee on the busy lawn. The extras were still milling around, taking up space.

'But why are the extras still here? It doesn't look like they'll be needed this late in the day, will they? Mr Langley's just filming with his leading actors right now.'

'You're right, of course. But Brian pays the extras by the day. Whole crowds of them. He expects them to stay the course. Just *in case* they're needed. In case he has to change the schedule. If they're not here at six-thirty, they don't get paid. Full stop. So they stick around.'

'I see.' Privately Posie was thinking how ludicrously expensive that sort of arrangement must be, and how Brian Langley must be shelling out crazy amounts for actors he simply didn't need. But who was she to question methods in an industry she didn't understand?

'You're on the trail of old Hector Mallow, are you? I expect Silvia told you all about her friendly stalker, did she?'

'She did.' Posie nodded. This was the first time Tom had mentioned Silvia by name, and she decided to probe further while the going was good.

'Do *you* think Hector Mallow is dangerous, Mr Moran? Have you seen him these last few days?'

Tom did not reply for a moment. He seemed to be

scanning the crowd. His one good eye came to rest on someone and his gaze lingered there.

'Quite frankly, I don't know the man at all, Miss Parker. I've only ever come across him once, when he was being carted off by some guards. And no, I haven't seen him these last few days, not that I've ever lost time or energy looking for him; Brian Langley keeps me quite busy, despite the silly job title – *Assistant to the Under-Director*! Besides, it would be like looking for a needle in a haystack: you do realise there are more than a hundred and fifty extras on the books each day? All dressed in very similar costumes. Usually thick brown sackcloth. Like hundreds of sacks of moving potatoes about the place. One man looks much like another.'

'That *is* a difficulty. I quite see that.'

'I'll say! You should ask Reggie Jones if Hector Mallow has been signing on as an extra this week. There he is now.'

Tom pointed over at a small, round, dark man with a clipboard and a tired look on a curiously fishlike face. Reggie was standing on the lawn, chatting to the dresser in the orange shoes. Tom signalled at the man to get his attention.

'But honestly, I don't think Mallow's your man. You might be wasting your time, Miss Parker.'

Posie was intrigued. 'Oh? Tell me, do *you* take the notes seriously, Mr Moran? Especially given the contents of this morning's note?'

Tom swung around to Posie and stared down at her, full-face. After a small, weighty silence, he spoke in a very low, hoarse voice and she had to stand very close to hear him.

'*Of course* I take the bally things seriously. I'm worried sick by these notes, frantic. And that terrible envelope today! That was completely uncalled for. What sort of sick person sends a finger?'

Tom lit another cigarette and inhaled deeply. 'The last

few days have been a living hell. I'm a bundle of nerves. I don't often speak about private things, but Silvia must have told you how things stand between us. She's the love of my life, has been for years. I don't know what I'd do without her.'

He laughed and splayed his hands.

'She's made me what I am: I owe her all of this.'

He whispered on, urgently now. 'I'm concerned that something will happen at tomorrow's party. I just wish Brian Langley would step up and get the police involved. Quite frankly, it makes me query his motives, or even his role in this. With all due respect – and no offence intended – I don't quite see how one lady detective can keep a fellow from committing cold-blooded murder if he's got his mind set on it and a gun at the ready.'

Posie shook her head reassuringly: 'Oh, please don't worry about offending me. *I* quite agree with you. I think the police should be involved too. And I might just get them involved. Undercover, of course. Without mentioning it to Brian Langley.'

'Oh? Well, thank goodness for that.'

Tom Moran heaved a sigh of relief and brightened visibly. 'That's the first sensible thing I've heard this week. You do that. Get them out here. At the party tomorrow. As many as possible. Please.'

But something he had said had caught Posie by surprise. She eyed the man keenly.

'Do you know who is behind these notes, Mr Moran? Who might wish Silvia dead? You referred to the writer of the notes as a "fellow" just now. If not Hector Mallow, then who?'

Tom hesitated, then shrugged uncertainly. 'I have no proof, Miss Parker. But I'd say that Robbie Fontaine should be high on your list of suspects.'

'He is. Apparently. He was first on the list recited to me by Silvia. But why?'

Reggie was now on his way over across the grass. Tom continued in the same undertone:

'Money. It's very unusual, but did you know that Silvia earns almost twice the amount he does, per picture? Has done since the war. She's very wealthy as a result, of course. With her out of the way his earning capacity will go up.'

'I see.'

Tom continued, his tone urgent now:

'You might also want to think about Brian Langley's part in all this. If Silvia dies, this new film will become a classic, instantly. Nothing sells better than death. And who knows, perhaps he has some other financial means of benefitting from her death? But I wouldn't say any of this in Silvia's presence. She's very loyal to Brian. Too loyal, some would say.'

Posie nodded bleakly. Tom's thoughts were echoing some of her own misgivings about the Producer and what he might gain.

'Thank you. Now, where can I find you and Miss Hanro later tonight? *If* I have to, I mean. I'll obviously try not to bother you.'

'We stay here at Worton Hall, generally. It's our base. It will be until Sunstar terminate the contract tomorrow. We both have rooms here, as have most of the film crew. When we go into London we stay at my, well, *our* flat in the Albany.'

Tom smiled proudly. 'You know it? It's in Mayfair, by the Royal Academy. It's useful for partying. But we haven't been there in an age. Silvia has kept her old family home, of course. But that's huge, and rented out, and not useful to us right now. If you have to, ask the Porter at the Albany for Mr and Mrs Delacroix. Top floor.'

'Fine, thank you.' Posie noted the address and the fake names down. 'I'm hoping to leave here soon. I'll see you again tomorrow for what I understand is the last day of filming.'

'Right you are. Hullo, Reggie!'

The secretary was upon them. He looked at Posie inquisitively, with frank interest. The complete unsuitability of her story as being a school friend of Silvia Hanro suddenly became apparent. Why had she been so stupid to accept it so blindly? Why on earth would a school friend of Silvia's be picking around a film set asking quite particular questions of various members of the company?

The thinness of the cover must have been apparent to Tom, too, because for just a second she saw what looked like a shadow of uncertainty cross his ghastly face. Frantically she scrambled for a plausible cover. But Tom got there first.

Was that a wink of the good eye beneath the shade of the glasses?

'It was a real pleasure, Miss Parker. If we can be of any further help with writing your story, you have my card, don't you? I know that Miss Hanro enjoyed your interview, especially given the personal connection; the fact that you were at school together really enabled her to trust you. I do hope that Sunstar's latest movie will be reviewed favourably by your magazine, especially as we've done you this favour of early admittance ahead of the other journalists. Goodbye.'

Journalists! She was being handed a safety rope and she took it gratefully as Tom Moran sauntered off back towards the dark studio.

'I'm Miss Parker, and I'm with *The Lady*, Mr Jones.'

'Press? That's unusual.' The small man spoke with the vestiges of a soft Welsh accent and he looked at Posie warily.

She nodded and fished in her bag for one of her very plain white business cards, which featured nothing more than her name in bold black type and a fake London address in Mayfair. She kept the cards for occasions just such as these, even though Len had laughed at her for her over-the-top ways when they had been delivered from the printers.

'I write features about different entertainments and I'm doing a big piece all about *Henry the King*, and what it's like to work on a film set, from lots of different angles. I've spoken to the leading lady; she's on our cover, naturally, and to some of the actual filming crew, including Mr Langley. And now I'm wondering, could I speak to you about the extras, Mr Jones? I'll only take up five minutes of your time.'

Reggie Jones had put the business card in his pocket without looking at it. At the mention of his Producer he had visibly relaxed and dropped his guard.

'Sure. What exactly do you want to know?'

****

Five minutes was all it took. Reggie Jones was more than forthcoming in talking about his important work as Brian Langley's secretary, and Posie gently steered him back to the subject of extras again and again, standing in the corner of the hot marquee, nodding and looking interested and taking fake shorthand notes throughout. She managed to swing the subject onto Hector Mallow as quickly as possible.

'Miss Hanro mentioned she had one particularly ardent fan. He works as an extra, too, whenever he can. Is he around to speak to at all? A Mr Miller? Or was it a Mr Mellow? Or was it…'

'Hector Mallow?' Reggie Jones replied, somewhat impatiently.

'Oh yes!' she said placidly. 'That sounds about right! Is he here?'

Reggie Jones tsk-tsked. 'Did Miss Hanro actually mention *him*? Think he'd be a good thing to write about? That creepy low-life?'

Posie nodded, delighted. 'Yes. She mentioned him. *I* thought it might be interesting to speak to him, and she didn't raise any objections.'

'As you wish. Although I've got a book full of lovely, dedicated extras you could speak to instead. Nice, *normal* people. We get two types of extras here, same as other film companies: we get those who live nearby and need the money, and we get real movie fans; those who live and breathe the movies and don't care a jot about the money. They're happy just being on set, being part of it all, having the chance to rub shoulders with the Miss Hanros and Mr Fontaines of this world.'

'I see.'

'Sure you don't want to speak to one of those second type of extras? I've got plenty here right now would be only too happy to get their names in a nice story for once. Nothing much else to do today, either…'

'Nope. I take it Mr Mallow's not your regular extra then?'

Reggie Jones blew out his cheeks in exasperation and wiped a hand over his sweaty brow.

'Not on your nelly. He might have been, *once*, but he's taken things a whole stage further, now. Once upon a time he was just a plain old movie buff, and a regular paid extra on Sunstar's books, nicely behaved as anything. But then he fell in love with our Miss Hanro and started playing dirty.'

'Dirty? How so?'

Reggie Jones sighed heavily. 'He started following her about. Lurking. Waiting in ambush more like. Then there were notes, and letters, and cards. And presents. You know the type of thing.'

'Notes?'

'Declarations of undying love. I seem to remember. I've had to throw away a fair few in my time.'

'But nothing dangerous?'

'*Dangerous?* Why would they be dangerous? You mean loaded with poison or something?'

'Well, no. I suppose I mean *threatening*, rather than dangerous.'

Reggie Jones was giving Posie a funny look, and for a minute she thought she might have laid it on a bit thick. She smiled hastily, tucking her dark short hair behind her ear in what she alone knew was a nervous tick.

'I'm just making sure he won't threaten *me*, Mr Jones, if I speak to him. I don't want to put myself in a small, enclosed space with a dangerous man. You never can be too sure.'

'Ah, I see.' He nodded, placated.

'Well, no. Be assured, Miss Parker. There's nothing obviously *dangerous* about Hector Mallow. But he's a creepy sort. He's banned from here now, but he gets in, all the same. It's usually me in charge of checking in the extras every morning, but occasionally I have the weekend off – I am a family man, after all – and then someone else steps in and does the register; someone not so experienced at seeing through all of Hector's disguises. And there we go again.'

'What was that about the weekends, Mr Jones? I don't understand.'

'Didn't I mention? It's only ever on a Saturday or Sunday that Hector Mallow appears. I've never known him show up for a weekday of filming. He must have another job, a regular job, perhaps, in the week?'

'So he's not around now? And he's not been around, say, Monday and Tuesday of this week at all?'

'No. He *was* around on Sunday, though. Chanced his arm and got through the replacement clerk's security checks. I was back here by early afternoon, thank goodness, and as soon as I spotted him – he had dyed his hair black this time and grown a pencil moustache – I got him escorted off the premises. He went with no objection, mind, quiet as a lamb.'

'How interesting. And do you have the contact details for this Hector Mallow?'

Reggie shuffled, a bit dubiously. 'I expect I *do* have them somewhere, Miss Parker. If you're quite sure you really must speak to him?'

'Quite sure.'

'Come this way, then. All the paperwork and money is locked up in Mr Samuelson's office. It's the only really safe place here on set. It's at the top, up the stairs.'

As they walked through the large crowd of underused extras, most reading magazines in the marquee, Reggie Jones gestured at them all appreciatively.

'On the whole we're very lucky.' He smiled. 'Fortunately the Hector Mallows of this world are few and far between. I suppose it seems odd to you, doesn't it? All these people sitting about with not much to do?'

Posie smiled winningly. 'Oh no,' she trilled airily. 'Mr Moran explained the arrangement. Most useful in case Mr Langley chooses to film something different to what he had planned.'

Reggie nodded knowingly. 'Or if he *can't* film what he had planned because of unforeseen events.'

'Like what?'

'Like this morning for instance. He was supposed to be filming Miss Hanro, alone, over and over in that execution scene, from the crack of dawn. What he's doing now. But she called in very early from home, in central London, with an urgent appointment: said she couldn't make it in to Worton Hall until coffee time. So then this great gaggle of extras were ushered into position for a big crowd scene at the last minute. Not planned at all. But it was jolly useful that they *were* around.'

'Quite.'

And in her head Posie was re-running something that Brian Langley had thrown out in anger at Silvia Hanro before she stepped in front of the cameras.

He had referred to '*your mysterious appointment*', something which had messed up his scheduled filming early this morning, delaying things, which had made him angry.

What had that been about? And why hadn't Silvia mentioned it to Posie earlier?

And why had Tom Moran insisted that the couple hadn't stayed at his flat in the Albany for an age, when in fact they, or just Silvia, had been there the very night before.

It could be something, and it could be nothing.

But Posie stored it up for later. In case it was useful.

* * * *

Eight

'You got the grand tour earlier, did you?' said Reggie Jones in his sing-song Welsh accent as they entered the house again.

Posie hadn't had any tour of any kind, but she mumbled something about having seen the studio, which was all she was really concerned about.

'Ah, well, folks are busy I suppose,' said Reggie wearily. He gestured around him, at the corridor where Silvia's dressing room was. 'Down here are the main actors' dressing rooms, and the props and costume rooms. This here is the centre of the house.'

They passed into the old entrance hall of the house, cool and inviting, if a bit dilapidated, where the telephone booth and a reception desk were now located. Everything was painted a sharp blinding white.

'Over there is the ballroom, and next to it in the old parlour is the staff canteen.'

Posie looked about as best she could as they started to mount the great curving staircase made of white planed wood. She could just see that several women and a man were standing on ladders in the white ballroom, fixing what looked like hundreds of strings of tiny lights and several rows of silver glittery decorations around the place, presumably in preparation for tomorrow's Wrap Party.

The canteen next door with its white walls looked more austere, rows of wooden benches and great tables, much like at a boys' boarding school. But it wasn't very big. At all.

'Does everyone eat in there?' Posie asked, puzzled.

'Nope. Only the film crew and the leading actors. The labourers and the extras either bring a sandwich and a thermos from home or else they nip off down the Royal Oak for lunch. It's a favourite haunt, and only three minutes' walk from here, on the Worton Road. They do a good sausage sandwich, mind.'

Posie felt her stomach growl at the thought, despite the halfpenny buns she had devoured.

They had reached the top floor of the house. Here everything was painted white, too. Rows of doors on long corridors led away in every direction from a round central landing, above which a huge skylight shaped like a giant flower allowed the light to flood in, illuminating what could otherwise have felt like quite a dark, poky space.

Reggie Jones jerked his head quickly in the direction of the rows of doors away to the right.

'Over there are a whole load of rooms for the main film crew and staff. It's a bit like a hotel up here, really. And there are a couple of little flats over there, too, for the principal movie stars themselves. A home from home.'

'I see. How cosy.'

'Brian Langley wanted exclusive use of this place when he signed the lease last year. Normally Mr Samuelson, the owner, he operates shifts here, so two films might be being filmed at any one time, by two producers, from two different companies; all day and all night, sometimes. Mr Langley didn't want that this time. Which means a condition of the exclusive use of this place was that he took the whole house, as well as the studios outside. That included all this accommodation. And he also had to take on Mr Samuelson's permanent staff, too.'

'Sorry? Permanent staff?'

'Yes. It was all set out in the contract. I should know, I had to study the thing until I was blue in the face! Brian had to take on the cook and an army of cleaners, plus the in-house carpenters and the scenery painters. The receptionist downstairs is Mr Samuelson's, too. As are a couple of cameramen, a projectionist and a couple of dressers for the main movie stars. You might have seen me talking to Elaine, who's supposed to look after Miss Hanro? She's one of Mr Samuelson's permanent staff and she's been helping me a bit with the extras. It's been very handy, actually; having someone who knows the place like the back of her hand and knows where everything is.'

'I can see that would be helpful.' Again, Posie was thinking what a huge waste of money and what a non-slick operation the whole film industry seemed to be, but just then she realised that Reggie Jones was looking more animated than she had seen him, and his face had lost its fishyness. He had stopped outside a big door with a large safety bar across its double width, and was motioning over excitedly.

'This here is the projection room,' he whispered in reverent tones. 'Right next to the cutting room. Care to have a look?'

Before Posie could utter anything, Reggie Jones had pushed the bar down, and was indicating that she should follow him inside. She did so gladly, and screwed up her eyes again as what met her for a second time that afternoon was pitch-black darkness, again punctured by the glowing ends of cigarettes here and there about the place.

As far as she could make out, the room was fairly large, and packed with rows of hard-backed chairs, like a mini cinema. The room was empty save for about five men mainly seated in the front row. A large screen, almost as full sized as in a real cinema, dominated the room. It was flickering madly just now, busy with nothing, just a crackly grey with blobs of black and snowflakes of white hissing in-between.

A sharp voice called over:

'Who's there? Who's opened the door?'

'Relax, Bernard. It's just me, Reggie. I'm showing a journalist from *The Lady* around. Thought she might like to see a bit of the final thing.'

'Brian know about this, does he?'

'Yep. He's authorised it all.'

'I see. Well, there's not much to see at the moment. Willie back there is changing the reel. Oh! Here we go!'

The invisible Bernard's voice softened instantly. It became almost dream-like.

'Atta-girl! Does anyone do that better? Betty Balfour eat your heart out!'

And Posie stared up and saw the screen had stopped crackling and that the now-familiar wide face of Silvia Hanro was up there instead; huge and blown up, with all of the focus of the camera trained intently on the kohl-rimmed eyes, dark and anguished and smouldering.

'I say!'

Posie saw at once that the camera loved Silvia Hanro; that the make-up which had looked odd and over-the-top in daylight was perfect on the silver screen. That the blonde wig and velvet clothes seemed eminently right up there. She understood too that when you started to look at Silvia Hanro, here seen pleading with Robbie Fontaine, you couldn't take your eyes off her.

'Quite something, isn't she?' said Reggie Jones softly. 'Cinema dynamite. And everyone here knows it.'

Posie nodded mutely. She agreed with him wholeheartedly.

'Let's get out of here. Bernard and his lads are busy putting yesterday's reels together so Brian Langley can view it late on tonight. Or in the early hours, more like. He can spend the whole night in here working, can Brian. Anything could happen outside and he wouldn't know about it.'

Out on the corridor again they approached a room at the very end with a glass-stencilled door. Reggie Jones took a key from around his neck on a bit of string.

'Here we go. This is Mr Samuelson's office. I'll have a look for that address you want…if you're certain…'

Posie nodded and stared around unabashedly while Reggie went over to a huge dark-wooded desk which took up most of the room, and retrieved a huge grey box-file.

He started to flip through the unwieldy file while Posie took in the oak-panelled walls, the green velvet sofa in the corner and the traditional British hunting scenes which lined the walls. There was a small humidor on the desk and a cut-glass ashtray, clean. The place felt much like a gentleman's club in Mayfair, a real man's stronghold perched high above the white and unreal fairy-tale blaze of Worton Hall Studios below. A window behind the desk gave on to rolling scorched countryside with a view of unbroken blue skies overhead.

'Here you go,' Reggie said, scribbling something down on a piece of lined notepaper and thrusting it at Posie. 'But you might rue the day you took this.'

'Thank you, Mr Jones. I appreciate it.'

If Reggie Jones had been about to say anything else on the subject of Hector Mallow, he didn't, for just at that moment the glazed door swung open and a huge figure entered the room, taking up all the space. The man who stood there was very tall, and very wide and very round. He was impeccably dressed in a three-piece suit, with a maroon dickie-bow tie and immaculate white spats over his shoes, despite the blistering heat. The man was surprisingly young, perhaps only a couple of years older than Posie herself, although the weight he carried lent him a much older aspect. He had a ruddy complexion with small blue eyes which twinkled with a crisp intelligence.

'Ah!' said Reggie Jones subserviently, 'Mr Samuelson! I'm just collecting some necessary bits from my box-file, sir.'

Mr Samuelson put up a large, fleshy hand as if stopping traffic. When he spoke it was in a booming voice:

'Carry on, by all means! No need to explain! I did give you the key to my office, after all.' He looked at Posie expectantly. She smiled and held out her ungloved hand.

'Miss Parker, sir. I'm here with *The Lady*. I've been seeing everything there is to see, and meeting Silvia Hanro, of course.'

'Ah, yes. Miss Parker. I know all about you! Would you like to interview *me*, too?'

He sat down heavily in his padded leather desk chair.

'Perhaps Mr Jones here could give us some time alone?'

Reggie Jones positively gaped, and as Posie watched him back out of the room hastily, she was just in time to see Mr Samuelson suppress a laugh.

'Be a good girl and go and peep out of that window in the door and check that Reggie Jones has actually gone, would you?' Mr Samuelson said, lighting a cigar. 'What we need to discuss has no need of an audience, now, does it?'

Posie did as she was told, checked the corridor outside, shook her head to confirm that no-one was around, and returned to a comfortable chair which Mr Samuelson indicated to on the other side of the desk. She looked up and saw that a tobacco-coloured cloud of brown had distempered the immaculate white ceiling right above the desk, presumably over a long period of time.

'I saw you in the projection room,' said Mr Samuelson between puffs. He spoke in a low undertone now. 'I thought "Aha! There's the lady detective Brian Langley told me about this morning." I've heard all about you anyhow, of course. You're that famous explorer's girlfriend, aren't you?'

Posie nodded fairly primly, hoping Mr Samuelson would just carry right on, which he did:

'I snatched myself away from the lures of Miss Hanro and came to speak to you.'

'Thank you, Mr Samuelson. Can you shed any light on these death threats?'

'No, I'm afraid not.' He shook his head. 'Don't know the first thing about them, except they keep on coming, apparently. Brian Langley thinks it's a known stalker: wants to keep things quiet, naturally, until filming is all wrapped up tomorrow. Can't say I blame him, either. Hopefully the whole thing *is* just a wretched hoax.'

'Mnnn.'

'You don't think so, Miss Parker?'

'I think we ought to be looking at these notes as serious death threats, Mr Samuelson. That's what I think.'

The eyes of the owner of Worton Hall no longer twinkled, and he held his cigar a moment too long over the tooled leather inlay on his desk. There was a horrible burning smell.

'I see. Well, in that case I'll give you this, then.'

Mr Samuelson had unlocked a small drawer in his desk, and reached into the back. He took out a plain-looking silver key on a length of worn string. He passed it over to Posie.

'This is a master key. It unlocks every single door in this place, the house and studios included. You have my full permission to look absolutely anywhere you please, in the course of this investigation.'

Posie put the key into the pocket of her yellow dress. She thought that the clues to the death threats lay elsewhere, other than at Worton Hall, but she appreciated the gesture of the key anyhow. Perhaps she might need it, who knew?

'Is there anything else I can help you with, Miss Parker?'

Posie had just spotted the shining black telephone apparatus on the desk beside Mr Samuelson's substantial right elbow. She had two calls to make, and she didn't really fancy making either of them downstairs in that public telephone booth again.

Mr Samuelson's eyes followed her gaze and he nodded enthusiastically. 'Please, be my guest. All of my facilities are at your service, use the telephone here as much as you like.

Just lock the door again to this office when you leave. I'll let you get on.'

'That really is most kind of you.'

Bertie Samuelson was rising now, making his way over towards his door. 'You're sure there's nothing else I can do for you?'

'Well. Actually, how often does the bus or train run back into central London? I need to go again fairly soon.'

Mr Samuelson smiled. 'That's typical of Brian Langley, not to have thought of getting you home. He's only got the one car and the one driver, and he can't really afford him, but I tell you what, have mine.'

He checked his watch. 'Fred, my personal driver, will be back here at five o'clock. I'll get him to wait up front for you. Tell him to take you to the moon and back, as far as I'm concerned. He's all yours.'

'Thank you.'

'Don't mention it. Now I'm back to that projection room. You know where to find me if you need me, right?'

But Posie was already placing her first call with the Operator.

* * * *

Nine

'Chief Inspector Lovelace's office, please,' she told the receptionist on the switchboard at New Scotland Yard.

'Wait a moment. I'm connecting you now.'

After a few seconds, Posie heard the familiar voice of the maverick Chief Inspector, Richard Lovelace, her long-time collaborator and her sort-of champion, come on the line.

He sounded more flustered than usual, as if he were in a hurry. When he heard it was Posie on the line she heard him let out a jagged sort of sigh.

'Oh, it's only *you*. Thank heavens for that.'

She imagined him standing in his horrible olive green office, paperwork everywhere, his tweedy waistcoat askew, running his hands through his thick, wild reddish hair, looking out through his triple-barred window with its sliver of a view over the Victoria Embankment, his mind wandering over how he would catch his next arch-villain.

'You don't sound very pleased to hear from me.'

'Oh, I am. I am. I thought it might be the Assistant Commissioner on the line asking to check my speech.'

'What speech would that be, sir?'

Richard Lovelace sighed again. 'Oh, just this blasted Police Awards Ceremony I'm having to go to this evening.' He mumbled over the next words a bit.

'Actually, I've been awarded a prize, and you know, I've got to make an acceptance speech afterwards.'

'Oh, my gosh! Congratulations! That's amazing news!' Posie wasn't that surprised. The Chief Inspector was fast gaining a reputation for putting away virtually every big-time criminal in London. And on more than a couple of occasions she had helped him do just that.

'Mnnn, well. I'm just about to go, actually. Got to get on over to the Inner Temple. So you've caught me standing here all dressed up in white tie like that dashing cad Robbie Fontaine: Mrs Lovelace is always going on about him, more's the pity.'

'I didn't take you for a movie fan,' said Posie cautiously.

'Nor am I. But the missus is.'

'Funny you should mention films, though. I'm at Worton Hall Studios right now. With Robbie Fontaine, as it happens.'

'Oh, yes?' said the Chief Inspector. 'Then by rights you should be having the time of your life.' Posie heard a rustling sound before the Chief Inspector resumed.

'So why are you calling me Posie, EXACTLY?'

'I need your help, sir. I'm in a bit of a tight fix.'

'Can't it wait until tomorrow? I'm literally just leaving.'

''Fraid not, sir. It can't really wait even a few hours. Ideally I need your help this very evening.'

The Chief Inspector groaned, and shouted something at someone in the background. 'Go on then. Give me your worst. But do it quickly.'

And Posie outlined the case of Silvia Hanro and the death threats as best and as quickly as she could, trying to explain who the suspects were as succinctly as possible, while not scrimping on detail. She explained that she was calling him for help against instructions.

Then she mentioned the grey, severed, frosty human finger.

When she had finished there was a silence on the end of

the line, and before she could break it Inspector Lovelace groaned again.

'Good grief! This is all we need. A dead movie star on our hands. It's not just a mare's nest, is it? You really think these notes are real?'

'I do, sir. There's a lot of venom behind them, especially the last one, and the timing is spot-on, what with this big party planned for tomorrow lunchtime. But I'm worried even before we get to tomorrow: there's lots here that doesn't fit. I don't think that Silvia Hanro is telling me everything, for one thing. She doesn't really want me here: that's what I think.'

'You think she knows who the notes are from?'

'Maybe. I'm not sure, sir. She's panicked, but not panicked enough, if you see what I mean.'

'Right. What do you want from me now?'

Posie heard a ripping noise as a piece of paper was torn off between teeth down the line.

'I'd like you to find out as much as possible about Miss Hanro's background, and also about Brian Langley, and Robbie Fontaine. And could you check on the official police files relating to this stalker fellow, Hector Mallow, and the sister, Pamela Hanro? And there's a fellow who works here – Tom Moran – can you check his records too?'

'You don't ask much, do you, Posie?'

'Sorry, sir.'

'I'm going to get Sergeant Binny to get this information for me, and bring it to me at the Inner Temple. Let me put my thinking cap on and we'll puzzle this out as best we can, shall we? Can you meet me there at nine o'clock this evening? By the Temple Church? We'll discuss it there. That's the best I can do right now, I'm afraid.'

She heard the rustling and shouting again in the background as the Chief Inspector barked out some orders.

'Don't hang up!' she called out desperately. She had a few hours to go before nine o'clock and she had decided to check out the people Silvia Hanro had told her about as quickly as possible, before the police records came in.

'What is it now?'

'Frightfully sorry, but is that Sergeant Binny just there? Can I speak to him?'

And within minutes Posie had spoken to the Sergeant, whom she also knew of old, and had got him to look in the Telephone Directory for the details of Brian Langley's house in Richmond, and any listed home address which might exist for Pamela Hanro.

The Sergeant quickly gave her the address details for Brian Langley, but he was less successful with Pamela Hanro. She wasn't listed.

On the off chance, Posie mentioned the suffragette connection, and asked Sergeant Binny to check whether there was any given address for Pamela in any of the old police files.

The Sergeant sighed huffily down the line. 'I'll call you back in ten minutes,' he said, trying to keep some of the annoyance from his voice. He had obviously been looking forward to an early escape homewards, and was now lumbered with all manner of extra work, all of it Posie's doing.

'I really do appreciate it, Sergeant.'

'Mnnn.'

Posie checked her wristwatch after she replaced the receiver.

Yes: she had time.

She picked the receiver up again and placed a call with the Operator to a huge double-fronted Mews House on Pavilion Road, Chelsea.

She was after her old friend Rufus, Lord Cardigeon. Dolly's husband.

When Manders the Butler answered, Posie had a moment of self-doubt. She hardly knew why she was pursuing this at all.

Was she losing her touch? Why was she so bothered about Dolly just now, and by those hulking great nannies? However much she had on her plate with the strange happenings at Worton Hall, and it felt a lot right now, those nannies kept coming to the forefront of her mind.

Posie made polite chit-chat with Manders and confirmed that the babies and the nannies had arrived home safely before coming to the purpose of her call. Rufus.

But it was not to be.

'He's not here, Miss. Was he expecting your call?'

'Oh no, Manders. Can you tell me where he is?'

'I can indeed, Miss.'

'And?'

'He's at The House, Miss.'

'The House? What house? Do you mean his club, Number 11, in St James's? I thought he'd stopped going there?'

'Oh, not *there*, Miss. *The* House. The House of Lords, Miss.'

'But it's the summer recess, Manders. Surely? They're not sitting just now, are they?'

'No, they are not, Miss. But the restaurant does a very nice three courser on a Wednesday by all accounts, and there's always the library, with that lovely view out over the river.'

'I see. Well, thanks anyway.'

As she rang off, Posie privately thought that Rufus had simply exchanged one sort of private men's club for another, perhaps to escape the noise of the two screaming twins, or to escape the baleful glare of the nannies, but she tried not to be disloyal and sounded as cheery as could be as she rung for the House of Lords and asked for Lord Cardigeon to be dragged from whatever hole he happened to be hiding in.

She hoped it wasn't a hole which involved drink.

Hopefully Posie wasn't about to unravel some awful great knot in the middle of Rufus and Dolly's private lives. It was the last thing she felt like doing.

He answered after a bit.

'What Ho, Nosy!'

Posie swallowed down her annoyance at this age-old nickname for her. Rufus sounded completely sober, thank goodness.

'You sound pretty chipper, Rufus.'

'Mnnn. What do you want, Nosy, ringing me up here? Bit bally odd, what? All quite all right, is it?'

'Fine. Look, Rufus. I'm in Isleworth, at a film studio, at Worton Hall, and I've got Dolly here with me.'

She heard a sharp intake of breath, a slight whirr of panic. So, there was *something*.

She hurried on:

'The babies are fine, safe at home: don't worry. But look here, it's really none of my business, but is everything all right with Dolly? She seems a bit down. And what's the score with those great man-lookalike nannies? Don't tell me they're just for fun, or to help with the nappies and the baby purees. You may have pulled the wool over poor Dolly's eyes but you haven't done so with me. They're not real nannies, are they? They're bodyguards, aren't they?'

There was silence from the other end of the line.

'Is Dolly in danger, Rufus? Is this your clumsy response to a kidnapping threat or something?'

There, she had said it. It was out. Her completely over-the-top hypothesis.

She was met with yet more silence. She felt distinctly uneasy. Posie found herself gripping the edge of Bertie Samuelson's immense desk.

'Rufey? Just what exactly is going on here?' she said sharply. 'You need to tell me.'

'I can't talk on this line. Who knows who might be listening? But all I can say is for goodness' sake keep a close eye on Dolly, will you? Don't let her out of your sight. Bring her home.'

'Now come on, surely that's coming on a bit strong?'

'No. It isn't. All I can say is that there *is* a real danger. I need you to help me.'

Posie felt all of the air go out of her, like a great balloon. So, her worst fears had been realised. What sort of trouble was Rufus facing now? Who exactly were they up against?

'Another thing, Nosy. Dolly knows nothing about this. Don't let on. She'll be scared out of her wits.'

Posie didn't exactly agree: the Dolly of old had been one of the pluckiest girls she had ever met, but who knew, perhaps things had changed? She had no choice but to help out. She sighed.

'Fine. I'll do as you say, Rufus. For now.'

'Thanks, Nosy.'

'Tell me, are the police involved? I'm meeting the Chief Inspector later, if you'd like me to put in a word…'

But the line went hissy and she heard Rufus ringing off. Seconds later the telephone rang again and she grabbed it, expecting to hear Rufus.

Instead, it was Sergeant Binny, sounding considerably happier. He had obviously made short shrift of the suffragette records.

'Got what you need here, Miss. It was surprisingly easy to find. Miss Pamela has been at the same place since 1918. And this address is definitely the current one, as she's required to report in once a year with all of her current details.'

'Why's that?'

'Proper little firecracker, this one is. Miss Pamela got bailed out several times by family members, but the seriousness of her crimes means she's on our records for life. Got up to all sorts, mainly in 1913. Proper little devil, especially with a packet of matches: arson, criminal damage, you name it, the lot. She ran with that crowd who were suspected of setting fire to the Tea House, at Kew Gardens. But she got away with it as nothing was ever proved. From a very good family too, by the looks of it. Top-drawer. A Hyde Park address for the parents, before the war, anyhow. Got a pencil for her current address, have you?'

'Yep. Go for it.'

The Sergeant listed an address in South Kensington, a street which sounded slightly familiar to Posie. She wrote it down carefully.

'Something juicy for you.'

'Oh?'

'Mnnn. Your Miss Pamela Hanro doesn't work by the way, not officially, despite the fact she's unmarried. But she *does* have a child. An adopted child. Says so on our records. From the Foundling Hospital in Bloomsbury Fields. Adopted in the autumn of 1918. A girl. Odd, isn't it?'

'Indeed.' Posie raised an eyebrow, just to herself. Pamela Hanro sounded just as interesting as her famous sister. Perhaps more so.

'I wasn't sure if you needed to know that, but it doesn't hurt to go armed with the full facts, now, does it?'

'Thank you. I owe you one, Sergeant.'

'You do, Miss,' said the policeman in a sad, beleaguered tone, as if he had heard it all before.

Which of course, he had.

* * * *

Ten

Posie checked her watch again.

She still had twenty minutes before Bertie Samuelson's driver could pick her up. She'd have to find Dolly, and steal her away from Silvia Hanro, a task she wasn't looking forward to.

Coming out of Bertie Samuelson's office, she pulled the door to and locked it with the master key. Outside, on the white corridor all was quiet except for muffled sounds coming from the hallowed grounds of the projection room.

Beguiling though she was, Posie had no desire to see Silvia Hanro on screen again quite so soon, and she stepped lightly along the corridor, away from the head of the staircase, in the direction of the rows of doors behind which lay the rooms and flats for the film crew and movie stars.

Without really knowing why, Posie found herself unlocking the first door she came to. Inside was a mean sliver of a white room, furnished with just a single white bed and a wooden desk, the small high window closed and curtained. It was obvious the room wasn't in use. The next room was identical, and empty, and Posie had almost lost interest by the time she automatically opened the third door.

This room was the same as the two before, but occupied, obviously by a man. A pipe and tobacco were thrown carelessly across the desk, and a stash of paperback novels were piled over by the bed. Rumpled, soiled, dark clothes were thrown across every surface, and a glass bottle of milk stood curdling on the windowsill. An unpleasant unwashed-body smell pervaded the room. She closed the door again quickly, feeling a terrible snoop.

The next door led to another occupied room, unremarkable but for the familiarly sharp smell of lingering pine-wood with that strange undercurrent of burning. A neat pile of white clothes had been left folded on the desk chair. This was obviously Tom's room, and Posie suddenly felt an awkward sense of shyness overcome her.

Even so, she crept into the tiny room and had a good look about, but there was precious little to see. The real-life romance between Tom and Silvia didn't encroach here; they were obviously very careful, even behind closed doors, for not a single bleached blonde strand of hair or a daub of kohl or anything remotely feminine was in evidence.

Next door was another occupied room, and there was more to see here, although it, too, was very neat. It was obviously occupied by a woman, and a small mirror had been set up on the chest of drawers, together with a musky Penhaligon's travel candle in a little leather holder, its wick burned almost right down.

A framed and signed professional photograph of a male movie star in the style of around the time of the Great War stared out moodily from the top of a desk, the man's jet-black hair swept back harshly from his face and a semi-scowl making his eyes look intense.

There were a good many magazines fanned out across the top of the desk, mostly the *Picture Post* but a few film magazines thrown in too for good measure. Coming closer Posie saw that a few of the magazines were opened on spreads which featured pictures of the royal wedding between the Duke of York and his bride, Lady Elizabeth Bowes-Lyon, which had taken place a mere three months earlier.

In several places the bride's fabulously daring dress, now being copied up and down the country by ambitious seamstresses, had been circled around with a pencil, and in another magazine the entire dress had been cut out.

Underneath all of this was a fat wedding scrapbook.

A bride, Posie breathed to herself, with very little joy and a jolt of what felt for a horrid moment like jealousy. *The person whose room this is is about to be a bride.* She skimmed through the magazines unhappily.

The whole royal wedding in April had passed Posie by in a cloud of awkwardness. She had tried to pretend to herself and to everyone else that it wasn't happening; despite the fact that the new royal couple had enchanted the nation, and that the Duchess of York's lovely face in its jaunty bridal cap and veil had looked out from almost every woman's magazine for a period of weeks on end. Weddings and high-profile weddings in particular, were just a little too close for comfort right now.

Just as Posie was replacing the magazines, a sharp, shrill voice caught her out:

'Who the very devil are you? And what are you snoopin' about in here for?'

A flabby, gingery woman of about forty filled the doorway with her very substantial form, blocking out the bright light from the corridor, her quivering arms placed firmly on her hips in a gesture of disbelief, anger blazing from her blue gimlet eyes.

Posie stared and then realised that she had probably invaded the woman's own room. The white cook's hat and institutional apron gave away her profession and Posie suddenly remembered what Reggie had said about Brian Langley having taken on all of Worton Hall's permanent kitchen staff. It made sense for the cook to stay in residence.

'I'm so terribly sorry,' Posie lied, if not smoothly, then she hoped convincingly. 'I'm a friend of Silvia Hanro's. I was invited onto set and I got the most atrocious headache. She gave me a headache powder and told me to come up here to her room to lie down for a bit. She gave me her key but perhaps it works for all the doors? I'm sorry – do I have the wrong room?'

'Oh,' said the cook. 'I see.'

The mention of the movie star's name had worked its usual magic and the cook stopped looking quite so fearsome. She indicated along the corridor with a great paw of a meaty hand.

'Yes, you *have* got the wrong room, Miss. Mere lowly mortals like me reside along this side. Miss Hanro and Mr Fontaine have *suites* down there. Her suite is on the left.'

The woman gestured along the corridor. The anger had gone from her manner but curiosity and nosiness had ebbed their way into the woman's voice, for she had seen a rare chance to take a brief look into the rooms of the famous movie star.

'Want me to show you, Miss? Won't take a minute of my time.'

'No, no. I'll be quite all right. Thank you, and a thousand apologies.'

Posie hurried away, very aware of the time now. She saw on the other side of the corridor that just two doors stood together, rather than row upon row of them. She opened the door on the left first, well aware of the cook still watching her back. Posie dipped inside.

This was an entirely different set-up altogether: a single room, but big enough for about eight of those smaller single rooms to fit into. A kitchenette and a small bathroom were included here, together with a bedsitting room furnished in luxurious white furs and glass bookcases. A perfectly round bed was raised on a dias in the centre of the room. An open window gave onto a calm view over the back of Worton Hall: the fields, the farm, the greenhouses.

Picking her way around the room Posie saw that there was nothing remotely personal here.

Don't these people live at all? Posie thought to herself unbelievingly.

Is there anything to learn here?

A silver-framed studio portrait of Robbie Fontaine leaning nonchalantly against a wall was placed strategically on the bedside cabinet next to a glass vase containing a mass of the same red and pink orchids as in the dressing room downstairs. Next to this was a large ceramic jar of Pond's Cold Cream.

Going over to the bedside cabinet, Posie saw that a tiny slip of carbon paper, no bigger than a thumbnail, was sandwiched tightly under the jar of cream, together with its counterpart, an orange piece of paper which looked like it had included signatures before it got ripped apart. It looked very much like the carbon paper and its original had been weighed down by the jar of cream, perhaps to prevent the document from fluttering away in the wind, and then picked up again in a hurry at some later point.

Hurriedly Posie took the snippets of paper and put them in the pocket of her carpet bag. There was nothing stocked in the kitchen and nothing to be seen in the bathroom, either.

Dashing away again with only a few minutes to spare, Posie locked Silvia's door. She had no time to go inside Robbie Fontaine's room, but she swore she could hear some low rumblings, like a radio or music on a gramophone, coming from inside.

Cursing to herself for her bad management of time, she hurried over to the dark studio.

* * * *

Posie found things much as she had left them back at the dark studio, although everyone was on a five-minute cigarette break. Most of the crew had taken the chance to stand outside, smoking as if their lives depended on it, clustered around the doorway. The two leading actors were sat smoking together in the scant shade, Silvia sitting on Robbie Fontaine's lap, the famous blonde head and the dark dipping and moving together in perfect unison.

Annoyingly, there was simply no chance for Posie to speak to either of them.

Robbie Fontaine looked over at Posie as if she had ushered in a particularly horrible smell and looked away again shiftily, his arms still circled tightly around Silvia's waist. Posie sighed. *What was it with him, anyway?*

And Tom Moran was simply nowhere to be seen.

Posie found Dolly inside the studio, squatting on the floor, happily re-stocking a large black make-up case.

Brian Langley was pacing around the stage area on his own in the darkness, checking the lighting. He looked like he wanted to thump someone, so Posie steered well clear. She called across to her friend:

'Dolly! Come here, I need you. It's important.'

'Can't move, lovey. I'm at a crucial stage with these lipsticks. *You* come here.'

Already exasperated and short on time, Posie explained in as calm a manner as possible and in a low tone of voice to her friend that Rufus had instructed her to bring Dolly home, with her, *now*.

'What you goin' on about, lovey?' said Dolly, looking at Posie from the floor, a kohl pencil now jammed in her mouth, squinting up at her in the gloom. '*Why* do I need to come with you now? I don't understand.'

Posie had sworn not to explain to Dolly about the grave danger she was in and she now felt a stab of well-contained anger at Rufus for putting her in such a ridiculous position. She had not been served a good hand, or any hand at all, come to think of it.

'I can't tell you I'm afraid. It's top-secret. You just need to come now. You'll just have to trust me on this.'

Dolly raised a painted eyebrow. 'I'm jolly well not goin' to. This is the best fun I've had in years. *Years!* You'll have to drag me away from here kickin' and screamin'. Literally.'

'Right, then. I'm going to have to blow your cover.'

And marching over to where Brian Langley was standing adjusting a lamp, Posie tapped him on the shoulder.

'Excuse me, Mr Langley?'

The Producer turned, his tiny eyes glittering menacingly. 'What? Oh, it's *you.*'

He stood up a bit straighter, as if remembering his earlier promise to help Posie, *if* necessary. He lit a cigarette and tried to smile.

'Finding your way around okay, are you? Asked lots of questions? Any the wiser as to these daft threats, are you?'

'I don't think they're so daft, sir. Miss Hanro should take great care. But I've definitely seen as much as I need to here. Please be assured that I'm going to carry on with this job when I get back to town; I'm going to pursue some other important leads, including investigating the stalker fellow you mentioned. I'll be back here tomorrow, first thing. But that's not what I wanted to tell you just now.'

'Oh?'

'You see your new make-up mistress over there, my friend from the car?'

'What of her? She's bally good as it happens. Better than that woman Samuelson insisted on supplying. Your pal's quick. I like that.'

'That's as maybe. But it could spell trouble for you, sir. She's actually Dolly, Lady Cardigeon, and her husband is Rufus, Lord Cardigeon. She's happy as anything mucking about here, but I don't think her husband will be when he hears about it. *If* he hears about it. So I'm just going to take her home with me, right now. Just so you know.'

Brian Langley looked thunderstruck for a split-second before recovering his usual angry stance.

'That so?'

He looked over at Dolly who was obstinately continuing to match tubes of orange Leichner into different rows according to their shade, with a determined expression on her face, pretending to be oblivious to their conversation. A telephone had begun ringing somewhere in the background and its shrill sound went on and on. Brian Langley swallowed and then stamped out the butt of his cigarette on the linoleum floor with his heel.

'Here, Dolly love,' he shouted across the floor. 'You happy working here, are you? Only your pal wants you to leave now with her.' His voice dripped with sarcasm and he gave Posie a quick smile which was really a jibe.

Dolly looked from one to the other of them and gave a small moue of distaste.

'I'm quite happy here, Mr Langley,' she called over. 'Quite happy.'

'Good. Well, carry on then. As you are. I don't intend losing you. Only, forget going to pick up your pay packet from Reggie at six-thirty. We have a marriage bar in this industry, so by rights you shouldn't be working at all. I don't want to do anything illegal. But if I'm not paying you we can just say it was for the thrill of the experience, can't we? And it means you can work late here, too, if we do it that way.'

Dolly nodded and grinned. Posie almost exploded with anger at the man's cheek, but short of dragging Dolly out physically she couldn't do anything. Humiliated, she glared at Brian Langley, who glared back at her and shrugged his shoulders as if he didn't have a care in the world.

Outmanoeuvred, Posie spread her hands helplessly in one final plea. 'You're supposed to help me, sir. Remember? Not put obstacles in my path. You're really not helping me here. Do you really dislike me that much?'

'Boo-hoo. Poor you. There's help and then there's *help*.'
Brian Langley grunted and turned back to his lamp.

'I'm not going to remove a well-oiled cog from the machine, now, am I? Especially if it's running for me for free. And no, I don't dislike you: but you're only here because your reputation precedes you and I thought you could fix things. I don't really like many people, as it happens.'

Really, the man was just *awful*.

The telephone started up again.

'Aren't you going to answer that, Mr Langley?'

Brian Langley harrumphed. 'What's it to you, anyhow? I *never* answer the telephone on set, Miss Parker. It's usually switched off. Some idiot has had it reconnected. Just sort out this mess of Silvia's, will you?'

He strode over to another corner without a second glance at Posie and tugged the black telephone violently from its socket on the wall. Tiny blue sparks flew in the darkness. Then he started yelling at everyone to get back on set.

Speechless at Brian Langley's bad manners, Posie turned on her heel in a barely-suppressed temper. It was almost inconceivable that it had been *he* who had called Posie in to Worton Hall in the first place: anyone would have thought it were *she* who had turned up as a thrill-seeker for the pure pleasure of the thing.

Posie found herself mentally advancing him up her list of current suspects into virtually pole position. She remembered that she had intended to visit his house on the way back to London, uninvited, and she decided now not to have any scruples about doing so.

As Posie passed Dolly she told her friend to make sure she got herself home to Chelsea safely, with a hired driver at the very least. Or else to phone Rufus and get him to collect her. But Dolly shook her head, determined.

'You must be jokin' lovey. I'm off the leash. And enjoyin' every minute of it.'

'Well, do *me* a favour then.'

'What's that?'

'Keep your eyes and ears peeled for me here. If you need me I'll most likely be at the office, but I'm meeting the Chief Inspector at nine o'clock at the Temple tonight. You can always find me there.'

'Fine. Right you are.'

'I'm sure nothing will happen before tomorrow but look out for anything odd.'

Dolly roared with laughter. ''Course I will, lovey. But this is the movies! *Everythin's* odd here.'

Posie sighed and left: she couldn't do more. And stamping across the grass and the cinder path and through the endless crowd of extras, towards Bertie Samuelson's driver, she found herself feeling very happy to leave.

She simply couldn't understand Dolly's enthusiasm to stay.

* * * *

Eleven

Posie sat in the silent agony of a strop all the way to Richmond. She hated it when a plan didn't come together, still less when she was subjecting her good friend to some unknown danger she had promised to guard her against.

There was nothing for it but to continue on with her evening's work. Posie had just taken out her notebook from her carpet bag and was studying it intently when she was interrupted by the driver:

'Miss?'

They had stopped, and Fred was rapping urgently on the glass divide.

'This is it, Miss. Brian Langley's place – "Globe Garden". I know it well: I've dropped Mr Samuelson here often enough. Shall I just wait here by the main gates? How long will you be?'

Posie looked through the window. They were parked up on a grass verge along the main road. On the right were shops and houses, all jumbled together, but on the left-hand side were more exclusive dwellings, all high-gated and with their own stretches of the river.

'Globe Garden', Brian Langley's lair, squatted behind prohibitively high gates. It looked to be a large white bungalow in a very modern, deco style. Lush manicured gardens surrounded it on every side, green and verdant despite the scorching heat, and snatches of the glittering Thames were visible beyond.

Forced out of her simmering discontent, Posie focused hard. She had no idea what it was she was searching for here, or what it was that she wanted to find out. Despite her strong dislike for Mr Langley, and her suspicions, she had nothing concrete at all which proved he would wish any harm to Silvia Hanro. Nothing.

And how exactly had she expected to get into the house at all, uninvited?

Fred, the driver, was looking at her in the mirror. He took her silence and her refusal to get out of the car as an invitation to talk. He smiled under his black driver's cap.

"Course,' he prattled in his estuary accent, 'I'm a gardening man meself. I've got a nice little garden attached to my property, just a terraced house, mind, in Isleworth itself. Nothing I love better than a free Saturday spent pruning my roses, or diggin' potatoes.'

Posie frowned uncomprehendingly.

'I don't quite follow you…'

'I'm sorry. I meant that I'd give up a month of Saturdays off to spend just ten minutes inside Mr Langley's greenhouse. They say he's the number one collector of rare orchids in the British Isles. They're his passion. He has quite the reputation among these posh gardening folks. Imagine!'

'Imagine indeed!' Posie recalled Silvia mentioning something about hot-house flowers, now she came to think of it.

'Apparently he has some gardener fella he's got in from the Orient to look after the flowers, the chap speaks to them and croons them lully-byes and what have you. Just like to little kiddies! I'd love to be a fly on the wall in that greenhouse! Mind you, someone's got to do it, haven't they? Old Langley's never here. He's probably here once a week at the most.'

'I see.' Posie stared at the gates again, her mind working sixteen to the dozen.

Fred nodded, warming to his theme, unaware of Posie's wandering mind.

'They say he gets written requests from dealers. And buyers for the big shops in London like Harrods, they all want to call and see his orchids. And buy some if they can. Apparently he turns them all away with a flea in their ear.'

Posie turned back to Fred in the mirror. He had unwittingly given her her entrance into the house. Or an attempt at one, anyhow.

'I don't know what you're here for, Miss, but I'm glad that old Langley isn't at home for you. I know I shouldn't speak out of turn, but the man's as sour as vinegar. Besides, I wouldn't want to get on the wrong side of him in that house.'

'Why not?'

'They say that in addition to the imported orchids he keeps, he has whole borders full of Foxtrots.'

'Foxtrot? Now you really have lost me.'

'Aye. Foxtrot or *Digitalis* orchids. I can see you're not a gardener, love. The most poisonous critters to be found. You'd just need to touch one of those beauties in the wrong way and you'd be making your way out of that house in a wooden box.'

'Let me get this right. The man grows poisonous orchids? For pleasure?'

'Aye. But to be fair to him, many plants are poisonous. But these are especially so, and they're in bloom right now, as it happens.'

'What should I look for?'

Fred smiled blissfully. 'Beautiful pink and red blooms, maybe spotted like leopard skin if they're feeling particularly healthy.'

'Right. Well. Thanks for that. I'll be about twenty minutes.'

'You'll let me know, won't you? What his greenhouse is like? And watch that Housekeeper of his: she's a sour old puss, and no mistake.'

* * * *

The gate was unlocked, but the front door was latched across so many times that it took the Housekeeper a good couple of minutes to open it.

'Yes?' said a voice with a soft indistinguishable lilt, many years buried, through a crack of doorway. It still had a chain across it. There was a hint of a dark, watery-eyed woman lurking behind it wearing a plain black service dress and apron.

But the thirty-second walk up the drive had prepared her. Posie knew exactly what she was doing now.

'This *is* Mr Langley's house, isn't it? It's just that Mr Langley sent me over here,' she said in an enthusiastic-sounding rush.

'Oh?'

The voice was disbelieving and the slice of doorway didn't get any bigger. 'I don't know who you are, Missie, but Mr Langley isn't in the habit of sending people over anywhere, let alone here. So perhaps you could go on your own sweet way?'

'Oh, he said you'd be like this: a first-class Housekeeper who keeps people away. It's Mrs Cleeves, isn't it?'

Somehow the unusual name which Silvia Hanro had mentioned had just implanted itself in Posie's brain. It must have been the *Henry the King* connection and the thought of that tempestuous monarch's doomed fourth wife.

The dark eye showed a second of nervous hesitancy, and Posie pressed on while the going was good.

'He said you were to ring him up in the studio if you were at all concerned about my identity. How's that? I'm quite happy to wait here while you do so.'

Posie was calling the woman's bluff, and she saw Cleeves swallow nervously and open the door a fraction wider. If she'd worked for Brian Langley for any length of time at all she'd know that it was more than her job was worth to disturb him on the set of one of his precious films, and she'd know too that such an action was futile anyhow. The telephone would either be disconnected or unanswered.

'There'll be no need for any of that, now. What is it you were here about, anyhow?'

'I'm one of Mr Langley's investors: or rather, my *husband* is.' The lies came easily now. Posie was sure Alaric wouldn't mind her taking his name in vain, *not* that he was her husband yet.

'Ah, I see, Madam.' The door opened a fraction wider. Posie felt that the word 'investors' had worked quite a bit of magic.

'Yes. We're staying at Worton Hall tonight before this big party tomorrow. Mr Samuelson sent his own driver with me, see?'

The woman craned her neck now, and obviously satisfied, she nodded.

'And to tell you the truth,' Posie smiled apologetically, lending an air of conspiracy to her words, 'movies bore the life out of me. I'm more of a gardening kind of girl, you see. The Chelsea Flower Show is really the highlight of my year. And when Mr Langley heard about my hobby, he asked if I'd like to look at his orchids. As a very special favour. I understand not many are afforded such a unique privilege?'

'Aye. That's correct, Madam.'

The door was unlatched and swung fully open.

The frown had now dropped like a falling curtain from Mrs Cleeves' face and she became amiability itself. Posie was surprised to see in the full light that Mrs Cleeves was only about forty. There was a glimmer of beauty beneath the black-and-white livery, although the years had not been kind to the woman; she was tall and too lean, and the skin around her eyes had sunken in, giving her the impression of one who permanently cries.

If she had been a looker in the past, now she was as sallow as a withered lemon.

'Do forgive me, Mrs…?'

'Mrs Brown.' The colour Posie wished she had worn today.

'Any friend of Mr Langley's is most welcome in his home. Now, I'll show you through here, shall I?'

Posie couldn't place the faint accent, and the woman dipped and bobbed and Posie found her yellow coat and yellow hat being taken expertly from her at lightning speed and being hung on a peg next to what looked like a long, slim, silver gun-cupboard by the front door. And then she was following Mrs Cleeves through the white bungalow at a sharp trot. The woman was flat-footed but fast and Posie hurried along, trying to keep up.

It was very bright inside the house, even in the late afternoon, mainly due to the huge glass windows on every side which let great shafts of light stream inside.

Posie made a rapid survey of the bungalow and noted that the place was enormous, but essentially it was just a big horseshoe, with its longest side running horizontal to the road.

Everything was open-plan, and a blinding white: the long, shaggy carpets; the walls; the lamps hanging low. It was decorated in the modern 'deco' style, and again, there was nothing personal anywhere. No photos or paintings or books or the usual bits and bobs which created a home and stamped a man's personality on a place.

Don't these people live?

In fact, there was nothing interesting here at all, and

Posie felt a sudden jolt of annoyance that she had even bothered to come. At the waste of her time.

They passed through a white 'study' area with a metal desk pulled right up against a plate glass wall which looked out over an internal courtyard, a sort of shaded atrium planted with vines and trailing trellises. A small fountain made of silver-and-white glass tinkled at its centre, the bubbles of water lending the place a calm, almost monastic air. The space was beautiful. Posie stopped and stared, transfixed.

She had not expected this sort of tranquillity, but then if you were a man with a temperament like Brian Langley's, perhaps you needed just such an oasis to return to, albeit occasionally.

'Madam?'

Mrs Cleeves had stopped ahead of her and was frowning. Posie realised that it looked as if she was snooping: she was standing directly in front of Brian Langley's big chrome desk, which was littered with his papers of a personal variety. It looked, unlike the rest of the place, a total mess: as if someone had been busy searching for something, and very recently, too.

Posie smiled. 'Sorry. Don't mind me. I was just admiring the courtyard. It's so peaceful here. Lovely.'

'I just thought you might think me a sloppy Housekeeper, Madam. All that mess there on the desk. It's a right midden. Bane of my life, that is.'

'I quite understand,' Posie nodded in a reassuring manner. 'My husband, Mr Brown, is even worse than that. He likes to leave all his papers around and I'm not allowed to touch anything.'

They moved off, Posie following the woman's straight-backed black-and-white figure through a sort of linking corridor. Posie thought about the absolute pit of a room in her flat which was Alaric's: it was more than the desk which was messy, it was every single available inch of space. She smiled at the memory of it.

'I suppose the only difference is that Mr Brown has his own room for his paperwork and affairs. I can close the door on his mess. We don't live in such a modern, open-plan sort of a house.'

Mrs Cleeves nodded. 'It's a strange layout here, I'll give you that. The worst thing for me is the kitchen, which is miles away from anywhere useful. Mr Langley has all his film work papers sent to him wherever it is that he's filming, and his secretary, Reggie, sorts it all out. But, as you can see, his own affairs are sent here. Good job he trusts me and that we don't have a large staff here. Prying wee eyes and all that…'

'Quite. Just you here, is it, Mrs Cleeves?'

'Aye. I do everything. That's how Mr Langley likes it. He employs Shay, of course, but that's mainly for outside.'

'Shay?'

'The Chinese gardener, *when* he bothers to put in an appearance. He often disappears, mainly at night. But I've seen him today: I'm sure he'll be along in a minute.'

Mrs Cleeves dropped her voice to a confidential whisper:

'Don't trust him, Mrs Brown. If you find yourself alone with Shay, even for a few seconds, be very careful. I've seen him meeting with different people in the grounds lately, passing across packages. A woman once, very fashionably dressed, and then a man in a straw summer hat. That was just yesterday.'

'Oh? What is he doing, do you think? Selling orchids without Mr Langley's consent?'

Mrs Cleeves tapped her nose. 'I shouldn't say this but I think he *arranges things*. I've definitely seen money being passed across. Drugs, I'll warrant. A nice little side-line. But then, what do you expect? I expect its opium.'

'Goodness! I didn't realise opium was still in fashion!'

'Oh, it's not. But its not being taken as a fashion statement now, is it? Just as a way to forget…like most drugs.'

Mrs Cleeves coughed sanctimoniously. 'Not that I'd know anything about any of that, of course. But there *are* rumours of an opium den having started up in Richmond. Who's to say Shay isn't running that and supplying private clients, too?'

The woman had pursed her lips up tight disapprovingly and moved off again before Posie could utter a single thing in response.

'Here we are then, Mrs Brown.'

Up ahead, Posie could see a huge glass room running horizontally to the rest of the bungalow, forming a sort of 'missing' arm of the horseshoe shape. It was a large specially-constructed greenhouse, and the view of the gardens and the spectacular view of the Thames beyond was almost obliterated by the hundreds upon hundreds of blooms which filled the place with their gorgeous colours.

Orchids trailed from the roof, grew up the sides of the greenhouse, rose in masses from specially-constructed tables and wall-stacks. Purples, reds, yellows, indigo: every colour imaginable was present, but by far the most common colour was white. It was like looking at a crazy theatre of dancing butterflies, running riot.

'My gosh!' Posie was genuinely moved. She wished that Fred, sitting patiently outside, could share in the marvel. 'How spectacular!'

'I'll leave you with Shay, then. He'll be in shortly. But remember what I said: don't let him sell you anything, a nice girl like you could be caught out. Would you like a drink, Mrs Brown?'

Mrs Cleeves half-curtsied. 'We do have coffee, if you like.'

Posie smiled. 'That would be most welcome, thank you.'

She moved towards a particularly violently-coloured yellow plant and made a show of looking at it admiringly, in case the Housekeeper decided to give her a look as she departed.

Posie hoped that it would take the woman a good few minutes to percolate the coffee. She also hoped that Shay would stay well away. As soon as she heard the sound of the woman's retreating steps die away, and remembering that the kitchen was, conveniently for *her* at least, a good way off, she darted back to the desk area which formed Brian Langley's study. She calculated she had about two minutes before she needed to get back to the greenhouse again and stand riveted, gazing at flowers.

Her heart pounding, her nerves on fire, she scanned the desk quickly. In truth Posie had simply no idea what she was looking for.

A bottle of green ink? Documents which would show that Brian Langley had taken out insurance on Silvia Hanro's life? Other missing body parts?

This was a game of chance. And a risky one at that. The paperwork was heaped up at least a couple of inches thick, in places held down by large round glass paperweights which, unsurprisingly, held dried specimens of orchids. She started to flick through.

The usual paper detritus of a normal man's life were all here: receipts from dentists, and doctors, and carbon copies of prescriptions for tonics against the flu, and advertisements for ridiculous products which had come in the post and never been thrown away.

There was strong evidence of the passion for flowers: a couple of magazines about gardening, and a brochure in French about growing orchids.

But there was nothing at all about Silvia Hanro, and nothing at all about films, or Sunstar Films, which was surprising, as this was Brian Langley's whole life, apart from the orchids.

But Posie remembered the division of mail which Mrs Cleeves had mentioned, and she supposed it made sense.

She had almost reached the layer of the blotter when something caught her eye. It was a neatly typed bank statement, a half-year's worth, from Hoare's Bank on the Strand. Posie grabbed at the thin blue sheet gratefully, aware of the time. She couldn't take it, but she read it quickly. It was a record of cheques sent out, and Posie noted that it was all fairly routine. But then something caught her eye.

It was highly unusual and stood out a mile.

A monthly cheque, paid out to QUEENSGATE SCHOOL.

The annotation typed next to it simply read 'SCHOOL FEES'.

Posie knew that Queensgate School was near to Kensington Palace Gardens and all the museums, and that it was a private school for privileged, rich girls, whose parents, rather unusually, had an eye to the education of their daughters as well as to their social manners. So whose school fees was Brian Langley shelling out for?

Posie dropped the bank statement and rifled through the rest of the papers, grabbing up a handwritten letter written in a large, looping hand.

In green ink.

But there was no chance to read it, or even to snatch the thing, for just then she heard the distinctive, flat-footed tread of Mrs Cleeves in the distance. She hurried to cover the letter and dart away back to the greenhouse.

But in replacing it she managed to read the signature at the bottom.

P. HANRO

****

Back in the greenhouse Posie accepted her coffee gratefully, and she ate the whole plate of lemon puffs which were supplied.

'Not been feeding you today, has she?' asked Mrs Cleeves, a downwards snag of the mouth lending her an even more worried look than before. Posie was fingering a trailing blue plant with studied awe.

'Sorry?'

'Mrs Thynne. The cook up at Mr Samuelson's place. They *say* she keeps a good table but then that can't be true, can it? You're obviously starving to want to eat a plate of shop-bought biscuits like that.'

Posie was about to admit that she was just a glutton when it came to anything sweet, especially biscuits, when an image of the very fat cook she had met earlier in the day came to mind, and the absurdity of the name almost made her laugh aloud. *Mrs Thynne!*

She sensed, however, that she was being tested. Her answer to Mrs Cleeves was important. Posie remembered just in time that Isleworth and Richmond were close, and that people employed roundabout were all bound to know each other, or *of* each other. So she should be careful.

'Oh, I'm being fed fabulously, thank you, Mrs Cleeves. Especially the homemade buns; far better than anything from Lyons, for sure. I'm afraid that as you can see I'm just a first-class pig. Truly, I am.'

Mrs Cleeves nodded and looked satisfied, even relieved. Posie realised she had given the right answer.

'I can't think what's got into Shay,' Mrs Cleeves was saying, going over to the window and looking down to the river. 'I *did* call him from the kitchen. I can't see him from here. Perhaps he didn't hear me? Shall I go out onto the lawns?'

Posie made a show of looking at her watch and shook her head.

'Oh, no. Please don't bother. I've seen plenty. Thank you so much. This has quite made my day.'

She made a move to turn and go, and then Mrs Cleeves called out again:

'Oh, there he is! He's cutting more of that Foxtrot! Wretched stuff. I won't have it in the house, although some fools like to have it all around them. It's deadly. For all its beauty. But then of course, you know that, being a gardening expert.'

And staring out of the window at the place she had indicated, Posie saw a neat little man dressed all in white, with white gloves and a pointed black beard and a white cap, dressed much like many of his compatriots who lived in China Town in London, where Posie often walked.

But it was not the oriental gardener she was staring at, it was rather the flowers he was carrying in his arms: huge bouquets of pink and red blooms.

Identical to those in Silvia Hanro's dressing room and in her borrowed flat at Worton Hall.

＊＊＊＊

Back in the car, Posie talked blithely about the wonders of the greenhouse, but her thoughts were already elsewhere, running over the strange papers on Brian Langley's desk.

She was thinking of green ink and school fees and strange and impossible connections between people she didn't know at all, but who were all linked together by Silvia Hanro, caught in a web in which the movie star sat presiding over, spider-like.

After a short silence, something struck Posie which she thought Fred, being a local, might help her with: a silly detail, but it nagged at her anyhow.

'I say,' Posie asked in a mild tone. 'Is there any reason why Mrs Cleeves would ask me about the cook, Mrs Thynne, up at Worton Hall? Does she know her at all?'

Fred laughed as he drove. 'I'll say: them two are thick as thieves. Best pals. Spend their days off together, too.'

'Oh?' Posie was slightly reassured that she had at least said the right thing.

Fred warmed to his theme. 'She's a funny fish, is Mrs Cleeves; bit of a mystery really roundabout. There's a lot of heartache there, same as there is for many a lass these days. Folks say she came down from Edinburgh to marry someone in London. Trouble was, he got himself killed in the war, didn't he? So Mr Langley took her on as his Housekeeper after the war, five years ago. They seem to rub along together just fine, though: both as dour as each other.'

'And Mrs Thynne?'

'Oh, Bertha Thynne is a local lass, married to one of the gamekeepers up at Richmond Park, a rum chap, always on the right side of the law, but only just, if you get my drift. Mrs Cleeves and Mrs Thynne go to the movies together when they're off on the same days: my Vera's seen them out and about, all dolled up apparently. But more often than not Mrs Cleeves is up at Worton Hall. I see her coming and going. Perhaps she's helping Bertha in the kitchens, but I've never asked. Not my place to, is it? Besides, it must be awful lonesome at that big house back there of Brian Langley's, just her and one gardener about the place. He seems a shifty sort, too. I don't blame her for wanting to get out and about, do you?'

'No, no. Not at all.'

Posie's thoughts drifted, then came sharply into focus again. Something that Fred had told her jarred: it wasn't quite right. But whatever the discrepancy was, it eluded her.

And anyway, there was no time for that. Right now she had to get her brain in order and think about the remarkable, elusive, estranged – and potentially dangerous – woman she was about to meet.

Pamela Hanro.

Just what was it that she was going to say to her?

* * * *

122

Twelve

Posie looked up and down the street.

She had bidden thanks and goodbye to Fred and was now standing outside a blue-painted front door which led to two flats upstairs.

The door was squeezed right next to the already steamed-up window of Tacy's, a fish and chip shop in the heart of London, SW7.

HADDOCK SPECIAL! screamed the sign in the window.

Tacy's was obviously doing a roaring trade, and their patient customers queued right back up the street past the blue front door, politely making room for Posie on the dusty pavement when she blundered through, shattering the queue.

It *was* half-past six, after all, and for most people that meant tea-time. Posie sniffed the air longingly: the perfumes of acidy vinegar and thick salty batter made her mouth water. But her hunger pangs would just have to wait.

Posie consulted the address which Sergeant Binny had given her again: *15, Bute Street, South Kensington.* Next to the blue front door were two handwritten name cards with two identical black bells: the first read 'SMITH–FLAT ONE' and the second read 'HANRO–FLAT TWO'.

She rang the second bell, conscious of the people in the queue behind her staring at her unapologetically. Too right: her stupidly bright yellow clothes invited stares.

Posie looked up nervously at the Victorian flats above, and saw no encouraging signs of life. The first flat seemed to have the curtains drawn already, despite the light summer evening, and the second-floor windows were too high to be seen properly.

Posie waited.

She had thought there was something familiar about Pamela Hanro's address when she had first heard it, and she had been right. In fact, Posie knew this street well. She had lived in a bedsit around here, in Nightingale Mews, until a couple of years back. She didn't miss the bedsit at all, but she did miss the location sometimes.

She rang the bell again and heard it trill out in the hallway.

South Kensington was a sparkly bright jewel in the sometimes dusty grey crown of London. And while it suffered from the same black smog as the rest of town, and its buildings were tarnished in exactly the same way, there was something wonderful about its little streets which boasted dozens of fancy boutiques and cafés, with snappily-dressed waiters on street corners urging you to come in and try one of their strange-coloured drinks.

A magnet for tourists, it was a fashionable, wealthy crowd who ran in this part of town, drawn no doubt to the oasis of the great parks which South Kensington could call its own, and London's first-class museums and concert halls which were crowded into a row just off the Exhibition Road.

But Bute Street was different again. It was like a seamy little artery running through the pure rich heart of South Kensington, close to the Underground station. This was a road you *used*; you came here to eat, or to shop, or to drink. And probably you did those things in a hurry. The street was merely functional. It would be fair to say that the smart crowd didn't run *here*.

At one end of Bute Street was the Zetland Arms, a pub with wooden tables spilling out onto the streets, frequented by commercial travellers staying in one of the cheaper hotels nearby. It was busy right now. Other shops crowding the street were fruiterers and grocers, and there were a couple of small luncheon restaurants of the middling sort, where secretaries and filing clerks ate hurried plates of ham and eggs for lunch, and drank strong tea from chipped green enamel mugs afterwards. Posie recalled how she had often swung along here when in need of milk, or biscuits, or even for a lonely meal for one, eaten after work with not much attention paid to either her appearance or what it was that was on her plate.

How things had changed.

It was certainly a strange choice of place for the famous Silvia Hanro's sister to live in.

'Yes? Can I help you?'

Lost in her reverie of the past, Posie hadn't noticed that the blue front door had swung open. A small beaky-nosed woman in her late forties was peering out. She was wearing an olive-coloured house-coat and had paper rags in her hair, attempting a poor copy of a Marcel wave. Thick half-moon glasses sat on the end of her nose. Posie concluded that this must be Miss Smith from the first-floor flat.

Posie had decided that honesty would be her best policy with a woman like Pamela Hanro. She was about to open her mouth and introduce herself by her real name to the neighbour when she was interrupted.

'I'm sorry, Madam,' said beaky Miss Smith, almost dropping a curtsey, 'I didn't realise that Miss Hanro was taking clients in the evening now. Normally it's just the daytime. Please come on in.'

The woman motioned her into the tiny dark entrance hall and Posie hurried in, thankful but completely uncomprehending. She turned to see Miss Smith latching the door behind her and drawing across two chains. Miss Smith stared at Posie in the muddy, dim light of the hallway, but when Posie looked again she saw that the woman's eyes behind their thick glass were actually taking in her yellow outfit rather than her person, her gaze lingering on the small gold 'H' logo on the bottom of Posie's fashionably short chiffon hemline.

'That's a fine outfit you have there, Madam. Miss Hanro's really quite something, isn't she? I hope you don't mind my saying so, but it looks like it could even pass muster as a genuine House of Harlow creation. A fair copy and no mistake!'

Posie gulped and nodded in what she hoped looked like genuine satisfaction. This had all been very easy so far. So Pamela Hanro was obviously a dressmaker, or a tailors' help, or something else dress-related.

'Quite. I'm very pleased with it. Is she in, Miss Hanro? Only, I have something which needs altering in my bag. Quite urgently as it happens.'

'Oh, yes. She's in all right. You know the way up, I suppose, if you've been here before?'

Miss Smith motioned upwards and they began to ascend a very narrow and depressingly brown-painted staircase. The smell of frying fish got stronger and more cloying as they rose higher.

'Miss Hanro's just been bathing the little 'un. We share a bathroom between the two flats, and Miss Hanro keeps exactly the same time for the little 'un's bathtime every day. Probably why she didn't hear you ring the bell. I only came down when you rang a second time. It's nearly time for the child's bedtime of course, but I'm sure Miss Hanro will be glad to see you. There you are, then. You go on up.'

The woman pointed upwards at a door at the top of another steep staircase. 'I'll bid you goodnight.'

Standing on the tiny uncarpeted landing in front of

Pamela Hanro's door, with great splashes of what must have been bath water all around her in little pools, Posie heard the sounds of laughing and running about inside, the tweak of old floorboards creaking and a child's uncontrollable, bubbling laughter. This must be the adopted child Sergeant Binny had told Posie about on the telephone.

Posie's brain scrambled quickly over the facts again: a child adopted in 1918 from the Foundling Hospital in London. An orphan. So Pamela Hanro was still flying in the face of convention, then. As an unmarried woman it wouldn't be easy to be raising a child all alone, and it wasn't an enviable lot.

Posie wondered how Pamela managed, both financially and socially. Perhaps there were lies or disguises involved – an imaginary husband killed in the front line of battle, for example – the same sort of deceptions which were part of many a woman's life since the war.

Just then Posie heard a voice call out cheerfully:

'I'm coming, Hilda! Ready or not! I'm coming to get you!'

A game of Hide-and-Seek was obviously in progress. Caught off guard, Posie stood, uncertain, not wanting to disturb. She had that pin-prickly feeling again and turned and saw that Miss Smith was standing watching her from the landing below, from outside her own flat, her eyes bright through the thick lenses.

'Just knock, Madam,' called out the woman. 'They do this every night. Could go on for another ten minutes, yet. You did say it was urgent, didn't you?'

So Posie knocked and there was an immediate silence on the other side of the front door. Then there was the sound of a banging door, things being thrown around, and then more silence. Just as she was about to raise her hand to knock again, still with Miss Smith watching her every move below, the door swung open.

'Can I help you?'

Pamela Hanro was tall, like her sister, but there the similarity ended.

This woman was dark, not blonde, and although she had the same china-blue eyes, they peered out from a sharp, foxy face which was full of suspicion. A stubborn little chin was prominently drawn up beneath a small, twitching mouth, painted out of all existence by a crimson slash of lipstick. Pamela Hanro had the outward appearance of someone who was chewing on a poisoned apple. The impression was saved, however, by a razor-sharp short haircut which would not have been out of place on a flapper, and an absolutely sumptuous pink brocade evening gown, cut rather like a kimono, which was quite unlike anything Posie had ever seen before. It was utterly magnificent, and not something you would normally wear to play games in with a child.

'Miss Hanro?'

'Yes?' Pamela Hanro said, crossing her arms over her flat chest defensively and checking behind her with a darting motion. Following her gaze, Posie saw a small but light-drenched interior, tidy and entirely child-free.

Posie whispered in an undertone:

'Please can I come in? I do realise that you don't know me. But if I tell you what I need to out here, that woman downstairs will know all about it, too, and then so might others, if I'm not much mistaken. And I don't think you want that. It's about your *sister*.'

Pamela Hanro took a sharp intake of breath and for a second Posie thought she might have the door slammed shut in her face. She pressed on, putting considerable top spin on her words:

'It could be a matter of life or death. *Please*.'

'I have no sister,' the woman whispered. But she held the door open anyway and Posie walked through it before Pamela Hanro could change her mind.

* * * *

128

Thirteen

The flat was tiny, just this one room really, but there were two closed doors leading off of it.

A dining table and a sofa and a small oak sewing table with a glossy Singer sewing machine in the corner filled it all up. Swatches of fabric were tidily packed under the sewing table and a dressmakers' dummy with a part-made wedding gown in the old style, hugely elaborate, was tucked right into the nook by the front door where normally a hat stand would sit.

'Tea?'

'Please.'

Pamela headed grudgingly over to a miniscule kitchenette on the left, just a gas ring in a cupboard with a kettle on it. She had curtained it off with a piece of thick baize on a string. As she made tea she kept throwing Posie nervous glances over her shoulder, and biting her lips wordlessly. You could have heard one of her dressmakers' pins drop.

The flat was very neat and clean and sparse, and although the furniture was of surprisingly good quality, it was quite obviously the flat of someone who had to eke out every penny of their income to make ends meet.

A bunch of white shop-bought roses, long past their

best, were placed in a vase on the table, and their decaying sweetness jarred with the smell of the fish-fat from below in the street. A beautiful yellow orchid in a white pot was placed on the windowsill, distracting the eye from the smeary outside glass of the window, and the grey greasy air of the street outside. Over in the corner on a small glass bookshelf was a good deal of correspondence stacked up in neat piles. Fresh writing paper and ink sat atop it all. A bottle of green ink.

And there wasn't a single toy or crayon or scrap of evidence of a child's existence in the place.

Was the child standing behind one of those two closed doors?

Posie sat on the sofa uncomfortably. She felt terrible that she had disturbed an enjoyable evening for Pamela and her daughter, but more so for the child who even now might be fearful or anxious or wondering just what on earth might be the problem outside in the main room.

As Pamela came over and handed her a cup of tea in a beautiful elaborate blue-and-white cup and saucer, Posie smiled in surprise and took it with thanks. Pamela herself drew up her high-backed sewing chair and sat, her neck arched with tension, waiting for Posie to speak.

'I'm truly sorry to disturb you, Miss Hanro. To disturb you *both*.'

Pamela raised a plucked-out-of-existence eyebrow.

'I had quite forgotten about children's early bedtimes and such like. I don't have any children myself. Not yet, anyway. Please accept my apologies.'

Posie was finding it hard to reconcile the laughter she had heard before out on the landing with this anxious silent slash of a woman. She ran over the facts she had received from Sergeant Binny again, flipping them over, looking for something she could use to break the ice.

She resumed in a hushed tone:

'It's no concern to me, Miss Hanro, about your being

unmarried with a child here. You don't have to hide her from *me*. I don't give two hoots for social stigmas. I understand you adopted your daughter in 1918? So that would make her almost five by now, is that right? That was jolly kind of you.'

Pamela Hanro flashed angry eyes over at the left-hand door of the closed pair ahead of them, and hissed at Posie in a frantic whisper:

'I don't know what this is about, but you can jolly well leave my Hilda right out of it. She doesn't have a clue she's adopted, and she never will. So you keep your voice down and a civil tongue in your head.'

Pamela Hanro stood up furiously. 'Who are you, anyhow, and what do you want? You can get out right now if you've come here to cause trouble. I only let you in because of your House of Harlow clothes; I thought you really *must* be a friend of my sister's in clothes like that. But perhaps I was wrong? Are you an associate of the woman who's been threatening us?'

The words were desperate, and tears weren't far away. Posie saw with dismay that she had gone about things entirely the wrong way. She had meant to use her knowledge of the child as a means of establishing a confidence, not as a way of threatening Pamela Hanro. She remained seated and put down her beautiful teacup.

'Please. My name is Posie Parker, and I'm a Private Detective.' She splayed her hands apologetically.

'I really *am* here about your sister. I don't know anything about any threats being made against you, and I'm sorry if that's how it seemed. I only know about your child because I asked for help from New Scotland Yard and you had given them that information yourself back in 1918.'

Pamela gulped and sat down again. She flushed unbecomingly. 'Okay.'

Pamela nodded. 'I've read about you, I think. Weren't you in the papers with your engagement snaps earlier this year? That famous explorer chappie is your fella, isn't he? Boynton-Dale?'

Posie nodded, feeling no joy at the mention of the photos.

'So why are you here then? What's all this about Silvia? And are you one of her film cronies?'

Posie pushed one of her real business cards across to the woman.

'I've been asked to investigate death threats made against your sister, Silvia. I'm working my way through any of her family and friends who might know something. Or be able to help. And I'm absolutely *nothing* to do with the film world, I can assure you. I'm a genuine Private Detective: my work is never usually this glamorous.'

She briefly explained about the threats to Silvia, and the nature of them, and the finger which had arrived that morning. She watched as Pamela Hanro followed every word, wide-eyed, licking her thin lips nervously.

When Posie had finished, Pamela seemed to consider what had just been said, and then seemed to visibly relax, as if satisfied as to Posie's real identity.

'Excuse me for a moment,' she said quickly, rising. Pamela went over to the left-hand door, opened it a fraction for a second and then could be heard speaking in reassuring tones to the child within.

Posie stood and admired an oil painting which was hung above the dining table of two small girls in distinctly Edwardian clothes. *Really* she was trying to catch a glimpse of Hilda. But she didn't see the child at all, just gleaned an impression of tall shelves stacked full of dolls and games, and overheard snippets of 'this will only take a few moments, darling,' and 'one of Mummy's ladies about a dress.'

Pamela Hanro took a small gramophone from the glass shelf, a good, expensive model from around twenty years earlier, placed it near the door to the child's room, wound it up and placed the needle on the record to begin. A warbling rendition of 'The Teddy Bears' Picnic' soon filled the room.

'That's better,' said Pamela, sitting down in her chair again. 'Children are highly perceptive and Hilda found it strange that I insisted on her staying in her room, hidden away. She usually has the run of this place. Apart from when I have customers, and then this is usual practice; she stays in her room until I'm ready again. The music is a treat. And it also means that little ears can't hear us talking. But let's speak quietly, anyhow.'

Pamela Hanro grimaced. 'I'm sorry about my nervy manner before. As I said, I've been receiving some threatening mail lately myself, about Hilda, as it happens. About her parentage. I thought you might be connected to that.'

'Oh? Do you want to tell me more? Could I help?'

Pamela made a dismissive gesture. 'It's nothing that I can't handle. It's happened before, last year. Twice, actually. I dealt with it then by paying up. A despicable woman showed up here, and I'm expecting a demand for money again any day now. You can see it's got the wind up me. I can't be too cautious about answering the door.'

'Quite. Very sensible. Tell me: coming back to your sister, do you know who could be threatening her?'

Posie didn't mention that Pamela herself was currently on a list of suspects for the death threats. It wouldn't help. The girl was thorny as an old red winter rose and only just beginning to accept Posie for who she was.

Pamela sighed. 'I'm afraid you're wasting your time here, Miss Parker. I'm surprised that my famous sister didn't tell you – we haven't seen each other now for years – and that won't change. I haven't got a clue about her life or what makes her happy or sad anymore, or what she might have done to annoy someone so much that they'd do such a gruesome thing as to send her a finger. That's revolting.'

'It is. I quite agree.'

A silence fell between the women. From somewhere outside came the tinkling sound of a bell and the hoarse calling of a rag and bone man.

'*Any bones? Any old iron?*'

He passed further on down the street.

Posie indicated over to the painting she had been admiring. Two little girls, both in white lace, almost the same age as each other, but one with a helmet of golden hair and a round rosy face, quite captivating, the other with dark, flat wings of hair and a sallow, worried face, looked out at the viewer, their arms forever wrapped around each other protectively.

'That's beautiful. A John Singer Sargent, if I'm not mistaken?'

Pamela raised the eyebrow again. 'You know your artists, then?'

'I know a little. My father dabbled in painting and taught me what he knew. He loved Singer Sargent's work: said he captured the souls of people. That's you and Silvia, right? When you knew what made her happy, and what made her sad. And you must feel something for Silvia to keep that painting hanging up there. I'm right, aren't I?'

Pamela smiled, just a tiny wrinkling at one corner of the mouth. 'Quite correct, Miss Parker. You're good. They were happier times. Much happier times.'

'So what went wrong?'

'Everything.' She pursed her scarlet lips. 'It would take too long to tell you.'

'Try. Please. I'm frightfully sorry but you never know what's important in my line of work.'

Pamela stared at Posie in a slightly disbelieving way. She shrugged eventually. 'Somehow, Miss Parker, you're the type of girl to whom one wants to tell the truth. Goodness knows, I have few enough people to tell it to nowadays. Or who want to hear.'

Pamela Hanro fetched more tea, and Posie got out her notebook and listened.

She heard how the Hanro parents had been famous bohemians, part of the London set; they had been friends with William Morris and early patrons of his work. They had also been extraordinarily wealthy, the money flowing from the mother's side. Mr and Mrs Hanro had known every famous artist in Europe.

Posie heard how Pamela and Silvia had been raised as free spirits in a huge house with many servants just off Hyde Park. Silvia and Pamela had been two little girls with the world at their feet.

'My parents were truly amazing. They took us everywhere on their travels. They believed their family was all-important, and worth defending: they never gave up on us, ever. I was wild in my pursuit of what I thought was right, and they backed me all the way. Getting me out of messes time after time.'

'You mean when you were a suffragette?'

Pamela nodded, her mouth a tight, grim line. 'That's right. If you've spoken to Scotland Yard I expect they've mentioned the rumours about me starting the fire at Kew Gardens. Well? Don't tell me that you disapprove?'

'Not at all. My best friend Dolly was a suffragette. Got locked up with the best of them several times over. I think you two might get on very well, actually.'

'Perhaps.' Pamela shrugged carelessly as if she had a surfeit of friends and didn't need one more. 'Anyhow, I was lucky. My parents were right behind me, pulling me out of hairy situations: paying for lawyers and forking out vast sums by way of bail fees to keep me this side of the law.'

'What about your sister, was she a suffragette too?'

Pamela laughed bitterly. 'No. Absolutely not. She had no interest in women's rights; probably felt she had no need of them; life was good enough already. You see, my elder sister Silvia was always beautiful, startlingly so, and she touched whatever she happened to do with magic: ballet, gymnastics, singing. By the time I was involved with the suffragettes she'd been bitten badly by the cinema bug. It was all she could think about: becoming a movie star. She persuaded my parents to get her an acting coach, and she was hanging around with every famous movie person she could. She met her first boyfriend at Flicker Alley before the war and that was that.'

'Flicker Alley?'

'Golly, you really don't know much about the film industry, do you?'

'Afraid not.'

'I like you all the better for it, Miss Parker. Just so you know, Flicker Alley is Cecil Court, just by Leicester Square, where all the aspiring actors and beauties of the day hung around, and still hang around, hoping to be noticed. It's where all the famous directors go and eat lunch. Quite a place.'

'I see.'

'Indulge me. Is my sister still with her original boyfriend? The man who was injured in the war, I mean, not Robbie Fontaine.'

There was a note of imploring curiosity in Pamela's eyes. 'It's okay. I do realise it's difficult. You've probably been sworn to secrecy. Are they together *unofficially*, I mean.'

Posie looked over at the Singer Sargent painting and back at the grown-up Pamela. She nodded.

'Yes. Yes, they are together. You know Tom?'

'Tom?'

'The injured boyfriend?'

'Oh, yes. Tom… Sorry. I *knew* him. At the time. I knew several of my sister's movie star crowd quite well, but I stopped seeing them when Silvia and I cut off contact. But that poor man, oh my goodness…'

Pamela looked shaken for a moment. She whispered, almost to herself:

'It was summer 1917. I was still talking to Silvia a bit when it happened, although she only spoke of it to me once. She told me he had survived, but with life-changing injuries. Silvia was traumatised: didn't think she could visit him in the hospital. But who knows if she did or not? I haven't seen him, of course, but it all sounded horrendous. What a huge tragedy for him, those injuries...'

'Quite.'

'Sorry, I digress. So Silvia and I began to see less of each other as she ran with her acting crowd and I had my own, more political chums. We'd always been very different, even as little girls. And then of course the war came along, and we saw even less of each other. I was helping out here in London with clothes for soldiers, and my sister was helping make movies with Brian Langley for showing to the troops. She got her lucky break then, as it happened. Became a cinema sweetheart. It was around about 1917. Of course, she was nothing like as famous as she is now, but it was a start.'

'Your parents must have been very proud.'

'They never lived to see her become really famous, I'm afraid.'

Pamela looked away quickly. She swallowed as if she had a golf ball stuck in her throat.

'My parents left for Vienna in early 1918, to visit some artist friends of theirs who were having a special exhibition. They caught the round of Spanish flu which was sweeping the city on just their second day there. By the third day they were both dead, as were most of their artist friends. It was very quick. We weren't even allowed for their bodies to be brought back home to London, for risk of the infection spreading, you see.'

Posie had stopped writing in her pad. She looked up, appalled.

'I'm so, so sorry.'

Pamela shrugged. 'And that was the end of the fairy-tale,

I am afraid. I saw my sister last at my parents' memorial service. Five years ago.'

'But why the estrangement?' Posie picked up her notepad again. 'Surely their deaths should have brought you closer. Not pushed you further apart?'

That mocking bark of laughter came again:

'Miss Parker, my elder sister really is a fine actress, and a beauty, and a fine woman too. The thing is, she let me down, twice, in the same year, in 1918. And I can't forgive her for it.'

'Oh?'

'The first time she let me down was over money, of course. You must be sharp as a tack; I'm sure you've wondered why it is that I'm living *here*, raising a child above a chip shop, sharing a bathroom with a drearily annoying snoop who serves tea to the drivers in the Kensington Bus Depot at the crack of dawn?'

'Well, it's not my place to wonder anything, but…'

'The answer is that this is all I can afford in a good area. I take work as a seamstress. I do piecework for Nathan's, the costumiers, when they need an extra pair of hands: theatre costumes, like that old-fashioned wedding dress over there; it's for a performance at the Royal Opera House in a couple of weeks. And I work for private ladies, too. I've been here since 1918. I need a place which is handy for the rich women who live in this area. It's also good for Hilda to be so central. She's well-catered for.'

'But how come…'

'I've fallen so low? Well, my parents had money, but it wasn't really *theirs* as such. It was all tied up in a big family trust, on my mother's side. You know about such things?'

'Yes.'

Posie knew all about trusts: how Alaric's family had been riven apart by the inequalities which had followed the portioning off of family money into trusts, with payments being made to some family members and not to others.

'In the absence of a male heir, this particular trust followed the first-born female's line. After my mother's death, the trust income went to Silvia. The trustees who run the trust were two male cousins of my mother's – awful old stick-in-the-muds – who were only too delighted that their beautiful and now-famous little cousin was going to benefit in this way. She played up to it, of course. Acted very grateful.'

'And you? What did you get?'

'From the trust? Nothing. There was a provision in the trust that *if* everybody agreed, then a portion of the trust income could be paid out to another family member; someone such as myself. But, despite my writing to all of them in late 1918 what I was ashamed to call "begging letters", in which I requested an income from the trust, however small, I got nothing.'

Pamela frowned at the memory. 'Worse than nothing, really, as I lost my home during the process. The Hyde Park house of my parents was made over to Silvia, who promptly ordered that I leave. She emptied it and announced that it was to be rented out for yet more income. Most of my parents' paintings were auctioned off, as well as their more expensive belongings. All of the money made from the sales was tipped back into the Trust Fund.'

'Golly.'

Pamela shook her head suddenly, at pains to get things right.

'Actually, that's not strictly true. I got a legal letter saying that after much consideration, the trustees and Silvia had decided not to pay anything to me as I had a criminal record and had brought shame upon the family, and that such actions shouldn't be rewarded. They did, however, invite me to take my pick of items, up to a maximum of ten things, from the house before everything was sold. You can pretty much see what I took all around you: the furniture, the crockery, the gramophone, the Singer-Sargent painting. I must confess I was surprised to see it still there, on the wall in the old living room. I had thought Silvia would have taken it, as she had first dibs on everything. But the painting – and what it represented – obviously wasn't important to her.'

'And since?'

'Since then I've lived by my wits alone, and my sewing skills, which are really pretty good, even if I do say so myself. But I'm not registered as such. I can't be an official seamstress, working in-house: no big fashion house would have me work for them, probably not even piecework stuff, because of my criminal record.'

You haven't really asked. And you're too proud to beg again, thought Posie sadly.

'So I moved here, which was cheap. And I've never bothered to tell my sister where I live, although she could get in touch with me if she really wanted, through the family lawyers, Carver & Nicholas, in the city.'

Posie nodded. 'I know them. Tell me, does Silvia still get the trust money?'

'As far as I'm aware. And as far as I understand, she'd get even more, the capital itself, hundreds of thousands actually, if she married. But of course that won't happen.'

'Oh? Why not?'

'Remember, Silvia is first and foremost a movie star. That's not something she's going to give up in a hurry, is it? Not while she's still beautiful and able to take star roles.'

'I don't follow you.'

'She *can't* marry. The film industry, like so many other stupid professions, has a marriage bar in place for women: once you're married, that's it. No more job. And what if the story leaked that she had married Tom and that the whole sorry story with Robbie Fontaine was revealed to be the fiction that it really is? It would be a disaster for her. And for Brian Langley. Nope. She wouldn't do it; couldn't risk it.'

Pamela sighed. 'So their lives are just suspended.'

'I see. I wondered why Tom and Silvia hadn't married.'

'Now you know.'

Posie stared at her notepad, at her scribbles there.

'Do you know what happens to the trust money if Silvia were to die now?'

Pamela shrugged. 'I don't, I'm afraid. I think it either goes to me, or to one of those awful male cousins who act as trustees.'

Pamela got up and put the needle back on the record again, and the jangly notes and false-jolly voices of children's music filled the room.

'You mentioned *two* things your sister had let you down about. What was the second thing?'

Pamela's face darkened and the initial anger Posie had seen at the start of their meeting returned. Then the woman drew herself up straight in her chair, almost haughtily, and she clammed up as tightly as an oyster.

'I'm very much afraid that I can't mention it. No offence, Miss Parker, but I swore I would never speak of it. It doesn't touch on anything *you* are looking into, believe me. It shouldn't change your opinion of Silvia, either. Most people who meet her believe her to be a really first-class professional. And they're right. Our disagreement was quite personal.'

Something in Pamela's voice made Posie look at her curiously, but then she nodded. She was disappointed, but she understood; Pamela had been more than forthcoming on many other matters.

Posie realised that Pamela Hanro was one of life's survivors, and that she would always have found a way of getting by, with or without her sister's help and with or without handouts from an old Trust Fund. Money hadn't been the pivotal thing in this second, personal row.

And although Pamela Hanro hadn't used the word 'hate' or 'hatred' when talking about her sister, the word, unspoken, bubbled beneath the surface of everything she said. Posie saw very clearly that whatever the second thing Silvia had done in 1918 to let her sister down was unforgivable indeed.

But was it anything to do with the death threats?

She glanced down at her list of suspects.

'Could you help me, Pamela? I'm looking into the motives and backgrounds of the various people who might have sent the death threats. You said you used to know her film crowd: do you think Brian Langley, or Tom, or Robbie Fontaine would want your sister dead? Do you know of any reason in their histories which I might not have come across yet?'

Pamela Hanro paused for a few seconds, her mind running backwards through the past, dredging it for memories.

'I'll tell you this for nothing: Brian Langley is like a sharp pain in the behind, but he's not a murderer. In fact, he's one of the most reliable and trustworthy people you will ever meet, although he hides it well. He'd do anything for those close to him, and Silvia, for all that she doesn't deserve it, *is* close to him.' She sniffed. 'Unfortunately.'

'You knew him well?' Posie asked this innocently, thinking of the mysterious green-penned letter she had found on the Producer's desk from the woman sitting just opposite her now. Obviously quite a recent letter.

'Oh, yes. Well, we don't have anything to do with each other *now*, of course. But I met him properly time and again in the early days, the Flicker Alley days.'

'And Tom?'

'If I were you I'd strike him off that list. He adored my sister. He'd have no reason to kill her, either. He's wealthy, too: he made a stack of money before the war. For all his injuries now.'

'And Robbie?'

'*That* cocaine head? He spends his life either snorting

the white-stuff or else looking for his next hit. And that's all between learning his lines and being the Eighth Wonder. Haven't you seen the magazines? I'd hardly imagine he has time to *think* about killing my sister, let alone composing letters about it, or organising severed fingers. No way.'

Posie blinked stupidly.

She had been called innocent by Chief Inspector Lovelace when it came to drugs on several occasions before, and she still didn't register their presence quickly enough now. So much made sense now about Robbie Fontaine: the general feeling that everything to do with the star seemed wrong: his lack of attention; his wild eyes; his shiftiness. Perhaps the drugs explained all of this, or was there something else?

There was little else holding Posie in that peculiarly-furnished room, and she started to rise and gather her things. Pamela Hanro handed her the House of Harlow yellow linen jacket, fingering the stuff and admiring the seam-work as she did so.

'That's beautiful. But you know that, of course.'

'Thank you. And this meeting has been really helpful, thank you for your time.'

Posie had been peculiarly touched by Pamela Hanro in a way she had not expected, and she also felt she had been caught a little off-kilter: she had liked the girl.

But Posie had to be careful: it didn't mean the girl wasn't a suspect.

And with the half-made revelations of hatred towards Silvia hanging tentatively in the air, and that tell-tale bottle of green ink sitting on the shelf, and the possibility of hundreds of thousands of pounds from a trust coming Pamela's way with her sister dead, Posie found herself asking the unavoidable question:

'Forgive me, but you must realise you are on my list of suspects?'

There was an unexpected wry grin. 'Naturally. I hoped I would be. I count it as an honour.'

'And if anything happens to your sister tomorrow, I'm going to be obliged to hand over your name to the police.'

'Oh, do. They know me of old.' Pamela gave a rather fearful smile. 'Have you got anything by way of evidence against me?'

'No. Only that you use green ink.' She pointed over at the bottle on the stash of paper. 'Feeble, I know. But it happens to be the colour the death threats have been written in.'

Pamela threw up her arms in mock horror.

'So lock me up for it. Do you know why I use green ink? And why half the nation does, I expect? No? That's because you don't need to use it; you with your wonderful clothes and your snappy boyfriend. Green ink is the cheapest type you can buy at the stationer's: it costs half the price of blue, and a tenth of the price of black. Cheap turns like me can only afford green ink.'

Posie flushed red. It was true, she hadn't known that.

Posie paused at the door. She chewed her lip. 'I can't work you out, Miss Hanro. And that's something I say very, very rarely. I don't believe you would wish your sister dead, and you certainly don't benefit by her death under her personal Will.'

'No, I don't suppose I would.'

'So I don't believe you wrote those notes, but maybe I'm wrong. After all, you've lied to me about something else this evening.'

'What was that?'

'You said you weren't in touch with Brian Langley. But I know for a fact that you were. Quite recently, as it happens. I saw a letter from you, to him, in his study. He'd left it there, on his desk, open. Unguarded.'

Pamela Hanro gasped and her face flushed crimson with anger and embarrassment, but she didn't deny it. And then her response completely surprised Posie.

'*Unguarded?* It was open? For all to look at?'

'Oh, don't worry. No-one could see it,' Posie assured her. 'He has no real staff, you see. Just the Housekeeper, really.'

The crimson flush diffused just a little, but the chin was drawn up again and Pamela's fingers plucked against the violent pink of her brocade gown. Any friendliness in the woman's manner was now gone.

'So *do* you have a connection with Brian Langley, Miss Hanro? I'm sure you do: just as I'm sure that that expensive and beautiful yellow orchid over there must be a present from him to you. And those white roses were probably a gift, too. So what is the connection between you? Are you lovers?'

'Certainly not.' The tone was prim, but almost wistful.

'So what is it?'

But the woman simply shook her head, refusing to answer.

'It's of no importance to you, Miss Parker. And it's of no relevance to this case. Whatsoever.'

Pamela was retreating into the room already. 'Good night to you, Miss Parker, and please don't bother to pass on any message to my sister. There's nothing to be said.'

And with that, Pamela Hanro shut the door.

* * * *

Fourteen

Posie munched away on her fish and chips, loitering in the hot shadows of an awning. At her feet were her carpet bag and a spare fish and chip supper which she had bought for Mr Minks, the office cat.

Under the awning it smelt like a sweaty tent, and the mingled scents of melting pavement tarmac and fried fish ran high. But the location for her meal was no coincidence; Posie was standing directly opposite Tacy's, with a full view of Number 15, where Pamela lived.

The long queue had now dispersed and Bute Street had become quiet, a shimmering haze of dust. Posie had decided to linger on as something had made her curious and she felt a real need to get at the truth. But she didn't know why exactly.

She had, however, kept her eyes trained on the windows of the upper-floor flat of Number 15 for a little while now.

She was just finishing, licking at greasy fingers and scrunching up her newspaper wrapper when she saw a ripple of movement in the very window she had been focused on. Posie stayed in the shadows, watching. And there it was again. Posie stared.

And stared.

A child's face, her nose pushed up tight against the glass

of the grimy window. Peering out from behind the yellow orchid. An anxious, worried little face, somehow.

A familiar face.

And then suddenly Posie understood. She understood everything. Everything about Pamela Hanro made sense.

'Yikes.'

Posie exhaled. She stood, frozen, and then the little girl disappeared. Then there was a flutter of pink and a glimpse of Pamela Hanro's dark, shrewd face and for just a second her eyes roamed the length of Bute Street and then met Posie's and widened in horror. The two women stared at each other, Posie's heart hammering violently in her chest, her breath coming fast. Pamela Hanro disappeared.

Posie stepped out of the shadows into the brightness of the street and ripped out a piece of thin paper from her notebook. She started to write quickly, her greasy fingers staining the paper. And then she crossed the road and rang the doorbell of Number 15 again.

Posie waited at the blue door, unsure or not as to whether it would be answered this time. But after a couple of minutes she heard running steps in the hallway.

'So?' Pamela's face was suffused with a vivid anger, caught out.

'I don't want to bother you. But please, for my own understanding, tell me if I'm correct. And I promise, this won't go any further.'

Posie passed across the note, and Pamela Hanro grabbed at it as if it could catch fire. She read what Posie had written there:

Silvia doesn't know, does she?
But Brian does.

Posie studied the woman's face, all the while seeking to understand, but mainly trying to reassure. She failed spectacularly.

'Blast you and your interfering ways,' hissed Pamela Hanro. She crumpled the note and thrust the greasy paper into a sleeve of her elaborate pink dress.

'Maybe I misjudged you, Miss Parker; told you too much. I thought you were a decent sort. Nice, even. But that's enough now; I'll not tell you anymore. I've nothing more to give you. Go away and leave us be.'

Posie was stunned, but she saw the fear shadowing the girl's face. She held her hands out apologetically.

'I can assure you I have no desire to cause trouble, or take anything from you. What you did was good; it was *kind…*'

But she was cut off.

'I might have been a troublemaker in my youth, but that was a long time ago now. I'm a mother first and foremost. And there was nothing kind about me adopting Hilda: she's my life. My Hilda's all the family I've got.'

And then the door was slammed firmly shut.

As she left, Posie saw a beaky spectacled face peering out from the first-floor flat of Number 15. And above, curtains now shut tight, a yellow orchid rammed unforgivingly close to the glass of the window.

Suffocatingly close.

* * * *

The heat got worse the higher you climbed up the building on Grape Street where Posie's Detective Agency was housed, despite the shady narrowness of the little street and the trees outside. By the time she reached the top floor, Posie was covered in sweat and feeling decidedly unglamorous.

As she opened the glass-stencilled door to the office, the heat inside hit her like a wall. The place smelt like burning carpets and she raced in, opening all the windows in the waiting room and dashing through and opening the window in her office, and in Len's. She hurried to the kitchen at the back, and hauled up the tiny sash window there, causing a tiny waft of stale hot air to enter. She moved aside the tatty red velvet curtains she had installed a few years earlier for Mr Minks to climb on.

In truth, they weren't really needed anymore. She had brought Mr Minks in a basket down on a train to London when her father, the Reverend Parker, had died unexpectedly in 1919, leaving Posie almost penniless and without anything much to call her own, least of all a family.

Mr Minks was her father's beloved cream-and-brown Siamese, and he had been spoiled rotten by the vicar on a daily basis, having the run of the Norfolk Rectory Posie had called home. But when it had come to it, Posie was all Mr Minks had, and he was all she had. Initially, he had been forced to live in her office, her first landlady having an aversion to animals, but Mr Minks had liked it at Grape Street, and had refused to move on.

He was an old cat now, and his curtain-climbing days were almost behind him. He hadn't even bothered to greet Posie tonight; he was too hot and bothered. But he suddenly caught a whiff of the now-cold fish supper and he purred and rubbed at Posie's leg as she fetched a plate and undid the newspaper.

'Good grief, Len! Don't bother next time!'

Posie moved aside a tin of sardines in a brightly-coloured tomato sauce which Len had left out for the cat, the tin lid jagged and bent back, at a dangerous angle for anyone to encounter, human or feline.

'Good job you don't like tinned sardines, eh, Mr Minks?'

But now the cat ignored her, intent on wolfing down his food. Posie sighed and went through into the main office.

The place looked okay, to be honest, but it wasn't up to the usual standards kept by her permanent secretary, Prudence Smythe. It looked like a slummy girl's bedroom: there were bits and pieces everywhere, out of place. Her recent and unread copy of the new Agatha Christie bestseller *The Murder on the Links* was on the floor by the secretary's desk, obviously being 'borrowed' without Posie's consent, a cheap bookmark stuffed halfway through. Posie gave a sniff of irritation.

Her aborted effort at a grey jumper for Alaric was still lying sadly beside the desk, and this irritated her beyond belief. Dolly's magazine, *The Lady*, was also lying around from earlier. Good job that it was high summer and that no clients would come and call out of the blue.

Checking the top of the secretary's desk, Posie saw there was a postcard in cheap gaudy yellows and blues from Prudence, and an unopened letter with Posie's name on the front of it.

She slit the letter open and perched there on the desk, kicking her yellow suede shoes off. The letter was an invitation to a Christmas Eve party from someone she had met at Maypole Manor, in Kent, the previous year, as 1921 had slid unhappily into 1922. She had liked the person and stayed in touch sporadically. Posie smiled in amusement and placed the invite carefully aside in the metal mesh 'FILING' tray: the location was intriguing and the invitee was equally someone who would have a good many stories to tell over a roaring Christmas fire.

'Interesting.'

But it would have to wait: there was Alaric to consult, of course, and besides, Christmas seemed such a long way off.

Just as she was shifting herself from the desk, the telephone rang.

'Yes?' She sighed into the receiver, checking her wristwatch. It was seven-thirty. At least she had plenty of time before meeting the Chief Inspector.

'The Royal Oak pub, Madam, in Isleworth,' the Operator said primly. 'Do you want to take the call, Madam? Shall I make the connection?'

'The Royal Oak?' Posie's mind scrambled.

She remembered Reggie Jones telling her about how the extras and some of the crew would take off there for a bite to eat, usually sausage sandwiches, leaving the more important members of the film crew to their canteen dinners.

So who was this calling her? Someone unknown who had realised who she was, and had some snippet of advice or information about the death threats? Or else someone who couldn't rely on the privacy of the telephone at Worton Hall and had sneaked off to the nearest telephone hoping not to be overheard?

'Fine. Put the call through.'

'Two minutes, Madam.'

Posie grabbed at a piece of paper and a pencil from the desk, idly bundling up the grey mass of wool at the same time. She threw it into the bin and missed.

'Blast!'

She picked up the copy of *The Lady*, its front page emblazoned with yet another wedding portrait of the unutterably beautiful Lady Elizabeth Bowes-Lyon.

WEDDING SPECIAL! screamed this particular cover in a predictable variation on a theme.

Posie was suddenly reminded of the cuttings of the Duchess in her bridal attire up in the cook's room at Worton Hall. She studied the cover again. Would the cook appreciate it if she took it with her to Worton Hall tomorrow? As extra material for the scrapbook? It was a lovely picture at any rate: the Duchess was dreamily serene, wearing her wedding dress and wrapped up in furs against the April chill. Stuffing the magazine tightly into her carpet bag Posie was again plagued by some sort of misgivings about the cook, about something which wasn't quite right.

Just then the Operator announced the connection. There was a sudden rush of whispering and whirring down the line. The voice when it came sounded very far off.

'Posie? Hullo?'

'Who is this?'

'Don't you recognise my voice?'

The whirring continued, more than before. Posie suddenly realised it must be Silvia Hanro, although the voice sounded only a tiny bit like hers. She seemed to be whispering. Posie remembered Tom telling her that the couple maintained a fake name at their address in town.

'I say. Is that Mrs Delacroix?'

A slight laugh could be heard amid the howls and rasps. 'That's right. It's me.'

'I must warn you, Mrs Delacroix, I don't think this is a very secure line, at my end, I mean. You might be being listened in on. I thought we agreed that we wouldn't speak unless in person? Otherwise why was there all that cloak-and-dagger stuff before?'

'Well, I'm not exactly in my usual place, am I? Who would know to listen in on this call? They'd have to be mightily clever to do that. I'm sure it's fine. Brian doesn't know I'm here. Tom doesn't, either, although I left him a note to say I'd gone out and would be a while. No-one knows who I am. I've come in disguise. It's a wonderfully liberating feeling, people not recognising you. I feel completely free. It's delicious! I'm sitting in the lounge bar drinking milk and soda.'

'Well, how can I help you?'

'I couldn't speak to you earlier, when Robbie and I were sitting outside the studio. I felt awful just ignoring you like that. And then I found you'd taken off and gone. Why did you have to leave so soon?'

'There wasn't much more I could do there, to be honest. I wanted to see if I could find out a bit extra in town.'

'Oh, yes? And did you?' The whispering voice was eager, almost desperate. *Oh yes*, Posie thought to herself.

I found out a good deal.

Just then Posie was almost drowned out by a wave of crackling, and she held the receiver away from her ear for a bit.

'I'm making a good start,' she assured the movie star. 'I'll tell you all about it tomorrow. I'll be with you first thing. Don't worry. Are you finished for the day?'

'Oh yes. It's a relatively early night for us. Brian's busy in the cutting room so we all get a break until tomorrow. We'll start again at nine o'clock sharp for any last bits and pieces which might be needed. Your pal Dolly left here with Bertie Samuelson's driver, by the way. I saw her leave about half an hour ago. Jolly good sport, isn't she? Especially given Brian's sharp tongue; she seems to take it all in her stride, though.'

Posie felt a stab of relief, and guilt. She had actually forgotten all about Dolly until now. At least she was homeward-bound with the reliable Fred, who was certainly earning his shilling's worth from Bertie Samuelson today. 'She *is* a good sport. And thank you for letting me know.'

'See you tomorrow then. And thanks awfully.' The pips went amidst a blur of whirring noises and Silvia Hanro rang off.

Posie went through into her own office, shutting the door gently behind her.

What she had said wasn't quite true, actually. She wouldn't be telling Silvia Hanro what she had found out today. Not at all.

It wasn't her place to.

* * * *

Fifteen

Posie stood by her office window looking out at the view, at the dirty, tall grey buildings which were just blank backs, where the only signs of life were the pigeons who circled around and around beneath the sliver of hot, clear blue evening sky.

Strangely enough, Posie loved this view of offices which others might have found claustrophobic, or depressing, even. It reminded her of her own independence, of what she had achieved, of her love for London.

Most of the office workers would now be at home, eating dinner. Not Posie. But then, she wasn't most people.

'Lucky blighters,' she muttered to herself half-seriously. She had a busy night's work ahead of her, and one which demanded a change of clothes.

She slipped gratefully out of her dusty yellow outfit and kicked off her stockings, now grimy with London soot. Opening the locked cupboard nearest her desk, she brought out her emergency change of clothes and her stash of make-up, which in days gone by Len Irving would have called her 'glamour-attack'.

But those times were definitely now past: the 'glamour attack' *had* been an embellished short black dress, complete with sequins and feathers and trimmings, daring in its hem length and neckline. Now that Posie was richer, older, wiser and perhaps – even if she didn't like to admit it, *fatter* – the 'glamour attack' had been replaced by a plain black House of Harlow dress. It was cut beautifully and on the bias; serviceable for both day and eveningwear.

Posie had longed for this handy dress on countless occasions today.

She tugged it on over her head and immediately felt better, inconspicuous, but beautiful, too. A squirt of Parma Violet and a dash of pink lipstick completed the change and she sunk with a sense of relief into her desk chair. She tugged her hands through her very short shingled brown hair and then sat, thinking nineteen to the dozen.

She thought of the movie star she had just spoken to.

Silvia Hanro wasn't done for the night either. Even now she was probably still sitting incognito, alone, drinking her milk and soda in a pub, pretending to be someone else. Not that *that* would be difficult for the girl: she pretended to be someone else day in, day out, and got paid for it.

Posie thought through the implications of what she had found out on Bute Street. How things were stitching themselves together.

She had discovered, quite by accident, a web of secrets and dark histories which had been imperfectly hidden. The question was, was there enough of a motive among all that mess for threatening Silvia Hanro with murder?

Posie thought again of the small face at the window of Number 15, Bute Street.

Hilda Hanro.

Posie smiled sadly to herself. 'A child with two mothers, both in the same picture. Which the child looks at every single day without realising.'

The girl who had looked out of the window had had Silvia Hanro's saucer-like eyes and golden hair, and had been reminiscent of the elder child in the painting by John Singer Sargent. But the wide face, although similar to the movie star's, bore more of a resemblance to Brian Langley's. There was no mistaking it: her anxious expression was his alone.

The child was quite obviously the natural daughter of Silvia Hanro and Brian Langley. Adopted by Pamela Hanro in the autumn of 1918, most probably without her sister's knowledge.

And to this day, Posie was certain that Silvia had no idea that her sister had the daughter she had given away.

It had been the work of a moment for Posie to put it all together, standing there beneath the hot awning of the shop, staring at the child. She ran through it again now.

In late 1917, or early in 1918, when Tom Moran was recovering from his injuries, Silvia Hanro had been rising to the top of the cinematic ladder, and part of this process had no doubt included some sort of affair with her Producer, the already-famous Brian Langley, resulting in a pregnancy.

Posie remembered Silvia's tinkling laugh earlier that afternoon when she had suggested that Brian Langley might be behind the threats, and the movie star's protests that there was *too much* between herself and the Producer for him to wish her dead.

'I'd say!' muttered Posie darkly.

In the late summer and autumn of 1918, Silvia Hanro had probably removed herself from the movie world for a while, given birth to Brian Langley's child, and, desperate to retain her movie career, she had secretly arranged for the child to be given to the Foundling Hospital in Bloomsbury.

How much Silvia had wanted to keep the child was anyone's guess, and Posie couldn't fathom that out, but she suddenly remembered Silvia saying that on her death her money would pass to a children's charity, and Posie was certain, sure as bread was bread, that the charity would turn out to be the Foundling Hospital in Bloomsbury. That somehow, underneath it all, the memory of it gnawed at her still.

The arrangements had probably all been fairly easy. After all, it had been 1918 and a good deal was up in the air: Silvia's parents were newly dead, and Tom Moran was still cloistered in some far-flung hospital. The Great War was entering its final stages and everyone was paying attention to that. It was a good time to have secrets and to conceal things. Even babies.

Quite what Brian Langley had thought of the pregnancy and the giving away of the child was uncertain. Posie remembered him saying earlier in the day that he didn't really like many people. That had been a lie: at some point in 1917 or 1918 he had liked Silvia Hanro. A good deal.

A thought struck Posie.

Brian Langley didn't know about the baby. He had no idea. The idea rang true the more it lingered there.

Had Silvia hidden the pregnancy from him? Perhaps she had requested sudden leave from her film work, or simply disappeared? Perhaps Brian had put her strange behaviour down to the cooling off of their love affair and left her to get on with it…

But somehow, in all this mess, Pamela Hanro had found out about the child and, without Silvia's knowledge, rushed like an avenging angel to the rescue. Pamela Hanro had discovered that the child was at the Foundling Hospital and had secured the child into her own guardianship. Despite being single, and unmarried, and with a criminal record to her name.

'How she managed it quite beggars belief,' Posie muttered to herself.

Posie had had some experience of dealing with the Foundling Hospital before, when she had been seeking records of children 'given up' by those who were later desperate to be reunited with them. And, sad cases though they were, they had been hopeless cases too, as the Foundling Hospital, although an exemplary institution, guarded its files and its children's real identities fiercely.

And Pamela had given Posie the key to why she had done it: it was even there in that haunting painting. Pamela had said earlier that evening that her parents had '*believed their family was all-important, and worth defending*.' Having lost her own parents, and her sister, she had grabbed hold of what she could. Her own flesh-and-blood.

Posie remembered Pamela's angry parting-shot, which had had the awful ring of truth about it: '*My Hilda's all the family I've got.*'

It was ironic that while the world had thought of Pamela as the rebel, it had been she, and not her famous sister, who had been desperate to stick to old-fashioned family principles and keep the child who had been unwanted.

Posie sighed. It was obvious that Pamela couldn't forgive Silvia for abandoning Hilda. That had been the final nail in the coffin of their relationship, the point at which they had become truly estranged, at which Pamela had turned her back on her sister. But did Pamela want to murder Silvia now, because of something which had happened five years ago?

It seemed highly improbable. But Pamela couldn't be ruled out as a suspect.

And it was the same for Brian Langley. Posie drummed her hands on her desk. What was his role in all of this *now*?

Pamela had insisted she hadn't had anything to do with the man in years, but that was quite obviously a lie. The yellow orchid in her house and the letter from Pamela on Brian Langley's desk told a different story.

Posie tried to force herself to recall anything which might be useful about Pamela's letter, but all she could remember was the signature. Her mind wandered over the memory of the bank account statement she had had sight of. She remembered the strange entry about school fees, a cheque paid out every month to QUEENSGATE SCHOOL.

'Of course!'

Queensgate School was near to Kensington Palace Gardens, but it was also very close to Pamela Hanro's flat. A two-minute walk away. Posie remembered how Pamela had said the area was good for Hilda because she was '*well-catered for*.' Hilda must have been in attendance at the school for almost ten months now, since last September.

'That's it! He's paying his daughter's school fees, which cost a pretty penny. So he *knows*. At least, he's known since before last September when Hilda started at that school. He now knows what Silvia did. At some point Pamela Hanro must have caved in and gone to him, swearing Brian Langley to secrecy and begging him for financial help for the school fees.'

Posie nodded to herself.

'She'd touched her sister for money on a couple of occasions, but it was unreliable, or else, it just wasn't enough. Silvia is stingy, that's what has shocked me in all of this: Silvia doesn't like to spread her riches around. Pamela needed more than the occasional hand-out. She wanted to bring her daughter up as a lady, despite the fish and chip shop. So somehow or other Pamela and Brian have muddled through, in a highly unorthodox way, raising Hilda. I wonder how well they get on? Or how often they see each other? Or if this is merely a financial agreement and Brian Langley never comes near the girl?'

Whatever the case, Pamela and Brian shared a precious secret. One worth protecting. No wonder Pamela was so protective of Brian Langley; he had come up trumps. Posie smiled to remember Pamela's defence of Brian Langley; her insisting that he was one of the most reliable and trustworthy people you would ever meet.

But that didn't fit with the angry man Posie had met today, a man possibly fuelled by the terrible knowledge that he had been deprived of a child, without having had any say in the matter. He had had that knowledge for at least ten months now, if not more.

Posie wrote 'HATE' on an empty page.

Was the Producer angry at Silvia still, after ten months?

If so that would be very awkward: Silvia was his ex-lover and his daily work colleague, not to mention the star keeping his company afloat. Could he afford to hate her? And was he angry enough to want to kill her? But if so, why now, exactly? Why not when he had first found out about Hilda?

Posie nibbled at her pen-lid and tried to think a little wider. Could it be that Brian Langley was still in love with Silvia Hanro? That he couldn't shake it off or forget it?

He hadn't married, and he didn't seem to have a girlfriend. A long-harboured love for Silvia would be equally inconvenient for a successful working relationship. But if so, why threaten her now? Surely it would be simpler and more effective to get rid of Tom Moran, the boyfriend who had had to be 'hidden away'?

She wrote 'LOVE' on the open page.

'No.' Posie shook her head reluctantly, pulling herself away from thoughts of Brian Langley hankering after some long-ago love affair. She half crossed the word 'LOVE' out.

'It doesn't figure. This thing isn't about love. He's not sentimental enough. More likely it's a case of Brian Langley cashing in on Silvia's death if he's got an insurance policy on her life; a simple motive of needing money to fix Sunstar. And Silvia can be replaced: it seems he's already scouting for someone new for the position of his leading lady.'

Posie wrote 'MONEY' on the same page, too.

She sighed. 'How utterly, utterly depressing.'

Whatever the story, in Posie's view, Brian Langley towered head and shoulders above everyone else as the most likely suspect, even though he had called Posie in to investigate the death threats himself.

But thinking of money as a motive, there was something about money in general in this case that didn't add up.

Everything pointed to the fact that Silvia was mean. Tight with a capital 'T'.

Posie had heard from Pamela how her sister had refused to give her money from her Trust Fund in 1918, and how Pamela had later received two hand-outs from her sister in 1922. For *what* Pamela had needed the payments Posie didn't know, but Silvia Hanro seemed, even in her own telling of the tale, to have given them very grudgingly.

She even seemed to have bought her boyfriend a flat somewhat grudgingly, using it more than he did, and not willing to give him anything else. But was this meanness a motive for murder in itself? Had it upset someone *that* much?

And what about the capital of the Trust Fund? Where exactly would that go when Silvia died? Was *that* a motive for somebody to be sending death threats?

Posie knew from experience that Trust Funds usually didn't go the same way as people's Wills, and that it would most likely have a separate destiny, all of its own. Posie might be able to find out from the lawyers, Carver & Nicholas, *if* she was lucky. They'd probably still be working: lawyers kept crazy hours, too.

Going through to Prudence's desk Posie placed a call.

Posie had told Pamela Hanro she knew the firm of solicitors, Carver & Nicholas. But that wasn't strictly true. She knew only the younger Mr Nicholas, in a personal capacity; she'd met him from time to time at formal legal drinks functions in the city, mainly with the Chief Inspector.

Sebastian Nicholas had reminded Posie immediately of Harry Briskow, whom she had been engaged to, before the war, another lifetime ago. The two men shared a wicked sense of humour, thin sandy hair and dark blue eyes which betrayed a hankering to run away from the very respectability they had sought out in their profession: for before the war and before his death Harry Briskow had been a lawyer too. A couple of years back the similarity had led to a handful of trips to a Lyons Cornerhouse on the Strand together and a few inconvenient weeks of Posie believing herself to be in love with Sebastian, until good sense and the rather more captivating thrills of Len Irving had convinced her of her mistake. Still, she smiled at the prospect of talking to Sebastian again.

'Wotcha, Posie. Long time, no hear! How lovely to hear from you. Bit late, isn't it?'

After they had exchanged a few more routine pleasantries in which Posie found out that Sebastian had married and was about to become a father any day now, and he, likewise, congratulated her on her own engagement, Posie asked him quite bluntly about the destiny of the Hanro Family Trust Fund. She didn't tell him about the death threats, of course. Instead, she spun what she hoped was a likely tale:

'I'm having a quiet patch at the Detective Agency and so I'm working for Silvia Hanro herself at the moment; you know, I'm a sort of glorified secretary, tidying up all her personal bits and pieces. She's getting everything organised in big black files and she needs to know about the Trust Fund. So can you help me, Seb? Where does it end up?'

'Yikes, Posie. You don't ask much, do you? I'm so sorry but you know I can't break client confidentiality like that. Not even for you. Not without written permission from Miss Hanro herself. Now, if there had been an *actual* death…'

Posie almost screamed in exasperation. She tried to remain unflustered. 'Well, let's hope not. Please? Pretty please?'

Sebastian Nicholas sighed in defeat down the telephone line. 'Tell you what, if you put your questions very clearly to me in writing, whereby I answer in plain 'yes' or 'no', that might be a way around this.'

'I don't have time to write you a letter, Seb, I really don't…'

'Sorry old thing. But you know, can't you just ask Miss Silvia Hanro herself? We *have* written to her about this exact matter, you know. She's been informed about things, very recently, in fact.'

Posie frowned. Had Silvia been in contact with her lawyers about her Trust Fund? If so, she hadn't mentioned it to Posie. But then, why would she have done? The subject of the Trust Fund hadn't cropped up at all in their conversations. It had been Pamela Hanro, not her sister, who had been more than forthcoming about the matter.

Posie rang off among a flurry of slightly insincere promises to meet up again soon and had just started to scribble out a written request for information to Sebastian Nicholas when she heard the doorbell to the office ring from the street entrance.

'Horrors!' she cursed. 'It's way past anyone's opening hours.'

She opened the sash window and craned her neck to look down into Grape Street below. She just made out a gleaming black Rolls Royce Phantom parked up on the kerb, its painted body glistening and gleaming in the evening sun, its flying lady symbol on the front a darting globule of silver catching the light.

A white-gloved driver was visible at the wheel and Posie saw a tall man in full evening dress, complete with black top hat and gold-tipped cane, walking impatiently backwards and forwards on the pavement below.

Her heart sank.

* * * *

Sixteen

It was Rufus, Lord Cardigeon. Dolly's ridiculously wealthy husband.

Normally Posie would have been delighted to see him; he was her dead brother's best school chum from Eton and one of her only links to her brother now. It was fair to say that she loved Rufus to bits.

And yet here was another conundrum, one she didn't have time for.

Posie remembered her promise to Rufus earlier about looking after Dolly and she grimaced: something else she had failed at.

Just what on earth was going on to make Rufus so worried about his wife? Perhaps he had come to enlighten her.

'Coming!' she shouted down, all falsely bright.

As she went, she was suddenly aware of the overwhelming stink of the fish and chip supper emanating from the tiny kitchen, a greasy fug of scent wafting through the airless office. Diving into the kitchen she saw that Mr Minks had curled up for a nap in a shadowy spot by the curtains. She grabbed at the odious bits of newspaper, scooping up the gobbets of fish all around the place, gathering the whole lot up into an oily ball. There was a large refuse collection point at the end of the road, where the lane hit Shaftesbury Avenue, and she'd put it there.

Out on the street she found Rufus still pacing on the piping hot pavement.

'What Ho, Nosy!' He kissed Posie in a distracted fashion. His eyes were darting up and down her office building in a kind of nervous panic, and peering towards her open doorway.

'Rufus, darling. Always a pleasure. It's been an age. I used to see you all the time.'

'I know, Nosy. Dashed sorry and all that. And how's the delightful Alaric? Chipper, is he? I thought you two were going to get hitched pretty quickly...'

'Don't you start.'

'Sorry, old thing.' Rufus put his hands up as if in mock apology.

Posie crumpled the fish wrapper.

Something wasn't right. Not at all.

She shot a quick glance at Rufus, noticing how his previously rakishly thin good looks were giving way to something else now: something more substantial, weightier, more serious.

His blonde hair beneath the top hat was shorn shorter than before and he wore a small clipped beard, which somehow suited him. His blue eyes were harder and clearer than before, and they burned with a fire which Posie couldn't quite place.

Posie's heart lurched: she hoped to goodness Rufus hadn't taken up drinking again. Despite having won the Victoria Cross twice in the Great War, for untold acts of bravery in the trenches, he had sunk into a deep depression and become an alcoholic after the war, as had many men who couldn't forget the sights they had seen, and were haunted in equal parts by ghosts of comrades lost and intense waves of guilt at simply surviving. But after meeting Dolly in 1921 he had stuck to his promise not to touch a drop ever again.

Posie was standing very near to him. She sniffed discreetly. She couldn't smell anything remotely alcoholic.

'So, what have you been up to, Rufey?'

'Oh you know, a bit of this, a bit of that. I've got more involved in the estate business up at Rebburn Abbey, now that the old devil is so ill and out of it all. I don't think he's long for this world, to be honest.' Rufus sniffed. 'Poor blighter, I actually feel sorry for him. Makes you consider your own mortality and all that. You know, the bally old future…'

'Oh? Yikes. Sorry to hear that.'

Posie hadn't heard that Earl Cardigeon, a curmudgeonly old buffer of an aristocrat was ill and on the wane. Somehow it had seemed that he would go on forever.

Posie was scared and fond of the old Earl in equal parts, once having worked for him in recovering a priceless family jewel. Having been terrorised by him throughout the whole case, she had found herself wishing never to set eyes on the man again, only to find herself rewarded so handsomely by the Earl that she was set up for life as an independent woman. She owed him an enormous debt for his generosity. It had changed her life, which before had been very uncertain.

Rufus was still casting glances up at Posie's office on the top floor. He looked at Posie, suddenly aware of her presence again.

'I'm getting more involved in government, too. I really feel it's my time to make a difference, Nosy. Help people out. I'm usually at the House of Lords at Westminster chewing the fat with the other fellas. I feel I've finally found my niche.'

'Nice.' Posie didn't really want to know about politics, or want to discuss it. Alaric had famously given up his aristocratic title to become a regular Member of Parliament back in the time before the Great War, and while he was now too busy being an explorer and had given up his duties as an MP, she still had to hear about politics a good deal, particularly when he got together with his best friend, Major Hugo Marchpane.

She tried to look pleased. 'As long as it doesn't involve drink I'm happy for you, Rufey darling. Now, cut the niceties and tell me what you want exactly. What's going on?'

'Eh?' Rufus reeled a bit. He seemed to be struggling for words.

'Well, it's a bit out of your way to stop off here. This is nowhere near being *en route* from Westminster to Chelsea, is it?'

Posie stole a look over at the driver of the car. He was probably well within earshot. You never knew who you could trust these days. She'd learnt that the hard way.

'Let's walk, shall we? I need to throw this fishy paper away.'

Rufus scowled.

'It's not Friday, is it? And it's hot as Hades. Why are you guzzling down a fish supper mid-week, Nosy? You want to watch that, you know. Don't you want to fit into your nice wedding dress for Alaric? You used to be quite thin once. And pretty. Almost beautiful. I fancied you myself for a bit there. A long while ago now, mind.'

The remark stung and Posie flushed red.

'And *you* used to be polite, once upon a time. So just you shut up.'

Posie cast Rufus a look filled with malice and took his arm anyway, giving it a good pinch beneath the Savile Row dinner jacket. They strolled in the direction of two huge, reeking metal bins at the end of the street. A boy of only eight or nine, all threadbare clothes and dirty elbows, was rummaging in the nearest bin, propped precariously on a step of an old soap box.

'Hey you! You clear off! Little tyke!'

Rufus waved his top hat madly at the boy, who climbed

down, stuck his tongue out and ran off. Rufus kept his hat off, raking his hand through his sweaty short hair.

Posie cast a loaded look at her old friend. 'I thought you wanted to *help* people,' she said incredulously.

'There's people and then there's *people*. Posie, you are a noddle sometimes. That boy was a little oik. When will you ever learn?'

'By Jove, Rufus. He was just a wee lad, looking for some dinner. You could have helped him by giving him something. Not everyone's as fortunate as you, or your well-born daughters, you know!'

Rufus had gone red and squirmed a little beneath her gaze but he muttered something about '*my daughters!*' in an undertone which Posie didn't quite catch.

Posie stuffed the paper in a bin and turned to look at Rufus. She wiped her fingers and crossed her arms in a business-like fashion.

'Now tell me. No-one can hear. Well?'

'I came here to collect my wife. I tried your flat first, but with no joy. She *is* with you, isn't she? In that office up there of yours?' Posie noticed how Rufus's jaw muscles were drawn tight.

Posie thought unaccountably of Mr Minks. Fed and satisfied.

She banished the real-life thought of Dolly, in Mr Samuelson's chauffeured car, speeding towards Chelsea. Hopefully by the time Rufus had turned tail and reached home Dolly would have got there first.

'She's fine,' Posie assured him. 'She had fish and chips with me and now she's having a catnap.'

'Ah.' A smile of sheer relief spread itself across Rufus's face. He lit a cigarette with more of his usual manner.

'That makes sense. Well, I'll get on over to dinner at the Carlton Grill then. I won't disturb her. Not in her condition.'

'Sorry? What condition?'

'You know, Nosy. Don't be such a dolt. *The pregnancy.*'

Posie stared at Rufus and whistled softly under her breath.

So *that* was it! That was why Dolly wasn't quite herself at the moment. But why hadn't she said anything? Posie smiled back, quick as anything.

'I'll get her home to you later tonight myself. She won't leave my side.'

Rufus nodded. 'Dashed decent of you, old thing. Keep her close. Not a second out of your sight, remember?'

Rufus replaced his hat and walked back to the car, Posie trotting beside him, trying to keep up with his long-legged stride.

'But what's going on with this plot you were so wound up about earlier? You haven't told me anything. I'm going to see the Chief Inspector in half an hour. Obviously I'll take Dolly with me. But shall I tell him to come and speak to you about some protection?'

Rufus looked down at Posie and she saw something flush his face with scarlet. She knew him well, but couldn't place it. Was it fear? Anger? He ground out his cigarette stub on the sole of his beautiful black John Lobb shoe.

'What is it, Rufey? What is it? Have these blighters warned you off involving the police? Is that it?'

They stood uncomfortably close together by the car. At his silence Posie sighed and checked her wristwatch.

'I've got to go, Rufey darling. Have a good evening, even if you're utterly maddening and won't tell me anything. But tell me this, is Dolly in real danger?'

Rufus opened the car door. But he turned and nodded and whispered earnestly:

'Oh yes. Real danger. Of the worst sort. But for goodness' sake don't let on. She's got enough to worry about and I don't want her worried, not in her condition.'

As she headed back into her Grape Street office to collect her bag and wash her hands, ready for her meeting with Chief Inspector Lovelace, Posie saw the poor lad from the bins slink out of the shadows opposite. He came forwards with outstretched hands, dirty and woebegone.

Up close Posie could see how tanned he was from the unrelenting July sun, and she realised how even the London weather was no friend right now to the homeless. White crease lines framed his small blue eyes, which sparkled out of his nut-brown face like two tiny sapphire lights.

'Penny for me supper, Ma'am? I'm right starvin' and I've no mam. Me dad died in the war. Got three little sisters down High Holborn way to feed tonight, too. 'Ungry bellies, Ma'am; all of us. Please 'elp me?'

There was something about the lad which reminded Posie of the stringer, Sidney, who Robbie Fontaine used, and she found herself feeling immeasurably glad that Sidney had managed to get himself some sort of paid employment and was at least off the streets.

Posie asked the lad to wait while she ran upstairs, fetched her carpet bag and tipped out the contents of her small change purse into his hands.

He ran away, delighted.

'A soft touch, I know,' said Posie to herself. 'But at least my heart isn't hardening and I'm not turning into a miserable old bigot.'

And she thought of Rufus, and how he seemed to have changed.

* * * *

Seventeen

Posie walked down to the Inner Temple instead of catching a bus or a tram. Her brain was hurting and she tried just to enjoy the walk through central London.

She'd forgotten to bring the note for Carver and Nicholas, and she was cross at herself. It would have to be dropped off first thing next morning.

She was carrying a big green and gold bag from Gamages, the famous toy shop on High Holborn. Inside was a beautiful and costly baby doll in a smart box. It had been sitting under her desk for a good couple of months now, waiting to be given to Richard Lovelace's daughter, Phyllis, for her first birthday, which had now been and gone. Posie was Phyllis's Godmother, although she hadn't managed to see the little girl for ages, and there was definitely an element of guilt involved in the value of the purchase.

Bloomsbury and Holborn and Aldwych all lay spread before her, dusty and hot and bothered, unprepared for summers such as these.

She made her way out onto the Strand, past a row of tiny fashionable cafés on the Aldwych with awnings still out and strings of white fairy lights tacked about the place. In them were youngish lawyers and beautiful girls dressed in pastel-coloured silks and chiffons. All of them seemed to be drinking hard and moving much faster, and Posie tried not to stare too much as she walked by. She looked down at her sensible black dress and pumps and felt old. She also felt unaccountably hot, despite the lateness of the hour. And the dress, sensible though it was, couldn't be said to be light as a feather.

She had noticed a pair of girls sitting on a man's lap, both drinking amber-coloured cocktails and she knew without giving them a second glance that these were 'Bee's Knees', the most fashionable cocktail in London right now, an American sticky-sweet treat of gin and honey mixed with lemon and orange juices. She'd kept meaning to try one, but hadn't had the time, or inclination, or company. Maybe she'd drag Alaric off to one of these bars and force him to buy her one, when he came home.

If he ever came home.

Her thoughts were interrupted by a wolf-whistle and she walked on, looking down at the pavement, passing a bank of black cars whose drivers were waiting patiently for their masters.

'No, *you*! You in the black! Come back! Please!'

Posie turned in surprise. A handsome man in his late twenties with sad eyes and a vivid scar on his chin was standing at the front of a café, cigarette in hand, his evening suit rumpled. He had evidently had too many drinks already. He smiled at Posie forlornly and raised a bottle of something in her direction.

'You're beautiful! You'd make my night if you'd only step in here and have a drink with me? Join us, won't you?'

Posie smiled gingerly and was about to reply when her eyes came to rest on a woman among a crowd behind the man with the sad eyes. Posie noted that something in the woman's manner was dashed familiar.

It was Silvia Hanro. It had to be!

The height, the stance, the long-limbed athletic grace

– these were all identical to Silvia. But suddenly the woman turned her back on the street, moving into the dim interior of the café, and in the swirling blur of her apricot-coloured dress, she revealed herself as having long dark hair in an unfashionable plait hanging down her back.

'How bizarre!' muttered Posie. 'My eyes must be playing tricks on me. And why would Silvia be *here*, anyhow? She's miles away.'

In the brief moment that she had been staring at the girl in the apricot dress, the man who had wolf-whistled had vanished, without knowing that he had somehow made Posie's night.

Posie carried on, more cheerful, aware of the bells of St Clement Danes striking the hour. Nine o'clock. She was just on time.

Right now the light was beginning to fade and London was taking on that peculiar twilight colour which was all its own: several shades of purple mixed as if by a lunatic hand.

Crossing Fleet Street by the Royal Courts of Justice and swinging under the old black-beamed Tudor entrance to the Inn of the Inner Temple, Posie felt like she was entering another world. She passed under the heavy oak door, which wouldn't have been out of place in a fortress.

The busy streets of London with their horses and carts and many motor cars had no place here, and she was struck, as always, by the other-worldliness of the place. It was as if time had stopped still. As with the other three London legal 'Inns of Court' the Inner Temple had a calm, unhurried air. In the dusky light, blowsy late roses in a rainbow of colours swayed along the cobbled paths which led down to a great square garden.

On the left-hand side at the end of the path was the famous Temple Church, a perfectly round pearl, which had sat there since the Templar Knights had built it in the twelfth century. Inside the church were a row of memorials of stone-carved Knights, tombs as big as real men, slumbering forever on the floor. They lay there complete with an assortment of dogs and lions and swords and chainmail. The Temple Church was famous for its carol concerts, as well as its Knights, and Posie remembered coming here to sing carols a few years running as a small girl, with both her mother Zelda and her father and her brother Richard. It had been part of a much looked-forward-to December 'day out' down in London, topped and tailed by shopping for presents at Harrods and then tea at Lyons on the Strand. She remembered being fascinated by those stone Knights. As Richard had been. Who then could have known that he too would be felled by war? That he too would be destined to sleep forever as a young soldier; not in white-marbled majesty, but lost on some godforsaken foreign battlefield.

Posie had reached the door of the church, now bolted fast, and she saw that an oil lamp was being lit in a glass lantern by a Porter in an official-looking dark and gold livery. She nodded in acknowledgement and sat down on a bench there to wait.

'You only just made it, Miss,' muttered the Porter self-importantly. 'The gates to the Inner Temple close at dusk. I'm just off to bolt them now. Let me know when you want to leave again and I'll unlock the door. I'll be in my office.' And he stumped off.

She didn't have long to wait.

'Posie!'

Chief Inspector Lovelace suddenly came into view, silhouetted against a lamp further down the path, towards the gardens and the river. When he came up closer he kissed Posie quickly on the cheek and she felt the rough stubble of his cheek and a sheen of sweat on his skin as he pulled away.

'Blast this weather. They say it's the hottest ever summer, don't you know? I'm positively melting in this get-up.' He pulled at his collar to let some air in and gulped a few times like a fish out of water.

'I know,' Posie agreed. 'It's unbearable, but it's *so* lovely to see you, sir. And thank you for meeting me like this. I'm mighty happy to speak to you about these death threats. I must confess I feel very out of my depth.'

She continued breathlessly: 'Oh, here, take this before I forget.' Posie pushed the green Gamages bag into his arms. 'This is for that beautiful one-year-old Goddaughter of mine. Give her a big kiss from her Auntie Posie.'

'Gracious, how lovely of you.'

Richard Lovelace smiled happily as he always did when his daughter was mentioned. He was in his early forties, and scrubbed up well. He was good-looking in a big, capable, freckly-gingery sort of way, and tonight his reddish hair was slicked back neatly and he wore immaculate white tie. Posie noticed that around his neck he wore a blue-and-white striped ribbon and on the end of it hung a very shiny and obviously new gold medal.

'Goodness me!' Posie indicated the medal. 'You said you'd won a prize but this looks top-drawer stuff. What's it for?'

Even in the failing light Richard Lovelace had the good grace to look embarrassed and a flush stole over his already reddish skin. 'Er, well. It's not that much of a thing, really...'

'He's only gone and got the highest honour it's possible to get in the police force without getting killed!' a familiar voice boomed behind Posie.

It was Sergeant Binny. He was carrying a big canvas hold-all and was dressed in the normal regulation year-round Scotland Yard attire of beige trench coat and dark flannel trousers. He put down the hold-all on the bench and nodded cheekily.

'It's only the Blue Plume, Miss! For extraordinary achievement! The Chief Inspector is quite the top dog now at Scotland Yard, Miss Parker.' Sergeant Binny then turned to Lovelace and tipped his dark homburg hat in a show of mock deference.

'*If* you don't mind me saying so, sir. Just a turn of phrase, mind.'

Posie smiled at Binny. He was one of the Chief Inspector's most capable right-hand men, and, as he had proved earlier that afternoon, he was extraordinarily good at his job.

'Good evening, Sergeant.' Lovelace smiled. 'And thank you for that charming elucidation. Not that I would have put it quite like that myself, mind. Now, let's get down to business. Let's stay here on this bench. No-one seems to be about and we can see anyone approaching. But let's keep it down, eh? Just whisper.'

They all sat. The light had nearly gone and the dark cobbles of the alley were lit strangely by the oil lamp, the shadow of the round church looming over everything like a dark cocoon. In other places the effect might have been sinister, but here in this safe place it was oddly comforting.

'Best give us an update so far, Posie. You seem to know a good deal.'

'Right-ho.'

And so Posie described as best and as quickly as she could what had happened today; the death threats and the strange atmosphere at Worton Hall and the many odd characters it seemed to harbour.

There was a short silence.

'I've been thinking this over, what you've told me so far,' said the Chief Inspector after a little bit, rubbing at the stubble on his chin thoughtfully. 'First, are you sure this isn't just Silvia Hanro instigating the whole thing? Didn't you say she has a new film out soon?'

Posie nodded.

'Well, then. Wouldn't this be the perfect way to generate a little extra publicity for it? And calling *you* in adds that little touch of credibility, Posie. And if so, no wonder she doesn't want to involve the police. We've known of such cases, both you and me. Eh?'

Posie thought of the capable girl she had met today who had given away a baby and carried on with her career. Whose single-mindedness obviously included personal sacrifice, a girl who was now holding onto her career by the skin of her teeth, but nonetheless a girl who, Posie firmly believed, did not engage in cheap tricks.

She shook her head firmly. 'No. With all due respect, that's utter rot, sir. I thought that might be a possibility at first; it was at the forefront of my mind when I met her. But it's not possible.'

'Mnnn. Well, what do you think of her?'

'Regardless of what I've since found out about her history, initially I rather liked her. I think Brian Langley is a jolly lucky man to have such a reliable leading lady. She's wealthy, too: massively so, aside from her own earnings. She's the beneficiary of a family trust. Not that she likes to share the money around. Not one bit.'

'I see. Binny? What did you find out?'

Sergeant Binny nodded in agreement. 'What Miss Parker says about the girl seems to be correct. I couldn't find anything against her in the police records, and by all accounts she's a dream to work with. High-class background and hell-bent on success, which she's achieved, of course. Up until now, anyway. Not a hint of the usual drugs and all that shenanigans. Miss Hanro seems squeaky clean.'

'So it would seem,' said the Inspector with an exaggerated nod. '*Too* squeaky clean?'

'I swear she didn't do this herself, sir,' Posie insisted. 'It's too complicated. Besides, the finger was really horrible.'

'Very well, then. I *had* to ask. But you don't think the finger was from a fresh corpse, do you? Rather like some crusty old specimen dug out from somewhere?'

'That's right, sir. In fact I could detect a distinct smell

of formaldehyde as a preserving agent. It niffed more than a bit, I'll tell you.'

The Chief Inspector sighed. 'Well, I don't think it sounds like we have a mass-murderer on our hands. Thank goodness. Just someone with convenient access to old body parts. However, there are two things that bother me in all of this. And one of them is that finger.'

'What's the other, sir?' piped up Binny, interested, from along the bench. Lovelace crouched forwards, his medal flashing in the dark.

'Actually it's the circle of foil around the finger, Sergeant. That worries me a darn sight more than the finger itself.'

Posie frowned. 'Why so, sir?'

'It gives the finger meaning, Posie. You said that this odious digit was the left-hand ring finger?'

Here he shot a quick glance in the dark at Posie's own pink-sapphire ring, as if to check he wasn't about to make some horribly tactless remark. Satisfied, he went on:

'Well, you know very well that by wearing a ring you show the world publicly that you are engaged, or married. It's a sign of belonging to someone, or, some would say, *possessing or having won someone*. It's a universal sign of the strongest emotion.'

'Love?'

'Yep. And we both know that love is often the driving factor behind murders. More often than not. Love comes in many shapes and sizes, often in dangerous and warped forms. I think the gold foil was a fake wedding ring, a sign: a symbol which was intended to deliver a message to your movie star, or else to hurt her. I think it might have meant something to Silvia Hanro. Perhaps something she didn't tell you? You said she was holding something back. A lover? A secret?'

Posie shrugged, all the while thinking. She hadn't thought of the gold-foil as a ring properly, and she was cross with herself because of it. It was so obvious. The Chief Inspector deserved his Blue Plume tonight.

She scrambled to remember Silvia Hanro in her changing room earlier that day, when she had passed across the finger. There *had* been something Posie had felt Silvia was keeping back, something about today which *had* been special, but what it was exactly had eluded her. The girl seemed to have a positive ton of secrets.

'I don't know if it meant anything to her, sir. But I do know she's not planning on getting married any time soon. She *can't*. Apparently it would be the end of her career. Not that she'd marry the man you'd expect her to, anyhow.'

She had struggled with herself as to whether or not to keep Silvia's secret about *not* being an item with Robbie Fontaine, and yet her concern for the girl won out, and she blabbed about the deception, and the real-life boyfriend. She had the satisfaction of hearing both Sergeant Binny and the Chief Inspector take sharp intakes of breath and Lovelace mutter to himself: 'Good grief! Well, I'll be blowed!'

'There are other secrets, too, sir.'

Posie then described how she had visited both Brian Langley's home and Pamela Hanro's. She mentioned the baby, Hilda Hanro, and about how Brian and Pamela Hanro now knew each other and were united in raising the girl, without Silvia's knowledge or consent.

After she had finished, they all sat in silence for a few seconds. Chief Inspector Lovelace groaned in disbelief.

'What a can of worms! Where do we start?'

'You're telling me, sir.'

* * * *

Eighteen

The oil lamp flickered.

'Are you certain that Silvia isn't in danger right now, Posie? It would be a devil of a thing to leave her alone tonight if she's in peril.'

Posie tried to suppress the thought of the girl in the apricot dress, turning back into the café, alone.

'I think the person who wrote the letters and sent the finger intends to kill her tomorrow, sir. It's very specific. For some reason, whether it's for the public nature of the party, or needing to have the film all finished, she can live until then. I think the murder is intended to be a big public gesture. Probably a shooting, unfortunately.'

'I agree with you there.'

'So my feeling is that Silvia is safe until then. The writer is a man, or a woman, of their word.'

The Chief Inspector nodded. 'I see. Good work uncovering the background. But what about the suspects you told me about earlier? Tell me where you're up to and let Sergeant Binny chip in with anything extra he may have found out. Is that what's in that bag, Sergeant?'

'Yes, sir,' Binny muttered, pulling out a notebook and various bits of paper and heading over to be nearest the oil lamp in order to read them.

'I've been scouring all sorts of things: our own police records; birth and death records; army records; newspapers. The full works.'

Dark shadows flickered across Binny's face, catching around the moustache he had grown to make people take him more seriously, and Posie saw him concentrating hard, not liking to look as though he had been caught on the hop. She knew that Sergeant Binny was studying hard for his Inspector's exams in the autumn, but he needed to make a constant good impression with the Chief Inspector in order to be entered for them. She felt for him and the pressure he was under, although she knew that Lovelace was a good boss and a kind man.

'Ready?' she asked, getting out her own notebook. Binny nodded.

Posie counted off on her fingers:

'Suspect one, Robbie Fontaine. He's a drug addict, sir. Cocaine, apparently. You now know, like me, that he's not really Silvia Hanro's boyfriend; he's married to a woman called Sheila who I'm yet to meet. There's no love lost between him and Silvia, for sure, but I don't think he'd stoop to murder. Anything to add, Sergeant?'

The Sergeant consulted his notes in the dim flickering light.

'Not that much, Miss Parker. He was already in the movies at the time the Great War broke out, although playing bit-parts rather than the romantic leads he now specialises in. He seems to have got his big break during the war, when other actors had famously signed up. He didn't volunteer for the army, by the way. He managed to wangle it that he was doing "necessary service" at home, making entertainment for the troops.'

Chief Inspector Lovelace raised an eyebrow. He checked his fob watch as the Inner Temple bell struck a quarter-past the hour. 'I see. Go on, Sergeant.'

'Nothing much more to add, sir. We had no idea he was

married – like the general public we believed in the sham relationship with Miss Hanro – but we *did* know he was a cocaine addict, although he has no criminal file and no charges have ever been brought against him.'

'How did *you* know he's a drug addict, then?' trilled Posie.

'Oh, Posie,' muttered the Chief Inspector, half-affectionately, half-exasperated. '*Honestly!* If an actress or a film star *isn't* a cocaine addict these days it's a pleasant surprise! Miss Hanro seems to be the exception to the rule. Surely you remember Amory Laine?'

Posie nodded. The beautiful, doomed film star had been trying to quit the drug when Lovelace and Posie had met her at a party on New Year's Eve, 1921, and Amory Laine's behaviour as a result had been both erratic and shocking.

The Chief Inspector resumed: 'Cocaine is about as widely used in that trade as bottles of ink and postage stamps are in our profession! Remember that film last year, *Cocaine*? Everyone says it was the most scandalous thing ever made, only just passed by the censors, but I'd say it was pretty darn accurate, actually. Surely you saw it?'

'Erm…' Posie was saved by Sergeant Binny.

'He's right, Miss. But the background information I have on Robbie Fontaine is a bit more certain. Do you remember the Billie Carleton case, Miss?'

She was on firmer ground and nodded eagerly. 'Of course I remember it.'

The Billie Carleton case of 1918 had been a huge scandal, a sensation. An actress, Miss Carleton, had died accidentally at the Savoy Hotel in London after attending a Victory Ball and the whole affair had cast a spotlight on how many of London's most glittering stars were using drugs. It had become a sensational court case, with many famous celebrities forced through the Courts to give evidence. The newspapers, looking for news which didn't focus on the horrors of the Great War, had lapped it all up greedily.

'Well, it seems that our Mr Fontaine was there, at the Savoy, on the fateful night. Part of a big crowd with Miss Carleton. But he was never made to give evidence, he was ferreted away and kept out of the whole thing. All hushed up. There are just a couple of references here and there to his presence being reported at the time.'

'How was it covered up?'

Sergeant Binny shrugged. 'I'd say it was your Mr Langley. He must have gone over and above to keep his rising star out of the gutter press.'

'You mean he paid someone, somewhere?'

'I'd say so, Miss. Or else he threatened someone with blackmail, or violence. He seems a very powerful man, your Mr Langley. He's used to getting his own way and he's able to do unscrupulous things. Unorthodox.'

Posie nodded. Unaccountably she thought again about the big black crow on the lawn at the Rectory.

'That sounds about right. Shall I tell you what I know about Mr Langley so far?'

'Go on,' said Lovelace encouragingly.

She checked her notes again and carried on: 'Brian Langley is a cross and angry man, and a weird one, too: his passion is to grow fancy orchids, several of them poisonous, and exactly that sort are decorating Silvia's dressing room just now. It's very strange. If I *had* to name the most likely suspect, at the moment it's him. But right now I'm still unsure if and why he'd want to kill his leading lady. And why now?'

Lovelace nodded. 'Sergeant? Anything more you know?'

'Yes, there is, actually. Something important.'

'Oh?'

'Brian Langley doesn't just grow orchids for fun, you know. He's a seller, too. On a *very* high level. He trades with America a good deal. No wonder he can afford to pay a full-time gardener to look after those things! He makes hundreds and hundreds of pounds a year buying and selling those hot-house beauties. The Customs and Excise boys have crawled all over his business several times now and by all accounts he's playing it all by the rules. Nothing untoward.'

'My gosh!' Posie thought of the glasshouse addition to the strange bungalow at Richmond with its rainbow of blooms. She had had no idea they were so precious, and now she appreciated Mrs Cleeves' Rottweiler-like security tactics and the fact that visitors were hardly ever admitted.

'Yes, indeed, Miss. It would seem that in some years Mr Langley has made more through selling orchids than making films for Sunstar! It supplements and keeps Sunstar Films going.'

'That's ridiculous!' snarled the Chief Inspector.

'But it's true,' said the Sergeant, a touch apologetically. 'Even if he doesn't advertise the fact. And that wasn't even the important bit I needed to tell you! There's something else you need to know. The man is even more complicated than you think. He's a first-class shot.'

'What! How so?' Posie said, flabbergasted. She saw the Chief Inspector's eyes had widened visibly. Brian Langley didn't strike her as someone who would go out shooting anything other than films.

Binny nodded, pleased at their reaction. 'He was a member of a gun club before the war, down at Richmond. In fact, he was more than just a member, he was Captain of it for several years; their star by all accounts. When there was a trophy in a competition to be had, he won it. He owned the lot: rifles, revolvers, pistols. Had quite a collection. We have a list of his firearms on our police records. It makes for extensive reading.'

'Gracious! Is he still a member of the gun club now?'

The Sergeant shook his head.

'He was just a little too old to serve in the war, of course. That was before things got desperate and the War Office started calling up absolutely everybody, even famous film directors. He was working on films all through the early summer of 1918 and went over to France as a very late entrant. He closed up Sunstar Films and went in as an officer with minimal training in early August 1918. He found himself leading his troops through the Battle of Amiens! He was there only for the end, but it was a bloody, horrible end.'

'Golly!' muttered Posie. 'That was the start of the end of the war, wasn't it?'

'It was,' interjected Lovelace, nodding. 'Fortunately. It was the start of August when it began. It was a terrible battle, by all accounts. Chap must be brave as hell.'

'He was,' said Sergeant Binny simply. 'He won a Victoria Cross. The highest award for bravery you can get. Although he doesn't ever seem to have spoken about it in interviews; he refuses to do so. It's a sort of strange unspoken-about secret.'

'My gosh!' Posie was stunned. And suddenly she saw how remarkably easy it had been for Silvia Hanro to hide the birth of baby Hilda from Brian Langley: he had been off at war in France and wouldn't have been any the wiser. She gulped.

'And then what?'

'I'm only guessing, mind,' said Binny thoughtfully. 'But he doesn't seem to have owned a gun since. Handed all of his firearms into the police in the amnesty just after the armistice. Doesn't own anything now, and he doesn't shoot.'

'He must have been affected pretty badly by what he saw at Amiens, poor beggar,' said Chief Inspector Lovelace, who had himself fought in the war and been invalided out after Passchendaele.

'Maybe,' said Posie darkly. 'But no-one can take away his ability to shoot well, can they? And you only have a record of what he *officially* gave back. Who knows if he's kept hold of some gun or other? A favourite, perhaps?'

'True, Posie. It's got to be borne in mind.'

She swallowed hard. Posie didn't want to give up her first impressions of Brian Langley too quickly in exchange for some sort of war-hero type.

They quickly discussed Pamela Hanro, and agreed that beyond the suffragette record and Posie's findings about the child, there was little more information to add.

Posie looked down at her list.

'Tom Moran? The real-life boyfriend? I must confess I don't have anything on him at all. Only his address at the Albany. I'll tell you what he's like though: he's devilishly handsome, gorgeous, even. And I can see why Silvia is mad about him, for all that he's missing half his face.'

'Oh?'

'He was injured out after the battle of Ypres in 1917. I'd say from our brief conversation that he's still coming to terms with it. He seems very proud and resentful, as if he's been handed a very raw deal.'

'Which he has, poor blighter,' added Lovelace.

'Quite. But there's a sadness or an anger there I don't understand. Something more than you'd expect, somehow.'

'Is *he* capable of sending these threats?'

'I don't know sir; truly I don't.'

Posie shrugged. 'I must say I don't envy his lot: he has to watch this ridiculous circus with his girlfriend and Robbie Fontaine on a daily basis. He can't let anyone know that he's Silvia's boyfriend. Plus, he can't marry Silvia, as it would end her career. And all the while he hangs around Sunstar Films doing goodness only know what. Even *he* was scathing about his job title. I *do* know he's paid a salary by Brian Langley, though.'

The Chief Inspector frowned. 'It sounds like it would be enough to drive a fella mad. A sort of strange torture, really. Why doesn't he just get another job away from it all?'

Posie paused for a moment. 'You know how hard jobs are to come by these days, sir. Every second man invalided out of the army is after a job just now. Maybe Tom Moran thinks he'll keep hold of what he has? And besides, people *are* prejudiced and frightened of bad injuries; it's true. Maybe it would be difficult to convince a new employer to hire him in a public position? And at least as it is with Sunstar he gets to be physically near the love of his life.'

'But would he gain anything from frightening his girlfriend, or by killing her?'

'He doesn't benefit under Silvia's Will; it all goes to charity. My guess is the Foundling Hospital, actually, where Silvia dropped off her child. But apparently Tom's already been bought the Albany flat, though. You know, instead of benefitting under the Will.'

Sergeant Binny whistled through his teeth. 'Jolly nice present! That must have cost a pretty penny! Even if it is small!'

Posie shrugged. 'Perhaps.'

'You mentioned a Trust Fund, Posie. Do we know if Tom gets *that* if Silvia dies?'

'I don't know, sir. But my understanding so far is that it only passes if there has been a legal marriage. So, no. You'd have to ask the solicitors though, Carver & Nicholas. They wouldn't tell me anything, at least not yet. Pamela thought it might even end up with her.'

'I see.'

A false and melodramatic coughing noise broke from Sergeant Binny's throat, echoing around in the darkness.

'Sergeant? Are you okay?'

'*I* am, thank you very much. But this Tom Moran fellow we've been discussing isn't. He's not okay at all.'

'What?'

'He's dead, actually.'

Posie gasped, incredulous. 'Please explain.'

'Tom Moran doesn't exist. He *did*; he was born in 1905. But he died five years later, in 1910. He was just a little boy.'

'How do you know this, Sergeant?' Posie didn't like the cold hand of fear which was just now clutching at her heart and pressing on her ribcage.

'I always request birth records first, Miss,' said Binny, rather smugly. 'Then you know where you are. Well, I knew straight away that the date of birth I was supplied with wasn't right for our chappie, and so I called up the Office of Births, Deaths and Marriages, to make sure they were not mistaken. There was no mistake: there were no other Tom Morans listed in the country, you see. They came back and told me that Tom Moran's date of birth was correct, and that he was dead, to boot. And do you know where he's buried, this little boy?'

'No.'

'Isleworth Churchyard!' piped up Sergeant Binny, enjoying his moment of triumph. 'Apparently it's right next door to the Royal Oak pub, and there's a shortcut through the graveyard to the beer garden. So you can see what happened!'

The Chief Inspector groaned. 'Our Tom Moran has just borrowed a handy name! Because he needed one. Quickly. Your man with half a face is also missing a name, and a real identity.'

Posie felt like choking. Her Norse God was all a mirage. 'Gracious. This doesn't look good for Tom at all.'

'I agree with you, Posie.'

Sergeant Binny explained that he had checked all manner of other records for a man named Tom Moran, including army records, and had found nothing at all.

'Question is,' murmured Lovelace. 'Who is the fella? And why's he using a fake name?'

Just then there was an almighty banging on the huge wooden door which opened out onto Fleet Street. The sound was frenzied and persistent.

'Open up!' came a male voice which sounded a tiny bit familiar to Posie.

'What the blazes?' muttered the Chief Inspector, standing up, followed quickly by Posie and Sergeant Binny, as the little Porter from before came bustling out of his hidden office to see what all the fuss was about.

The Porter opened a little window next to the door and chatted to whoever it was out there. Whoever it was must have been important for he turned tail pretty quickly and trotted back over to where they were standing and did a mock-bow.

'Lady Cardigeon, Chief Inspector. She wants to see you, and this lady, too, if she's a Miss Parker?'

Lovelace nodded and waved a sweaty hot hand as if directing traffic. 'Let her in, of course. You didn't need to ask me, you silly fella.'

'What on earth is Dolly up to?' queried Posie. She stared over. Why was Dolly not at home?

'Posie, lovey!'

Seconds later Dolly was crossing the cobbles, in the same attire as earlier, but this time hatless, and her blonde shingled head seemed to shine like a little light in the darkness. Posie noticed that Dolly was followed, as across a lit stage, by the dark figure of an unknown man.

Dolly shook hands with both policemen and turned to Posie, almost completely out of breath.

'What's happened, Dolly?' asked Posie quickly, dreading hearing more of the possible plot which Rufus was worrying about.

The man at Dolly's side suddenly appeared out of the gloom and materialised as Sam Stubbs, a now-prominent journalist at the *Associated Press*. He and Posie knew each other quite well; they sometimes worked alongside each other, trading information and stories as needed.

'Sam!'

'Wotcha, Miss.'

The Chief Inspector stepped forwards in the darkness, wary of the press. 'Now wait a minute, young fellow,' he began. 'I'm not sure you should be a party to our conversation here. Could you just wait over...'

But Dolly cut Lovelace off: 'Oh, no point in sending Sam away, Inspector! He knows all about mostly everything. You'll never guess what!' breathed Dolly, turning to Posie, her voice sounding raspy.

The excitement and nerves were palpable on her face even in the dim light and Posie was about to suggest she sit down and calm down for the sake of her baby, but then she remembered that she wasn't supposed to know, and she held her tongue.

Dolly rummaged in her big bag and was suddenly flapping something around in her hand.

'It's about Tom Moran!'

'Oh?' said the Chief Inspector. 'That's timely! We were just discussing him, weren't we, Sergeant?'

'That's right, my Lady. Turns out he doesn't exist. At least he's not who he says he is.'

'Oh!'

The wind had gone out of Dolly's sails a little, and she looked slightly put off for a couple of seconds. Posie reached out and took Dolly's hand and held it, soothingly, she hoped. 'What is it, Dolly? Do you have some information?'

Dolly recovered a little. She nodded gleefully.

'I'll say I do!'

* * * *

Nineteen

'I'd been thinking most of today over at Worton Hall that there was something familiar about the man,' said Dolly breathlessly, her pale face luminous in the heat.

'Go on,' said Posie encouragingly. Her heart was racing.

Dolly waved the paper maddeningly around in the air.

'And then, in the car on the way back into town, I remembered who it was that Tom Moran reminded me of! But it was late, and I had to be sure. So I got the driver, Fred, nice fella actually, to swing past the *Associated Press*' office on Fleet Street. I asked Sam here if I could use their archives room, and, do you know what? I was blimmin' well right!'

Everyone except the journalist groaned.

'And?'

'Oh, didn't I say? Sorry! Tom Moran is, or rather *was*, the famous film star, Mark Paris!'

'Mark Paris?' repeated Posie softly. Even *she* had heard of Mark Paris.

'Here.' Dolly had thrust her paper, which seemed to be a photograph, under the light, and both policemen looked at it quickly.

The Chief Inspector whistled softly. 'I thought Mark Paris had died in the war.'

'I think everyone thought that, Inspector.' Dolly nodded, lighting up. She turned to Posie.

'I know you ain't really got a clue who Mark Paris is, or *was*, lovey, except by name. But he was a wonderful actor; a *real* movie star in the old days, before the war. Half the world was in love with him, or wanted to *be* him, before Robbie Fontaine or Silvia Hanro meant anythin' to anyone. When Mark Paris signed up to fight on the front line there was a big story about it in all the papers.'

'That's right,' said Sam Stubbs, with a tremor of barely-suppressed excitement. 'It was before my time of course, but looking at the archives it seems clear enough that thousands of girls worried about him, and sent Mr Paris fan mail via our offices: none of which ever got sent on to him, of course.'

'And hundreds of girls mourned him,' Dolly nodded, blowing a smoke ring, 'when it was reported in July 1917 that he had gone missin' in action. Seems like he's been missin' ever since. Huh?'

Posie took the photograph which Binny passed to her, almost warily. She didn't know what to expect. Binny edged over, trying to be helpful. He lit a match and stood with it near the black-and-white studio portrait so Posie could see it better.

She looked at it with a sense of trepidation. The man who looked out at her was scowling moodily, his face turned to the left very slightly, his finely-chiselled features captured beautifully by some long-gone photographer. He wore his hair waxed thickly back, its raven-black curls making him look like some sort of Byron. Posie felt when looking at the photograph that there was indeed something familiar about it, but she would never have put the blonde god with the shattered face and this dark heart-throb together; never connected them as being the same man. It would have taken an expert to see through it.

She said as much.

Dolly shrugged. 'I went to see nearly every one of Mark Paris's films, so I suppose I'd pick up something. Look at his eyes, then you'll see. It's just the hair really which makes him look so different; that was the fashion back then, of course, and Sunstar Films must have told him to wear it like that.'

She patted her own bleached crop mournfully. 'He must have had the devil of a job dying it black all the time: the man's a natural blonde of course. Lucky so-and-so!'

Posie looked up. 'Hang on a minute,' she said sharply. 'Did you say he was working for Sunstar Films way back before the war?'

Dolly nodded. 'Yes, of course. They're the biggest film company goin'. Have been since movies started in this country. So it's only natural he'd have been workin' for them, isn't it?'

Thoughts crowded Posie's mind. She pictured Tom – she couldn't think of him as Mark– working for Sunstar Films as a major movie star, back in the old days.

She thought too about how it must be for him *now*: to be unknown, when before the war he had been at the very centre of the business. What must it be like to be ordered around by Brian Langley, who had known him in his prime? And the shame of being paid a small salary for doing pretty much nothing, when before the war he must have commanded vast sums for flaunting his very presence on screen? Pamela Hanro, who had known the truth, of course, had spoken of the riches Tom had accrued before the war.

Posie felt an ache of pity for the man.

Some things fell into place; things heard but not understood at the time. Posie remembered Tom's bitter words to her earlier about his lot in life, about his terrible wounds. No wonder the man was resentful: his face had quite literally been his fortune and now he was without it.

She remembered too Silvia Hanro's awe and love for

her boyfriend, who she had met in her early acting days, when *he* was the star. Her description of him being '*movie star material...sort of*', now made much more sense.

The 'sort of' was important.

Of course Tom could never be a film star again. That much was obvious. Pamela Hanro had been entirely correct when she had described what had happened to Tom as a tragedy. It *was* a tragedy if one knew who and what the man used to be. It also explained his powerful presence and the aura of entitlement which somehow still hung around him, even in his diminished role.

But why pretend to be dead and pick up another identity? Was it just simpler? Was the pride Posie had detected in the man too great to endure pity and the inevitable outpourings of grief and sympathy which would surely come? And why return, like some poor tormented soul, to the industry, even the very company, which he had been a star of? A move which would surely rub self-inflicted salt into the wounds of his obviously-delicate ego.

Strangely Posie felt peculiarly defensive of the man. She remembered his providing her with a fake identity for Reggie Jones' benefit, and she had admired his quick-thinking. And, it had to be said, she had fallen for his shattered good looks. She stuck her chin out, ready to be challenged:

'I suppose it's not a crime to change one's identity, is it?'

Lovelace shook his head steadily. 'Nope. Poor blighter might just be looking for a quiet life. Nothing wrong with that. It explains a lot.'

'After all,' continued Posie, 'he's never actually *said* he's dead, has he? I suppose that's what people just *presumed*?'

'I suppose so,' said Dolly uncertainly.

And then Posie remembered with a sudden jolt where she had seen that photograph of Mark Paris in his heyday before. It had been just hours earlier. At Worton Hall.

It had been framed, and on a desk, surrounded by

cuttings of wedding dresses. In Mrs Thynne's little bedroom.

Posie turned to Dolly quickly.

'Do you think anyone else knows who Tom really is at Worton Hall? Apart from Brian Langley and Silvia, I mean?'

Dolly shook her head and ground out her cigarette underfoot. 'Nah. You said yerself that he isn't recognisable anymore. Besides, the crew are different now from those who worked before the war. Brian Langley is famous for having made public the fact that most of his film crew and his old hands died in the trenches.'

'It's just that I saw that photograph earlier today,' said Posie in a puzzled tone. 'In the cook's room.'

'Probably just a coincidence,' said Dolly. 'I had a photo of Mark Paris up for years, tacked up by my bed when I was nursin' out on the Western Front. Ironic, really, innit?'

'Mnnn,' said Posie. But she didn't like coincidences. Not one little bit.

She looked over at the Chief Inspector who was looking at her thoughtfully. But he suddenly turned to the journalist.

'How come you're here, anyhow, Stubbs? Surely not just as an escort for Lady Cardigeon?'

Sam Stubbs shook his head and proffered something from his pocket. Again everyone shunted around into the light from the oil lamp.

'What's all this, then?' Lovelace demanded, taking what looked like a standard cream-coloured telegram from the journalist's hands. Posie read over everyone's shoulders.

GET YOURSELF OVER TO WORTON HALL TOMORROW.
MIDDAY.
THE BIGGEST SCOOP OF YOUR CAREER AWAITS YOU
— SILVIA HANRO IS TO DIE FOR.

Posie took a sharp intake of breath. It was an invitation to murder.

'This looks to be more than a simple invitation to a party,' Lovelace said sharply. 'I don't like the sound of that at all.' He turned the telegram around in his large hands.

'Posted at Richmond, tonight,' he confirmed. 'Eight o'clock. Not that that helps us particularly. The world and his wife seem to be at Worton Hall, if I understand correctly, and the nearest telegram office open would be Richmond.'

'I've telephoned to a few colleagues at other newspapers,' said Sam Stubbs with a tremor of excitement in his voice, 'and they've all received exactly the same thing, too. It's a rum do.'

The Chief Inspector looked at Posie. 'Do you think Brian Langley might have sent these out? You know, elaborate party invites to muster up some press excitement?'

'It would be decidedly odd. He doesn't want any press near. This party is a big deal: it's for financial backers and people who might carry this new film in the future. He's no time for journalists at the best of times, let alone at an important party.'

Lovelace's mouth was pursed into a grim line. 'Then this really is serious,' he said quietly. 'It means that our writer of death threats has decided that keeping things nice and quiet wasn't enough: he, or she, wants a public stage, with a very public audience.'

After some discussion and having sworn Sam Stubbs to absolute secrecy about the things they had spoken of, especially Tom Moran's real identity, the journalist left, buoyed up by the thought of a good scoop coming his way. He had declared firmly that he *would* be attending the Wrap Party, and that no-one would or could stop him from coming.

The Inspector sighed heavily. 'I daresay I won't be returning to the rest of this Awards Ceremony tonight. It seems we'd better get back to the Yard, Binny, and get plans in place for tomorrow to cover Miss Hanro at this glitzy party. I'd say that invited or not, this has just become an official police matter.'

'Hang on a minute,' said Posie. 'Before you go, Sergeant, did you find anything out about Hector Mallow, this stalker? I haven't managed anything at all. All I know is he turns up as an extra at the weekends at Worton Hall.'

Sergeant Binny rustled around with his notebook, flicking a few pages to and fro. He nodded.

'Hector Mallow is a well-educated fellow, trained as a Science Master back in the day. Bit of a sad case, actually. He worked at one of the major public schools but got dismissed as he took a fancy to the wife of the Headmaster; pursued her all over the place. Same story a few times over, at various schools, until he seems to have become absolutely unemployable. He seems to scratch a living these days and is quite down on his uppers. Fallen pretty low, I'd say.'

'And the stalker bit?' asked Posie, trying to tamp down her impatience.

'Yes. The fella is a first-class nuisance. He's been reported by Miss Meggie Albanesi, just a couple of weeks ago. Apparently he keeps sitting in the same café as her after her current show ends. A place called Ciro's. Our lads investigated it: he *is* doing that, but it's not a crime, and there's nothing we can do.'

'What does he do exactly?' asked Posie, curious.

'It seems he just drinks tea and stares at the poor girl. He gives people the creeps. But he's more of a pest than a danger: unrequited adoration and all that. He lives over on Nassau Street in Soho in a scruffy bedsit, and works in the week at the teaching hospital, the Middlesex, on nearby Mortimer Street. He *must* be odd, though. He works as a morgue assistant.'

'A *WHAT*?'

Both Posie and the Chief Inspector stared at Binny in horror, thoughts of the horrible severed finger at the forefront of their minds. It dawned on Binny a jot too late:

'By Gad!'

'Exactly,' nodded the Inspector. 'This chappie could well be our man. He certainly has ample access to a cartload of corpses at that old teaching hospital. We need to look slippy about it and get him in: lock him up before he wreaks havoc tomorrow at this party.'

Inspector Lovelace was already busying himself into action, pulling off his smart medal briskly and pocketing it and tugging off his tight white collar. 'Where did you say he lives – Soho?'

Binny frowned doubtfully. 'But sir! We don't have a case against the man, do we? We have no *actual* evidence linking him to that finger, which, by the way, we are yet to see for ourselves. At the moment it's tenuous as anything. He's done nothing wrong, not yet. Nothing criminal, anyhow. What charges can we possibly bring against him?'

Lovelace groaned. 'We can't always do everything by the book, Sergeant. I know you're studying hard just now for your Inspector's exams and your diligence is to be praised, but you'll have to think a little wider on the job.'

'How much wider, sir?'

The Chief Inspector, clearly flummoxed, groped around wildly for an answer. 'We can say he's hindering a police enquiry…'

'There *is* no enquiry, sir. Not yet.'

'Or charge him with disrupting the peace at this café, where he's spying on this Meggie Albanesi woman…'

'He's just drinking tea, sir.'

Lovelace flapped his hands and turned crossly from his Sergeant, calling out to a man Posie hadn't clocked before, standing in the shadows further down the alleyway.

'McCrae! I need you to get the car. Pronto. Bring her out front, Constable. We're off to…now where did you say, Sergeant?'

'Wait a bit,' said Dolly, stepping forwards and jabbing the air with her cigarette holder, a fresh cigarette already loaded. 'You said he's spying on Meggie Albanesi just now?'

'That's right, my Lady. What of it?'

Dolly checked her tiny and priceless Cartier wristwatch which sparkled with diamonds as she moved it in the darkness, a bauble from Rufus.

'Well, it's coming up for a quarter to ten, and Meggie Albanesi is in *The Lilies of the Field* just now over at the Ambassadors. It's a long-running bestseller, so she'll definitely be performing tonight; it's doing so well that the cast and crew are not even having Wednesdays off, which is almost unheard of. They're about the only show making any money this year!'

'And, my Lady?'

'Well, it would make more sense to get on over there. If this stalker fellow wants to get up close to Meggie Albanesi he'll be queuin' by the stage door, waitin' for her to come out. She'll be out at about ten minutes past ten. Betcha! You'll have more of a chance to grab him there in the nice quiet darkness than at Ciro's, which is where she goes on afterwards. That place is like a goldfish bowl. I know it, and you'll have about a hundred spectators.'

The Chief Inspector smiled approvingly. 'Nice work, my Lady. It seems you are a veritable mine of information. Hear that, McCrac? The Ambassadors Theatre, pronto.'

The man disappeared into the darkness.

'Shall we come too, Inspector?' asked Posie dubiously. She was genuinely interested in taking a peep at the odd Mr Mallow, but somehow she had the feeling, more than ever now, that Hector Mallow was a red herring. It was far too neat, somehow. Come to think of it, hadn't it been Brian Langley, of all people, who had mentioned Hector Mallow in the first place as posing a danger?

Posie frowned, lost in her tangled thoughts again, as Richard Lovelace nodded at her.

'Of course you should come. A nice neat end to a bally strange day's work for you, eh?'

Suddenly the policeman, McCrae, was back, running.

'What is it, Constable?'

He reached them, panting a little. 'A police post boy, sir, from Scotland Yard. Brought you this message. He was waiting like a wee young idiot outside that great door there. I've given him a cuff around the ear for being so slow.'

He passed it across. Lovelace read it and groaned, pocketing the message. 'It's from your pal, Posie. Brian Langley.'

'He's no pal of mine, I can assure you.'

'Well, he evidently wants to involve *us* now. Make this a proper police case. Officially.'

'Why?'

'He telephoned in. Apparently Silvia Hanro has gone missing.'

****

Twenty

As they belted up the Strand with Constable McCrae at the steering wheel, Chief Inspector Lovelace was thinking aloud to Posie and Dolly, whom he was squeezed rather uncomfortably between on the hard back seat. The large Gamages bag and Binny's canvas hold-all were crushed right up against Posie's knees. The smell of petrol was strong and filled the inside of the car, which was close and stuffy.

Posie rolled down a canvas blind and took in deep breaths of London's thick night air, which was treacly on the lungs at the best of times.

'Of course, there's nothing we can do just now about her having gone missing,' Lovelace said decisively, but a touch defensively. Posie could tell he was actually quite worried.

'We'll get on over to Worton Hall tomorrow, at first light. Chances are she'll have shown up by then.'

'Work is due to start again at nine o'clock tomorrow. If I know anything about Silvia Hanro, sir, it's that she's punctual. She'll be there at nine if she can help it.'

Lovelace nodded. 'Thanks, Posie. Besides, a missing person, even a movie star, isn't officially missing until she or he has been gone for twenty-four hours.'

'Even now, in the circumstances, sir?' trilled Binny from the front of the car.

'Even *now*, Sergeant.'

'So we'll pick you up early tomorrow at your flat, Posie? Seven sharp?'

'Mnnn.'

Posie was thinking of the apricot-clad figure she had seen melting away inside the café on the Aldwych earlier. Chances are that it *hadn't* been Silvia, but Posie had had a good look inside on the way back to the car anyhow. Of course, by then the string of cafés were completely empty, shutting up for the night, their glittering crowds of revellers moved on to nightclubs further on into the town.

Posie thought of Silvia at the Royal Oak pub earlier, drinking incognito. Had that been the start of a night out alone, unaccounted for? And was that so unusual or surprising?

Why did Brian Langley think Silvia had gone missing, anyhow? It wasn't exactly late, so why was the Producer worried enough to make it an official police matter? Did Silvia usually stay in all night at remote Worton Hall, like a wallflower, learning her lines?

Maybe tonight was different for some personal reason? Maybe the girl was celebrating the end of the movie in her own way? Or celebrating something else entirely.

Posie's thoughts were interrupted by her friend.

'Can I come too tomorrow, Inspector?' asked Dolly in a cheerful, helpful way. 'I can make myself jolly useful, you know.'

'Well…'

'I think I'll stay with you tonight, Posie, if you don't mind? Then we can travel out together, can't we?'

Posie frowned. It seemed that everything was being decided for her just now.

'*Only* if you telephone Rufus when we get to the theatre, or call your Butler at home,' she said in a resigned voice. 'Go inside and call from the foyer. I promised Rufus I'd send you straight home. Tell him I took you to the theatre as a treat.'

'Fine. Thanks, lovey. Although I 've seen this show at least three times; *not* that he'll remember.'

They jerked onto West Street, which was brightly lit and full of cafés and smart restaurants, just off the Charing Cross Road. The Ambassadors Theatre was up ahead of them, the name of the play, *The Lilies of the Field*, picked out in silver spotlights.

'Here we are, sir!' called McCrae with a dash of excitement. It was coming up for ten o'clock.

There was already a small crowd of perhaps ten or fifteen people gathering at the side exit, at the stage door. Others were joining them steadily. Some people were holding scraps of paper for signing, or bunches of flowers for their favoured star.

'Park up here on the kerb, McCrae. We'll lurk here just now, Posie and I. Lady Cardigeon, you go and make your telephone call, and take Sergeant Binny with you: pretend you're a couple, if you don't mind. As you go in and out of the theatre check out which one of those chaps could be our fella Mallow. When you find him, tell him to come over here for some nice friendly questions in the back of the car. So ditch that homburg and trench coat, Sergeant: nothing says "policeman" more than those.'

'Right you are, sir,' said Binny, a bit ruffled. He shook himself out of the offending articles and turned around.

'There are several men over there, sir. Have we got any clue what he looks like?'

'You'll have to use your gut instinct a bit more when you're an Inspector, you know, Binny. *If* you get made an Inspector, I mean.'

'I understand, sir.'

'Hector Mallow disguises himself often,' chipped in Posie, keen to help. She remembered Reggie Jones' description. 'But I *do* know that just three days ago he had dyed black hair and a pencil moustache. And he's quite short, in his forties.'

Lovelace nodded appreciatively. 'That's quite a description, Sergeant. Certainly enough to be going on with.'

'*I'll* find him, Inspector,' said Dolly, desperate to get going. 'I think I can see a chap from here who fits the bill.'

'Wonderful, my Lady. And McCrae, I want you to stand by the car, and get ready to run if you have to: our fella Mallow might make a wild dash for it if he's feeling a tad overwhelmed.'

When the three of them had got out of the car, Posie watched Dolly trotting towards the lights, back in her world. She held onto Binny's arm as easily as if he really *were* her husband. Posie groaned.

'What's up?' said Lovelace, his eyes never leaving Binny and Dolly for a moment.

It was obviously a night for the spilling of confidences, and Posie found herself telling the Chief Inspector about Rufus and his worries about a plot against his wife, how she had promised to keep Dolly safe.

The Inspector turned quickly to Posie in disbelief before staring out again. 'Goodness, you really are spreading yourself thinly today, Posie. You think there's anything in it?'

'I don't know. It's unusual for Rufus to be paranoid, though. He seems quite worked up about it all.'

They watched Dolly and Binny dip inside the theatre foyer.

'For what it's worth, I heard his father's dying.'

'I heard that too, sir.'

'Maybe Rufus isn't thinking quite clearly at present. Imagining things?'

'Maybe. It's odd though.'

'If it makes you feel easier, I'll get McCrae to stay over at your flat at Museum Chambers tonight, Posie; to keep an eye on Lady Cardigeon. You don't mind putting him up on a sofa? Or he could sleep outside the front door, I suppose?'

Posie breathed a sigh of real relief. 'He can have Alaric's room. That would be wonderful, sir. You seem to like him, McCrae? He's new, isn't he?'

'He is.' Lovelace nodded approvingly. 'Down from Glasgow. A poor boy done good. Bright and helpful and as resourceful a chap as you're ever likely to meet. He'll become my next Sergeant if I can help it, at the end of the year. When Binny goes his own way as Inspector, I mean.'

'He'll definitely get it, then, sir? Only, you seem to be casting doubts on it every now and then. That's all.'

The Chief Inspector grinned. 'Of course he'll get it. He's got no family to distract him, not like Rainbird. Poor Binny's spending days and nights studying his socks off. But even so, it doesn't hurt to keep the fella on his toes, does it? Look sharp, what's this?'

Dolly had rounded on someone in the crowd by the stage door who was out of their line of view, and she was earnestly chatting away, clutching at a programme she must have grabbed in the foyer. She was looking animated, flicking through it. Binny was hanging a little behind, looking a tad embarrassed. Then, Posie saw Dolly grab at Binny's arm and nod certainly. A second later he had looped his arm tightly around a small dark man who was now in full view. McCrae went bounding over, although Hector Mallow hadn't shown any sign of wanting to run, wildly or otherwise. Instead, he looked bemused, blinking from Dolly back to Binny, and then to McCrae.

Within seconds the man was being frogmarched over to the car, the two policemen on either side, Dolly tripping along behind, taking deep drags on a cigarette. The man put up no resistance.

Lovelace and Posie got out of the car. They were standing in a small pool of light from the nearby street lamp, but it was still dim. And still stifling hot. Overhead Posie thought she heard a crack of thunder, but it could have been a passing Underground train.

'Evening, sir. Care to answer a few questions which are bothering me?' said the Chief Inspector, nodding at Hector Mallow in a friendly manner and leaning against the car, before crossing his arms authoritatively.

'What the deuce is this all about?'

The small man seemed nervy, but there was a self-righteous defensiveness about him, too. He was fumbling with a large canvas hold-all which he eventually put down at his feet. A large straw hat was squashed into it.

A strange waft of sweat and something even more rancid – formaldehyde or formic acid, perhaps? – drifted across from the man to Posie and she swallowed hard, trying not to look as if she minded. The smell must have met the Chief Inspector's nostrils too, for he made no more mention of getting inside the car and stayed put.

'I take it you *are* Hector Mallow, morgue technician at the Middlesex Hospital and sometime admirer of the movie star, Silvia Hanro?'

'That's right.'

When Hector Mallow spoke it was with a good, educated, middle-class accent, but he wheezed on the last breath of each sentence, as if he were consumptive.

'What's the problem? You are the police, I take it?'

He looked over at Dolly and then took in Posie with some surprise and a hint of scorn. 'So who are these lovely pair of lassies?'

'New Scotland Yard, and our associates,' said the Chief Inspector, indicating towards Posie, before stating his name and rank. His tone carried a tiny undercurrent of menace, and Posie saw Hector Mallow visibly wince. But Mr Mallow didn't seem afraid: didn't seem like the sort of man who had been caught doing something illegal.

'The Yard? What have *I* done to warrant that sort of attention? Are you hounding me? What is all this?'

He was still being held tightly by either arm.

Up close and under the lamplight Posie could see that

Hector Mallow was distinctly pug-like. He had very dark round eyes, set too far apart, peering out from a pale moon face. The eyes were accentuated by his too-black moustache and patchy hair on either side of his face which had been dyed the same colour. On top he was completely bald. He had small hands and little fat fingers which moved ceaselessly against his trouser pockets. His fingernails were too long, and curling, and dirty, and Posie shuddered, remembering his job.

His clothes, a dark blue flannel suit and what had once been a good-quality white shirt, were shiny with age. The hot weather obviously didn't agree with him, either, for he was soaked in sweat. He gave off a distinct scent of weakness along with the embalming chemicals.

'Tell me, do you have any evidence against me for *anything*?'

Posie knew that Lovelace had a difficult job ahead of him; with no criminal case or real evidence against Mallow, all he could do was question the man. Lovelace stayed very calm, almost friendly.

'You're an admirer of Meggie Albanesi, I hear?'

Hector Mallow shrugged. 'Nothing wrong with that, is there? Many fellas admire her. You going to question all that lot over there queuing for autographs too? You lot were onto me only last week, and you went away empty-handed then. So what's changed now?'

Posie felt the lack of any good answer hanging heavily in the air between them all. Suddenly Dolly came right up, nodded at Mr Mallow and then asked, as if she were really interested:

'They're quite different, aren't they, these two actresses you favour?'

'What do you mean, Miss?' Mallow sniffed, uncertain.

Dolly flapped the programme she had procured. 'Well, little Meggie Albanesi here is small and dark, and sort of nimble; known for dancin' and jitterin' and such like. And yet, Silvia Hanro is quite another kettle of fish: blonde and big and like a real screen Goddess. Besides, I've never seen her dance. She looks like she belongs on the prow of one of those great big ocean liners!'

Posie smiled: she liked Dolly's description of Silvia. It was very apt.

'So?' wheezed the little man, frowning at Dolly. 'Is this any of your business?'

'Usually a fella likes the same type of girl. He's consistent. Or not you, Mr Mallow?'

After a few seconds of silence Hector Mallow shrugged again. 'A man can change his mind, can't he? I've admired Miss Hanro for months now, years even, but that was before Miss Albanesi became famous. Have you seen her on stage? She's really quite something. Mesmerising. The deuce of a thing! Very *now*. About to go into films, in a big way. Done a few already.'

'Do you only stalk women who are fashionable, or newly-famous?' interjected Lovelace with a note of scorn in his voice. 'Does that mean we can safely assume Miss Hanro's star is on the wane?'

'Yes.' Hector Mallow sniffed. 'She's rather old news, actually. And she's getting on a bit now, too. Almost thirty if she's a day!'

Posie scowled: before this she had found the man slightly comical, almost an object of pity. But the truth was, the jibe about the age cut deep. Posie was a year older than Silvia Hanro, at least. Now anything resembling sympathy went right out of the window and she found herself hardening her heart against Hector Mallow.

'A glory hunter!' said Dolly decisively, and with a snip of derision in her voice. 'That makes sense.'

'Call it what you will,' said Hector Mallow, wheezing. 'I don't do anyone any harm.'

Posie frowned. She edged closer, less keen on being an impartial bystander in the discussions. 'But you *were* at Worton Hall on Sunday, Mr Mallow,' she said sharply, commanding instant attention. The small man turned and stared at her, and she continued:

'You were seen, and escorted off the premises.'

Hector Mallow started. 'Eh? How the deuce do you know that, old top?'

He looked over at Lovelace and smiled a strange, slow smile which went from ear to ear. 'Got yourself a pretty little policewoman doing your dirty work for you, have you, Chief Inspector? Unconventional. But a nice little arrangement, I'm sure.'

Posie ignored him, as did Lovelace. She ploughed on:

'But you still thought something of Miss Hanro *then*? On Sunday? She wasn't quite old news, then? You can't deny that, surely?'

The man shrugged. 'No point denying anything, is there, old top? Yes: I was there. Old Jonesy spotted me and turfed me out of the place. Good thing too, as it happened. He saved my bacon.'

Posie frowned, she didn't follow him. Hector Mallow stared at Posie intently with his goggly black eyes. He sniffed and continued:

'I signed on for a bit of money, actually. Sunstar pay pretty well, and goodness knows my pay packet needs an uplift now and then. I spend everything I can get on theatre tickets or travelling out to Worton Hall. I'm virtually broke, old top.'

'My heart bleeds for you,' snapped Posie. 'And don't you dare call me "old top" again.'

Mallow ignored her and turned to first Binny, and then McCrae. 'I say, could you fellas let me go for a bit? It's the deuce of a thing being held here like a prisoner. I'm not going to run anywhere, I promise you. I'm terribly asthmatic. I can't run. Even if I wanted to.'

Lovelace seemed to consider this news, then nodded his head.

'Carry on. Let go of his arms but stand by, Constable. Now, Mr Mallow – about Sunday. Continue, please.'

'Yes, well. It wasn't just the money that saw me over at Worton Hall again. Rumour has it that old Langley can't afford the place for much longer. I intended it to be my last trip out there. Although I wish to goodness I hadn't gone, actually: everyone was at each other's throats and the atmosphere was prickly as the proverbial paw-paw. A horrible day.'

He sighed dramatically. 'I knew the filming was coming to an end, you see, and I wanted to see Miss Hanro again, just one last time. Although I shouldn't have bothered, should I?'

'Why not?' asked Posie.

'I've just learnt from one of the chaps in the crowd that Miss Albanesi herself is going to some fancy party tomorrow at Worton Hall. Apparently Brian Langley wants to make her his new star! Imagine! So I'll do my utmost to be there for that. Midday sharp, apparently. So I'll see Silvia Hanro again, after all. Two birds with one stone, and all that.'

'Even if one of the birds is getting on a bit?' hissed Posie bitterly, regretting it as soon as the comment had left her lips.

Mallow gave Posie an intrigued look and smiled. 'Exactly, *old* top.'

Posie narrowed her eyes and stared hard at Hector. She had known much, much worse, but this man really did take the biscuit. Chief Inspector Lovelace cut in quickly:

'Actually, I don't think you'll be going anywhere near Worton Hall tomorrow, my man. In fact, unless you tell me exactly where you've been over the last three days, with full and reliable alibis, you're coming with me, to the cells at New Scotland Yard, at his Majesty's pleasure. Got it?'

'But you still haven't told me what I'm supposed to have done!'

And Posie held back a smile, finding herself unaccountably pleased that Hector Mallow might have to spend a couple of days in the small, bleach-stinking holding cells for male prisoners which ran around the back of Scotland Yard, and which she had had the dubious pleasure of visiting on a couple of memorable occasions. Even if he did have no real reason for being there; even if he was being held on false charges or without evidence. It might take the horrid little man down a peg or two.

But when she looked at Mallow again he was rustling around in his hold-all.

'Never mind. Don't tell me. Keep your reasons all to yourself, then. Here you go.'

He brought out a thin blue sheet, similar to a doctor's prescription page for medicines, and shoved it in front of Inspector Lovelace with a funny little bow and an exaggerated flourish.

'All *yours*, Chief Inspector. I'll think you'll find that covers the time period in question. Alibi-wise, I mean.'

'What is it?' asked Posie sharply.

'You should have listened carefully to me, old top, shouldn't you?' Hector Mallow had swivelled his gaze back to her. 'Weren't doing your homework well enough here, were you?'

Posie tamped down her anger, waiting for Lovelace, who was reading and re-reading the same short sheet over and over again. His almost-handsome face was bathed in shadows, and she couldn't read his expression. In all her time of knowing Richard Lovelace, she had never known him lose his temper. He was always distinctly unruffled. Even now.

Overhead there was a sudden short crack of thunder, clear as a bell this time. Everyone looked up in surprise and a fast wind came up from nowhere, growling around the street corners, cooling everything.

'If you'd listened to me properly you would have heard

me tell you that old Jonesy saved my bacon. When he forced me to leave Isleworth on Sunday I turned tail and trotted back to London. I don't know if it was the heat or the exertion but just as I was going into my building – I had the key in the door – I had an asthma attack: my worst ever. Fortunately there are some medical fellows living in my building and they rushed me to the Middlesex Hospital, where I recovered. I've been there the whole time. I was discharged tonight, in fact, and I came straight here, to see Miss Albanesi.'

Posie stared. It explained the sour-smelling clothes, the bag, the man's careless attitude to their questions. She turned to the Chief Inspector, whose face, as ever, was neutral.

'Thank you for your time, Mr Mallow,' he said calmly, handing back the blue paper. 'The time in question does indeed seem to be covered by these discharge papers.'

Posie noticed that he seemed to be speaking through gritted teeth. He needed to stay calm, though. Fellows such as Hector Mallow were the type to bring a suit for harassment against the police, just to prove a point.

'My pleasure, Chief Inspector.'

The small man was positively brimming with his own self-worth.

'I wish you a very pleasant evening,' Lovelace said firmly, indicating to Binny and McCrae with a quick sweep of his hand that their work here was done. He motioned to Posie and Dolly to get into the car.

Just then the growls of thunder gave way to rain. Big raindrops like pennies started to hit the dusty pavement.

'Quick, in you get!' Constable McCrae was holding the door open at the back.

'What a nasty piece of work. He made my skin crawl,' muttered the Inspector softly, getting in after Dolly.

'Hang on.' Posie had remembered something. It could be something, but it was probably nothing. But worth checking on, regardless.

She turned and saw that Hector Mallow had started to turn back to the theatre, holding his bag up over his head for protection from the rain.

'Wait!' she called, running over to the stage door through the rain which was now falling in sheets. She was instantly soaking wet.

'Mr Mallow!'

He turned, and a gloating smile was on his face again within seconds.

'Back for more, old top?'

Posie swallowed down the anger. 'You mentioned that Sunday was a particularly bad day. A prickly atmosphere? Can you tell me exactly what was going on at Worton Hall that made it so bad?'

There was a slight ruckus at the stage door as an older female actress came out, blonde and still beautiful and very glamorous. Some men pushed forwards, proffering flowers. Checking it wasn't Meggie Albanesi, but keeping an eye on the stage door regardless, Hector Mallow only gave Posie half his attention. He shrugged at her question, as if it was of no importance to him.

'It started first thing, at coffee time. I was in the Green Room, where the extras hang around. In the corridor, that new fella with only half a face...'

'You mean Tom Moran?'

'That's right.'

'Why do you say "new"?'

'He's only been working at Sunstar for a few months, only since this last film started up, actually. Never saw him before.'

'Oh? I see. Carry on. Please.'

'Well, he was having a blazing row with a woman. We all heard it. They obviously didn't realise we could hear everything, but that house has very strange acoustics.'

'Was he arguing with Silvia Hanro?'

'No, definitely not. And why would he? Fella like that

doesn't know her from Adam! Wouldn't hope to get near her!'

'Of course not. Any idea what the row was about?'

Hector Mallow made a dismissive gesture. 'I think it was about money. We heard him shout: "*I don't care! Do you think this means anything to me at all? I'm not giving you a penny!*"'

Posie thought quickly. Was someone trying to blackmail Tom Moran about his true identity as Mark Paris? And if so, who?

'Do you know who the woman was? Or did you hear what she said?' Posie prayed that Meggie Albanesi would take her time coming out tonight.

'No idea who she was. I only heard fragments of her conversation, which didn't make sense. Something like "*squalid little carry-on!*" We did see the woman, though. She ran past the open Green Room door. I'd never seen her before. She was dark, not beautiful. Thin.'

'Thank you.' Posie nodded appreciatively, storing up the information for later. 'And was there anything else which happened that day?'

'Oh yes!' drawled the man with relish. 'Plenty! Silvia Hanro was not at her finest. Later that morning when we saw her it was obvious she'd been crying; even the Leichner couldn't disguise her sad puffy eyes. She was all over the place, too: couldn't remember her lines and had to keep re-doing "takes" again and again. Awful!'

'Any idea why *she* was out of sorts?'

The man shook his head. 'I managed to get up very close to her during the coffee-break, though. I know her ways and where she goes. She was in a thicket of trees behind the dark studio with Brian Langley. Very close together.'

Posie's brain was racing: had Silvia and Brian resumed their affair?

'And?'

'They were arguing, too. I couldn't hear what she was

saying, but Brian Langley was irate; I mean worse than usual. He was pipped about something or other. He kept shouting "*Pull yourself together*," and "*Not now!*" and "*No way!*"

'*No way?*'

Hector Mallow nodded. 'That's right. He said it several times. The only thing I really heard at the end was him saying "*Over my dead body. Or yours.*"'

Posie stopped herself from gasping aloud. 'You're sure he said that?'

But she had lost the man's attention and he surged forwards as a tiny, dark-haired girl stepped out from the dark, grubby doorway towards her adoring fans.

Posie turned back to the police car, soaked, oblivious to the rain and the high winds and the promise of more thunder in the air, thinking through what she had just heard and whether it helped anyone at all.

* * * *

Twenty-One

London was up to her old tricks again. As Posie and Dolly leant out of the window of Posie's living room, the air outside was tangy with brine, and it smelt as if they were by the sea.

'It's a relief, innit? After all that sun.'

Posie nodded.

They sat on the window seat and watched the rain falling heavily on the rooftops opposite, on the thin, dark, dusty street which led up to the British Museum, and they watched the lightning crack the sky apart in furious riots. A cool salty breeze rushed in at them. Dolly was smoking and had been very quiet since they had arrived back at Museum Chambers half an hour before.

'Can't say I like the police guard much, lovey. Even if he *is* a nice lad. Was that your idea? Still think one of us is in danger somehow? You *are* funny!'

'Mnnn,' Posie lied. 'I might be over-egging it somewhat. But it's only for tonight.'

Constable McCrae had taken up residence in Alaric's room, picking his way courteously through stacks of paper and piles of discarded travelling clothes, maps and even a stray dog basket in order to find the bed. He had very properly kept a respectful distance from the two women, and had taken a mug of cocoa and a plate of buttered toast only when Posie had insisted, and he could now be heard flicking through Alaric's vast collection of travel magazines, with the door only very slightly open.

'Do you want a slug of whisky in that hot chocolate, Dolls? Help you sleep? It's been a long day.'

'Go on then. This is nice, just you and me, Posie. Like back in the old days.'

If truth were told, Posie desperately wanted to be alone. She was bone-tired and her body, wrapped as it was in her comfy blue dressing gown of shot silk, ached all over.

As she made her way over to the drinks cabinet she realised that all she wanted was to think: to try and make sense of the many and varied pieces of information she had heard today about Silvia Hanro and Worton Hall.

She started to pull out bottles and decanters, without paying the least bit of attention to what she was doing.

'Rats!' Posie spilled some of the amber-coloured drink all over her hands and sleeve.

'Here you go.' She took the drink over to Dolly, who seemed wrapped up in her own thoughts. Posie sat down with her pepped-up drink at the formal dining table, next to the serving hatch of frosted glass which led into her tiny kitchen, and rubbed at her eyes. She winced as the whisky hit her throat and burned.

As she listened to the rain, Posie wondered where Silvia was right now. Had she made it back to Brian Langley and Tom Moran and Worton Hall all ready to wrap up *Henry the King* at nine tomorrow morning? Or was she still enjoying a night out alone, the freedom of pretending to be someone else? Or had something more sinister befallen her?

Posie shivered and tried to put the thought from her mind: she hadn't been hired as a watch-dog, after all. She thought fleetingly of the other people she had met for the first time today, too.

Pamela Hanro, the second sister, was undeniably a brave and gutsy woman. But how involved was she in all of this? And had *she* been the dark woman Hector Mallow had seen arguing with Tom Moran on Sunday at Worton Hall? She was unquestionably '*dark, not beautiful.*' Pamela undoubtedly knew Tom's secret; that he was the famous Mark Paris. What other secrets or hidden knowledge did she possess? Was it possible that the blackmail victim had turned blackmailer?

Posie thought also of the beautiful Robbie Fontaine, probably off his head on drugs somewhere right now, and his odd, hostile conduct towards her today. What had been behind that? If anything?

And what of Brian Langley and his many attributes, manners and cheerfulness not among them? Was he still busy on the cutting-room floor, or in that projection room, genuinely worried about Silvia? Worried enough to have called the police.

Posie's mind flickered briefly over the unwelcome thought of Tom Moran – or Mark Paris – all alone at Worton Hall tonight, he too perhaps out of his mind with worry over where Silvia had got to.

And lastly, her thoughts turned to Hector Mallow. Right now he was sitting in Ciro's café, making Meggie Albanesi feel uncomfortable…

On top of all of this was the problem of Dolly.

And Alaric.

In fact, when Posie thought about Alaric now, because she was guiltily drinking his good, expensive Scotch single malt as a mixer, the same cold feeling was back, worse than ever. She remembered the dream from the morning again, those horrible words:

'*Look, darling, there's something I need to tell you. Quite urgently.*'

'*Bad news? It must be. What is it?*'

Posie looked around briefly, to calm herself down.

It was an odd thing, and she didn't think of herself as materialistic, but the fresh apple-green living room always made her feel pleased as punch.

The room wasn't furnished in the current chrome-and-glass silliness. It was minimalist and uncluttered; a sanctuary, furnished with just a few personal touches here and there.

A framed Egyptian hieroglyph hung on the wall above the fireplace, between two well-stocked bookcases. A small enamelled console table in the corner displayed a photograph of Posie's dead brother, Richard, and a more recent addition; a photograph of people raising their glasses in celebration at an engagement party which had taken place earlier that year, in January.

Her engagement party.

Bradley, her daily woman, had been busy and had already set the table for breakfast. Posie stretched and cursed as her leg accidentally brushed against a large silver-and-white cardboard box under the table, causing it to topple over and cascades of white silk and tissue paper to fall out.

'Oh, dash it all.'

She had quite forgotten it was there: a neat, nautical-styled cream wedding outfit made by the House of Harlow, and now stowed away out of sight, gathering dust since she had ordered it months before, with no fixed wedding date being mentioned.

Posie had even been to the local Registry Office, the Camden branch, and filled in the flimsy orange marriage forms and the carbon copies which came with it, thinking they might be needed at any given moment. But now those forms had expired. Of course.

That breath of unease seemed to blow over her again.

'What's that?' trilled Dolly, turning from the window, alert now, seeing the fancy box and recognising the mark of the House of Harlow.

Posie popped a piece of cold toast in her mouth irritably.

'My wedding outfit,' she munched, sadly. 'It was beautiful. I got it a few months ago. I doubt it will even fit me now.'

Dolly came and sat down at the table with a packet of cigarettes, looking very much like a strange and tiny sprite with her weirdly luminous white hair and dark, magical eyes, all at odds among the cool green stillness.

'What's really happenin' with Alaric, lovey?' Dolly asked gently.

'I don't know.'

Posie shrugged. 'We don't really make plans, just suggestions. But those suggestions never seem to go anywhere.'

That spilling of confidences, again. At last. But somehow, strangely, it felt good to put a voice to these fears.

Posie bit at her lip savagely: 'In my world when a fella says he'll marry his girl he gets on with it pretty sharply. But we had that great engagement party, and then... nothing. Since he's been away I've been lucky to get one postcard or telegram every couple of weeks. It's like I don't exist anymore.'

Posie looked over at the framed hieroglyph, thinking about the time she had met Alaric, on the continent, when everything had seemed so new and glamorous. She thought she might cry: she had never cried in front of Dolly before, and she didn't fancy starting right now. She rushed on quickly.

'I think Alaric may have found someone else. I wouldn't blame him, really. I just feel such an idiot.'

Dolly was genuine enough not to reach out and offer mock sympathy. She looked at Posie carefully and lit a cigarette slowly.

'He's very lucky, you know.' She exhaled, her eyes never leaving Posie's face for a second.

'Not the other way around. So don't you *ever* make yourself feel small compared to him. I know he's famous, but so are you now, lovey. And you earned it all yerself.

You're funny, and clever. Not to mention flippin' beautiful: half the men I know would gladly become *Mr* Posie Parker; the Chief Inspector included. I've seen the way he looks at you with those great green eyes of his. With a sort of longin' in them.'

'Rot! He's happily married. You're just trying to make me feel better!'

Dolly shrugged. 'It's the truth. I swear it. And don't let's start on *Len*: that idiot knows what a fool he was, lettin' you go. It's written plain as anythin' on his face every time he even so much as sees you! No, mark my words, Alaric's a lucky man havin' you. Besides, he's onto a very good deal, here.'

'What do you mean – a *deal*?'

Dolly nodded, warming to her theme. 'Financially, I mean. Don't get me wrong, Alaric's wonderful. But it seems to me he takes more than he gives. He lives here rent-free, doesn't he, when he's in town?'

'Well, that's right. But we're engaged, aren't we? I can hardly ask him for money, can I? It would be odd…'

'Pah! Fellas like Alaric always fall on their feet. I know he gave up his aristocratic title and his great house in Oxfordshire and all that, but that was out of choice, wasn't it? And he has a good income from all the talks and books and things he does, doesn't he? Not to mention that Trust Fund you told me about!'

'Mnnn.' Put like this, Posie saw Dolly's point. 'But his travelling and exploring take up nearly all the income he has! He's quite broke much of the time,' she protested.

'Don't you believe it.'

'I swear, he's not just trying to get a cheap room out of me.'

'If you're sure, honey, then all well and good. But it might not be such a bad thing that you've had a few months as an engagement, you know. Gives you both a chance to think about what you really want. If *you* really want him or not.'

'I *do* want him! But right now I feel like he's out of my grasp,' wailed Posie. 'I want him more than anything. I have a tendency to go for elusive men, always chasing a will-o'-the-wisp, and Alaric's a case in point. He's a wanderer. And I'm not.'

'Mnnn.' Dolly carefully stubbed out her cigarette on Posie's plate of half-eaten toast. There was a far-away, longing look in Dolly's heavily-painted eyes. 'I might know how he feels. I'm a wanderer at heart myself, you know.'

Posie frowned, looking at her friend intently. 'Dolly? What do you mean?'

Just then there was a ring of the doorbell.

'*Who* on earth can that be?' Posie checked her wristwatch and saw that it was coming up for midnight.

More than a bit worried, she got to the front door at the same time as Constable McCrae, who had evidently just been nodding off, still in his full policeman's uniform, despite Posie's insisting he borrow something more comfortable of Alaric's.

She placed a finger to her lips, hushing the policeman, and looked through the fish-eye spy-hole.

She needn't have worried. It was only Ted, the trusty and unflappable Porter at Museum Chambers.

'It's all fine, Constable. We can relax. For now.'

Breathing a sigh of relief, Posie opened the front door.

'Ted! It's a bit late, isn't it? Is something the matter?'

Ted tipped his cap at Posie and then goggled at the sight of the blue-uniformed policeman lurking behind her.

'So that's *your* police motor parked up outside the front door, is it?' he asked, curiously. McCrae simply nodded.

'Couldn't it have waited until the morning, Ted?'

Ted pulled his eyes away most reluctantly and proffered a silver salver with a cream card upon it, a trick he had learnt from a Butler somewhere, and one he always used to full advantage when he was after a tip or two.

"Fraid it couldn't wait, Miss. This 'ere telegram is

marked "URGENT" and "PERSONAL". I only saw it just now, as I'm newly-arrived for the night shift and I'm going through all the evening post. This telegram obviously arrived earlier tonight and the Duty Porter just put it aside when you weren't in. I hope all is in order, Miss.'

He mock bowed. 'Here you go.'

'I'm much obliged, Ted.' Posie scrabbled around in the bowl of change on the hall table for a tip and passed it across. 'Good night.'

When the door was closed and Constable McCrae had withdrawn to Alaric's room again, Posie sunk down on the vivid green Lloyd Loom chair in the hallway and opened the telegram, her heart in her mouth.

It was two lines long, and it was from Alaric. The telegram had been sent from Paris, at six o'clock.

DARLING. COMING HOME.
WE MUST TALK ABOUT SOMETHING QUITE
URGENTLY. AL.

* * * *

Twenty-Two

Posie went hot and cold and shivered all over. She tried to calm herself, but the butterflies in her stomach were fluttering up in great gangs into her throat, making her gag. And so her horrible dream *had* meant something; the ominous feeling she had carried around for days now really did spell out trouble.

It could only mean one thing.

The end of it all.

At least he was coming home to tell her in person, she supposed. She rubbed at her eyes, but they were gritty and dry. She was too scared to cry. She wanted to scream, but that would have been unladylike and undignified, and besides, she had guests.

A quick movement at the door and a soft step on the shining parquet flooring of the hallway, and Dolly hung in the doorway like a little ghost.

'What's that?'

Taking the telegram from Posie's hands she read and re-read the message. Dolly made a moue of distaste and cast the card aside on the hall table.

'Men!' She disappeared back into the living room for a couple of seconds, then re-emerged, hauling Posie up out of the wicker hall chair.

'You know, he probably dashed that off in an instant at some tiny Post Office in the station. Didn't have time to think about the words he was using.'

'You agree, then? It looks bad?' Posie gulped, blindly following Dolly through into the living room. She noticed with only a smidgen of surprise that Dolly was dragging along the wicker chair behind her.

'If *I* was to get telegrams from Rufus I'd have my heart in my mouth most of the time. He'd use the wrong words, or *no* words at all, come to think of it. Fortunately, we never need to write to each other.'

Dolly had now placed the green wicker chair by the window, where the wind was still blowing.

'Sit here,' she commanded. Posie did so unquestioningly, in a daze, her mind a racing whirl of unhappiness.

'Look, two good things,' continued Dolly resolutely. 'First, he called you "darling", and second, he's coming home. Right? So stop pondering. It won't help anything. Now, wait here a minute.'

Dolly had run off, and Posie thought she heard her in the bathroom. Sure enough, Dolly was back within seconds carrying an armful of fresh fluffy white towels.

'What's going on?'

'Well, Alaric will be back tomorrow night, won't he? Maybe tomorrow evening, even. Why don't we give him a nice surprise, show him how fashionable and gorgeous you are. Still.'

'*Dolly?*'

Posie saw a washing-bowl of water on the floor, together with a china cup and a spoon, and Dolly's big purple bag, propped open. She also spotted one of Alaric's Penhaligon's shaving brushes. She gestured at the floor.

'What's all this for?'

Dolly sighed, as if Posie had just pricked her party balloon. 'I thought we'd turn you blonde. Just for a few days. I can change it back if you don't like it.'

'A *BLONDE*?' Posie almost squeaked and her hands went up to her short, dark-brown hair almost involuntarily.

Dolly nodded. She was pouring something from a paper twist into the china cup, and now taking out a tiny corked vial, opening it and counting out drops.

'One, two, three. Perfect.' She was mixing up her solution, her face determined, a mask of concentration. A sharp chemical rush hit them both and both women nearly gagged.

'Hold on, I haven't said you can do anything yet, Dolls. Hold your horses.'

Dolly grinned. 'But you haven't said I *can't*, have you? Just think, it will be lovely to have a new look. Especially for this glamorous party tomorrow. It will give Alaric something to think about, won't it? Show him you can still run with the bright young things.'

Posie had never been part of that fashionable, dare-devil crowd who lurched around London from nightclub to nightclub, buoyed up on a fuzz of drugs and drink and gossip, but she thought suddenly of the crowds of pastel-coloured girls she had passed on the Aldwych earlier, flitting around in the bars like throngs of hummingbirds.

Dolly frowned, as if reading her thoughts. 'You don't want to be a frump, darlin', do you? And while we're on the subject, I didn't like that yellow dress today *or* that black thing you were wearin' earlier. They make you look old. Where have your fun clothes gone? You're only just thirty.'

Posie almost gasped. She had actually turned thirty the previous year, in the autumn of 1922. She was closer to her thirty-first birthday now, and she wasn't in a mad hurry to mark the occasion.

She made her decision in a split-second.

'Fine.' Posie nodded. 'Go ahead. As long as you know what you're doing. Why have you got that stuff here, anyhow? Is it the same stuff *you* use?'

'Nah, I wish,' said Dolly, rigging up a towel around

Posie's shoulders and then checking the time on her diamond watch. 'This is superior stuff, from America. Costs an arm and a leg. But I'll see how it goes on you and then I might place an order myself. It should turn your hair a real movie star silver blonde.'

Dolly had made a fluff of white in the cup, rather like an egg white, and was now coating Posie's hair with the stinking stuff using Alaric's shaving brush. She slavered it on quickly. The smell hurt Posie's eyes.

'I borrowed this, today, from Silvia Hanro. She keeps a stack of it in her dressing room. I asked her if I could try it and she said I could take some. She uses it once a week.'

'Goodness, what a lot of work!'

'Worth it, though. She looks a dream. So you'll be the exact same colour as Silvia. Like two peas in a pod!'

Posie laughed uncertainly. Dolly seemed to have finished and was checking her wristwatch again.

'Now we have to wait exactly ten minutes.'

Dolly started dabbing frantically at the green chair, where Posie now saw a big dollop of the white hair dye had landed. It had burned through the lacquer on the chair and turned the green colour a horrible orange. Posie gulped, thinking of her scalp.

'You never liked this chair anyway, did you, lovey?' asked Dolly breezily before flitting across to the window seat and taking great gulps of fresh air. Posie could have done with some, too.

'You stay where you are. Don't move.'

Posie looked at her friend. She was sitting with her eyes closed for a second, and she looked tired and drawn, despite her constant action.

It was now or never.

'I know about the baby, Dolly. The *new* baby. Rufus told me.'

Dolly opened her eyes and stared at Posie in a blank, unreadable way. She didn't say anything at all.

'Is that what's wrong? Only you don't seem yourself much lately. For all your carrying on as if nothing were the matter today.'

Dolly sighed and pulled herself up into a tight ball on the window seat. She looked out, longingly. When she looked back into the room her face was filled with sadness.

'I wish I could have a smoke,' she said quietly. 'But that stuff on your head is flammable, and we'll both go up in flames in an instant.'

'Better not, then. Don't change the subject, either.'

Dolly gripped herself. 'If you wanna know the truth, lovey, it's a bit unpalatable. It's the sort of thing I *feel*, but I shouldn't feel. It's not an acceptable thing to feel, or to say aloud. Not conventional.'

'Since when were you conventional, anyway?'

Dolly paused. The light seemed to have gone out of her eyes.

'Don't get me wrong. I love being Rufus's wife, and I know I'm a sort of Cinderella story: there's hundreds of girls would change places with me in an instant.'

'*But?*'

'But I'm not cut out for it. And what I'm *really* not cut out for is being a mother. I love my girls, of course I do. But I've spent more than a year, since they were born, in a sort of dull fug. A sort of sadness has hung over me all the time.'

Dolly wrung her hands in barely-contained misery. 'I love visitin' them in the nursery, but I love closin' the door on the nursery even more. And walkin' away. And I feel horrible sayin' this, but I don't long for them and want to be with them every second. If I'm honest, apart from the occasional party and theatre trip, this last year has been hell. A living hell. I've had a great black cloud hangin' over my head for fourteen months now. I've felt a terrible failure. Sometimes I wanted to run away.'

'Goodness, Dolly. Why didn't you say anything? It

sounds terrible. You should have spoken up before.'

Dolly shrugged. 'Oh, I put a brave face on it, and I just kept thinkin' it would get better, that it would pass, that I would suddenly love being a mother. And now I'm goin' to have to go through it all again! The birth; the same performance of pretendin' to be a good mother. All the while hatin' every minute of it. I can't bear it.'

'Have you spoken to Rufus about how you feel?'

'How can I, lovey? He's almost never home, always at the House of blimmin' Lords! And then when he's not there he's up and down to Rebburn Abbey, worryin' about his father.'

'I heard things aren't so good there.'

Dolly shook her head. 'He's not got much longer, poor devil. The irony is that I used to hate the Earl and we still rub each other up the wrong way. But since the babies were born we've become quite close. He's been terrific with the twins, much better than me, in fact. Loves them to bits: spoils them rotten. He's an old softie underneath, and I'll miss him terribly.'

Posie nodded sympathetically. Dolly was looking out of the window again, lost in thought. Posie looked around the room, and noticed without knowing quite why that something significant had changed. She saw now that the engagement party photograph on the lacquered table had been removed.

Dolly must have hidden it out of sight when the telegram had come, fearing bad news. Looking over to the dining table Posie saw that the wedding dress box, too, had disappeared out of sight. This hiding of things depressed her wholeheartedly: Dolly was not one for meddling, and it was indicative of the fact that she obviously thought things were beyond repair.

Posie was jolted sharply back to the present by Dolly's voice, sounding sad:

'Do you know, I think I only got through this last year

because I had the most wonderful nanny lookin' after the girls. She was French, her name was Violette. She was from Paris, as it happens.'

'Ah, that must have been nice for you,' said Posie, remembering that Dolly's own dead mother had been French, and that Dolly was fluent in the language, but that she never made a big deal of it; scarcely mentioned it, even.

'It *was* nice.' Dolly nodded. 'We'd chat away merrily. And of course just recently the girls have started to talk too, in French. Only a few words, of course.'

'Ah.'

Dolly looked at Posie imploringly. 'Can you believe I've never been to Paris, despite the fact my mother was from there? Violette told me all about it. We'd even planned a weekend away there, so she could show me the sights.'

'What's happened to Violette? You're speaking in the past tense.'

Dolly got up, checking the time. She nodded and dragged Posie through to the bathroom where she proceeded to pour buckets of cold water swiftly over Posie's head. Quite roughly.

'Rufus sent Violette away. About a month ago now.'

'I see,' said Posie, between having her head drenched and then pummelled by scratchy towels. She thought about the timing: about how the French girl had been kicked out and the nannies who were really watch-dogs had been brought in to make sure nothing untoward happened to Dolly. It must have been a month ago that Rufus had received threats, and he had realised that the French-speaking nanny was no help at all when it came to protecting his family from the worst sort of danger. Not that she could tell Dolly *that*.

'I think it was when the babies began speaking in French. He hated that.' Dolly threw the towels in a big heap in the bath and looked at Posie quizzically.

She took a step back.

'It looks good,' Dolly said. 'But you'll need to wear a tad more make-up to pull it off. Bright red lipstick, perhaps. You'll look washed out otherwise. Now, where are your curling tongs? Let me do you a nice Marcel wave. Don't look in the mirror yet.'

Posie sat quietly, curiously uncaring, having her hair crimped.

'Of course,' said Dolly with a mouthful of pins, 'what Rufus was really worried about is that French would become our family language. And if we have a boy next, which is what he really wants, he's terrified that little Lord Cardigeon will be speakin' froggy-froggy.'

Posie laughed. 'Oh, come on! Rufus doesn't care about that, and still less if you have a girl or a boy. Besides,' she added, but less certainly now, thinking of his surprising conduct with the street urchin earlier, 'he's not like that.'

Dolly gave her friend a serious look with raised eyebrows. 'Pah! Don't you believe it. He's *only* concerned that this baby is a boy. This baby *must* be a boy for Rufus. What with his father dyin' I think it's really brought it home to Rufus what will happen when he himself dies: who will become the next Earl, and who will take over Rebburn, and such like.'

Posie looked at Dolly disbelievingly. 'But you've got years ahead of you!' she said, surprised. 'Why the urgency? At this rate you'll be having one baby a year! A boy will come along sooner or later.'

Dolly shook her head meekly. Without warning she had grabbed a pair of sharp scissors from the cabinet and cut a thick fringe across Posie's face. The bang tickled.

Dolly indicated that she had finished and got Alaric's small round shaving mirror down from a shelf and started swivelling it around behind Posie's head.

'That's where you're wrong, lovey.' Dolly smiled sadly. 'We *don't* have forever. I don't think I ever told you how old I am, did I?'

Posie stared at Dolly, not looking at her reflection. 'I say, what do you mean? Er, no…I don't think we ever spoke of it.'

'Well, save your embarrassment. I'm forty-one. Old. Older than you knew. Older than Rufus knew when he met me. Which means the twins and this baby I'm having right now are some sort of miracle. But miracles don't go on forever, do they?'

And Posie, completely wrong-footed, and not knowing what to say, made a big show of admiring Dolly's handiwork in the mirror, smiling along.

But secretly she didn't recognise herself at all; that strange halo of silver which surrounded her face, making her large blue eyes seem even more anxious and scared than they really were, and her cream English-rose skin looking frightfully pale.

She had met a real ghost once, although she hadn't known it at the time, and he had seemed much more colourful and full-of-life than the way she currently looked.

'It's lovely,' she lied.

* * * *

It had been such a long day, and although she was so tired, Posie found sleep elusive. As she turned and turned in the coolness of her bed, she listened to the rain and the thunderstorm which continued on outside. She had left her window open and the long muslin curtains fluttered in the wind like tattered doves. Her small case containing a red cocktail frock for the Wrap Party was already packed, and a smoke-grey linen day dress, *not* a House of Harlow number, and her old glacé sandals were waiting ready on her airing rail for her to simply slip into early the next morning.

But her brain couldn't turn itself off, and she started, without meaning or wanting to, to think about all the people she herself had loved and lost.

Those who had died: her father; her brother, Richard; her first fiancé, Harry Briskow.

And then those she had somehow lost along the way without meaning to, while both parties were still very much alive: her mother, Zelda, who had left her family when Posie was just twelve years old, never to return; Len Irving, her business partner, who had at one time become an almost-boyfriend, but who had cried off at the last minute, deciding instead to remain with his childhood sweetheart; a nephew, Harry, who lived and breathed in nearby Cambridge but couldn't formally be acknowledged as her dead brother's illegitimate son.

And now Alaric.

Posie looked at the black-and-white framed photograph of Alaric which lived next to her bed, beside her cold cream and her glass of water. Uncharacteristically dressed up in immaculate black tie for a long-ago ball, Alaric's hair was slicked back and he was clean-shaven. His magnificent eyes were creased up in a beaming smile which asked the photographer not to be so silly: to *stop* taking a photograph, right now.

She had found the photo among his papers on the floor one day and he had said she could have it.

That old thing? Of course you can have it, darling.

Posie loved that photograph, although it was from a time before she had known him, and she didn't know who it was who had teased out that laughing look. But what was certain was that Posie had never managed to make Alaric smile like that, not in all the time she had known him. Not even in bed.

It had probably been taken with Cosima Catchpole, a flame-haired beauty who had been Alaric's lover for several years, an ill-fated and dangerous love affair which had left a bad taste in everyone's mouths and a lingering, rusty sense of betrayal, as Cosima had been Hugo Marchpane's wife. The wife of his best friend…

Posie tried not to think of Cosima, hoping that she was a piece of the past which would happily stay there for ever.

Annoyingly, Posie's scalp itched like mad and she tried not to think about the 'new look' which Dolly had created for her, reaching instead for a hair cap which she hardly ever used and throwing herself back irritably on the cushions.

Sleep started to come heavily, and just as it did the black-and-white photograph of Alaric flashed though her mind again, in waves, as if it were being flung at her on a tide, and then pulled out of reach, time and again. She sank gratefully under the water of the almost-dream, drowsy.

And just as sleep came, another photograph, this time of a raven-haired moody movie star, imprinted itself on top of Alaric's image. It stayed there, vivid, etched on the surface. It was Mark Paris.

Tom Moran. Mark Paris. Tom Moran…

'Oh, go away,' Posie muttered drowsily. 'I want to *SLEEP.*'

Mark Paris was washing backwards and forwards in a framed photograph, in a sleepy white frothy sea of wedding dresses and cuttings from magazines.

And then Posie sat bolt upright in bed, absolutely and horribly wide awake.

'The deuce!'

She saw again the photograph of Mark Paris in the cook's room at Worton Hall, surrounded by the magazine cuttings, clear as day.

She remembered too the conversation she had had with the driver, Fred, in the car back to town earlier. She remembered how he had described the cook, Mrs Thynne, as being married to a gamekeeper in Richmond Park, and, judging by the woman's age, she had probably been married for several years.

What had struck Posie as being unaccountably wrong earlier was now very clear to her. Why would a seemingly unromantic, middle-aged, married cook have a crush on a dead movie star?

And why would she be making a schoolgirl's scrapbook about weddings and dresses?

It didn't make sense. Not one little bit.

* * * *

PART TWO

(Thursday 26th July, 1923)

Twenty-Three

She was woken by the banging of a door somewhere outside. And a dog barking.

Possibly.

It was very early, judging by the colour of the light shining through the thin curtains, and it was crazily hot again, already.

Posie told herself she had just imagined the noise, and was just hunkering down again, sliding under the cosy enveloping sleep which she longed for, when the door of her bedroom burst open. She sat up, startled, still half-asleep.

It was Alaric, bronzed all over and covered in oil and stinking of petrol.

He was standing in a shaft of bright sunlight. And at his heels was Bikram, his liver-coloured pointer.

'Darling!'

He was grinning, and as she watched, she saw him pull off his crumpled linen shirt in one easy move, straight off over his head. He revealed a rippling chest and torso tanned dark with a southern sun. He started to pull off his belt, and a groan escaped his lips.

'By Gad, how I've missed you.'

She stared at him sleepily. Was he *real*? Without knowing what she was saying, she mouthed, blearily, ridiculously:

'You snuck into my room?'

'Yep.' Alaric laughed. 'We *are* engaged, after all. And Bradley isn't here yet to be shocked. It's early, darling. Not yet six o'clock.'

Bikram, seeing which way the wind was blowing, took himself off into the shadiest part of the room and curled up in a ball, his back to them both.

'My gosh! But I didn't expect you back so soon. And what was so urgent, anyhow?' Posie forced herself sharply awake, rising quickly through the layers of sleep to hear his answer.

'Sorry?'

'You know; the urgent thing you mentioned in your telegram?'

'Mnnn?' Alaric shook off his linen trousers and kicked them aside and stood as naked as the day he was born on the warm parquet flooring. He was beautiful.

Posie gulped.

'Dash it all, let's not talk about *that* now, eh?' Alaric smiled and it cracked across his face from side to side, almost but not quite like in the photograph. He bounded over to Posie and dragged off her cotton counterpane, kicking aside the sheets. He got in beside her in bed.

He tilted Posie's disbelieving face up to his and kissed her, on and on. His caramel-coloured hair, which was too long, flopped into her face and he raked it back impatiently with his long, tanned, weather-beaten fingers. He smelt of cigarette smoke and coffee and sweat and petrol and the scents of travel and hot, exotic climates. It was quite intoxicating.

Posie pulled him closer and closer, thankful and relieved and desperate for him. Her pink sapphire ring with its bevy of petal-like diamonds caught the sun as she grabbed greedily at him and it glittered happily, sending small rainbows of arching lights dancing across the room. Alaric moaned, urgently unbuttoning her camisole, but then he stopped, frowning.

'By Gad, what's this, anyhow?' Alaric had only just noticed Posie's sateen sleeping cap. He laughed and ripped it off in a trice. And then his strangely green-bronze eyes widened like saucers and he looked aghast. He sat up, shocked, lust on hold.

'What the blazes?'

He swallowed in a stunned fashion. 'Darling, what on earth have you had done to yourself?'

Posie patted at her silvery-white hair as if to make sure it was still there. 'Oh, *this*?' she said, mock-casually.

But actually she was worried. Alaric, quite disturbed, was sitting quite apart from her now, frowning and swallowing in disbelief.

'You...you don't like it, I take it?'

'Er...well.' Alaric paused, still staring. 'I suppose it takes some getting used to. You look quite different.'

But then he smiled. 'Actually,' and the lust seemed to flood back into his eyes, which gleamed greener than usual, 'what shocked me at first was quite how much I *did* like it. Gracious, you look just like...'

'Just like who?'

'Just like Silvia Hanro.'

'Is that a good thing?' Posie frowned. 'I didn't know you liked her.'

'There can't be a man alive that *doesn't* like her. I'd be lying if I said otherwise. Not that she's a patch on you, mind. Now come here, you gorgeous girl. It's been too, too long.'

He grabbed her urgently, and the movement caused him to knock over the glass of water and the photo on the bedside table and the items went clattering, smashing to the floor.

And just as Posie was wondering quite how much she liked being compared so directly with Silvia Hanro, and wondering too if Alaric remembered meeting her as a schoolgirl, Bikram stopped giving them their privacy and started barking like crazy.

'What the…'

The door to Posie's room banged open.

'Let's be havin' yee!'

And there was Constable McCrae, rumpled of uniform and red-faced with broken sleep, wielding an old cricket bat of Alaric's before him.

'Oh, oh! I say! I'm sorry, Miss…'

Constable McCrae had managed to put on his policeman's helmet in all the fracas, but had, in his hurry, put it on back to front, and the effect was comical. It almost covered his eyes. Posie felt her face flush with shame, but at the same time she wanted to laugh, hysterically. It was all too, too much.

'Lady Cardigeon and I, we heard a noise and thought there must have been an intruder in yer room. I'm so sorry.'

Behind him peeped Dolly, deathly pale without her make-up on and looking nervous, already clutching at an unlit cigarette.

Alaric looked at them both in disbelief, before throwing himself aside in the big bed, grabbing at a sheet to cover his modesty.

'*Some* things haven't changed, I see.' He smiled, in weary resignation.

* * * *

Ten minutes later, newly-dressed and quite fit for proper company, Posie and Alaric sat at the dining table in the living room, having breakfast.

Posie was wearing much more make-up than usual, and while she had been dabbing black kohl pencil around her eyes in the bedroom, she had outlined her current case to Alaric, and he had given her a potted version of his adventures in Morocco.

Alaric had also protested, at Posie's questioning, that he *had* written to her quite a bit, at least once every two weeks. What more had she expected?

Posie had thus resigned herself to Dolly's way of thinking; that men and letters simply didn't mix. She was so, so delighted to have him back, and to have rid of that terrible sense of unease which had clung to her now for weeks. Except…

Except there still was some niggling little doubt fluttering there, like a lonely balloon stuck in the branches of a tree.

And marriage – and that pesky wedding – still hadn't been mentioned, like an elephant in the room. Later, perhaps.

Soon they were joined at the breakfast table by both Dolly and, at everyone's insistence, by Constable McCrae.

'You look very fetchin', lovey,' said Dolly, nodding approvingly. 'Nice young dress. *For once.*'

Over a bag of yesterday's croissants and slightly squashed Madelaine cakes from Paris, and a pot of piping hot coffee, because no-one could face kippers or anything much, Alaric told them all how he had planned to get back to London even earlier, how he had been due to arrive before midnight.

He'd got a plane ready and waiting at Le Touquet airport, and his old friend and ex-flying partner Major Hugo Marchpane had organised him an evening landing slot at Croydon Aerodrome. It should have been a short flight across the English Channel, not more than an hour.

'Thing was,' Alaric said, sipping coffee, and feeding bits of Madeleine cake to Bikram beneath the table, 'this wretched storm stopped me from doing anything. I had to hang around the airfield in northern France until about two o'clock this morning, when the storm had died out and I was cleared for take-off. Good old Hugo, he was still waiting for me at Croydon; I think he'd slept on a bench there, in fact. He's a dear friend. He was waiting with Bikram here, who seems pleased to see me again.'

'He's not the only one,' said Dolly in a knowing voice, with a raised eyebrow, looking over at Posie in an exaggerated tell-tale fashion. Posie flushed red and Constable McCrae spluttered into his coffee. Posie noted that the engagement photograph was back out on display this morning, although the white box was, suitably, of course, well-hidden away.

'We were just talkin' last night,' continued Dolly, casually flicking her purple nails against the bone-china mug, and Posie's heart dropped, for this spelt trouble, 'about a date for your and Posie's wedding, Al. You know, my diary is so busy these days, and I'd want to be there for it, even if it *is* a small wedding. So? Any news, lovey?'

Alaric laughed easily.

'I take the hint, Dolly. Thank you.' He looked at Posie next to him, squeezed her hand under the table and looked into her black-rimmed eyes, quite seriously.

'Yes, we do need to talk about that. It's just that it's been so darned busy these last few months, and with me being away in Morocco it didn't exactly help. I daresay those wretched orange marriage forms from the Camden Registry Office which kept fluttering around the kitchen have now expired, have they, darling, worst luck?'

'Mnnn, I think they have,' said Posie, from between a mouthful of croissant. A thought had occurred to Posie, but it was stuck somewhere, inconveniently lodged in the dark recesses of her mind. It twanged now, like an itch.

She came back to the present. 'I think once you apply to be married you can use them within forty-eight hours, but they expire after a month. And that month was a lifetime ago.'

Constable McCrae was now down on the floor, picking up imaginary crumbs to stem his embarrassment.

'Well, I was going to talk to you about it later;'

alone.' Alaric threw Dolly a half-comical look which was nevertheless laden with mind-your-own-business meaning, and turning back to Posie he continued:

'But as it happens why don't we talk about it now? I've had an invite to Venice, for the end of November and the whole of December. Why not come with me? Len can handle the Grape Street Bureau, and you can stop taking work for five measly little weeks, can't you? Why don't we get married out there? It will be easy as anything. *That* was what was urgent, in the telegram.'

'Really?' Posie muttered, incredulously. Then, more hopefully, 'Venice?'

'You've never been, right?'

Posie shook her head; she had travelled around Italy before, but the magical city of Venice had not been one of the places she had explored. It had been on her list of places to discover for a long time.

'Fine,' she breathed. And she smiled. 'It's a deal.'

'Can we still come?' asked Dolly, nosily, from across the table.

'Of course.' Alaric grinned. 'It will be easy enough. Where we'll be staying has plenty of rooms. It's a palace. In fact, it has views right across the main lagoon. It sounds a dream.'

'A palace?' asked Posie, slightly surprised. '*Whose* palace would that be?'

'Oh, you've probably never met them,' said Alaric breezily. '*I* hadn't until recently. I met a chap called Dickie Alladice while I was out in Tangiers. Nice bird, as it happens. He's got a sister; she married an Italian Count, and the whole Alladice clan will be out there in November and December. He invited me. And you, Posie.'

'Why?' asked Posie.

Alaric shrugged and finished his coffee. 'Simple courtesy? Sheer interest?'

Dolly was smoking a thoughtful cigarette. She narrowed

her eyes suspiciously. 'You're not on about Bella Alladice, by any chance, are you?'

'That's the girl!' said Alaric happily. 'You know her? Then it will be even easier!'

Dolly let out a scornful laugh. '*Nothing* is easy with Bella Alladice. Great fat frump of a girl, all tarted up in the current fashions as if that could help her at all!'

'Dolly!' said Posie, shocked. Dolly wasn't normally so harsh on people.

Dolly shrugged. 'Oh, you'll see. I met her on a committee for a theatre project last year. We were both trustees. She was awful: questioned every last penny spent, and questioned everything, in fact; so much so that the project, which was for penniless jobbing actors, fell apart and never got anywhere. I think that's what she wanted! And then she upped and moved to Italy. She's a nasty piece of work. I'd watch her, if I was you. And watch her with Alaric, for all her fancy Italian Count. Who, rumour goes, only married her for her sticky sweet fortune. It certainly wasn't for her fat face! Although I will allow, she has beautiful eyes...'

'I see.' Posie absorbed this new information and finished her coffee. The morning was taking an unexpected turn and it wasn't yet six-thirty.

She dabbed at her mouth, liking the feel of Alaric's hand on her leg beneath the table, the steady weight there.

'What sticky sweet fortune are you talking about, anyhow, Dolly?' she found herself asking, hating the fact she was clinging to a silly detail. 'I don't follow.'

'Humbugs!' said Dolly, almost triumphantly, grinding out her smoke. 'The Alladice family were industrial barons on a grand scale: sweets and chocolates and that type of thing. Humbugs, mainly. As I said, sticky sweet. They had a great factory up in the north somewhere, apparently. All sold up now, of course. Not that that's stopped Bella from eating all the sweets she can get her hands on, by the looks of things.'

Alaric intervened, in a half-hearted sort of way: 'The deuce! Dolly, perhaps you could try and be a little *kinder*, you know. Not everyone is as blessed in the looks department as yourself, or Posie, for that matter...'

Posie turned to Alaric suddenly, not taking on board his easy compliment.

In fact, she was frowning, her mind running through all this new information; she was actually thinking about timings and time in general. And now she tried not to wail, or sound desperate:

'But darling, there's simply ages between now and November. Couldn't we get a shuffle on before that?'

Alaric shook his head and his tanned face flushed red. ''Fraid not, darling. I'll definitely be staying here until my birthday party in two weeks' time, because I'm doing some talks for the Royal Geographical Society in Kensington, but after that I'm heading to Delhi.'

'Oh.'

Posie was just running through this latest and surprising news bulletin, working out exactly how she felt about it, when there was an almighty banging at the front door. They all jumped.

'OPEN UP! OPEN UP, I SAY!'

Constable McCrae had darted out, once again armed with his cricket bat, and Alaric had risen, serious and worried, his arm stretched out to shield Posie from whatever trouble might come.

Then the door to the living room was opening and the Chief Inspector was standing before them, Sergeants Binny and Rainbird hovering behind him like twin dark shadows. They were all distinctly ashen-faced and Lovelace looked more dishevelled than Posie had ever seen him. Which was saying something, considering they had been in a few bad scrapes together before.

'What?' Posie asked shrilly. 'What is it?'

'It's Silvia Hanro,' said the Chief Inspector, his face flat with dread.

247

'She's dead. She's just been found murdered.'

Posie gasped, a sickening feeling rushing through her. She thought she might gag. Alaric squeezed her hand.

Lovelace nodded.

'In her dressing room. The call came in twenty minutes ago. We were all in for an early meeting to plan for this big Wrap Party, and we beetled over here as quickly as we could to pick you up.'

Lovelace was pulling at his hair frantically. He saw the coffee pot on the table and poured the pithy last dregs into an empty water glass and swallowed the lot without waiting for any milk.

'You ready, Posie? And you, Lady Cardigeon? Let's go. And I want you, Lady Cardigeon, to stick like glue to one of Posie or myself. Got it?'

Dolly nodded meekly.

'I can't deal with anything else going awry today,' muttered the Chief Inspector. 'This here murder is probably more than my job is worth, as it happens. Blue Plumes don't count for much today, eh? Especially given the fact that Miss Hanro was reported missing last night. It doesn't look good for me. Not good at all. It's catastrophic, actually.'

'For me too,' said Posie softly.

The Inspector continued in a calm but numb voice:

'They've sealed up the room for now and not entered it. Mr Samuelson, who I understand owns the place, is watching the room, with a couple of his own employees. I thought it was best to have a so-called third party to man the fort until we get there. Of course, I've arranged for some of the police at Richmond to attend but they'll only be arriving there now, I guess.'

'Well, those arrangements all sound eminently sensible, sir,' said Posie reassuringly, but with a frog in her throat. She was trying to banish the thought of the apricot-wearing swirling figure from her mind.

'As a matter of interest, sir, who found the body?'

'It was the Producer, Brian Langley.'

'Very convenient.' Posie nodded, her face setting in grim lines, trying to imagine the scene.

'Apparently he'd been up all night, but upstairs in the projection room. He was going to grab some early breakfast downstairs when he saw the door to the dressing room was ajar, and he looked inside. Fella's in a bad way, apparently. It was his secretary, this Reggie Jones, who called the thing in.'

The Chief Inspector seemed to gather his wits together and barked out his usual orders:

'Right, let's go. We need to look snappy. Constable, you drive me and the ladies. You two,' he motioned to his Sergeants, 'follow in the other car.'

The Sergeants nodded. Posie grabbed at her bag of party clothes automatically, without thinking. But the swirling girl in apricot refused to dance away from her thoughts. She looked over at Binny and Rainbird.

'Sergeants, can you stop on your way at Piccadilly?'

'Posie,' growled Lovelace, 'we really don't have time for some unnecessary fact-finding mission. That can all be done later. We need to hop to it. We have a national tragedy on our hands, and both our reputations are on the line.'

'I know, sir. But this is important. Crucially so. I just need the men to look for two items at the Albany. And it's a tiny flat, sir. They'll be not more than ten minutes, I swear it. It could help us to work out why Miss Hanro was getting death threats in the first place, and help us to work out what she was up to in her final hours.'

Lovelace sighed testily. 'Oh, go on then.'

And Posie told the Sergeants just what the two items were which she wanted them to look for.

'Tell the Concierge that you're there for Mrs Delacroix, if they're funny with you,' she said.

'Right you are then, Miss.' Binny nodded unquestioningly and the two men left.

The Chief Inspector put on his hat again. 'You're staying here, sir, are you?' He looked across to Alaric, both men knowing each other a fair bit but not having as yet acknowledged each other in all the panic.

'Yes,' said Alaric, frowning, running his hands through his hair again. 'I'm not sure there's much *I* can do at Worton Hall. I knew the girl, as it happens. But that was almost twenty years ago. A lifetime ago. Beautiful creature, even then. But there's no help in that, is there?'

'Not much, sir. No. Have a good day.'

And then Posie, Dolly and the Inspector left in a mad swirling flurry of bags and Bikram's barking.

As they went down in the birdcage lift, the flickering electric lights dappled everyone's faces through the golden metal. Lovelace stared hard at Posie.

'I say.' He frowned. 'Are you feeling quite all right, Posie?'

'Right enough, sir. Why?'

'Oh, I don't know.'

The Inspector looked at her in an unseeing, confused fashion.

'You do look like yourself. But not *quite* yourself, somehow. Like you have a cold, perhaps. Or flu? No. Never mind. It must be my eyes.'

* * * *

Twenty-Four

The dressing room corridor was thronged with people when they arrived at Worton Hall an hour later.

It was almost eight o'clock and someone somewhere had been cutting grass and the usually friendly scent lingered in the air, at odds with the ghoulishly expectant atmosphere. Young excitable policemen from the Richmond Constabulary and a bevy of Scotland Yard employees of various professions were hanging around irritably in the already heavy heat, waiting for directions.

Bertie Samuelson was sitting, implacable and calm, his large bulk square and immovable on a foldable deckchair patterned in blue-and-white stripes, placed right outside the closed door to Silvia Hanro's dressing room. He looked relieved when Chief Inspector Lovelace introduced himself with a brief handshake. A temporary cordon of string was put in place, slicing the corridor apart. The Chief Inspector turned to the mass of people and boomed authoritatively:

'Everyone back, please. Clear away. There's nothing anyone can do. I just want Dr Poots the Pathologist to stay here for now, please. And Miss Parker.'

Inspector Lovelace started talking to Dr Poots in an undertone, going through some sort of police checklist between them.

Posie was trying to take everything in, storing up the details for later, her eyes darting up and down the hot glass corridor. She noted that Brian Langley was standing on the edge of the circle of people who had been pushed back, and he was watching Lovelace carefully. He looked more rumpled than ever, and his face was as white as driven snow. He was biting down hard on his lip and folding and unfolding his arms, and Posie noticed how dark and hollow his small eyes looked in his face, which seemed full of dread.

Or was he just a good actor? Perhaps he could be as good an actor as a Producer, or flower-grower? Or military medal-winner?

He kept swigging from a small silver hip flask. Beside him stood Reggie Jones, the secretary, pale and sweaty, muttering reassurances. On Brian Langley's other side stood a thin woman in an inappropriately-heavy winter hat and smart navy linen coat. Posie found herself thinking irrelevantly how hot the woman must be, in such formal clothes. The woman was staring intently, almost hypnotically, past the policemen and down the empty corridor. What was she looking for?

On a second glance the woman was revealed as Mrs Cleeves, Brian Langley's Housekeeper. Posie was surprised. What had Brian Langley called *her* in for? Moral support at so early an hour? Or was Mrs Cleeves more than just a Housekeeper?

Turning to follow the woman's gaze, Posie saw Robbie Fontaine lumbering along the now-empty corridor, obviously just awake, wearing a burgundy quilted dressing gown and with a bleary look in his eyes, which were very white and crazed.

'What the devil is all this?' he started shouting, before a burly-armed policeman leapt across the cordon and held him back. And then, and Posie felt her heart lurch, from behind Robbie Fontaine, from the silent staircase to the apartments above, came the running footsteps of Tom Moran. He was nimble on his feet and easily ran past Robbie Fontaine with his policeman, almost rugby-tackling them aside.

He seemed to have forgotten all caution, all need to play-act his role as impartial colleague of Miss Hanro.

He, too, had obviously just woken up, and he was only half-dressed, his naked torso riddled with shrapnel scars, his eyepatch on but almost askew, the blue sunglasses at an angle. Lovelace pushed him back gently with the flat of his hand.

'You can't go through, pal.'

'Is it true what they're saying?' Tom Moran gasped desperately, his voice still thick with sleep. 'She's actually dead?'

'I'm sorry, sir. We're still investigating. Please wait.'

'This is all *your* fault!' Tom Moran was shouting over at Brian Langley, watched by a fascinated crowd of perhaps twenty onlookers. 'You could have protected her! You fool!'

Brian Langley said nothing, but Posie saw him gulp and look down at the floor. And then in an instant, Tom Moran was down on the lino, curled up in a shaking ball, being violently sick, over and over. Retching as if he had just ingested poison.

'Pull yourself together, man,' said Dr Poots curtly, moving an immaculate spat-covered shoe out of harm's way and scrabbling in his bag for a twist of smelling salts. 'Buck up a bit. Some sort of mad fan, are you, lad?'

And then the Chief Inspector was ushering Posie into the doorway of the now-opened room and she looked around, her heart racing.

The girl was lying in the tiny, dim dressing room, flopped over her chair. She was face-down, dangling, a blonde and plaited wig covering her whole head. Her arms hung, flailing. She looked like she had drowned and been pulled from the sea.

The movie star had obviously been dead for some time.

They came out together, and Dr Poots who had come in at their insistence, stayed within.

'It's not her,' said Chief Inspector Lovelace to the waiting crowd, shaking his head. The relief he obviously felt was palpable in his words.

'I can confirm that the dead woman inside the dressing room is *not* Silvia Hanro.'

Posie stood beside him, trying to fill her lungs with normal air, staring mainly at Brian Langley. He had straightened up, put away the silver hip flask but was still gulping wildly and looking deathly white. He kept shaking his head disbelievingly. All around were mutterings and gasps and the general sense of people melting away, relieved, but robbed of a sensation.

Lovelace continued brusquely:

'We have a good idea who the dead woman is, but for the moment we are treating the whole incident as suspicious. Mr Samuelson, can my team take over one of your rooms here as an incident room? As a base?'

The large man, normally so smiley, looked very grave but nodded and indicated backwards, further along the corridor.

'Be my guest, take the Green Room, it's by far the most comfortable and is set up with all the necessary comforts: tea, coffee, paper, pens. I'll send in one of my lads to clean it up a bit.'

He looked over at the Producer. 'You won't be needing it today for the extras, will you, Brian?'

Brian Langley shook his head numbly. 'No,' he whispered. 'Everything is practically finished. I don't need extras today. I just needed one last take for a scene which we filmed in the wrong light, but it's just between Silvia and Robbie. And unless she turns up we can't even do that…'

254

Lovelace nodded at the Producer. 'I haven't forgotten, sir. For now, Miss Hanro continues to be listed as a missing person. She is a priority and we'll look into it and talk to you in just a little while. We just need to sort out this current situation first.'

'Of course.' The Producer was nodding obediently, but then something in him seemed to snap. He frowned and his dark eyes seemed to regain a spark of their usual angry fire.

'But what about the party?' He checked his watch. 'I'll have the cream of the London glitterati arriving here in less than four hours' time. Are you requesting that we cancel the whole thing?'

Posie was certain that the Chief Inspector was about to order that it couldn't go ahead, and she almost fell out of her glacé sandals when he shook his head.

'No. I'm not ordering any such thing. Please proceed. We can contain this incident here, and as far as I understand, the danger centres around Miss Hanro. As she's a no-show, I don't see a problem. My men, plus the Richmond Constabulary, will be on guard here anyhow. I insist upon that, at least.'

'Fine.' Brian Langley nodded. 'Thank you. I'll be in the editing suite if you need me.'

'I'll need to speak to you later, sir, but for now, I want Miss Parker and my Scotland Yard team in the Green Room. Oh, and Mr Samuelson, please. Nobody here is allowed to leave these premises. Please register your names with Constable McCrae over there.'

Posie looked around her but noticed that Mrs Cleeves, and Reggie Jones, and Robbie Fontaine, and Tom Moran had all disappeared, presumably to recover from the shock of the false alarm. Dolly, too, had also disappeared. Posie felt her heart skip an unwelcome beat.

While they were loitering outside the Green Room, waiting for it to be cleaned, Posie allowed her mind to dwell once again on the body in the dressing room.

It had been the glimpse of orange beneath the green kimono which had done it. The orange shoes.

And then Posie had known. It wasn't Silvia Hanro lying dead in that room at all. She had almost shouted in her eagerness:

'It's Elaine, Silvia Hanro's dresser!'

The girl was dressed up as Silvia. And pretty convincingly at that.

The wig, the kimono, the parasol, all the paraphernalia of the movie star, had elaborately masked the woman's true identity at first glance. And when that was discovered, it had been the work of a second for Dr Poots to come in, roll the girl over and validate things.

Elaine's frizzy long hair, revealed from under the inaccurate Anne Boleyn wig, had trailed out over the floor, in a sort of rebuke that anyone could have mistaken its owner's true identity.

'What was the cause of death? What do you think, Poots?' Lovelace had growled. 'Suicide, or murder?'

Dr Poots had huffed and puffed his way around the nasty little room, holding things up by the light of a torch and smelling things. He had picked up the water glass and had sniffed at it quizzically.

The Chief Inspector had paced on. 'Or a murder made to look like suicide?'

Refusing to be drawn, after a couple of minutes Dr Poots had covered Elaine's face up with a piece of green hospital muslin from his bag and put his hands on his hips and sighed.

'You always want it all, Lovelace, don't you? All I can tell you for now is that she was poisoned, but whether or not she ingested the stuff voluntarily, or whether someone forced her to drink the stuff, or whether they hid it surreptitiously and fed it to her without her knowledge or consent, I can't yet tell you. She died last night. I'd guess about midnight.'

Lovelace frowned. 'Poison? You're sure?'

'Yep. There's a bluish tinge to the mouth and tongue. A plant poison, I'd warrant. Belladonna? *Digitalis*, maybe?'

'Is *Digitalis* the name for an orchid? *That* orchid?' Posie indicated to the reddish spotted flowers in the corner. The big vase they were standing in was empty of any water.

'Mnnn.' Dr Poots nodded and stared at the plant. 'It could be. I won't know for sure until I can check the body back in my laboratory. What are these things doing in here, anyhow? They're deadly! I see the water is missing. Even drinking that could have caused death. It would certainly explain the blue tinge.'

Dr Poots had gone on: 'She'd only have had to drink a very little bit to die. She might not have noticed it, although the taste of Foxtrot orchid is bitter. This water glass smells like it's had lemon or orange in it, to me. Or honey? Maybe with gin, too. Perhaps one of those new fashionable cocktails? That would have masked the bitterness all right.'

'My gosh! A Bee's Knees!'

The Chief Inspector had harrumphed. '*If* we're treating this as a murder. She could have concocted the stuff herself, and drunk it herself.'

Posie had turned, disbelieving. 'You think so, sir? It seems an unusual way to choose to die. Poisoning oneself is a terrible way to go.'

'She might have been unhinged. A mad, crazed sort of a fan, despite her professional affiliations here. That's my initial guess. Explains the outfit, anyhow.'

Dr Poots had snapped his bag shut. 'I'm inclined to agree with Miss Parker, Lovelace. *For once*, mind. It's not for me to tell you how to do your job but there are certainly easier ways to die; she would have suffered a good deal of pain, plus terrible hallucinations and palpitations before expiring here. Poor lass, whoever she was. I'll have more for you later. I'll send my report directly to you.'

Posie was re-running the Pathologist's words over and

over as they entered the Green Room, led inside by Bertie Samuelson. A police constable from Richmond stood guarding the door.

Inside, the place was spacious and lived up to its name: every couch and rug in the place was a different colour green, and the muslin curtains hanging at the windows which blotted out the bright morning sun made the place feel like a murky fish-bowl. It felt distinctly underwater, and it was very hot.

Lovelace had been joined by Constable McCrae who was holding his pad aloft, eagerly awaiting the taking of notes. They all sat down quickly and without ceremony around the coffee table. The Inspector got straight to the point.

'I'm afraid that the dead woman is one of *your* employees, Mr Samuelson. A Miss Elaine Dickinson?'

The big man looked aghast. Beads of sweat were breaking out all over his face. 'Elaine? Elaine? Goodness me.'

He had balled his hands up into fists and was rubbing at his eyes. He composed himself and took a cigar from his pocket, taking his time to cut and light it. He took a drag. 'Please excuse me, it's rather a shock, that's all. How did she die?'

'We don't know as yet, I'm afraid. You knew her well, sir?'

'Not well, no. But she was with me from the off, you see. She was always in charge of the female movie stars here, for dressing and personal needs and the like. When I opened up here in 1914, just before the Great War, she came and asked me for work. She was never the brightest spark, was never going to set the world alight, and in truth, I felt sorry for her, but she was a decent worker and a real film fan. She lived her life through the cinema: knew all the stars and the movies like the back of her hand. She would have worked for free if I hadn't paid her her wages.

She once told me she felt she was really at home here, living a sort of dream.'

Posie thought of the drooping little woman with her bright shoes and wondered what sort of dream it had been to end up like that. She bit her lip.

'What can you tell me about Miss Dickinson, sir?' asked the Chief Inspector. 'Did she seem quite herself of late? Any mood swings? Depressions? Anything which might have meant she wanted to end it all?'

Posie sighed: Lovelace was obviously sticking to his guns about it being an elaborately-dressed up suicide.

Bertie Samuelson was puffing away. 'Gracious, no. I wasn't with her all the time, of course, but I'd say quite the opposite was true.'

He thought for a ponderous minute.

'It's only been these last couple of months, since Brian's been filming *Henry the King*, in which I'd noticed the change in her. A change for the better, mind.'

'I see.'

Constable McCrae was writing furiously, but Posie hadn't got her notebook out. She was too busy thinking. She jumped straight in:

'Two questions, sir. You don't happen to know if she had taken to wearing an engagement ring, do you?'

Bertie Samuelson shook his head. 'No, I don't. Sorry. But you can look in her room here, of course. Maybe you'll find what you're looking for up there?'

'Her room?' Posie spoke more sharply than she had intended to.

Bertie Samuelson nodded. 'That's right. She's had the same room since we opened up here. Nine years now. She didn't really have a family to speak of, that was one of the reasons I felt sorry for her in the first place; just a brother in a very unfashionable line of work. As I said, this was her home. What was your second question, Miss Parker?'

'Would you say that Elaine Dickinson got on well with

her current female star? Silvia Hanro? Enough to want to dress like her, to pretend to be her?'

The owner of Worton Hall looked at Posie and then shrugged. 'I really couldn't say, Miss Parker. I know she respected Miss Hanro and tried to serve her well, but I don't think it went as far as copying her. Adulation, you mean? A fixation?'

Posie nodded.

'No.' The big man shook his head. 'I think you're barking up the wrong tree. If anything it was the male stars Elaine had a crush on. She was besotted with Robbie Fontaine. She was known for it, these last three months. Well, all women are, aren't they?'

Posie managed a smile.

'Thank you. That was most helpful.'

Lovelace nodded approvingly. 'Indeed, sir. Most helpful. That will be all. We'd better call for Mr Langley now, as the man who discovered the body. Can you go and find him, McCrae?'

But before Mr Samuelson could leave, there was an almighty ruckus outside. The Richmond policeman on sentry duty put his head round the door, chortling.

'There's someone outside, sir, claiming she's a Lady-so-and-so. A likely story! You should see what she's wearin'! But I thought you should know. She insisted on seein' you. Says she's got somethin' important.'

'Dolly!' gasped Posie. 'Thank goodness!'

'Let her in, Constable. And that Lady so-and-so is Lady Cardigeon, and you'll get a dashed good talking to about this later, lad, you mark my words. I don't think we need your sort of cover on the door: best be without you if you're going to act like that. You're discharged.'

The bobby retreated, shame-faced, and Dolly rounded the door, looking small and bright and triumphant. Her arms were loaded down with several items.

'What is it, my Lady? And please, in future, stick with

either Posie or myself. We've got enough on our plates without losing you into the bargain.'

'Fine,' said Dolly merrily. 'Sorry! You asked what I was up to: well, I put two and two together and made five and realised it must be Elaine, that little frump, who was in the dressing room, dead as a doornail. So I did some fishin' of my own.'

'Where?' cried the Chief Inspector. 'What are you talking about?'

'Up in her room, upstairs, of course,' said Dolly, a touch defensively. 'And you'll be glad I did. Because look what I found.'

She came over to the coffee table and tipped the contents of her haul over it.

'That could have been key evidence from a crime scene, my Lady!' bleated the Inspector uselessly. 'What were you doing up there, rootling around?'

'He's right,' said Posie, but without much conviction. Instead, she was staring hard at the collection of things on the table. The objects were damning.

A bottle of green ink and a pen.

A few pieces of script paper of the same type and size and with the same writing on them as the death threats which had been received by Silvia Hanro, but these had blottings-outs and lines and marks on them: practice versions.

A small roll of gold foil, the same as had been wrapped around the severed finger which had been sent, and the same as which had been found wrapped around the finger of Elaine herself.

A few scrappy pieces of paper with many attempts at a signature on them. The same signature, over and over:
Silvia Hanro.

And most tellingly of all, a small sheet of headed notepaper with a quick scrawled note below it, which had obviously accompanied a grisly little cargo all of its own.

J.R.R. DICKINSON

– FUNERAL DIRECTOR, RICHMOND

Elaine,

Can't think what you want this for.
Practical joke, is it?

It won't be missed here, but you owe me, big time.

Joe.

'See?' said Dolly. 'As well as a dead body we've found our person making the death threats and sending fingers!'

'It certainly looks like it,' said the Chief Inspector grimly.

* * * *

Twenty-Five

'I told you her brother was in a distinctly unfashionable line of work,' said Bertie Samuelson, picking up the Funeral Director's note distastefully.

He nodded. 'I remember now. Elaine was going to have to join him as an assistant if I didn't give her a job. She said it gave her the creeps – dead bodies, I mean.'

Dolly raised an eyebrow. 'Obviously she changed her mind, though, didn't she? If she was prepared to send bits of bodies to the woman she worked for? It couldn't have affected her that much, could it?'

Bertie Samuelson was splaying his hands. 'This doesn't make any sense. It's strange. I just can't imagine Elaine would be behind something like this.'

The Chief Inspector tsk-tsked. 'Once you've been in a job like mine for long enough, Mr Samuelson, you've seen it all: strange things, odd things, things there don't seem any motive for.'

'But that's just it,' cut in Posie sharply. 'Why would Elaine go to the trouble of sending elaborate death threats to Miss Hanro – which, I admit, it looks like she has done – only to kill herself before she could bring the plan to fruition? If those telegrams to Sam Stubbs and his friends at the other newspapers are to be believed, she had wanted as big an audience in place as possible for her final showdown. So why end it all before that? Seems a lot of work for nothing, if you ask me.'

Inspector Lovelace shrugged. 'I stand by my initial theory that Miss Dickinson was somehow not quite right in the head. Maybe the movie world had got too much for her? Or maybe she felt guilty about what she had done, and decided to end it all.'

'Mnnn,' Posie muttered in a quietly disbelieving sort of way. She was unconvinced. It was very neat. Or neat-ish, anyhow. She only half-heard the snippets of conversation which continued around her:

'I'll ask this brother, Joe, to come here now, to tell us whether or not this is actually Elaine's writing on the death threats; then we'll know, wont we?' nodded the Inspector. 'And while he's about it he can formally identify the body.'

'I'll call him if you like.' Mr Samuelson nodded bleakly, turning towards the door, 'I *was* her employer, after all.'

Posie kept thinking of the gold-foil ring around Elaine's finger, and she couldn't shake the image off. Why would a girl like Elaine, a nobody, try and threaten a star like Silvia Hanro? What exactly had she hoped to achieve with the threats and the finger?

What was it that Posie couldn't see? Or what was it she wasn't *meant* to see, something which was obliterating the truth?

'I'd like to see her room, sir,' Posie said, and Lovelace simply nodded at her.

'I'll show you up, lovey,' said Dolly, keen to help. But just as she and Dolly were about to leave with Mr Samuelson, Lovelace put a finger to his lips.

'Shhh! Listen. What's that?'

And sure enough, a strange and whispered argument between a man and a woman could be heard going on somewhere outside in the corridor. But every word came through clear as a bell. Posie remembered the talk she had

had with the odious Hector Mallow, how he had overheard an argument out in this very corridor while waiting in the Green Room, how by the chance of some strange acoustics at Worton Hall secrets didn't always remain secrets.

Posie, listening, felt a sharp sense of relief flooding through her.

'Can it be?' cried Posie. 'Is it *her*? Oh, praise be!'

It was Brian Langley arguing outside, with Silvia Hanro. They'd obviously just bumped into each other by accident.

'Where the very devil have you been? I was going crazy with worry!'

They all listened in intently, eager eavesdroppers. Brian Langley sounded largely relieved, but more than anything, furious:

'I reported you missing to the police, you little idiot!'

Silvia Hanro replied snappishly, her cold whispers not quite masking her fear. 'Is it any of your business where I go or what I do?'

'I'd say so, wouldn't you? Today of all days! Today can make or break both of us. As you well know!'

'Well, I'm here now. You said nine o'clock, and I'm here on the dot, ready for filming. Like usual. Ready to face what may come: death included. But *you'd* know all about that, wouldn't you?'

'I can't think what you mean.'

'Yes, you do. I know what you've done, Brian. Those notes were meant to scare me, weren't they? All that wretched symbolism designed to frighten me. Well, you haven't succeeded. It's done now. You'll just have to deal with it. Like it or lump it.'

'You absolute fool. How could you? You succumbed? I warned you about this on Sunday, out in the woods. You don't know what you've done.'

'I know absolutely what I've done. And for once, I'm not playing by your rules or listening to your advice. What's going on here, anyhow? Why are policemen crawling all over the place? Surely you didn't call them all in for me? Or for the party? Bit over the top, isn't it?'

'Not everything revolves around you, although most things seem to, admittedly. I found a body, this morning. I thought it was you, initially. It was awful. There's a rumour going around the place now that it's Elaine Dickinson.'

'Elaine? What? *My* Elaine?'

And then the voice of Constable McCrae could be heard outside, asking Brian Langley to step into the Green Room.

'Blast!' Posie groaned at the Constable's efficiency. It had all started to get interesting. And surprising.

'Stay,' ordered Lovelace, motioning over at Posie and Dolly, although Bertie Samuelson was allowed to leave.

Brian Langley entered the room looking harried and threw himself down on an old couch, and crossed his arms. He stared at Posie for a second, as if seeing her anew for the first time, then he looked at the Chief Inspector.

'Is it Elaine, then?'

'We believe so, Mr Langley.'

'How did she die?'

'I couldn't say. But I think I heard Miss Hanro just now outside, so that's a relief for all concerned, isn't it?'

The Producer blew out his cheeks and finally nodded. 'I'll say.'

The Inspector continued: 'Especially for Mr Fontaine, I'd imagine. He looked positively off his mind with grief, or *something*, this morning. It must be the devil of a thing, having a fiancée go missing on you. He must be over the moon just now. As are you, I expect.'

Brian Langley stared at the policeman through narrowed eyes but refused to be drawn. If he suspected that the Chief Inspector knew the truth about Silvia Hanro's relationship with Robbie Fontaine then he kept his cool and stayed silent. He lit a cigarette.

266

After answering a few routine questions about where he had been the evening before, particularly around midnight, to which he replied he hadn't left Worton Hall all night, and whether he had known the dead girl at all, to which he had replied in the negative, he sat sulkily smoking.

Posie cut in.

'I understand that it was you who found the body, Mr Langley. And you thought it was Miss Hanro, without any doubt?'

Brian Langley shrugged. 'Well, don't forget — I didn't get very close — I saw the body and then I called for help.'

He seemed to think for a second or two. Then, removing his cigarette, he spoke softly, so Posie had to lean right in to hear him.

'But take note of this: I'm not often fooled, Miss Parker. And I have a sense for what looks convincing or not, otherwise I'd be in a different job. Which means when I say I found that girl and thought it was Silvia Hanro lying there, I'm telling you that it looked pretty darn convincing.'

He took a deep, thoughtful drag. 'I had no idea the girl could dress herself up so well: she obviously had an eye for detail. And the dramatic. It looked like the work of a professional. It's a shame,' he continued smoothly, 'I could have used her as a cheap double in one of my films if I'd known she was that good.'

He looked at Posie in a frank, appraising way, as if he was buying fish, or meat, or maybe one of his prize orchids in a special market. 'You too, maybe.'

Posie shuddered.

'I like your hair, Miss Parker. Very *now*. You look quite the ingénue. Maybe lose some weight and I'll think of hiring you on my next film as an extra, or, if you're lucky, as a double. *If* you've given up detecting by then, of course. Which you might well do: I've seen precious little evidence of your work so far in what I asked you to do. I've half a mind to ask for my money back.'

Posie flushed with embarrassment and stifled down the urge to slap the man but before she could do so the Chief Inspector jumped in:

'Miss Parker has been absolutely instrumental in finding the source of the death threats made to Silvia Hanro. I think you will find that the danger is now past, absolutely never to return.'

'*What?*' Brian Langley stared from Posie to Lovelace in what looked like disbelief.

'You mean…'

'That's right, sir. We have strong evidence to suggest it was Miss Elaine Dickinson herself who was making the death threats. You can rest assured now, can't you?'

Posie was about to protest, to spew out her misgivings about it all, when the Chief Inspector cut in again:

'I'd just like to ask, sir, why were there Foxtrot orchids in Silvia Hanro's dressing room? I understand you grow the things, but they make an unusual choice of gift, wouldn't you say? Rather risky. My understanding is that one tiny lick of that plant is enough to cause serious illness, and that death can be caused by ingestion of any part of the plant.'

Brian Langley laughed:

'Oh, come. What are you going to do? Arrest me? Death is all around us, all of the time. They were there for the simple reason that they are Silvia Hanro's favourite flower. When they are in season I send them to her, fresh, every few days. I always have done. For years now, since we met before the war. No harm has come before. And she's a big girl; she knows not to touch them. She listens to my advice, you know.'

Not always, thought Posie to herself, remembering the scene in the corridor, *and evidently not about everything*.

'Is that all?' asked the Producer impatiently. 'Only, now that Miss Hanro has bothered to show up, I've got one last take to film, then a party to host, and then we're packing up and leaving this place. I've paid up to today, and I'm not going to pay for tomorrow. So I'd like to get on.'

'We'd like to speak to Miss Hanro, herself. Is she around?'

'Oh, she's around. But I've sent her straight off to the studio. You'll have to wait until I've finished with her.'

And then he left.

'I'm sorry about not noticing your hair before, Posie,' muttered the Inspector. 'Langley's right, it's very fetching. I kept thinking there was something not quite right about you.'

'What a compliment. Thank you, sir.'

'Oh, you know what I mean.'

'I do, sir. Absolutely.'

* * * *

Twenty-Six

Dolly and Posie trudged up the white stairs.

To Posie it seemed like years, not just the day before since she had been there last, among the little rooms occupied by crew and cast members. The cook, Mrs Thynne, was loitering in the corridor. When she saw Dolly approaching she gave a curmudgeonly smile and almost dropped a curtsey. Dolly had obviously given the woman a large tip beforehand and leech-like, she was hanging around in the hope of another one. Posie felt nauseous.

'M'Lady,' said the cook. 'I've been waitin' here for you. Like I told you I would.'

'Thank you, but that will be all for now.'

They turned into the doorway of the same small room Posie had seen yesterday, and the cook melted away, backwards.

'Hang on a minute, isn't this your room?' called out Posie, confused.

'Nope. I'm next door, Miss. That there is Elaine's room. Sorry, that *was* Elaine's room.'

The cook made an elaborate gesture of crossing herself.

'God rest her soul. We were neighbours, when I stayed over here, anyhow. You've changed yer hair, haven't you, Miss? You're the girl from yesterday? When I saw you prowling around yesterday afternoon I happened to be on the way to *my* own room. I just wondered what you were doing nosing around in here. So I made it my business to find out.'

'I see.' The confusion over, Posie looked about her. Here on the desk were the scrapbooks, the magazines with the cut-out wedding dresses which had haunted Posie the night before.

In the corner under the small window was the neat white-covered bed, but the dresser with its set of drawers was a diabolical mess of papers, pens, clips and stationery, mixed together with clothes and underthings, mainly of the sad grey washed-out-looking variety, thrown around and heaped about as if a burglar had been through it all, searching for something. The drawers were all pulled out and askew. Posie remembered how neat it had been the day before.

'Did you do this?' she asked Dolly, pointing at the drawers.

'No, lovey. I'm not that stupid. Although that's where I got the stuff from, it was all mixed in with a lot of hair-tonic and curlers and stuff in the bottom drawer.'

'I see.'

Posie turned to the desk. The same magazines were still there, and that same matinée-idol photograph of Tom Moran in the days when he had been Mark Paris, but her eagle-eye now noticed other photographs, too. Four or five photographs of Robbie Fontaine, not framed but pasted above the wall nearest the desk, and there, on the floor, under the desk, a very large photograph of Silvia Hanro, probably in the days when she was just starting out, with longer hair and less make-up and less years under her belt to worry herself about.

The famous eyes looked out at Posie from under a layer of smashed glass: the photo had been framed, but looked as if had been thrown under the desk in a rage.

Posie got on her knees and looked at it, careful not to touch. She saw that the photograph had a slight white powdery dusting all over it. And at the back of the under-desk area, she found a small twist of paper. Putting her gloves on, she pulled it towards her, out into the light. She smelt it, licked it. Inspector Lovelace would be proud.

'Cocaine,' she whispered to a wide-eyed Dolly. 'I'm pretty sure of it. I think the room should be thoroughly searched by the Forensics team. I can't think why it hasn't been done yet. I suppose it's all the chaos of the morning.'

'But what are you hopin' to find out, lovey? The girl was obviously a crack-head and a bit of a nutter, that much is evident. Bit too reliant on the white-stuff for her own good, maybe?'

Posie crossed her arms, thinking. She kept remembering Inspector Lovelace's initial theory that Elaine was obviously an unhinged fan of Silvia Hanro's, and here was evidence beyond doubt to show she was obviously not quite in her right mind.

But the room bothered her.

Elaine's room today was so unlike the room she had seen yesterday as to be like night and day. Elaine Dickinson, frump though she had been, was not the kind of girl to leave her sad grey underwear hanging out on show. She had a peculiar sort of pride. And nor was she, Posie felt, the sort of girl to use drugs.

'*It's all wrong*,' Posie breathed to herself. 'This is all being cleverly directed.'

She stepped outside again. As expected, Mrs Thynne, the cook, was still lingering. Posie fished in her bag and made sure the glint of her money caught the sunlight this time.

'I say,' she called. 'I made one mistake concerning you yesterday, and I don't want to jump to any more wrong conclusions.'

Posie smiled in what she hoped was a friendly fashion.

'I wonder if you can tell me if Miss Dickinson had any visitors here last night? It looks as if there might have been a fight, or some unpleasantness, in here? If you were in the room next door you might have heard something? Anthing?'

Mrs Thynne drew herself up to her not-very-tall full height and puffed out even wider. 'I'm not one for tittle-tattle,' she said pompously. 'I can't tell you I heard anything. She was very quiet. Like usual.'

'Did she ever have a boyfriend here at all? Did you know of anyone?'

Again, the puffing.

'None that *I* knew of. But this is a decent place, Miss. Not a place to have fellas back for the night in, if you know what I mean. It's not a *hostel*. Mr Samuelson wouldn't abide any of *that*. And Elaine was a decent sort of girl.'

'Of course. And did Elaine keep her room tidy, do you know? As I saw it yesterday?'

'That's right. Neat as a new pin she were.'

'Well, thank you. That's most interesting.'

'There is one thing, Miss. If you're interested…'

'Yes? Go on.'

'Late last night, must have been past midnight, I heard a banging around in there. It was unusual, but I didn't like to interfere. But I *did* make it my business to open my door a crack when the visitor left.'

Posie's stomach was a knot of twisted dread. She had known something wasn't right. 'And? Did you get a good look?'

'I did. It was Brian Langley. He looked furious. Fit to burst. Worse than usual, I mean.'

Posie drew in a deep breath. 'I think you'd better come with us, Mrs Thynne. What you've said is very interesting. It could be crucial. You'd better repeat it for my friend the Chief Inspector, downstairs. In a witness statement.'

The woman pursed her lips. 'Very well. If I must. Is that there money for me?'

Posie pushed the coin across. 'Aren't you busy today, Mrs Thynne? I'm surprised you have time to be hanging around up here what with the catering for the party going on downstairs.'

The woman glared at Posie and gave her a look which implied that she found her very wanting. 'Haven't you heard? This 'ere party is beyond the likes of my skills, apparently. Old Langley's brought in Harrods to do the catering. Imagine! They were already arriving with their fancy hot trays a few minutes ago.'

Posie ushered the cook and Dolly along the corridor, making sure to close Elaine's door behind her. As they tripped along, she suddenly saw the door to the next room, Tom Moran's, was very slightly ajar. Pausing, she registered a slight movement within.

'Dolly,' she whispered. 'Can you take Mrs Thynne downstairs and hand her over to the Inspector. Tell him what we've heard. I'll be along in two ticks. Tell him to send the Forensics boys upstairs to Elaine's room, too.'

Waiting until the nosy cook and Dolly had disappeared, Posie knocked at the door.

****

There was no reply, so she pushed the door open anyway. The room inside was bright and white and hot. And immaculate. The window was right open but it smelt strange inside the room, a perfume of sesame seeds which were sweet and hot and burning. Like very sweet cakes which had been incinerated.

Tom Moran was curled up on the small bed, facing the wall, rocking backwards and forwards. He gave no impression of having registered Posie entering the room.

'I say,' she began awkwardly. 'I couldn't help but notice the door…'

Sitting up abruptly, Tom Moran's half-face was a mass of red, blotchy puffiness. He wore no coverings at all and looked frightful.

'What do you want?' he slurred. He seemed as if he couldn't quite wake up.

'I just wanted to see if you were all right. It must have been an awful shock, earlier.'

'It was,' Tom snapped. He put a strange metal bowl and some spoons and matches and what looked like a piece of paper covered in brown tar quickly under his bed.

'The scent of death is with me even now. I thought I'd escaped it when I was invalided out, but it's here too. And I thought it was Silvia! Imagine!'

Posie nodded sympathetically. 'You know, I think she's returned. She's safe: I heard her voice downstairs. I'm not sure if you know or not? But I think she's filming already so she probably hasn't had a chance to come up here yet.'

She registered a spasm of relief and utter misery pass across Tom Moran's face.

'Thank heavens for that!'

He groaned and rocked himself back into a ball, facing against the wall again. He seemed almost sick. Posie came closer. She felt terribly and unaccountably sorry for the man.

'Tell me, is there anything I can do? Or get you?'

'No, but thank you. I'll get along to the studio in a minute.'

'I hope you don't think I'm prying,' she continued, while she still had the nerve, 'but it must be terribly difficult working here, for Mr Langley, bearing in mind your past history. It must be an awful strain.'

Tom Moran sat up again, looking wretched.

'What do you mean?' he half-whispered. 'What do you mean "my past history"?'

'The whole Mark Paris thing. I know you were him. But don't worry. Only a couple of us know, and it's more than our jobs are worth to reveal your true identity.'

'Ah.' Tom Moran reached into the drawer in the cabinet by the side of his bed. Shook out a thin navy packet of foreign cigarettes from what seemed a lot of other apparatus. He offered one to Posie and, on her refusal, lit one for himself. He took a deep drag.

'I thought you meant where I had been since 1917.'

'Pardon?'

'Well, I told you I lost my face in the war; you can see that for yourself. If you looked for long enough, you'd see I shake, too. Shake like the devil: can't even hold a knife and fork very well anymore. I take medication of course, for that and for the pain. But what you *can't* see is that I lost my wits too. I was in a hospital for men who'd lost their minds. Until fairly recently, actually. I discharged myself from there about three months back.'

'Gracious. Poor you. That must have been awful.'

Tom Moran shrugged and took another drag. 'It was. It was Silvia's idea that I come back to what I know best: work in some capacity on a film set. Brian set it all up of course, when she asked. Better than sitting at home alone all day, twiddling my thumbs, isn't it?'

'You took on a new identity?'

'Yes. Wouldn't you have done in my position? It was sloppy, really. I didn't think too much about it. I saw a name on a gravestone and thought it would do when I first arrived here. The thing I've realised is that when you're quite a lowly minion in a film crew, no-one really pays you that much notice. And no-one wants to look me in the face anyhow. So no-one guessed at who I was. Or who I *used* to be.'

'Golly!'

'So, yes: it's tough. But not more than working elsewhere. The after-effects of war cling to many men I know. We can't move on. Even if you can't imagine it, Miss Parker.'

Posie was on the verge of confessing that her first fiancé, Harry, and her brother, Richard, had both been casualties of the Great War, their lives cut short in all that unspeakable horror, their hopes and loves and dreams untold, when she stopped herself. It was a confidence too far.

She nodded respectfully. 'I'll leave you, Mr Moran. You must be desperate to get downstairs to Miss Hanro now. But just quickly, can you tell me, staying in the room next door, did you see Miss Elaine Dickinson last night at all? Or Mr Langley, leaving her room?'

Tom Moran screwed his one good eye up in surprise. 'Elaine? Silvia's woman? They're saying it was her lying dead in that room. Is that right?'

Posie nodded.

Tom shrugged. 'No, I didn't see her. But I'd taken a good deal of medication last night, slept like the dead. She was always as quiet as the proverbial church mouse, although a good deal mousier, wouldn't you say?'

'Mnnn, maybe. But I don't like to talk ill of the dead.'

Tom Moran smiled a watery sort of smile. 'No. Neither do I, mostly. I'm sorry, but my nerves are pretty frayed today.'

'Understandably.' And Posie bowed out of the room.

* * * *

Downstairs, the glass corridor was still packed with Scotland Yard's finest, including Dr Poots, who was talking excitedly to a blonde man with a shock of leonine hair. He was obviously junior to Dr Poots, but medical nonetheless.

Out of the corner of her eye Posie saw smartly-dressed caterers in green livery, and men with what looked like hundreds of silver balloons, thronging through the main hall and foyer. The death of the lowly dresser and the macabre circus of death that followed in its wake was a mere side-show to the main event, the Wrap Party.

But even here, in the corridor with the only-just-removed corpse, there was already a jovial feeling. Not celebratory, exactly, but light-hearted, for sure. A tangible feeling of relief was hanging in the air.

Posie felt slightly sick in her stomach: did Elaine's strange death not mean anything to anyone? Did anyone have anything nice to say about her?

Opening the door to the Green Room, Posie saw a buzzing confusion of people within: Dolly, Mrs Thynne, and both Sergeants Binny and Rainbird were swarming around the Chief Inspector, all trying to get his attention. Satisfied that Dolly was staying put, Posie stepped out again, her thoughts a swirling mass of contradictions.

I need my own room here, she thought desperately. *A place to think clearly.*

As if he had read her mind, Constable McCrae, accompanying a small, almost transparent-looking man in his mid-thirties, stopped suddenly in front of Posie.

'We were told we could use the props room, here, Miss. You want it?'

Constable McCrae opened the door of the room next to the Green Room.

'I'll tell the Chief Inspector you're in here, shall I? I think there's a wee table and chairs inside. Shall I get you a coffee, Miss? You look fair wiped out, or ill, if you don't mind my saying so. Definitely off-colour. Green about the gills.'

Posie sighed, her mind made up that the silver-blonde hair colour was doing her no favours, except in Brian Langley's mind, which didn't count for much. But she nodded eagerly at the offer of the room and the coffee.

Inside, the props room was small and dark and packed

to the gunnels. It was also airless. But the privacy was very welcome, just the same. Its plimsoll-rubbery scent reminded Posie unaccountably and comfortingly of the changing rooms she had been ushered through as a small girl on visits to her brother Richard's schools, on her way to admire hard-won cups for cricket, stored in ridiculously out-of-the-way trophy rooms.

She sunk down at a very small and rickety desk, which had a mis-matched white-painted chair beside it. She sat with her head in her hands.

Posie was overjoyed that Silvia Hanro had arrived back at Worton Hall safe and sound. But that was just the start of it. The start of *everything*. Everything which could now go wrong.

What on earth was going to happen at the Wrap Party? Posie was pretty convinced that Elaine Dickinson's death, and her apparent role as the person sending death threats were just too convenient a distraction. How on earth could Lovelace be so unquestioning of what was potentially a murder and falsely-placed evidence?

Posie had never really clashed with the Chief Inspector before. Once, on one case, she had found his conduct surprising, and a little wanting. But that was with the benefit of hindsight, which everyone knew was a wonderful thing. He was truly an excellent detective, deserving of his accolades and plumes, and he was usually spot-on.

Posie drummed her fingers lightly on the table, her mind racing. She wanted to get the party over and go home; leave the world of movies and movie stars and carefully choreographed secrets behind her. There were secrets here aplenty, papered over with the thinnest of thin coverings. And the war, that most awful shadow of them all, seemed to loom largely over nearly everything. Even here.

There was a knock at the door.

'Come in.'

Sergeant Rainbird popped his head around the door

and grinned. 'This your new headquarters, Miss Parker?' he joked. 'A broom cupboard? Rent got too much at Grape Street, has it?'

'Ha. Ha. Very droll. The Inspector wants me?'

'Nope. *I* do. You were right. That hunch you had.'

Rainbird held out a large brown envelope to Posie, who gulped and swallowed down a strange feeling of excitement and dread at the same time.

She had entertained this notion earlier that morning, but not fully believed in it until now.

'Oh. Goodness me. *Now* I'm finally beginning to understand. And it wasn't a hunch, Sergeant. It was rather a pathetic little stab in the dark because I had nothing else to go on.'

'A good stab, anyhow,' said Rainbird, smiling. 'So now what do you want us to do?'

But Posie was miles away, staring at two of the things she had shaken out of the envelope onto the tiny desk. Both were of orange-coloured hues. The first was a very damp dress, the same apricot-coloured dress she had seen a girl wear the night before, out on the Aldwych, which Sergeant Rainbird had picked up off the floor in Tom Moran's flat at the Albany.

And the second was a ripped but almost-intact orange form, with an inky carbon counterpart below it. The perfect match for the tiny sliver she had found in Silvia's apartments here at Worton Hall. It was also identical to the forms Posie had collected from Camden Registry for herself and Alaric back in January.

This particular form was from Westminster Registry Office and it was a licence for a marriage to take place on a given date. It had been granted on Monday. And the actual date for the marriage to take place on was the day before, on Wednesday 25th July at nine-thirty in the morning.

It granted a marriage to take place between Silvia Hanro and Mark Paris.

Silvia's mysterious appointment which Brian Langley had raged about yesterday, and why Silvia had missed her early filming slot yesterday morning were now explained. She had gone to get married, instead.

It all made sense.

* * * *

Twenty-Seven

Posie snapped into action. 'Will you help me, Sergeant?'

'What do you need me to do?' asked Rainbird, his joking manner now completely gone.

'Can you go and telephone for me? But use Mr Samuelson's office upstairs, the line is secure, not like in that foyer along there. *You* have the authority: *I* don't. Call Westminster Registry Office and find out if the marriage really did take place, and if so, fetch me Silvia Hanro. She's filming just now out in that dark studio at the back. Don't tell her a word of what we know.'

'Will do. By the way, the Chief has just finished with Elaine's brother; this Joe Dickinson fella, the Funeral Director. He's confirmed the body is his sister. It's still here, by the way, in a mortuary van out front: Poots seems to be running a few more tests, actually. He's called some specialist crony in. Oh, and Joe says that it *was* Elaine's writing on those cards, and she did use green ink normally.'

'And the finger?'

'Yes: she did ask for a finger to be sent to her here at the studios.'

The Sergeant made a loopy sign to indicate that the girl obviously wasn't quite the ticket.

'Joe Dickinson admits his role in that. Of course, action

will have to be taken against him for contravening health and safety rules and breaking a whole gamut of other funeral industry rules. Apparently it was received by Elaine on Monday, a courier delivered it. So she seems to have pre-meditated the whole thing: obviously she kept the finger on ice until yesterday. Seems the whole thing was planned out. The Inspector's more convinced than ever this is a case of a fan gone wild.'

'Really? So straightforward?'

'You don't think so, Miss?'

Posie shrugged non-committally. 'Is anyone checking her room? The drugs I found up there?'

'Yep. Just more fuel for the fire, we think.'

'Fine.'

But it *wasn't* fine. Posie stood at the door and watched Rainbird's retreating back in a sort of blind panic. Some of the puzzle pieces were coming together, but not all. And what was missing was the most dangerous part of all. She felt a terrible sense of foreboding.

Just then Posie saw the thin, colourless man from earlier drift listlessly along the corridor on his own, a dim shadow of a man, whose thin sweaty suit hung off him like a sheet. He seemed to be in a world of his own, tottering along in a brittle, tragic manner.

'Mr Dickinson?' she called out, almost certain that the man was Elaine's brother, the Funeral Director. She leant against the door frame of the props room.

He turned and gave her a look full of sadness, but it was full of awe and respect, too.

'Yes? Who are you, Miss? Do I know you? Are you one of the actresses here?'

Posie shook her head. 'No. I'm just frightfully sorry for your loss, that's all.'

'Did you know my sister?' The man sounded eager.

'Not well, no. I'm part of the investigation into Elaine's death. I'm not going to ask you anything the police haven't already, but I wondered something…'

'What?' Joe Dickinson came nearer, and up close Posie could see he was extraordinarily like his now-dead sister, save for the long frizzy hair. Posie cocked her head, tried to look as if she was going to keep anything he said confidential.

'I'm wondering if your sister was happy, Mr Dickinson?'

The brother nodded quickly. 'She was, Miss. She *was* happy. In fact, she was a changed girl. She was stepping out with a fella from here, and she told me all her dreams had come true. They had even spoken about getting married. So, you see, she wasn't very likely to kill herself, if that's what you mean.'

'Ah. I see.' Posie nodded reassuringly, although this was all news to her. 'And you never met this gentleman?'

Joe shook his head. 'To be honest I was never much up here. It's not my world. But Elaine loved it all. It was all she had. You could barely get her away. If we met it was for a quick sandwich at that pub down the road. She almost never came into Richmond, or went up to town: maybe once a year for Christmas shopping. But I think she bought everything from magazines, from those order companies who deliver.'

'So as far as you're aware Elaine wasn't in Richmond last night, about eight o'clock?'

The man shook his head. 'Why?'

Posie ignored him. 'And she didn't ask *you* to send some telegrams for her from Richmond Post Office last night?'

The man looked dumbfounded and shook his head again.

'And you don't know if she had any other friends who might have done that for her?'

The man looked sad. 'As far as I know she didn't have any other friends. Not any out of this place, anyhow. It's a sad thing to say but my sister was never popular. And she was a loner. Well, I am, too. But it doesn't matter much in my line of work, does it? Is that all, Miss?'

Posie summoned all of her courage, not wanting to knock the man when he was already down, but she had to know the truth.

'I'm sorry to ask, but did your sister indulge in drug taking at all?'

'Drugs?' The man looked crestfallen, as if his last certainty had been taken away. 'Nobody mentioned anything of that sort!' In fact, he began to look outraged.

'It's just a line of enquiry, sir.'

'Well, take it from me, my sister would never even take a Beechams pill for a headache unless she was at death's door. She had a fear of anything she termed "unnatural". So, the answer is "no". No drug taking. Absolutely not.'

The man walked off sullenly, and Posie bit her lip, sensitive to his pain. Sergeant Rainbird almost collided with him as he hared along to Posie at breakneck speed. He gave an elaborate thumbs-up sign.

'Yes. It *did* take place. All signed and sealed and married. Yesterday morning. They just dragged two witnesses in off the street, apparently. No-one else was present. Helpful?'

'Very.'

'Miss Hanro will be with you in a few minutes. She said by ten thirty, for certain.'

'Fine. I'll stay in here for a bit. Can you make sure that Lady Cardigeon stays put, too? And if she shows any signs of wandering, come and get me?'

'Of course.'

Posie turned and noticed that some wag had pinned a scrap of paper to the props room door saying:

POSIE PARKER
– ON LOAN FROM GRAPE STREET.
KNOCK AND COME ON IN!

Without bothering to take it down, Posie disappeared inside and paced backwards and forwards. She was irritated and angry, but above all, scared. Several events and reactions she had not comprehended before could now be explained. But it was all simply background information which she should have been supplied with in the first place, to make her job easier.

Why were the very people at the centre of this strange case going to such elaborate lengths to conceal things? She was sure Silvia Hanro wasn't sending herself death threats, in some mad attempt at publicity, but Posie had to face the fact that she couldn't really trust the girl. And didn't like her much, now, either. Not even a bit.

There was a loud rapping at the door. She puffed aloud, desperate for some thinking space, minding the intrusion.

'Come in.' *If you must.*

She nearly fell off the rickety white chair in surprise as a citrus musk crowded the room. It was the last person she had been expecting.

It was Robbie Fontaine.

****

The film star was still wearing full make-up and his Henry the Eighth beard, but had obviously changed and was now dressed in his own immaculate white tennis clothes. He was looking much calmer than earlier that morning.

He kicked the door shut behind him and stood, his arms folded.

At first Posie found the gesture quite threatening, but then she realised the man probably stood like this normally, when not bothering to act for people. She remembered the comments Silvia Hanro had made about the young riveter who had wrestled on the Glasgow dockside and she could imagine him as he had been twenty years before, before drugs and money took over.

'Can I help you, Mr Fontaine?' Posie had got her notebook out in a desperate attempt to look professional under the man's scrutiny.

'No,' said the movie star at last. His big golden wristwatch glinted in the gloom of the cupboard as he ran his hands through his thick black hair and fake beard. He began to pull the beard off in great chunks, wincing at the pain. Eventually he shrugged and seemed to make up his mind. 'Och, no. It's *me* who can help *you*, actually.'

'Oh?'

'I've come to apologise for my behaviour towards you. Yesterday, I mean. I meant to come first thing but we've been filming this last take until it was perfect. You know how Langley is...'

This unexpected gesture demanded a seat, and Posie looked around quickly, fearing the man might bolt otherwise. A bashed-up stool which had once been painted gold with seashells stuck all over it was the only choice. She pulled it out and offered it. Fontaine took the seat wordlessly.

'I'd light a cigar but it's so darned airless in here,' he said, looking about curiously. His gaze rested on Posie's face and he lifted a famous eyebrow.

'Nice hair, by the way. You look like a wee American doll.'

'Thank you.' She flushed. 'Is that a good thing?'

'Aye.'

Feeling wrong-footed, Posie got up, turned and fiddled with a long, hooked pole designed for opening the one tiny window, high up in the room. She didn't feel like a doll at all, American or otherwise. She felt hot, and bothered, and like she was in over her head. She struggled with the pole and at last she got the window open.

'Guess you can smoke now, Mr Fontaine.'

He nodded and took out a cigar tin. 'You know, from behind, you're an exact double for Silvia? With that new hair, I mean.'

'Mnnn. You were saying, before?'

'I was rude to you yesterday, Miss Parker. It was inexcusable. I know you're a smart wee cookie, and I guess I was afraid.'

Posie frowned, remembering the way the movie star hadn't wanted to speak to her at all; how he had even seemed to avoid eye contact with her, as if he was guilty of something or other.

Yes. That was it. *Guilt*.

'Afraid of what, exactly, Mr Fontaine? Smart women?'

'I'd be in trouble then, Miss Parker. I'm surrounded by wee smart women. I love them, too. Wouldn't have it any other way.'

The man laughed a great bear-like belly laugh, and Posie realised it was the most genuine, attractive thing about him.

Posie had given up any thoughts of taking notes, and simply flicked the pages of her notebook nervily. It fell open on the page where she had scribbled 'HATE' and 'LOVE' and 'MONEY' on the previous day. She snapped it shut quickly, before Robbie Fontaine saw anything.

'Are you trying to tell me you had something to do with the death threats to Silvia Hanro, your, er…your co-star? Is that why you were afraid? You thought I'd find you out?'

'No,' Robbie said, carefully. 'But I think you know that, otherwise you'd have questioned me by now. Although I'm pretty certain you know a whole lot more about me and Miss Silvia Hanro than you're supposed to. Isn't that the case, Miss Parker?'

'About your relationship, you mean?'

'Aye.'

Posie nodded, non-committal. 'I might know about it. Yes.'

The man splayed his hands. 'Well, even if you know nothing about movies, as you don't seem to, you'll have realised by now that she is much the bigger star. *I* ride on her coat tails. If she died, my career would die, too. I don't like the lass one wee bit but I don't want to kill her. I need her too much. So why would I send her death threats?'

'That's what I thought. But why don't you like her?'

Robbie Fontaine snorted and shrugged. 'Well, apart from the fact that she's a terrible wee snob, and never lets me forget where I'm from, she shows me up. She's the lassie who's always perfect: always on time, always knows her lines, always gets things right first time. She's too perfect. It's all show.'

Posie could see the man was a good deal stirred up.

'A show?'

'Aye. In addition to *our* pretend relationship, which is bad enough, everything that girl does is a lie. She's a hypocrite.'

Posie thought for a second that Fontaine knew about the child, Hilda, but he resumed bitterly:

'Take that fella of hers, Tom. Mark, as *was* – for I'm sure you know that, too – well, he's had it tough, poor devil. And he's a first-rate chap, but nothing can be as tough as being in a relationship with someone who doesn't love you.'

'I'll just call him Tom to make it simpler. So you're saying Silvia doesn't love Tom? How come?'

'Maybe she did *once*. But we were all different back then, weren't we, before the war? No: she doesn't love Tom. Not that she can leave him, mind. She's got staying power, I'll give her that. Obviously she feels she's got to stick by him.'

'How do you know all of this?'

Fontaine made a choking sound. 'I have the suite next to hers, don't I? Upstairs? The walls are paper thin in this place, everywhere: you can hear everything. In three months all I've heard from that room is them acting like polite, perfect strangers towards each other.'

'Maybe they knew you were listening in? Maybe they went to *his* room?'

'Maybe. But Silvia and I, we dance this crazy tune together: you don't spent hours every day with someone and not know what's preying on their mind.'

'And what's on hers?'

Fontaine looked at Posie as if she might be stupid. 'Why, I thought someone with your skills would have realised – *our esteemed Producer* is on her mind. She's been madly in love with old Brian Langley for years. God knows why. You should see the way her eyes follow him about, like she's haunted by him or something. I think they must have had something between them once, and she's not forgotten it. I'd guess that she was going to leave Tom for Brian Langley, but then Tom got cut up the way he did in the war. She couldn't exactly leave him *then*, could she?'

Posie stared. 'And does Mr Langley reciprocate her feelings?'

'No,' said Fontaine, putting out his cigar. '*Professionally* she brings in wads of money for him, but on a personal level he hates her. I don't know why but he can't stand to be in the same room as her. It's like she's committed some awful crime. Like she stinks or something.'

'Ah.'

'Complicated, eh?'

'A bit messy. But I still don't see why you were apologising to me.'

Robbie Fontaine looked at Posie full on. He took a deep breath. 'I think you know a good deal of what's going on here, Miss Parker, and that includes knowing about my addiction. Yes?'

'I had heard rumours. Yes.'

'You can't repeat this to your policeman friend who fancies you next door, promise me.'

'What?'

'The Chief Inspector.'

Posie paused, then swallowed. She flushed. 'I promise.'

'You know that every addict needs a good dealer? Especially an addict who is as famous as me. What I need, and what I pay handsomely for, is *discretion*.'

'I'm not really following you…'

'I have a dealer. His name is Johnnie Roslington and he lives in a flat in the Burlington Arcade. He's top-drawer, a man of international business, but his real line is in cocaine. I see him personally about once a month, and in between times I get Sidney, my runner, to go to the Burlington Arcade and collect parcels of the stuff for me.'

'And?'

'Yesterday, when Langley ordered me to fetch you in town, like some common errand boy, I was angry: Silvia had disappeared off somewhere earlier, ruining the schedule, and yet it was *me* who was doing all the running around. I'd been ordered not to call you or leave any trace, but I wasn't going to waste my time on a fool's errand, especially if you weren't even in London. You could have been off at the sea like everyone else at the moment, on holiday…'

'You decided to call ahead at my office?'

'That's right. Just to check it was worth my while coming out. And then, the next thing I know, just as I'm leaving, is that an urgent telephone call has come for me, here. And it's Johnnie Roslington, my dealer, on the line.'

'And?'

'He said he knew I was going to meet you, and that he'd been wanting to meet you now for quite a while about a big job, but that it was important he wasn't seen entering your offices, as people might get the wrong idea. Or he might get photographed.'

Posie scowled.

'He told me to collect you and bring you back here to Worton Hall where he'd come and have a chat with you. He said to get parked up, and then to leave you alone. He'd jump in the back seat. I was surprised when he didn't show up. He's normally a man of his word.'

'That was why you were so nervy the whole time?'

'Aye.'

Posie stared. She felt like nothing was quite real anymore, and a horrible tiny doubt had entered her mind. *Was Johnnie Roslington actually Caspian della Rosa, in disguise?*

Caspian della Rosa: her nemesis, the man who had not been seen on British shores since New Year's night, 1921, who had somehow managed to escape the clutches of the police on all continents. But it was unthinkable that he could have re-entered England without being found out: every port, harbour and airfield had strict instructions to detain the man under arrest until Scotland Yard arrived.

But Posie knew that Caspian della Rosa was a chameleon, with a vast international network of connections and untold, unspeakable riches stacked up behind him. And until fairly recently, somehow, he had wanted Posie all for his own.

She suppressed a shiver.

How else could she explain the mechanics of how Johnnie Roslington had known that Robbie Fontaine had been going to meet her, unless this same Johnnie Roslington had been listening in on calls made to and from her office on Grape Street?

'What's he like, this Mr Roslington?'

'To look at? He's tall, thin, dark. Good-looking, I suppose. Easy on the eye. Wears fancy tailored clothes and tweeds. Very English.'

Posie breathed a huge sigh of relief.

Caspian della Rosa, while very good at acting and disguises, was short, tubby and not at all good-looking, and such attributes couldn't really be faked. The only jarring note now was the phone being intercepted, but hopefully Len was sorting that all out.

'Thank you for telling me, Mr Fontaine. I'm sure it's nothing to worry about. Please tell Mr Roslington I am at his service, when and however he wishes to meet me.'

'I will do,' said Fontaine, rising. 'I felt a rat, that's all; like I was selling you for a thousand pieces of silver. It all seemed peculiar to me but I couldn't really *not* do as he said. I'm in debt to Roslington, you see. In a big way. And he could expose me as being a drug addict at any time: it's a big power he wields over me. Fortunately, I have my Sheila.'

He smiled sadly. 'It's my Sheila who bails me out, time and time again. When I've got through the pay packet at the end of the month. I don't know how she does it, but she does. I think you've met my wife, haven't you?'

'No,' Posie said, shaking her head.

Sergeant Rainbird knocked. 'Can you come next door when you have a second, Miss? It's about Elaine Dickinson, of course.'

He vanished, looking harried.

'A bad business, this,' said Robbie Fontaine, sighing.

'Did you know her, then? Elaine? I'd heard she was a big fan of yours. She didn't stalk *you*?'

Robbie shook his head. 'She never bothered me. Asked for autographs and photographs a good few times, but she was a nice polite lass, I always thought. Now they're saying she sent those awful letters to Silvia and topped herself out of remorse. Poor kid. It's not for everyone, this business. That's why I'm getting out.'

'How so, sir?'

'This is highly confidential, so don't repeat it, but after this film is done I'm quitting. I've had enough. I owe it to myself and to Sheila to make a new start. Maybe have some kiddies before it's too late. Maybe I'll do what Tom Moran did, and take another name.'

'I thought you were contracted for the next three years to Sunstar?'

Robbie Fontaine chortled.

'Yes, legally I am. But after this film premiers there won't even *be* a Sunstar Films company anymore. The good old days are gone, even if others pretend they haven't. Brian Langley is on the brink of bankruptcy and nothing will save him. Every fool knows that America, Hollywood really, is what people want. They don't want a crummy little film made at Isleworth anymore! This Wrap Party is the end. Langley won't even make back the costs of filming. Even if both Silvia and I died together today, the insurance he has on both of our lives wouldn't cover much of his outlay.'

Posie tried to disguise her sharp intake of breath. 'How do you know this? About the insurance, I mean? You've seen the documents?'

Robbie Fontaine tapped his nose authoritatively. 'No,' he said. 'But someone I trust has. I have my sources,' he said, smiling. 'Same as I know that although he's supposed to have given up all of his firearms after the war, Brian Langley kept his wartime revolver: a silver-coloured Webley. A Mark IV. Kept it out of sentiment.'

'Golly.'

'And I tell you what,' Robbie Fontaine said, his smile now gone. 'I have to say that *I* thought it was old Langley making those death threats himself: I thought he might go as far as having Silvia Hanro and myself killed on the same day, for the money. I can't tell you how relieved I am to hear it was all down to poor little Elaine. I was even thinking of doing a bunk today, I was that afraid. Now I'll attend, of course.'

They stepped out together and the movie star sauntered off, his big form taking up most of the corridor, his cloud of citrus ebbing away, the policemen from Richmond stepping away from him in awe as he moved.

Posie was thinking through everything Robbie Fontaine had just told her when she saw Silvia Hanro herself, still dressed in her ridiculous Anne Boleyn costume, hurry down the corridor.

'Sorry, Posie,' she called, full of nervous energy. 'Got held up at the studio. Now, what did you want me for?'

Posie asked her to wait in the little props cupboard for a minute and dashed into the Green Room where a heated argument seemed to be going on.

****

Twenty-Eight

'What's going on here?'

Posie noted in a split-second that Dolly was still in situ, idly flicking through a magazine on a turquoise velvet couch, looking bored. The others, the Chief Inspector, both Sergeants, Dr Poots and the blonde man Posie had seen the Pathologist talking to in the corridor, were standing in a tight circle, obviously disagreeing about something. An elderly clock on the wall reached half-past ten, and was obviously meant to chime the half-hour, but wheezed it through instead.

Chief Inspector Lovelace looked harassed but stayed silent.

Sergeant Binny turned, slightly imploringly. '*You* didn't think it was clear-cut, the death of the dresser, did you, Miss Parker?'

'No. Why?'

Dr Poots, an unlikely ally, stared at Posie from behind his horn-rimmed spectacles for a second, as if wondering whether or not to waste his breath. He mopped at his brow. He evidently decided it was worth it:

'Speak some sense to this Inspector friend of yours, Miss Parker.'

'How so, sir?'

'I've had that body on my hands now for more than two hours. In this heat! Which is normally a bad thing, but it's helped me this time. The heat has accelerated the normal breakdown processes, and I've been able to see quite clearly – in fact, I'd stake my job on it – that the girl, Elaine Dickinson, was murdered.'

Posie gasped. 'Really?'

Dr Poots nodded. 'Really. There are now clear, livid hand marks around the girl's neck, as if she was held down. Clear as day! I'd say she was forced to drink that poison orchid concoction, by violent means, and it cost her her life. And someone intended that to be the case.'

'Was it a man, sir?'

'I couldn't tell, Miss Parker. That's the Chief Inspector's job, or should be, *if* he'd only accept my findings. All I can say is that it was someone strong and powerful.'

Posie thought briefly of Brian Langley's hands, twisted and with their long fingers, but strong, nevertheless. Unaccountably she thought too of Silvia Hanro herself, her strong physique, her big hands. She turned to Lovelace who had folded his arms angrily, a gesture she was unfamiliar with.

'You don't accept this, sir?'

'I find it unconvincing, Posie. Not evidence enough for murder. Not yet. Not until Poots here has got the body back to the mortuary for a proper post-mortem. This heat could cause any number of strange side effects in a body. I've known doctors be wrong before.'

'True.' Dr Poots nodded. 'But not me. I just think you should think about it, Lovelace. It's not my place to do your job but since being here this morning I've heard all manner of strange rumours about how this poor mite was responsible for death threats against a certain famous movie star. I'd say a good many people seem relieved: as if a danger had been averted somehow. I just think you should know that this woman may not have been that danger. She *encountered danger* herself.'

Posie nodded, grateful beyond words. The panic and fear she had been feeling since entering that dressing room filled with evil early in the morning now seemed as if they had been caught and given voice and shape. And delivered by an esteemed Police Pathologist, no less.

'Please, sir.' She nodded urgently. 'I think Dr Poots is right. You must call off this Wrap Party. At once. Make it official. Silvia Hanro is still in mortal danger.'

'That's not a given, Posie. Our evidence boys have taken away enough drugs to dope a horse with from the woman's room upstairs, and she obviously had some sort of screw loose. How else do you explain the finger and the death threats? Evidence which is clear as a bell!'

'I can't, sir.'

'Well, then. There you go. We go on. Clear this little lot up, and offer a subtle level of protection at the party. Then we leave. End of story. We can look more into the life and death of this sad girl when we get back to the Yard.'

'I hate to tell you this, Lovelace, but you're making a big mistake,' growled Dr Poots.

Posie stared over at the Chief Inspector who was looking angrier by the minute. He shook his head stubbornly and went over to a large scuffed-up table, pouring himself a hot drink from a thermos flask there, turning his back on everyone.

Posie had hardly ever seen him so rattled.

Dr Poots made exasperated noises and put his black bowler hat back on, stuffing paperwork into his large leather bag. 'I'll deliver my report later, then,' he called out in a resigned fashion. 'Sometimes I don't know why I bother. I even got a specialist in.'

'A specialist, sir?' said Posie, with interest.

Dr Poots barely looked at her, clipping his bag shut. 'Yes. This is Dr Andrew Netherton. I called him in when I saw that the girl had probably ingested plant poison. He's a specialist at Kew Gardens, close by. He specialises in poisonous plants. He's a toxicologist.'

'And? Did you find anything interesting?'

'It will all be in my report later,' said the Pathologist stiffly.

But the man with the leonine hair nodded excitedly at Posie, anxious to get his tuppence worth's in.

'I did add a minor detail. Could be significant, later. At the Coroner's Inquest.'

'Oh?'

'The original time of death was estimated at around midnight,' the blonde man nodded. 'But that type of plant poison – *digitalis*, or orchid poisoning – has a strange effect on the body after death. It delays all the usual effects by several hours: slows down rigor mortis. So we were able to deduce that Miss Dickinson, rather than dying at around midnight, had been dead for at least four hours before that – say by eight o'clock last night.'

'It will all be in my report, Miss Parker; Dr Netherton's findings too,' repeated the Pathologist moodily, swinging out, ushering his medical colleague out apologetically. But for Posie the minor detail was game-changing.

She stared hard at both Sergeants as if they were very stupid, and then across at Lovelace who was scrawling through notes in his own notebook, his back still to the room. She looked around desperately.

'Am I the only one who can see this?' she cried. 'If Elaine Dickinson was dead at eight o'clock last night then she can't possibly have been the person sending death threats, can she?'

Dolly, on the sofa, stopped flicking through another magazine and looked up thoughtfully. 'I see,' Dolly cried out at last. 'I'm with you!'

'Thank goodness! I think the heat is getting to our esteemed police force!' said Posie, roused to the point of anger.

'You mean the telegrams sent to the press, don't you?' said Dolly. 'They were sent at eight o'clock from Richmond.

But the doctor just told us that Elaine was dead then! And how can a dead girl send telegrams?'

'Exactly!' said Posie, and had the satisfaction of seeing the Inspector turn back into the room, pale and sweaty beneath his temper and his fear.

'You might have a point,' he conceded, irritably.

'I think you have to seriously consider the idea that it could be Brian Langley behind all this, sir,' Posie begged.

'We've fresh evidence that he was seen leaving Elaine's room last night, about midnight, and he could easily have killed her and then rearranged her room, making it all look like a crazy suicide. It's his job to make things look right, he said so himself. He hasn't really got an alibi for the night, either; he was just here, apparently reviewing the film so far. No-one can vouch for him specifically.'

Posie continued, more urgently now. 'I'll warrant that Brian Langley only reported Silvia missing as a smokescreen, to divert attention elsewhere. No-one else seemed worried she'd left Worton Hall, not even Tom. I also now know that Brian Langley still keeps a gun, a Webley. And that he definitely has insurance on both Silvia Hanro and Robbie Fontaine's lives. How much more evidence do you want?'

'I'll admit it's quite convincing,' said Richard Lovelace gruffly. 'What is the source of your new information?'

'Robbie Fontaine, sir.'

The Chief Inspector rolled his eyes. 'Then I'll not cancel the party.'

* * * *

'Sorry about that,' said Posie to Silvia Hanro, back in the props cupboard. The girl was sitting at Posie's desk and idly pulling out pins from an elaborate headdress she had been wearing. She took it off to reveal her own artificially-enhanced hair, the exact colour of Posie's.

Posie sat down hard on the small stool.

'I think congratulations are in order.' Posie smiled, letting the words, laden with meaning, fill the tiny space. It did the trick.

She saw the china-blue eyes of the movie star widen perceptibly. 'I'm sorry? What can you mean? I'm not sure I understand you.'

'Oh, I think you understand me just fine, Miss Hanro. I'm congratulating you on your nuptials, yesterday morning, at nine-thirty at Westminster Registry Office. When you mysteriously disappeared so that Brian Langley had to re-jig his filming schedule. Your marriage to Tom Moran, or should I say, to Mark Paris?'

The movie star stared, then flushed red, and looked down at her hands.

'How do you know this?' she whispered in a low voice.

'Oh, there's not much I don't know.' Posie smiled placidly. 'I don't want to be your judge, and I don't really give two hoots what you do, but I do wish you had told me all of this from the start. It would have made my job easier. That's the trouble with this place: literally nothing is quite as it seems. Did you think I was stupid?'

'NO! It's just…'

'*No-one* was supposed to know, is that right? I get that.'

Silvia Hanro narrowed her eyes and crossed her arms. 'You're good,' she whispered icily. 'I'll give you that. What else do you know? Or think you know?'

'A good deal.'

Posie took the opportunity to shake out the contents of Sergeant Rainbird's envelope again and the orange forms and the damp orange dress and a dark, long expensive wig, also damp, flopped out onto the desk. Silvia gasped.

'How dare you! You went into my home?'

'I thought it was *Tom's* home?'

'You know what I mean.'

'I didn't actually. The police did.'

'But you have no right! *They* have no right to!'

'They do actually: you were formally listed as a missing person, and they were looking for evidence as to where you might have been. I *saw* you, you know. On the Aldwych. Alone, on your wedding night.'

'Tell me what you know,' rapped Silvia, her knuckles white with anger.

Posie nodded calmly and listed her discoveries in chronological order: the early affair with Brian Langley; the birth of their illegitimate child in 1918 without Brian's knowledge, and Silvia's subsequently giving it away; the very recent plan to marry Tom Moran.

Silvia had gone white under the Leichner.

'You were worried when you saw that finger with its gold-foil ring, weren't you? It meant *everything* to you. Not that you bothered to tell *me* that.'

A strange calm descended on Posie and she resumed cautiously but certainly:

'You believed the threats and the finger were from Brian Langley. It was a crude but important symbolism which you immediately recognised. Why! His leading lady being married would have spelled huge trouble for Brian Langley! I expect, but I don't know, that Langley warned you it was professional suicide on Sunday, when you were outside in the woods, when he said you would marry *over his dead body*. And then the threats started up on Monday.'

Silvia Hanro didn't say a word.

'I think you probably thought it was funny at first, and then, slowly, you got a bit worried. But you kept thinking it was Brian Langley sending the notes, even when I got called in. You thought it was a warning; that was all. I expect you thought he was double-bluffing you, involving me in the case to make out he was worried! You must have thought I was someone to choreograph, a bit-part: hardly someone to explain things to properly.'

Silvia Hanro had the decency to flush red. 'I didn't think that, honestly…'

'You even threw me a couple of completely dead-end suspects, going on especially about Robbie Fontaine. And that stalker fellow. You wanted to deflect attention away from Brian Langley. Because, when all's said and done, you love him. Madly.'

'I don't have to listen to this,' said the movie star, furiously, rising. She grabbed up the envelope on the table, stuffing in the orange dress and the wig haphazardly.

'No. You don't,' agreed Posie. 'But all I'd say, Miss Hanro, is that my advice to you right now is not to go to that Wrap Party. Please don't attend. You *are* in danger, and I can't assure you you'll come away unharmed. Or even alive.'

'Don't be a fool. If you're so smart you'll know I need to do everything I can right now to hold on to my fame. Besides, Brian's already told me it was that little idiot, Elaine. So I was wrong all along, anyhow.'

'Not necessarily. Sometimes these things aren't as clear-cut as they appear at first. I think that your initial thinking may not have been that wide of the mark. I'd be jolly careful if I were you.'

Silvia dismissed Posie's words with a wave of the hand. 'You can't be serious! Brian? Brian won't touch me. Not really. Horrid letters might be one thing, but *killing*? He wouldn't touch a hair on my head.'

'Please reconsider. It might not be all bad for him and for Sunstar Films if you were to die this afternoon…'

Silvia Hanro paused at the door. 'You're wrong,' she said. 'Way off the mark. Even if you do think you understand everything, Miss Parker.'

'Oh, no,' said Posie, feeling her heart heavy in her chest, knowing her warnings were being disregarded in the most blatant of manners.

'I never said *that*. I said I *knew* everything: not that I *understood* everything. It's completely different. There's plenty I don't understand.'

'Like what?' spat Silvia Hanro.

'Why you were in such a mad hurry to marry Tom Moran *this week* – so urgently? What was the reason? You've been with him for years, and yet you only do it now! And also, if you got married yesterday, why were you going out into the small hours, disguised, in the city? You were alone, walking in the rain, without your new husband, on your wedding night. Why?'

'Confound you!' Silvia Hanro hissed. 'You think you're so clever, don't you? Who the blazes do you think you are anyhow? Coming in here and trying to look like me? I thought it was just Elaine who was a mad fan!'

But Posie didn't get a chance to answer. There was just a bang of the door and a resounding silence which carried none of the usual comfort.

Posie sighed and rubbed at her too-heavily pencilled eyes. The Wrap Party would have to be got through somehow.

Alive, preferably.

****

PART THREE

The Wrap

Twenty-Nine

The ballroom lay like an oversized bubble before them, shiny and glittering and not quite real.

Posie had only seen the place in broad daylight before, and now, at twelve noon exactly, as she stepped into it, she realised she was completely unprepared: the place was blacked out like a club, despite the bright, hot daylight outside. Dolly let out an exaggerated gasp.

'Good grief!' Inspector Lovelace muttered beside her.

Glitter-balls sparkled eerily, hung about like mistletoe, and silver balloons festooned the walls. Tiny rows of lights were lit high up in the blackness, hung from the corniced ceilings. It was very dark, save for an enormous screen which was set up at the far end of the ballroom, where a makeshift stage with a lectern was also rigged up.

The screen took up nearly a whole wall, and already, snippets from the current film *Henry the King* were playing on it, the same frames, again and again. Hypnotically.

Anguished eyes, Silvia Hanro's, of course, stared out at the room, an unspeakable horror and sadness reflected in them, and the tight, merciless smile of Robbie Fontaine, a close-up curled across the frame, splashed up over the screen again and again. These were interspersed with a couple of crowd shots, with a fairly convincing painted backdrop of what Posie supposed was meant to be the Tower of London.

Posie turned to see two men at the back of the room working the projector, both dressed all in black, replacing the loops of film hurriedly. They would be doing the same thing now for hours, over and over again, if Brian Langley wanted such a clipped, dramatic effect as a backdrop.

'This is a logistical nightmare,' Lovelace hissed in Posie's ear. 'Do you remember that club we ended up in once, the La Luna Club, underground?'

She nodded. It had not been a place for claustrophobics.

'Reminds me of that. It's like a bad dream. An ideal spot to try and kill someone in. Every corner is a possibility.'

Guests were already drifting through the doors, into the darkness within. On one glittering podium a jazz band were playing, and on others girls were dancing, all in matching silver dresses. All down one side of the room a long table was set up with Harrods food, and a bar had been created on the right-hand side, with waiters and drinks brought in especially from the Café Royal on Piccadilly. No expense had been spared. No-one could guess how badly Sunstar Films were doing, how much of this must be being paid for by Brian Langley's orchids.

Lovelace, his two Sergeants and about ten other policemen from Richmond were all wearing black tie, the Chief Inspector having insisted they remain to patrol the party, and Brian Langley having begrudgingly ordered in last-minute costumes from Nathan's, who had arrived in one of their blue-and-gold vans in a tearing hurry.

The policemen melted now seamlessly into the room, hands engaged in the usual poses of holding drinks and buffet plates and cigarettes, eyes trained on anything untoward happening in the semi-darkness.

'Just keep your eyes peeled,' warned Lovelace. 'And stick like glue to Silvia Hanro. Where is she, by the way?'

Robbie Fontaine, in an immaculate dinner suit, had

already been besieged by women, and his presence could be felt powerfully, rippling out through the room, even across the noise of the pulsing music and the darkness. Brian Langley, looking unusually pristine and handsome, was holding court near the big screen with a group of men, all identically dressed in tuxedos, and all puffing away on cigars. Posie presumed these must be the important investors he so wanted to please.

'She's there,' said Posie, with relief. Silvia Hanro was entering the room from a hidden back entrance, and all eyes were immediately on her, darting between the real-life woman and the huge black-and-white snatches of her face on the screen behind her. There was a collective intake of breath.

Silvia Hanro certainly did look quite something, dressed in a red sheath dress, her blonde bob gleaming and decorated with a matching tasselled ribbon.

Inspector Lovelace eyed the movie star keenly. 'Mnnn. Hang on a minute…'

He turned to Posie and frowned. 'Forgive my stupidity, but don't you two look just exactly the same?'

Posie gulped: it was true. In her attempts not to look so fusty and to look young, she had got out a daring red dress bought from Peter Jones on Sloane Square a few years before. It had come with a matching headdress and she had last worn the outfit back in 1921, in the days when she was still very much in love with Len, her working partner. The dress hadn't been expensive, but it had made her feel a treat, slinky and almost thin. Posie had put it away when their romance hadn't come off, fearful it would bring back bad memories. And it had languished in her wardrobe until now.

It was a miracle it still fitted her at all, and she had smiled to herself happily as she tugged up the crimson zipper.

But the Chief Inspector was right: it was an *exact* match for Silvia Hanro's red dress. Posie felt mortified.

'There's not much I can do now, is there?' she whispered crossly. Posie was aware that she looked as if she were trying to be a carbon copy of the movie star; a cheap trick if ever there was one.

'You look better in it, though, lovey,' declared Dolly, loyally, who said she felt sick and must have been telling the truth, for she hadn't bothered to change and she looked distinctly off-colour in the strange light. She wasn't even smoking. Posie had ordered that Dolly accompany them, though. There was to be no hanging around in Green Rooms alone today.

'Look who's coming in,' hissed Dolly, sounding a bit more like herself. They all swung around and saw a man entering the room, surrounded by a crowd of adoring fans. Other people looped back to get a look.

'Ivor Novello!' Lovelace murmured. They had all three seen Novello before, on stage at the La Luna Club in early 1921, playing the piano. But he had gone on to bigger and better things since then, mainly films.

'They say he'll be the greatest movie star of all!' whispered Dolly. 'And he's only just startin' out in this game!'

The man radiated presence, and looked a good deal like Mark Paris, back in the old days, only more handsome, impossibly so. Lit with an inner fire and possession, the black-haired slim man had a sparkle and glow which seemed almost unearthly. He seemed to hold all who looked at him in a hypnotic sway, his wide, sensuous mouth curled up naughtily at each corner, promising delight.

'Never mind. Get to it, Posie,' said Lovelace, breaking the spell. 'We're covering you all the way. Lady Cardigeon will stay with me.'

And Posie darted forwards just as Robbie Fontaine was planting himself at Silvia's side, both stars smiling gleefully and arching into each other as if for warmth, their mask-like faces presented to the world as a perfect dream.

Posie hung like a small shadow behind the couple as

cameras began to snap and the acid stench of flashlight filled the air.

'The press!' Posie breathed to herself fearfully. Among the swirling mass of people who were now moving about in the room, eating and drinking and dancing, the 'invited' journalists and their accompanying photographers stuck out like sore thumbs.

The journalists began to surge forwards like a plague of locusts, engulfing the couple. Eventually they stopped, forming a tight ring around the movie stars, and some men began firing off questions; mainly about whether or not the couple planned on ever getting engaged.

Posie saw Sam Stubbs, accompanied by his photographer, and she looked away, pained. Sam looked very red in the face and excited, like a child at a funfair who didn't know which ride to go on next. She thought of the telegram he had been sent about Silvia's death, which was probably right now burning a hole in one of his pockets, its contents etched firmly in his mind.

He, like his colleagues, was after much more than news about the forthcoming film or about an engagement. And they all knew it. They were prowling like hungry vultures, sniffing at the wind.

She looked about her in disgust, all the while keeping Silvia Hanro well in range.

Her senses heightened, as if the whole scene was suddenly brought into sharp relief before her for the first time, Posie saw that the group of investors had now broken up and that Brian Langley had gone.

She saw too that many people were peeling back, allowing a dance floor to take shape over near the screen, and in the very centre of it, under the glittering spotlights, dancing like a banshee, alone, was the figure of Meggie Albanesi. She was utterly lost in a world of her own.

Scanning the faces of the shadowy people watching the girl, Posie gave a sudden start, for there was Hector Mallow.

He had got in after all, and the expression of his face as he watched his prey was enough to turn a girl's stomach. It was quite revolting.

'Confound the man.'

And there too, under another dip and turn of a light, was a glimpse of a vivid flamingo-pink kimono sleeve. A kimono which Posie had seen the evening before; a dress probably made especially for tonight, which had been given a trial-run at home the evening before.

Here was Pamela Hanro, trying too hard, holding aloft a drink in one hand, her dark hair scraped back brutally and her face made up heavily in the fashion of an ancient Egyptian queen; violent pink hoops, big as fists, dangling daringly from either ear.

So Pamela couldn't be bothered to explain that she would be attending this Wrap Party at which her estranged sister is the star-turn, thought Posie wryly to herself.

Why was Pamela here? For what exactly?

Pamela was standing next to a tall man in the shadows, and she seemed to be hanging on to every word that he was saying, trying to keep his attention. Her rapt eyes never left his face. But the man hardly seemed to know she was there.

And then the tall man leant in to her at last and Pamela beamed. And when he turned from Pamela to watch the dancing Meggie Albanesi, Posie saw with some distaste that the man was Brian Langley.

She loves him, Posie realised with a jolt. *How complicated.*

Brain Langley had forgotten all about Pamela by now, that much was obvious, and Pamela knew it. The Producer was grinning broadly; obviously eyeing up his next box-office star, pleased with what he saw. Pamela was the invited but unwanted party guest, hopelessly uncool. It was as if she had been thrown a crumb of Brian Langley's favour. She stood slightly apart, humbled.

An investor was suddenly at Langley's side, pointing

to the whirling Meggie Albanesi in an animated fashion. Both men turned their backs on Pamela in her shockingly pink dress and laughed appreciatively.

Posie saw Pamela's defeated gaze move on from Miss Albanesi, straight on to her own sister who was still fawning for various photographs. Pamela's eyes lingered on Silvia for a few seconds, but her face appeared unconcerned. Her gaze then wandered off casually, listlessly, across the room. For something to do.

Suddenly Pamela's eyes widened in something like horror or astonishment and her mouth opened in what must have been a silent scream.

Posie followed Pamela's gaze behind where she herself was standing, but only managed to see a mass of people getting food or drinks, or turning inwards into the room, all of them dark as shadows.

She just made out the cook, Mrs Thynne, carrying an empty punchbowl, her face like thunder, followed closely by a woman in a navy hat-Mrs Cleeves-who also seemed to be carrying away something of a culinary nature; dirty plates, maybe.

Tom Moran, wearing an unexpected black hat set at a rakish angle, which covered most of his face, followed the two women and skirted around the dance floor. He came up to Pamela Hanro and embraced her. And although Posie couldn't hear the words, it seemed as if the two were meeting genuinely again for the first time, not as if they had argued bitterly earlier in the week outside the Green Room. They hugged each other for a good long while.

Although, as she watched, Posie saw that Pamela kept looking urgently around the room, nervily, past Tom's shoulder. And past Silvia, whom she almost ignored. Pamela was like a woman possessed, and an angry fire had lit up her gaunt, plain features.

This is a roll-call of every last one of the people who could possibly want Silvia dead, Posie thought to herself dismally.

And this is the worst possible sort of occasion at which they could all assemble.

The crowds, the darkness, the flickering lights, the press…

Just what had the Chief Inspector been thinking of? Allowing it all to proceed?

'The deuce!' Posie muttered, noting that the photos and press attention now seemed to have come to an end. She was filled with a dreadful sense of the inevitable.

The movie stars were hissing at each other in well-practiced undertones. Posie drew closer to listen in:

'Brian said twelve-thirty. Not a minute later.'

'He's busy. Can't you see that? With the money men…'

'He'll expect us up on that podium now, with him, to speak about the film. You know it always runs like clockwork with him.'

'Och, relax a wee bit, won't you? A minute earlier or later is no big deal. He hasn't given us the sign yet, has he?'

'Confound you and your relaxed ways. Who needs a sign? Let's move over to the podium now. I want to shake this wretched limpet of a detective off me, too. Dreadful girl: have you seen what she looks like today? Just like *me*.'

Robbie Fontaine chortled with mirth. 'She's done quite a good job of looking like you,though, hasn't she? A proper wee stunner there, and no mistake. You're only jealous of that!'

'As if! Now, hold me close and let's move. Closer, Robbie. But don't crush my orchid spray, you fool.'

'*Where is* Brian?'

And at Robbie Fontaine's question, Posie found herself looking around again sharply in the dipping, nightclub-esque lights. The three of them started to move towards the screen, to the podium, Posie bringing up the rear, twisting her head all around.

Going up the steps of the small stage with its wavering backdrop of the film images, Posie caught sight of Brian Langley. He was still with the investor, in front of Pamela

Hanro, talking seriously. He had caught sight of his two main actors and looked as if he were trying to finish up the conversation. He looked over and nodded at Posie.

And then the lights, mad and crazy and insufficient though they were, went out completely.

And somebody screamed in the pitch-blackness.

* * * *

Thirty

There was a whizzing, jolting noise. A man shouted aloud:

'What is *this*, now?'

The lights came on again, but just for a second or so. It was enough for Posie to see, as if in one of the movie freeze-frames which had now stopped playing, that Brian Langley was still standing exactly where he had been, arms outstretched in front of him, one of his hands clutching at a silver revolver.

Could it be this simple? The Webley?

Posie turned and saw that the Chief Inspector and his trusty Constable, McCrae, were moving right into Brian Langley's line of fire.

The lights went off again. The darkness was terrible.

'Everybody get down! This is a police command!' Inspector Lovelace was shouting through the darkness.

A woman screamed again. Just then a terrible sound of gunshots started up, a staccato sound echoing around the enclosed space, and Posie heard a man shout out. She could have sworn it was Tom Moran:

'Stop it, you fool. You're not in the trenches now, are you?'

'Get down!' Posie hissed at the two movie stars ahead of her in the blackness. She pulled at Silvia Hanro's red dress and heard a ripping noise and felt the girl wobble and fall.

Posie was on all fours in the darkness on the podium, behind Silvia, breathing shallowly, trying not to panic more than she was already, when suddenly she felt a hot whizzing breath of a thing sizzle past her left ear, burning its way through her thick chemical-smelling hair and right through her crimson headdress. She didn't have time to scream.

The bullet went on, leaving her more or less intact.

Up ahead came an impossibly heavy thump, a dull falling sound.

'Robbie?'

Silvia Hanro was whispering. Then screaming:

'*Robbie?*'

Brilliant light suddenly flooded the room as someone with a smidgen of sense had realised that they could quite simply pull down all the black-out blinds and end the chaos without fixing the electricity. It was a summer's day outside, after all.

A reassuringly authoritative command pierced the suddenly-illuminated chaos:

'Everybody out! Out now! Through the French doors. A danger is still among us.'

And in that split-second of brightness Posie saw Robbie Fontaine up ahead of her on the podium, on the spangled gold sheet. Blood surrounded him.

He was dead.

His body was twisted and lifeless, his eyes were half-closed and a look of genuine surprise was etched on his handsome face.

And then she saw it: the back of Robbie Fontaine's head was gone where the bullet had hit him. Silvia Hanro was holding onto his arms, cradling him, pulling at him, as if there was a thread of hope left for him. Dark blood was everywhere, all up her arms and neck and seeping through the front of her red frock.

Posie looked about her, trying not to shake. Down on the dance floor two hundred people were climbing over each other in an effort to escape, like rats from a sinking ship, while a meagre crowd was gathered in the centre of the room where another body was lying.

Who was it?

Posie looked about her in panic. *Where was the Inspector?*

Tom Moran was suddenly beside them on the podium, on his knees, trembling violently, jolts going right through his body. Silvia clung to Robbie, frozen somehow. She seemed to barely register Tom's presence. She looked at him with unseeing eyes.

'Are you all right, my darling?' he was whispering at Silvia urgently, making a visible effort not to reach out and touch her; to keep in character, even now, as someone who didn't know her and love her, who wasn't her real-life husband.

'I'm here, Silvia, my love. It will be all right.'

Posie almost did a double take as she realised that Tom had lost his hat and his eyepatch and his blue glasses in all the chaos and his exposed face, lacking its eye and nose and cheek, was raw in the stark sunshine, and almost as gruesome as the back of Robbie Fontaine's head. Posie tried not to stare.

A woman was screaming shrilly from the group by the body on the dance floor, in a fit of panic, the same words, over and over again:

'*That* woman! That woman! She ruined my life!'

Posie stared. It was Pamela Hanro.

She was standing rooted to the spot, crying and shaking. Posie thought that Pamela must be referring to Silvia, and then she noticed that Pamela was held tightly on either side by men in black tie, presumably policemen.

A couple of seconds later, Chief Inspector Lovelace, recognisable by his rusty-red hair, had joined the group in the centre, where he muttered something inaudible to

Pamela, showed her something in his hand – something which seemed metallic – and nodded brusquely at the two policemen.

There was a glimmer of handcuffs as they were clamped into place on Pamela's wrists. The Chief Inspector looked very sombre.

Lovelace was shouting again at the crowds: 'Everybody out. Now. No point hanging around in here. We have contained the danger and we need you outside.'

To his men, Posie heard Lovelace utter the words 'Langley,' and 'Grape Street,' and 'place of safety for the actress.'

And then Pamela was led away.

Silvia Hanro was staring over at her sister's retreating back, her mouth open in complete surprise. Tom Moran had melted away in the confusion, presumably anxious not to be seen with Silvia.

'What in heaven's name? What on earth is *she* doing here? Is she the one who fired the shots? Has my sister just been *arrested*? Again?'

Posie was about to reply that she simply had no idea anymore, when the movie star seemed to recover herself, and, looking down at the body she was cradling in her arms, and the pooling blood, she stared across at Posie in a sort of stupefied horror.

'What is Sheila going to do?' Silvia hissed fearfully. 'She *lived* for Robbie. She loved him beyond anything. What will I tell her? This is all *my* fault, isn't it?'

Posie sat, uncomprehending: 'Sheila?'

And just then the swirling mass of journalists, their senses sharpened to the scent of calamity, seemed to converge in a swell up the steps to the podium.

'It's murder!'

Silvia Hanro froze, cat-like, her huge eyes blinking, still holding on to Robbie Fontaine as if she couldn't move. The crowd of trench coats assembled before her. Flashbulbs started to go off.

'MURDER!' shouted another journalist again.

'MURDER OF A MOVIE STAR!'

Posie stood up. She walked to where the two actors were sitting in their odd tableau, picked up what she could of the gold sheet and tried to block the view of the journalists as best she could.

'Get away!' she snarled. 'Get out of here.'

'I thought it was Miss Hanro who was supposed to die!' One small dark man tried to stare Posie down, hopeful for a reaction. He had his pen and notepad at the ready, and smiled gleefully.

'That's what we were all told, anyhow!'

'This isn't a game,' Posie heard herself say authoritatively, although she felt like almost sobbing. 'You're sick. Sick in the head. Get away.'

And suddenly there was Chief Inspector Lovelace, looming up before her, his reassuring figure ushering the press away. The room below was now empty.

Posie suddenly saw that Lovelace was covered in blood.

'What's *that*?' she whimpered, touching the bib of his shirt-front. 'Are you hurt, sir?'

The Inspector's eyes clouded a little but he pursed his lips in a grim line.

'It's not my blood,' he said in a low, tight voice. 'It's McCrae. He was standing right in front of me. He got hit. He didn't make it. He was murdered. Like Mr Fontaine here.'

Posie gasped. 'I'm so sorry. And what about…?'

'Langley?' Lovelace nodded bleakly. 'Clever trick, wasn't it? About the lights. It was rigged up this way: I should have listened to you, Posie. A fine shot like him! He'd placed himself in an ideal spot for it, too. He's scarpered, of course. I've got my lads searching the grounds now. Everyone else is being questioned or patched up or comforted out on the lawns. Good old Bertie Samuelson is calling for more back-up as we speak.'

'Are you sure it was Langley, sir?'

'Aren't you? You saw him with that gun, clear as we did. Didn't you?'

Posie nodded mournfully. 'What was that with Pamela Hanro, just now?'

Lovelace nodded again. 'Can't be sure just yet. But when the light flooded the place just now she was standing there holding a Webley in her hands, Langley having made a run for it. It might be something, or it might be nothing. She might have just picked it up from the floor, but it's likely she was in on it with Langley. Aiding and abetting, most likely. Why else was she here? Seems jolly odd. She's got form, remember? And all that guff just now about her sister ruining her life. It doesn't look good for her, I'll be honest.'

Posie grimaced. Lovelace's features softened. He was quite fond of Posie. More than a bit fond, actually.

'You don't look so good yourself right now, my girl. I think our Mr Langley must have aimed at you, thinking you were Miss Hanro. You do look very alike from behind. Especially in the darkness. Good thing was that he missed you both. But Mr Fontaine here obviously wasn't quite so lucky. Nobody knows about Robbie Fontaine just yet.' He grimaced. 'Well. They *didn't.* Those dratted journalists won't take long to go spreading the news.'

'What shall *I* do now, sir?'

'I want you to take Miss Hanro here to Grape Street. Quick as you can. Binny will drive you and protect you. He'll be here any minute. Keep her safe until I'm with you. You hear me? Keep her safe. We can't know where Langley has got to, or if he plans on carrying out his mad plan to fruition. Don't attract any attention: just go.'

'Why don't we head to Scotland Yard, sir? It seems the obvious place.'

'Exactly. That's what Langley will expect us to do. We'll do what he's not expecting. Besides, I've got most of my team out with me here.'

The Chief Inspector sniffed momentarily. 'What's left of my team, I mean.'

'And Dolly, sir? She's got to be kept safe. You can't let anyone get at her. That would be disastrous.'

'I know. Lady Cardigeon is safe with Sergeant Rainbird and he'll take her home.'

'No. No, don't do that, sir. Deliver her direct to Rufus. I don't want the risk of any mysterious third parties getting at Dolly. Far better Rufus meets her directly. He'll be at the House of Lords, as usual.'

'Fine. As you think best. Now, could you step away from the body now, Miss Hanro? I'll have to get Dr Poots, the Pathologist out here.'

'Of course. Give me a second.'

In the silence that followed, Posie was aware suddenly of two voices, both familiar to her in a very vague, implacable way, cutting through the silence of the huge room.

'I told you he was mean, didn't I?'

'You did, Sheila. There's no denying it. All I've done for him, too. Promises, promises and nothing happening. No more money. I can't find him anywhere. He deserves whatever shocking fact it was that you told him; so he does.'

'He does indeed.'

And Posie saw that it was the fat cook and Mrs Cleeves, both now over at the buffet, helping themselves to plates of food. They were obviously completely unaware of the presence of those up on the podium.

A strange sound seemed to emanate from Silvia Hanro. A strangled cry. She stood up and let go of Robbie Fontaine at last. She stared at the women by the buffet.

The Housekeeper in her navy clothes had turned casually and had been looking over, but now she seemed galvanised into action. There was a hissing sound and a dropping of a plate. A smashing noise and a wild and inhuman scream.

'*Robbie?*'

The Housekeeper was screaming and flinging herself up the steps while the cook stared on, stupidly. Silvia Hanro stepped respectfully aside.

'Now, now,' said the Chief Inspector dully, tiredness and weary wretchedness breaking through his voice. 'It's not the time or place for wild shows of affection for your favourite star; you'll have to mourn from afar like all the rest of them. Step back, madam. Please.'

The Housekeeper howled and dropped to her knees. Her hat had fallen off and she pulled out the pins in her dark hair instinctively, as if it could ease her hurt. Dark hair fell around her face in little coils and she instantly looked younger, prettier.

She was on all fours, clambering over to the body in its gold shroud like a woman possessed. And something clicked in Posie's mind.

'*Idiot!*'

She cursed herself for not having spotted it before. *This* was the reason why Robbie Fontaine knew Brian Langley's secrets.

The Housekeeper snooped for him when Brian Langley was away, had rifled through the Producer's personal correspondence: in fact, Posie had caught her red-handed.

The Housekeeper did other things, too. She had kept Robbie Fontaine in drugs; had fed his habit and got him money when he had run out. Had done anything, in fact, to make the movie star happy. She had done it for years. Robbie Fontaine had described her as a wee clever woman, and undeniably she *was*. Silvia had spoken the truth, too: this woman had obviously *lived* for Robbie Fontaine. She had loved him beyond anything. And he had loved her, too. Had been about to give it all up for her sake. For their future. For the children who now wouldn't be born.

Now the woman was holding onto her dead husband and rocking him back and forth. Her sobs were pitiful to hear.

'Sir,' Posie said softly. 'Sir, you're all wrong, sir. This is Sheila. Robbie Fontaine's wife.'

'*What?*'

And just as the situation couldn't get any worse, they both turned as a strange and piercing cry came from the doorway of the huge empty room.

A lad stood there, and Posie recognised Sidney, the stringer, small in the grand doorway. He seemed much younger than his twelve years and a look of horrified doubt was spreading on his pasty face.

'Is it true, is Mr Fontaine dead? That's what they're all sayin' out here. What'll I do now?'

He looked for reassurance to Sheila, but she didn't bother to raise her head and instead his eyes scanned the podium for someone else he knew in among all the confusion. They settled on Posie.

She was reminded of the song the boy had been whistling the day before, 'In and Out of the Dusty Bluebells,' when many things had seemed brighter.

Who will be my master?

'Tell me it ain't true, Miss. He were the best. Please? What'll I do now, Miss?'

****

Binny had brought the police car right up to the doorway of the ballroom. The car was parked outside one of the big windows, on the grassy lawn, the motor throbbing. A young policeman in uniform was now with the body of Constable McCrae and another was with Sheila, and Chief Inspector Lovelace ushered Posie and Silvia Hanro down the steps.

'Hurry,' he said, his green eyes scanning the room

anxiously. Silvia Hanro slipped through a glass door, her head bowed, looking as if she might weep at any second, and she got up into the car.

'Wait,' said Posie, turning back into the room.

'What is it now?' snarled the Inspector. He followed her gaze: Sidney was still in the doorway, unmoving. Posie fished in her handbag. She found her money clip which still had all of Brian Langley's crisp pound notes in it. She peeled one off the top. She called the boy over. The Inspector went out to speak to Binny in the car, considerably peeved.

'Sidney,' she said, seriously, looking into his eyes. 'I need you to work for me today, all right?'

The lad stared, rubbed his eyes which were still teary, and then nodded and wiped his nose on the back of his hand. He stood up a bit straighter.

'You know how to use a telephone, don't you?'

The boy nodded. ''Course, Miss.'

'Go upstairs, now. Tell Mr Samuelson that you need to use his telephone. Give him this if he questions you.' Posie grabbed one of her real business cards and wrote on it:

In haste – I sent this lad to use your telephone.
He needs your driver too.
All best,
Posie Parker.

Below it she scrawled:

Holborn – 1267
Westminster –7788

She thrust the card at Sidney:

'I need you to call two places. My office, that's the first number on the Holborn exchange. Speak to Len Irving, and don't be fobbed off. Say it's urgent. Tell him to dismiss the secretary for the day; get her to go home. Tell him Miss Hanro and I are on our way with a police escort, and to expect trouble. He needs to be on the look-out, and to be prepared. I need his help.'

'Okay, Miss. I've got it.'

'Good. Then call the second number written there. It's the House of Lords, so mind your manners. Ask for Lord Cardigeon and mention my name. Tell him his wife is going to be dropped off there in about an hour and to wait for her *personally*.'

'Fine, Miss. I can do that, no problem.' The lad nodded, brightening a bit although he kept casting looks over to his former boss' body.

'Then what do you want me to do?'

Posie handed over a fistful of coins. She accidentally on purpose let the white brightness of the pound note show in her hand. Sidney's eyes widened and he stared at Posie, drop-jawed. A pound note was a fortune to him. A year of living adequately, at least.

'Here's some money. Get Mr Samuelson to send you to the address on that business card, with his driver preferably. Buy some chicken on route, nice stuff, and bring it with you to my office. Len, my partner, is first-rate, but not when it comes to feeding cats.'

'Cats, Miss?'

'Never mind. Just bring the meat in a butchers' wrap. Come to the office as fast as you can; it's up on the third floor. Be prepared to muck in. You might get sent on more errands.'

'Dangerous stuff, Miss?' The boy looked excited.

'Hopefully not. But I could do with a lad like you today.' Posie waved the pound note. 'There's this in it for you, at the end of today, if you do everything I just told you and show up for duty at my office. Think of it as payment for today and as compensation for your job ending with Mr Fontaine.'

The boy nodded eagerly, a thin sheen of excitement glowing in his eyes. 'Right you are, Miss. See you later, then. I promise.'

Posie turned to see the Chief Inspector looking in at her. He rolled his eyes in disbelief. He had seen the white brightness of the note, too.

'Always were a soft touch, weren't you, Posie Parker?' he said, barely bothering to conceal his fondness.

* * * *

Thirty-One

They travelled in an uncomfortable silence as Binny drove as fast and as smoothly as he could along the burning heat of the small tarmacked road back to London.

For a while they had the road all to themselves, but after twenty minutes or so a blue-and-gold Nathan's van appeared behind them, dipping in and out of view every few minutes. The rest of the time the roads were totally deserted, the fierce heat keeping most people inside.

Posie studied her fellow passenger, who was looking pointedly out of the window, as if for privacy. Silvia Hanro was obviously lost in a cloud of sadness or regret for a man she had claimed to have hated.

'Couldn't you just have told me?' asked Posie, matter-of-factly, as they were entering the outskirts of London again, the car passing through Earl's Court with its metal rush and blur of railways and squiggly junctions.

'About Mrs Cleeves being "Sheila", I mean?'

Posie felt ruffled and insulted, somehow. Like she had deliberately been kept in the dark about nearly everything. She hated that. That feeling of being taken for a fool.

But she *was* a fool. A stupid little fool.

Silvia turned at last to Posie. She had a thinly veiled look of contempt on her face.

'You're supposed to be the Detective. Why should I have told you? I told you that Sheila was part of the scenery, and I also told you that Brian kept a Housekeeper. Did I have to spell it out for you?' Silvia shrugged. 'I thought you knew everything, anyhow.'

They had come to a stop at a level-crossing and waited as a steam locomotive screamed through. Silvia shifted in her seat. It was very hot and sticky in the car and the railway-scented air outside brought no freshness. The gates lifted.

'Besides,' said Silvia, 'I didn't tell you any lies. And if you want the truth now – although I feel sorry for her in her current predicament, of course – I despised Sheila. Not for where she came from, as Robbie always thought. It was her *nature* I hated.'

'Oh?'

'Sheila was friends with that horrible fat cook, wasn't she? And they suit each other very well. Both of them are money-grubbing horrors. It was well known at Worton Hall that if you slipped Mrs Thynne the right amount of money she would go out of her way to see you were well fed. Her husband's a notorious poacher and she was always trying to offload his ill-gotten wares to people on set. In fact, rumour had it that she'd do pretty much anything for cash. Sheila was always after money, too.'

Posie puckered her brow. 'But what did Sheila have to offer people at Worton Hall? Not food or favours, surely?'

Silvia's face darkened. 'No. Worse. She traded in secrets.'

'Secrets? You mean blackmail?'

Silvia sneered. 'I wouldn't go as far as that, no. That would be acknowledging that the things she said had some truth to them. The things she said were ludicrous, absolute drivel. Can you believe she had the gall to tell me that Tom – my own dear Tom! – was having an affair with the dresser?'

'Elaine?' Posie repeated.

'That's right. She said she'd give me evidence if I'd give her ten pounds. I told her to sling her hook! You can imagine that Tom and I laughed ourselves silly about it later!'

'When was this?'

Silvia hunkered down at the window, shrugging, losing interest.

'Oh, goodness. I can't remember now. Saturday? Sunday, maybe? But it was typical of her, I can tell you that for nothing.'

They were driving through High Street Kensington now, and the smart shopping street lay deserted. A cinema next to the Underground station had a small crowd of people around it, and a queue was snaking down the street in the cool shade of the shop fronts. A glossy poster advertised the name of Brian Langley and one of Sunstar's most recent films, and Silvia Hanro and Robbie Fontaine were superimposed in a tight, passionate clinch on a grand scale high above the entrance to the cinema.

Silvia recoiled in horror from the image, her eyes filling with tears.

But what the crowd were paying attention to mainly was a large bill poster which said:

AIR CONDITIONING HERE!

Silvia groaned. She seemed, now she was talking, in the mood for conversation. And sympathy.

'I still can't believe he's dead. Robbie. And while I loathed him, it felt as if he'd always be there, you know?' She shivered. 'I can't get that image to go away. His head like that…'

'Try not to think of it.'

'And that Brian could do that? *Really* do that, I mean. Kill us, or kill *me*. In cold blood. It's horrible.'

'But you thought the same, earlier this week? You thought Brian was behind the threats, didn't you?'

'Yes, but I didn't think he actually meant anything by it.

And you think it was for money? To save Sunstar? It just doesn't make sense…he has all of his orchid income. And does that mean he killed Elaine, too? Or was she actually a suicide?'

At Posie's unhelpful silence the actress frowned. 'And I can't understand what my sister Pamela was doing at the party, either. Those two have no connection to each other. Brian barely met Pamela back in the old days…'

She turned, seeking some sort of reassurance or explanation from Posie. But Posie said nothing.

She was thinking about Pamela. And blackmail.

She remembered Pamela's comments about someone blackmailing her over Hilda's parentage. The threats had started up again very recently. But she had also mentioned that it had occurred before. Twice before. Last year. It had been a woman. And Pamela had dealt with the threat by paying up.

Posie remembered that Pamela had written to Silvia asking for money last year. Twice. Money which had been grudgingly paid out. What if that money was paid out to stop someone from spilling a secret? What if the person doing the blackmailing had been Sheila?

It all fitted together.

Sheila had somehow got wind of the existence of the child, Hilda, presumably by rifling through Brian Langley's personal mail; a letter from Pamela about school fees, maybe. Sheila had hunted down her prey and blackmailed Pamela, no doubt secretly ecstatic at finding such a complicated and potentially devastating state of affairs, injurious to so many people. Sheila had gone back to Pamela for more money, a second time over, and had obviously been about to do the same thing again.

Posie knew the one thing about blackmailers was that they were greedy: they always came back for more.

And suddenly, and clear as a bell, she knew she was right.

She remembered the distracted manner of Pamela on the edges of the dance floor, how she had been staring at someone uncertainly, and then in a horrified way. Posie remembered the howl from Pamela on the floor of the ballroom when the lights had come on. Her words, over and over again:

'*That woman! That woman! She ruined my life!*'

Pamela had spotted Sheila, and had recognised her. She hadn't been talking about Silvia at all.

And if that was correct, Silvia Hanro was wrong: Sheila wasn't a woman in possession of stupid tittle-tattle. In her dealings with Pamela she had shown herself quite capable of using big, dark secrets. Secrets which ruined lives. Which *cost* lives.

A clever wee woman, after all.

****

Grape Street was slumbering fitfully in the heatwave. It was very quiet and dirty-looking.

'Is this where you work?' said Silvia Hanro in a shocked-sounding voice. Posie didn't bother to answer, getting her key out of her carpet bag, thinking instead of Bute Street and Pamela's neatly pristine flat above the fish and chip shop. Where Silvia's child had spent her life.

She could just imagine Silvia's words:

'*Is this where you live?*'

Sergeant Binny parked the car up against the entrance to the Grape Street Bureau, and told the women to go on up. Posie informed him that Sidney, the stringer, might be along at any moment, and Binny nodded. He then revealed the fact that, completely against normal Scotland Yard policy, he had been authorised by the Chief Inspector to carry a handgun, and felt he was best suited to stand outside the entrance on the street level with it, watching and waiting, until further police back-up came. They left him, still in his black tie, looking somewhat nervously up and down the tiny dusty street.

Up on the third floor it was terribly hot. Dust motes were dancing in the sunshine out on the landing with its faded blue carpet and somehow it made the place look even more grubby, even more third-rate than it really was. Posie didn't look at Silvia, just put the key in the lock of the glass-stencilled front door to the Detective Agency.

Inside, the client waiting room and the tiny offices were deadly quiet. No-one was about. Posie locked the door behind them and thought anxiously of Len, and his gun, which he always kept with him. She needed both of them right now.

Where was he, anyway?

It dawned on her in a strangely inappropriate manner that it had been *Len* that she had requested to help her in her hour of need, when she had asked Sidney to make a call, not Alaric, who would, no doubt, be fretting about getting his upcoming talk for the Royal Geographical Society ready just now.

She brushed the thought quickly aside.

It had been because Len was so firmly associated with this place, of course. And because of the gun. That was it.

Not that Len had bothered to hang around, though, by the looks of things.

'What was that *noise?*' whispered Silvia, looking about the place in some trepidation. She had hung her red headdress and bag up on the hat stand in the waiting room as if the piece of bland furniture might bite her. Her arms and her hands were still covered in bits of dried, encrusted blood.

'There it is again. A moaning noise? A kicking sound?'

Posie cocked her head and listened. A second later she

dashed across to the tiny kitchen out the back and opened the door. Mr Minks sprung out, mewing, vastly annoyed. He came up to Posie and ran his talons up her leg, ripping her stockings to shreds. On purpose.

He suddenly saw Silvia and hissed, arching his back. It was an acknowledged fact that he vastly preferred men to women. Any man would do. And if no men were around, then Posie had to suffice.

'It's only my Siamese, Mr Minks,' said Posie, slightly apologetically, although her nerves were strung out tightly and she felt like screaming. She picked up the cream-and-brown cat, stroking him as much as he deigned to allow.

'Mr Minks needs feeding and my partner, Len, has obviously been remiss. Len doesn't keep him in the style to which he has grown accustomed.'

Posie grabbed a clean towel and a new bar of Pears soap from the cleaning cupboard and indicated towards the kitchen sink. It was slightly more presentable in here than the tiny horrible bathroom out on the landing with its cracked sink and chipped mirror. 'Do you want to clean up?'

Silvia nodded, and tried as best she could to wash in the confined space. Her mouth was a prim, grim line and Posie wondered like mad what she was thinking about. Robbie Fontaine, presumably, and his blood which she was washing off her hands.

Mr Minks was hissing furiously.

'Don't mind him. Shall I make us both a cup of tea while we wait for Scotland Yard to arrive?'

Silvia eyed the cat with some distaste but nodded. While Posie prepared cups and tea, Silvia stood on the scratched lino of the tiny kitchen and stared out of the high sash window with its ragged red velvet curtains.

'Nice view.'

From the little kitchen window it was a sheer – and fatal – drop down to the courtyard.

'We keep the window closed at all times,' Posie explained, indicating towards the cat, while simultaneously remembering that there was no milk for the tea, as it was simply too hot to keep it out on the windowsill.

'Blast and botheration.'

And Posie didn't have the luxury of an ice-box. Or biscuits, come to think of it. With Prudence away mostly everything came a little undone.

'Do feel free to smoke. Be my guest.'

Posie passed across the black tea in a blue china cup and saucer normally kept for clients, and the sugar jar with the silver tongs which she normally kept for best, too. Silvia nodded a thanks and lit a cigarette, shaking out her match in great exaggerated gestures.

'How long will I have to stay here do you think?'

'I really couldn't say.'

Hopefully not much longer, Posie thought to herself, jumpily. She took a hopeful slurp of tea from her mug and almost choked; it was too hot without milk.

Mr Minks had now slunk to the opposite end of the kitchen, as far away as possible from the two women. Seeing as how there was no food on immediate offer, he had given up any semblance of affection.

'I couldn't keep a cat like that,' the actress said, turning from the window at last and sitting languidly in a kitchen chair across from Posie.

'Oh?' Posie said automatically, a tad defensively. 'Well, I didn't really have a choice. He was my father's. He would have been homeless without me. But he's wonderful, in his own unique way.'

'You remind me of my sister a bit, you know.' Silvia took a careful sip of her tea and grimaced at the taste. 'You know, the girl in bright pink whom they just arrested?'

Posie hadn't bothered to mention that she had actually met Pamela, in her own time. Or that Pamela had helped supply a good deal of Posie's knowledge about Silvia.

'She was always hunting down lost causes, too. Injured animals, sometimes. Or helping with workhouse fundraisers. All that. She always did that; she thought it was the noble thing to do. Those lost causes never brought her anything but hard work though, and no thanks in the end. And she would have been better off without them. Happier, probably.'

Posie tried to stop the anger bubbling over. She gripped the edge of the tiny, cheap wooden table until her knuckles turned white.

'Perhaps it runs in the family, then,' Posie whispered, too loud.

Fool.

'I'm sorry?'

Posie snapped.

'Lost causes. It's obvious, isn't it? You've just married *your* lost cause. Tom – let's call him that – and all because you think it's the noble thing to do. You went out of your way to tell me you were in love with him. But you're no more in love with him than I am!'

'How dare you!'

'But you're not going to be happy, are you? And all you will get is hard work, and no thanks. You might be better off without him, don't you think? Like your sister and her stray dogs. Or was it cats? Or workhouse children? I'm paraphrasing, obviously.'

Silvia stood up. She stubbed out her cigarette in the nice blue saucer. Anger was written all over her beautiful face.

'I don't have to listen to this. You're crazy. Completely.'

Posie continued to sit. She continued in the calmest, coolest voice she could muster:

'Am I though? It's the only way I can explain it. Although I still don't know what the rush in marrying Tom this week was for. You feel guilt that Tom lost his looks and his career in the war, and that he almost lost his mind, too; especially since your career is still going strong, *for now*. Even though you're about to be replaced by some new young thing…'

'How dare you! I'm only turning thirty next month!'

'Happy birthday. But I'm right, aren't I? About Tom? And the guilt? Guilt is stamped all over this. You feel guilt for involving him in Worton Hall and Sunstar Films again, after him being such a long time away from the industry. You feel guilt about your affair with Brian Langley while Tom was away, and guilt about the child you had. Brian's child. A lost child with the man you *still* love.'

Silvia gasped and stood rooted to the spot.

Posie stood at last. 'And I'm guessing that you feel guilt at not loving Tom. Worse, you feel guilty because you feel disgusted, repelled by Tom.'

Posie felt terribly tired, and sad:

'So you ran away on your wedding night, didn't you? Because you were desperate to be alone: to walk in the rain in a disguise; to party hard as if you could blot out the marriage you had just entered into. A marriage you saw as your duty, as Tom's right. You weren't reconsidering it, were you? You knew you had made your uncomfortable bed, and you knew you had to lie in it. But you wanted one last night of freedom. You told me you'd left Tom a note when you rang me from the Royal Oak. I think you told Tom that you wanted to be alone in that note, didn't you? That's why he wasn't worried about you, but he must have been embarrassed, not to mention hurting like hell inside. He knows why you don't want to be with him. Is that why you don't help him more financially? Why you're so wretchedly mean towards him?'

'You don't know what you're talking about.'

'I bet I do. Poor man. Isn't that what happened?'

Silvia was reaching for the door of the kitchen, but Posie was faster. She slipped through it and pushed it shut again behind her and quick as a flash she had used her office key to lock the door. Silvia was locked inside the kitchen with only Mr Minks for company.

'Good,' Posie breathed, panting. 'Serves her jolly well right. Cold-hearted harpy.'

'Let me out!' shouted the actress furiously. She hammered on the door uselessly.

Posie didn't feel guilty. Not at all. The Inspector had given her clear instructions to keep Silvia safe. Not entertained, or happy.

Just safe. Posie thought about the sheer drop from the window and how Silvia couldn't go anywhere right now. That was safety.

Sort of.

* * * *

Thirty-Two

Posie stomped through into the cooler interior of her own office, dragging the fan she had seen Len hauling up the stairs earlier. *Where on earth was he?*

What kind of idiots did she have to put up with on a daily basis?

At her desk she threw down her carpet bag huffily, and tipped out its contents. She got the fan to start. She hurled herself into her chair. However, there was no comfort to be had from studying the crisp unruffled interior of her office today, or the jaunty little watercolours which her father had painted on his holidays in France.

Instead, there were increasingly cross-sounding noises coming from the kitchen, as Silvia had obviously lost her temper and had decided to hurl furniture or herself about the place in a spiral of anguish.

Posie didn't feel sorry for her. Not one bit. The woman had suffered a shock with Robbie Fontaine dying practically in her lap, it was true, but then so had they all.

So Posie sat, head in hands, staring at her notebook, mainly focused on the words 'HATE', 'LOVE' and 'MONEY'.

Before she knew it, she had written a fourth word: 'GUILT.'

Posie was running over and over her diatribe at the movie star in her locked kitchen. Had she gone too far?

She pushed away her singed hair and bits of burnt headdress – where the bullet had whizzed by – in a preoccupied fashion. A spot of dried blood fell off her cheek and flaked onto the open notepad before her. The smell of the burned cloth and hair and the dried blood on her hands was rancid and unpleasant.

It lingered horribly.

Suddenly something struck Posie as familiar. Like a bell was ringing somewhere in her mind, but from very far away. A warning sound.

Her brain scrambled, twisting up quickly through the gears, trying to find an equilibrium, a solution.

And while her thoughts didn't follow any obvious direction, several ideas crept, unbidden, into her mind: five unrelated details which she hadn't focused on before now blazed before her.

She breathed slowly, counting the five details off on her fingers, in no particular order:

The first was the memory of a scent.

The second was a sudden and clear understanding of the skills of an expert blackmailer.

The third was a fact: a person's age.

The fourth detail which came to Posie was Silvia Hanro telling her in the car on the way back to Grape Street that the cook, Mrs Thynne, would do most things in exchange for money.

And the fifth detail was the memory of a phrase which she had heard very recently, not more than a couple of hours back. A man shouting: 'What is *this*, now?'

Posie stood, her heart hammering in her chest. She pulled at her horrible blonde hair in exasperation.

'*Can it be?*'

The telephone rang suddenly from the waiting room. Posie raced through, just in time to see the shadow of a boy standing silhouetted outside the glass-stencilled front door.

Posie hurriedly let Sidney in, and gave him the key to lock the door behind him, while she was answering the telephone. The Operator announced a call from Worton Hall Studios, which she said would take a couple of minutes to put through. Posie nodded over at Sidney, who was staring around with interest.

'Old policeman plod let me in downstairs. Nice place you got here, Miss.'

He put the butchers' wrap of meat down on the edge of Prudence's desk with a couple of unspent coins. 'Need me to cook that for you, Miss? I'm a handy turn with a fryin' pan and a knob o' lard.'

Posie shook her head and started to write quickly on a jotter. She wrote down two separate points.

She gave Sidney the note and another of her business cards, holding on to the receiver all the while.

'Take this, will you? I need you to get to Number 11, Lincoln's Inn Fields. Five minutes' walk from here. You know where that is, Sidney?'

"Course I do, Miss. I ain't stupid. Next to that big bit of park where the tramps get their soup at night, innit?'

'That's right. Fast as you can, there and back. Ask for Mr Nicholas of Carver & Nicholas Solicitors. Tell him it's urgent and I regret that I can't come myself. He's nice. He told me to put something in writing, and here it is. Ask him to just write "yes" or "no" to the two questions written there. Got it? Tell him I can't leave here. I'm under strict police instructions to stay put.'

The lad nodded. "Course, Miss.'

He edged towards the door but turned, perturbed. 'I say, Miss. There's some mighty funny noises coming from out here. Banging. What sounds like a mighty kickin' goin' on.'

He motioned towards the landing.

Posie clicked her tongue irritably. 'Oh, don't mind that.

It's only Miss Hanro and a cat locked together in the kitchen. They're just getting to know each other better.'

Sidney looked doubtful for a second, but then thought better of it, shrugged, and disappeared. Posie heard a voice ask for her in the receiver amid a cacophony of hissings.

'That you, Posie?'

'It is, sir. Who else?'

'You can't be too careful at the moment,' continued Inspector Lovelace. 'And this is a bad line. What a lot of background noise! I'm just checking all is in order.'

'All fine, sir. You-know-who is safe and sound.'

'Thank goodness. We've managed to clear most of the lot who were here, including your pal, Lady Cardigeon, who has gone off with Sergeant Rainbird, safely back to Westminster, but the journalists are another matter entirely: we can't stop the story about Robbie Fontaine from leaking out. Dratted fellows! It will be all over the early evening papers in just a couple of hours.'

'I wouldn't expect anything less, sir. Are you coming here now?'

There were some clicks down the line and some more hissings. Then all was quiet again.

'I am, Posie. I'm just about to leave. I've been held up. Would you believe that Poots was still here monkeying around with Elaine Dickinson's body, together with that blonde fella from Kew? So I got him to come and look at Fontaine's body, too, quick as he could, to speed up the process and so he could take the two corpses away together. But there was a problem with Fontaine.'

'Oh? What? I would have thought it was straightforward, surely?'

'Not in the *way* Fontaine died: Poots confirmed that Mr Fontaine died of a gunshot wound to the head. It was the gun itself which was the problem.'

Posie swallowed uncertainly. 'The Webley you took off Pamela Hanro, you mean?'

'That's right. Brian Langley's gun: a Webley Mark VI. It's definitely his. I've checked it out at the Yard: the serial number matches one issued to Langley in 1918. But it turns out that the gun which killed Robbie Fontaine wasn't the same sort of Webley at all. It was something much earlier, a large .455 model. Apparently the bullet, which nearly got you, and which Poots recovered from Fontaine, didn't match Langley's model. The two Webley's use different bullets, but only an expert would know that.'

'So what was Langley's gun doing there?' Although the words were simply mechanical.

For Posie knew the answer already.

'Search me. And I've still no idea as to where Brian Langley has fled to, either. We've had to let Pamela Hanro go, of course. She's not connected to the crime at all now. No direct evidence.'

Posie groaned in disbelief. 'Did you *have* to let her go?'

The Chief Inspector sounded startled. 'She's not a suspect any more for anything. Or is she, in your opinion?'

'She'll come here,' moaned Posie. 'She'll get here somehow. She's resourceful. I think she heard you tell your men that Silvia was coming here to my offices.'

'Surely not! Don't let her in. Stay calm. I'll be with you shortly.'

Posie sat motionless after the line went dead and the double click-click of the Operator's line went down. She replaced the shiny black receiver in its cradle and collapsed into Prudence's chair. The silence of the little office engulfed her. Even Silvia had now given up protesting and the kitchen was quiet.

Minutes ticked by.

Ten minutes. Twenty minutes.

Posie sat, digesting the recent news from the Inspector. She needed to wait for Sidney to come back with the response from the solicitor, but she was fairly certain of things now: who the killer was.

She ticked through her five unconnected details again. She tried to stay calm, as the Inspector had directed, but she felt like howling in anguish.

The truth had revealed itself as if the layers were being stripped back like a poisonous onion. But she had understood it all too late.

And she had made a huge, unforgivable error. A blunder of the worst sort. And lives had been lost in the process.

What will I do now?

The little clock on Prudence's desk struck two-thirty, bringing Posie back down to earth with a jolt. And then she jumped: the bell from the street entrance was being rung for her attention.

She marched to the front window, pulled up the sash and stuck her head out. The London plane trees, so lush and verdantly green despite the city smog and dust, formed an inconvenient barrier between herself and the caller at the door.

'Sergeant Binny?' she shouted down, as calmly as possible. 'Where are you? Is that you?'

There was no reply.

'Sergeant Binny?'

A nasal voice, unknown but cheerful enough called up. It was the voice of a Londoner, born and bred:

'Miss Parker? Is that a Miss Rosemary Parker of the Grape Street Bureau?'

Posie frowned and then called out snappishly. 'Who's asking?'

'My name is Davey Price. I'm a telephone engineer, from the telephone company, come to look at your line. Your colleague, Len, he asked me to call at two-thirty today. I had a free time-slot. Arranged it all yesterday, we did. He said you'd been having problems: maybe worried your line was being compromised? I can check it out for you. But I can come back another time if now isn't convenient? Next week for example?'

Posie thought for a second. It wasn't at all convenient. But it *was* necessary.

It was true: just the day before she had complained massively to Len about the telephone, and surprisingly he had actually done something about it. Besides, the Chief Inspector wasn't due at the office for at least another three-quarters of an hour, and Silvia Hanro was safely hidden in the kitchen.

And Len would be along anytime soon now. Hopefully.

She leant out of the window again. 'How long will you need up here?'

'Oh, only about ten minutes, Miss, give or take. I'll just prepare my tools if that's okay with you? I've got rather a heavy bag to bring up. I need to sort it out down here. It's in a bit of a mess from my last job. So if you could buzz me in and I'll come up when I'm ready. Probably in about five minutes' time?'

Posie thought. It all sounded plausible enough.

'I say,' she shouted down again, 'is my pal down there? His name's Binny and he has a black Ford motor car.'

'Do you mean the fella in tails?'

'That's right.'

'He's at the end of the street, where it joins onto Shaftesbury Avenue, by the pub. He's lookin' this way and that, like he might be expectin' company. That the fella? Shall I pop over and ask him to come on up?'

Posie thought of poor nervous Binny.

'No,' she shouted down, reluctantly. 'Don't bother him. I'll let you in and you just come up as soon as you can.'

Posie stepped away from the window and pressed the entry bell. She stood, nervously, and all of a sudden heard quick, unknown footsteps on the stairs.

It was just Sidney.

Breathing a sigh of relief, Posie opened the front door.

'Oh, it's *you*, Sidney. What a relief.' She drew the boy into the room. 'Thank you for being so quick. And?'

Sidney passed across the piece of notepaper, tightly folded and tied with a bit of lawyers' pink ribbon. Sidney nodded, his eyes gleaming with the satisfaction of a job well done.

'I would have been quicker, but I 'ad to wait for him to finish with some clients. Mr Nicholas sends his regards.'

'Good lad.'

Posie was about to open the notepaper when there was yet more running on the stairs. Both Posie and Sidney stopped, turned and listened. It was unmistakeably a woman running up the first set of stairs. Heeled shoes were tapping on the lino down below.

Posie groaned.

The office door was pushed open and there was Pamela Hanro herself, dishevelled and desperate-looking, her bright kimono slipping off her thin shoulders. Her heavy make-up was smeared all over her face and her hair was wild about her face. She stared at Posie like a woman possessed, her red lipstick eerily vivid in her pale face.

'You've left your door downstairs to the street wide open, you silly girl.' Pamela Hanro gasped for breath. 'You've made a big mistake, Miss Parker. Or haven't you realised that, yet?'

Posie had grabbed Sidney, and the piece of chicken, and the key to the kitchen, all in one easy movement.

'I need you to disappear,' she hissed at him under her breath. 'Feed the cat and don't panic. Lock the door behind you with this key and guard it with your life. Guard Silvia Hanro with your life, too. If you hear gunshots out here don't come out. Wait for the police to arrive. You'll be fine. Just fine. Now, through you go.'

'You gonna be all right, Miss?' the boy whispered. 'This woman looks like a right crazy one to me.'

'I'll be fine.' Posie nodded, without any certainty. Unlocking the door and shoving the boy through into the kitchen was the work of a second.

Turning back to Pamela, Posie did her best to hold on to her calm.

'Now, what was it that you were saying?'

* * * *

Thirty-Three

'You've got my sister up here, haven't you?'

Posie stared at Pamela hard, paralysed with fear, and she could feel the blood booming in her temples. No words came.

'It's okay.' Pamela laughed. 'I heard that dishy Inspector chappie tell you to bring her here, when he arrested me. He got *that* wrong. And you got it *all* wrong, didn't you, Miss Parker? I thought I'd better come along and tell you that.'

Just then a loud bumping sound could be heard from way down below, like a hearthrug or a big heavy mat being tugged along strenuously into the entrance hall of the Grape Street Offices. Then there were some bangs.

'What's that noise?' whispered Pamela in a sudden panic. She was at the window in a trice, looking down, licking the last of her red lipstick off nervily. 'Is it the police?'

Posie shook her head, not entirely truthfully. The cockney voice called up the stairs:

'Sorry I'm taking so long, Miss Parker. We'll be with you in a minute.'

'Fine,' Posie shouted back. 'No hurry.'

Posie turned to Pamela. 'It's just the telephone repair man,' she explained, hugely glad for the interruption, 'bringing his tools up from his van.'

'I see.' Pamela was back again at the window, pacing, restless.

In those few seconds Posie quickly unwrapped the note Sidney had brought her from the solicitor. She unfolded it and read the answers to her questions:

1. Does the main capital of Silvia Hanro's trust fund go to Pamela unless Silvia marries by the age of 30?

—Yes.

2. Was Silvia informed of this situation by you?

—Yes, she knew about it. She wrote asking for details and we supplied them.

Posie scrunched the note into her pocket. It all made sense now and this was the confirmation.

The banging and bumping downstairs had stopped. There was now a slow dragging sound from the stairwell.

Pamela had turned and was staring hard at Posie, almost accusingly.

'Hang on a minute. *What* telephone repair man are you talking about? There was no such van down there when I came up. There was a Nathan's van. You know, the costumiers? There was a black car, too. A Ford. But no-one was in it and all the doors had been left hanging open…'

Posie frowned. 'Nathan's? A Nathan's van?'

There had been a Nathan's van following them, on and off, all the way into London. *Had she got this badly wrong, too?*

And then she remembered her telephone conversation with Len, at the public booth at Worton Hall. A man had been waiting patiently behind the baize curtain. A man who, sure as bread was bread, had probably heard her whole conversation. Including her request for a telephone engineer to come to Grape Street. A man who had been wearing bright white.

But then, all the men at Worton Hall wore white. She felt sick in the pit of her stomach. Just who or what had she let in to Grape Street?

'Hello?'

But just then the strange dragging noise stopped. Whatever it was, was out on the landing. Both Pamela and Posie turned together to look over at the glass door. But they couldn't make out the figure there. It was just a big dark mass with no distinctive shape.

'Hello?' called out Posie again, making an attempt to sound normal. She was shaking and couldn't get it under control.

There was an odd clinking noise in reply. Something metallic was clicking into place.

'Hello?' Posie was horribly aware of Pamela Hanro beside her, breathing dangerously close, and of Sidney the stringer and of Silvia Hanro, not six feet away behind the kitchen door. Frightened, most probably.

As well they might be.

The glass door pushed open. And two men, both in black tie, could be seen. It was a bizarre and confusing spectacle, bruising on the senses.

'What the…?'

Pamela darted forwards, but Posie, heart racing, grabbed at Pamela before she could do anything else she might regret later.

The two men moved strangely together, as if they might fall over, as if they were propped up in some sleepwalking nightmare.

'Brian?' Pamela was screaming. 'What happened to you?'

And then, before anyone knew it, the door to the kitchen had burst open, and Silvia Hanro was standing there, flustered and gripping the kitchen key in her hands as if in a strange triumph. But her face fell in a second.

'Tom?' she shouted, rooted to the spot. 'What the blazes is all of this? Blood? Who did this to you? Good grief! Was it Brian? Or was it the police? What on earth…? *Cuffs?*'

For it was true.

Brian Langley and Tom Moran were indeed standing together, a pair of silver handcuffs linking them. Tom Moran's left hand was chained to Brian Langley's right hand. They moved as one because there was no other option.

But this wasn't the strangest thing about the men.

Tom Moran was wearing his blue glasses again, but they were cracked and broken, and even his good side was now bloodied, and a deep gash ran down his good cheek. He seemed distinctly unsteady on his feet.

Brian Langley wasn't quite so badly harmed. There was a residue of blood about his face, but he looked terrible. His eyes were red and bleary, unfocused, rolling desperately in his head. He was trying to hold on to his balance, as if he were a man out for the first time on a boat at sea.

Both men seemed as if they were under the influence of something.

'Here you go! Sit here.'

Before anyone could do anything, Sidney had darted forwards and dragged two office chairs out. Both men collapsed down into them. They sat near Prudence's desk in a heavy silence, panting and breathing heavily. Silvia dashed to her husband's side.

'Sorry, Miss,' the lad whispered to Posie. 'I couldn't keep Miss Hanro from getting at that key. Like a woman possessed, she was, when she heard that crazy woman in pink call out Mr Langley's name. But these two look like they've been hitting the snow.'

'Snow?' Posie said, too loudly.

The boy nodded. 'You know, *cocaine*. Like Mr Fontaine – God rest his soul – at his worst, they are. Addled. Although Mr Fontaine told me that he thought Mr Moran here had all the signs of an opium addict.'

'Opium?'

Posie was remembering the strange bowl and apparatus Tom had tried to hide in his room, the strange burning sweetness of the air, his grogginess. He had mentioned taking medication, but maybe it was an altogether stronger concoction than those prescribed by his doctors which kept him going now? It all fitted.

Again, a drug addict she had failed to spot. Were the drugs the real reason Silvia was so stingy with her money towards her husband? Why she had bought him a flat but nothing else? Was she scared he would blow all her money on drugs? Had Posie, in fact, judged Silvia too harshly?

'Well, who'd blame him, eh, Miss?' cut in the lad. 'But this isn't opium which has done this. Sweet tea and water will get them going again.'

Sidney cleared his throat lustily. 'Anyone for tea?'

Not receiving any obvious reply he scurried off to the kitchen and made a lot of noise with water and kettles and cups.

Posie stared with barely-seeing eyes at the ring of people in her waiting room. They were placed around the desk as if waiting to start acting out a scene in a play. Or a movie. But Posie didn't have a clue as to what would happen next, despite understanding how it was they had all ended up there. There was no obvious script.

And she seemed to have been handed the role of director...

Where was Len?

And where was the Inspector, come to think of it?

Posie breathed deeply and willed herself to get a grip of the situation. But there were so many unknowns.

Tom Moran leant forwards in his chair, as if about to be sick, and Posie remembered his violent retching when he had believed that his wife, Silvia, was dead.

Hastily she grabbed at Prudence's wastepaper bin and placed it conveniently in front of him and tried not to look. She took in Brian Langley, who was staring hard around himself, his gaze visibly awry, his pupils going in and out of focus.

Pamela was squatting at Brian's side. Thoughts of cocaine were obviously not far from her mind, too.

'Who did this to you, Brian? You don't take drugs, do you? Never in your life.'

Silvia Hanro suddenly stood up, frowned angrily and snarled at her sister:

'What do *you* know of Brian Langley, Pam? Nothing! You don't know him from Adam! And I'd watch it, if I were you, coming over all the good Samaritan again. The man's a killer. He killed Robbie Fontaine in cold blood, and wanted me dead too: just ask Miss Parker here. The police are after him. Looks like they had him too, but he obviously got away. Got away with Tom, maybe as a hostage?'

Pamela looked about ready to physically attack her sister, when Posie emitted a shriek of relief at the sight of the stocky, familiar man standing in the doorway.

'Chief Inspector! How good of you to join us!'

Lovelace came into the room, also still in his bloodied dinner suit, staring around himself with a professional smoothness. 'Good afternoon, everyone.'

Posie realised that he had certainly earned his Blue Plume if he encountered danger calmly like this, time after time. His gaze, when it took in the two men in handcuffs, and Pamela, wild-eyed, betrayed no real emotion or panic, no confusion. He focused hard on Posie, as if willing her to give him his next move.

Here was a calm in the storm, and, more practically, a loaded gun in a trained hand.

Posie was trying not to think of at least one other loaded gun which she knew was in a pocket in that very room: the gun which had cost Robbie Fontaine and Constable McCrae their lives; which would undoubtedly be trained on Silvia – and maybe everyone – at some point soon. How much time did they have left?

What could she do? What could she say to warn him about the killer?

She smiled brightly at Richard Lovelace.

'I say, sir. Did you see a telephone repair man on your way up? He seems to have gone missing.'

****

Thirty-Four

Sidney came in with the tea, handing it around among a false sort of calm.

He certainty made himself very handy, Posie noted subconsciously, in amidst her rising panic. Did Sidney realise, poor lad, the danger he was really in? Posie cursed herself now for having placed him in that danger.

But it was too late.

Lovelace was regarding Brian Langley, who was now looking slightly more awake, and Tom Moran, who was shaking violently.

'What happened to you two, anyhow? You look like you've been in a fight.'

Lovelace advanced, and picked up the two men's hands, chained together. 'And who chained you together? These look a good deal like...' He examined the handcuffs at close range. 'Sergeant Binny's!'

He dropped the men's hands as if the contact had burned him. His voice was calm but there was an undercurrent of panic in it: 'Where *is* Sergeant Binny, by the way?'

He looked at Posie who shrugged helplessly. Lovelace turned, anger breaking through the calm façade.

'You two fellas need to give me some answers. *Now.* Langley, you go first. Why are you chained to Mr Moran and why does he look as if he's been in a fight? Let me tell you, you'd better talk soon. Things don't look good for you. Not good at all. I've half the London police force out looking for you for the murder of Robbie Fontaine and for the attempted murder of Miss Hanro here. Which means you'd better speak up. *Right now.*'

Brian Langley looked like he was having trouble moving his head. Looked like he was having trouble full stop. Like he certainly couldn't speak.

'Sir,' cut in Posie. 'I think he's drugged. I don't think he *can* talk. Or do much at all just now.'

'Oh? Well at least he can't wave a gun about, then, can he?'

And before Posie could answer, Lovelace was at the door of the office again, on the landing. He shot Posie a look full of genuine concern, but then seemed to make his mind up.

'You're safe enough up here for the moment. I'm going to check on Sergeant Binny, make sure he's all right. I have a bad feeling about this. I also need to retrieve my gun. I gave him my only revolver to accompany you here with. Two ticks and I'll be back.'

'No, sir, please…'

But he was gone.

It all happened very quickly after that.

For a split-second Posie could have sworn that there was a presence over at the doorway, a fleeting outline of a man – Lovelace returned, perhaps? – but when she craned her neck to look again there was no-one there.

And then there was the hideous, surprising crack-shot sound of a gun going off in the room and glass all around them breaking.

'Gunfire! Take cover!' shouted Tom Moran.

Then a volley of shots, on and on.

The gunshots seemed to be being fired right into the centre of the room, where they were all gathered. From somewhere around the front door. *Was it possible?*

The whole waiting room had become a white-fogged mist of falling paint and plaster, and crystals of glass from the windows and picture frames were dancing like treacherous icicles in the dangerous air.

Posie was down on the floor. She saw Sidney, frozen, look at her with panicked eyes, and she managed to mouth 'RUN AWAY!' at him.

He dropped to the floor and, crab-like, got himself to the kitchen, pulling the door tight shut behind him. Silvia Hanro was running, uselessly, away, through the office into Posie's room.

The shots rained on. Posie screamed:

'STOP THIS MADNESS!'

Suddenly there was silence.

The room was still clouded with white powdery debris, but the strange double figure of Brian and Tom was now becoming clearer, crouched down next to the desk, hunched over and panting. Pamela Hanro slowly became visible too: she was also on the floor by the desk, shaking and crying, but still alive.

There was a terrible stillness about the chaos of the office. The intense heat made the situation even worse, and the broken plaster and paint got in the back of Posie's throat and itched horribly. Everyone was coughing.

Seconds later the figure of Silvia Hanro could be seen, her red dress now white, her face a deathly mask but seemingly unharmed, coming slowly back through the falling plaster. Her arms were outstretched in a pleading gesture.

'Who *was* that?'

'That's it!' declared Posie resolutely, angrily. She had had enough.

'One of you here in this room knows very well who did all this, just now, because it was YOU who were doing the shooting! I don't quite know how you worked that bit of magic from over near the doorway, but enough is enough!'

Posie marched around to Prudence's desk and sat down heavily in her chair. She found she was moving around like normal, fuelled by a snappy anger.

Posie could see all four of them from here, everyone covered in debris and looking scared. No gun was visible anywhere.

'The game is up,' Posie declared, crossing her arms over her chest, willing the crispness of her anger to continue: it made it sound as if she knew what she was doing.

'Not that it was much of a game in the first place. In fact, it's ludicrous.'

She took in all four white powdery faces.

'I know everything,' Posie said softly. Strictly speaking, this wasn't quite true: Posie could see only the outline of the story, but she could fill in the gaps easily enough. But could she hold her nerve until the Inspector was back?

She thought about the words she had written in her notebook, the truth they had contained together:

HATE, LOVE, MONEY, GUILT.

'I told Silvia Hanro yesterday that this case would all hinge on either love, or money,' she began, 'and then later I thought it might be about hate, and then later still I thought it might be about guilt.'

Posie paused for effect, heart still racing. 'But actually, it's about all four. Equally. So I was wrong.'

'You've been wrong about a lot,' slurred Brian Langley, finding his voice at last. He still looked terrible, and he was also now coated in a film of white grit, his small angry eyes peering out like a malevolent snowman.

'I know.' Posie nodded. 'And you'll get your fee back, I promise. I didn't solve this correctly at all. Not until this afternoon.'

'So you *know* who murdered Robbie?' demanded Silvia Hanro, looking all about her warily as if for a stray gunman to jump out at her. Then she stared hard at Brian Langley, narrowing her eyes, accusingly.

Posie nodded. 'I do. And I know who wrote the horrid death threats, too. I also know all about the complicated little drama that led up to that. It was better than any film you could make, Mr Langley, at Sunstar Films. And that's a fact.'

'What drama?' whispered Tom Moran hazily. 'And more importantly, are we still in danger? What's happening here? Who was that who was trying to shoot us? There was a man at the doorway over there, I swear it!'

Posie gulped. *Could it be? Was that even possible?*

But she shook her head and carried on.

'I think that we're safe for now,' said Posie authoritatively, although she felt far from safe. 'We might be lucky enough to enjoy a little interlude. Although I think our killer will start up again for sure. It's Miss Hanro, Miss *Silvia* Hanro, who they want, after all.'

There was a small whimper of fear from the movie star. But Posie ignored it. She sensed a slight movement out on the landing again – that intangible presence – and hoped against hope that Lovelace was lingering in the hopes of overhearing a confession.

But she daren't call out his name in case she blew his cover. 'I'll start, then, shall I?'

Four faces watched her intently, but silence reigned.

'This started out with blackmail. As these things often do. A good while ago. Didn't it, Miss Hanro?'

Posie looked at Pamela, whose blue eyes were pooling like a fox caught in its hide, crouched down pathetically on the floor. Slowly the girl stood up and made an attempt to brush herself down.

'Do you mean that despicable woman in the hat, today?'

'Robbie Fontaine's wife, Sheila. Yes.'

'His *wife*?'

'Yep. *And* Brian Langley's Housekeeper. The two were the same; another bit of ridiculous disguise. You see, Sheila loved Robbie so much she would do anything for him, including staying in the background as a drudge so her husband could pursue a successful career as a professional eligible bachelor. She paid for his drug habit. So she needed money, and lots of it: more than Brian Langley paid her; more than Brian Langley paid Robbie, even. She turned to blackmail. Had probably done so for years.'

Pamela nodded. 'Nasty woman. She blackmailed me over Hilda. Last year. Twice. And again, recently. Said she'd tell the world, and Silvia, about her. I couldn't risk losing my Hilda. I paid up.'

'Who on earth's Hilda?' snapped Silvia.

'There'll be plenty of time for that later, *if* you get out of here alive,' said Posie. 'It's not my place to explain. But everyone else here knows who Hilda is, and that, as it turned out, was fatal for you.'

Posie turned to Tom Moran. 'You know all about Sheila Fontaine, too, don't you? In her capacity as a blackmailer, I mean?'

Tom shrugged, as best he could in handcuffs. 'I suppose so.' There was a pause. He seemed to summon up an inner reserve of strength from somewhere.

'She said she'd reveal my true identity – as Mark Paris, I mean – to the world, unless I paid up. She was quite ruthless.'

'Tom!' Silvia sighed. 'How awful! You should have told me!'

Tom shrugged again. 'And made myself look even more pathetic in your eyes?'

Posie nodded understandingly. 'This case foxed me all along. There were so many facts; so many suspects; so much going on. *Too much* going on. I realised after a bit that that was all on purpose. You're all artists, in a way, making disguises. You're all used to making movie magic. Used to obscuring the truth.'

She paused and looked about herself, buying time.

'The *truth* was what finally led me to understand everything.'

'What truth?' asked Silvia, stupefied.

Posie drummed her fingers on the desk-top.

'It was one of five key things I realised today. Sheila Fontaine was an expert blackmailer, but I suddenly understood how good she really was. Quite the professional. She used the currency of *truth* to get money. Nothing less. No rubbishy half-stories or rumours for her.'

'What are you getting at, Miss Parker?' Pamela Hanro looked confused.

'Simply that if Sheila Fontaine said she knew a story and was prepared to blackmail with it, it was almost certainly correct. It was the *truth*.'

'How fascinating,' snarled Brian Langley, his words just about distinguishable by now. 'But we already know that she knew all about Hilda. She must have snooped around my desk and followed me to Bute Street one day, I suppose. I keep my desk and my mail at home locked up, but I suppose Sheila must have got a skeleton key to open my desk with on a regular basis. If she's as immoral as you suggest?'

Posie nodded. 'It almost certainly happened like that. But I'm not referring to her blackmailing Pamela over Hilda. I'm talking about a different truth entirely. I'm referring to Sheila attempting to blackmail Miss *Silvia* Hanro.'

She looked over at the actress, who was standing by the fireplace.

'Weren't you just telling me in the car over here how Sheila had spun you some ludicrous yarn and expected payment for the telling of the tale?'

The actress was puffing on a smoke, jittery as a cat. She laughed contemptuously. 'You mean that stupid little story about Tom carrying on with Elaine?'

'That's the one.' Posie nodded casually. It had been a crucial realisation, and everything else had stemmed from it.

'I thought to myself *"what if that actually happened?"* and then I understood.'

Posie turned to Tom and smiled.

'Because it *had* happened, hadn't it, Mr Moran? Your affair with Elaine Dickinson? Over the last three months? Sheila Fontaine spoke the truth to your not-yet-wife.'

'Be quiet!' roared Silvia Hanro, stubbing out her cigarette furiously on the marble top of the fireplace. 'Tell them it's not true, Tom!'

But Tom simply smiled lopsidedly. 'What makes you say that, Miss Parker? Why would you think I had an affair with that little woman at Worton Hall? It doesn't make sense.'

Posie sighed heavily.

'Because when you left the specialist hospital where you were being treated for mental health issues, just over three months ago, you were a wreck. You came back to Worton Hall at Silvia's insistence, not knowing what else to do. But everything was different; *too* different, wasn't it? Even Silvia was different with you, and your physical relationship had dwindled to almost nothing. You suspected she was only staying with you out of pity, and that was confirmed to you last night, in her note, when she ran off, wasn't it? It was terrible. Awful, really.'

Posie looked over at Silvia who she saw was licking at her lips nervously. Posie turned back to Tom.

'You were completely unprepared, and the situation you were in hit you like a steam train. You weren't a superstar anymore, but you didn't want to be Mark Paris in his new altered state, did you? Didn't want the world's sympathy.'

'Can you blame me?'

Posie shifted in her seat, tried to look sympathetic. If truth were told she was finding the going pretty sticky. 'Yours was truly an unenviable lot, I agree, but it might have been better to be truthful. For yourself, I mean. You took another, slipshod identity and you got on with things. Only, you weren't happy, were you?'

At Tom's silence she continued:

'It felt awful pretending to be someone else, didn't it? So when Elaine Dickinson told you that she knew who you *really* were, and that she had loved you for years – you had been her hero – you were flattered. Bertie Samuelson was right when he told me that Elaine didn't have a crush on Miss Hanro, only on the male movie stars. But he got it slightly wrong: it had only ever been *you* for Elaine, never Robbie Fontaine. She had loved you like no other in those giddy, glamorous pre-war days. You were relieved that someone knew who you were, what you had *been*. And then you took things to the next level.'

'No!' whispered Silvia, rooted to the spot. 'I don't believe it!'

Posie was focused on Tom. She nodded. 'And then you kept the affair going, didn't you? You couldn't stop it once it was in full-flow. Elaine was intoxicating in her adoration for you, even if she was dreary, laughable, even. And she adored you completely. Isn't that right? Why, she told her own brother that all her dreams had come true at last! She started to dress more glamorously, to wear what she thought were fashionable things to keep your attention. Her brother told me that she was a changed girl. Elaine couldn't believe her luck.'

'Tom?' shrieked Silvia, a good deal choked up. 'Is this true?'

The man turned, looking pained. His shattered face was screwed up and tears weren't far off. He took off his broken blue glasses and rubbed at his one good eye with his right hand.

'Of course not, my love.'

'Oh, but it *is*,' said Posie in a low, carrying voice, looking over at Silvia. 'Although I'm sorry to have to tell this tale. This affair with Elaine was the reason Sheila wanted to blackmail him. She tried on Sunday.'

Posie looked back at Tom. He shook his head slightly. Posie carried on, regardless:

'It wasn't anything to do with Sheila revealing your true identity as Mark Paris, was it? She had found out all about your little tryst on one of her jaunts up to Worton Hall, or, more likely, her friend, the cook, Mrs Thynne, had observed what was going on and had told her. She had the room next door to Elaine, after all, and apparently the walls there are paper thin.'

'You mean Sheila Fontaine tried to blackmail Tom over a tin-pot affair? And then she told my sister about it later?' cut in Pamela incredulously. Tom Moran was now shaking his head over and over.

'That's right.' Posie nodded. 'Sheila Fontaine *tried* to blackmail both sides. But she failed straightaway with Tom. You wouldn't play ball, would you, Tom? I think I'm right in saying that you laughed off her accusations by saying Silvia would never believe it – they sounded ridiculous – and you had a big row with Sheila Fontaine outside the Green Room at Worton Hall on Sunday morning. It was overheard by an extra – Hector Mallow – who mentioned it in passing to me, not quite understanding what was being said. He had heard the words "*squalid little carry-on!*" But Sheila was vengeful, wasn't she? She realised that if she couldn't blackmail you, she'd hurt you instead. She'd ruin you with a piece of devastating information, and tell you it out of spite.'

Tom continued to regard Posie in a stiff, hurt, silence. *Golly, this is just awful*, thought Posie to herself.

'She told you about the baby, didn't she?' Posie stared at Tom now. He choked for a moment, and then whispered:

'Baby? What baby?'

'Don't play dumb. About the baby Silvia had borne Brian Langley, in 1918, while you were away recovering from having your face blown apart on the front line.'

'DON'T!' Silvia shrieked and covered her eyes, her face burning visibly red beneath the paint and powder. 'This is too, too much!'

Tom Moran turned and looked at Silvia for a few seconds, willing his wife to look at him. He looked like he was pleading with her, silently.

Brian Langley was making strange swallowing noises, as if in real discomfort, and at his side Pamela Hanro crossed her arms. She stared at Posie with venomous eyes.

'I can't bear this. Is it really necessary to drag everyone's secret stories out into the light, Miss Parker? Can't we leave it there and all go home?

'Not really, I'm afraid. Because that piece of information, about the baby, triggered a chain of events which have led to at least three deaths since then. Have led us *right here, right now*. And we're only just holding on by the skin of our teeth. But it's not over yet, is it?'

Posie paused.

'Is it, *Mr Langley*?'

* * * *

Thirty-Five

The Producer stared at Posie.

'You still think all of this was me, do you? Foolish girl! All because of that ruddy gun in my hands when the lights went up?'

'No.' Posie shook her head. 'I realised, later admittedly, that it was you who shouted out "*What is this, now?*" when the lights first went off at the Wrap Party. That was crucially important to my understanding of all of this. You had been thrown the gun under cover of darkness, hadn't you? It was your own gun admittedly, which the killer had managed to take from your house, from your gun cupboard, by bribing your oriental manservant. It was dashed clever. You were fixed up and it looked as if you were caught red-handed.'

Brian Langley brightened visibly. 'Thank goodness! You believe me!'

'And the handcuffs? Was that your idea? I'm all agog for details.'

Brain Langley's eyes creased in vexation. He shook his head. 'I simply can't tell you, Miss Parker. I can remember nothing beyond staring down at my gun in my hands in complete surprise…the rest is a total blank.'

'How convenient,' muttered Posie. Then aloud:

'But you knew very well when you called me in to

Worton Hall what you were dealing with. Those death threats: you knew who was behind them, didn't you? You knew what the writer was capable of, and you wanted to protect Silvia and you wanted to protect them *from themselves.*'

Brian Langley hung his head.

'It's the same reason you reported Silvia officially missing last night. You were genuinely worried about her, weren't you? As you believed her to be in grave danger. We overheard you this morning telling Silvia that she was an absolute fool, that she didn't know what she had done, when she told you about her marriage.'

Posie continued:

'That outburst wasn't just a question of professional annoyance; *you* realised the danger Silvia had put herself into. You're a good man, Mr Langley. Even if you do stick a horrible stinking mask over your kindnesses: even if I couldn't see it in the first place. It's why both of the women in this room love you more than they can ever tell you. Why you're a national hero and you've been decorated. Even if you can't bear that. You're a good man.'

Posie stood up sharply.

'Not like the monster chained at your side.'

Posie stared down at the man with the wrecked face in front of her, the man she had found wonderful, a ruined fantasy. She was barely able to say the words. They came out quietly and slowly, as if she had a furry tongue after a bad cold.

'It was you, Tom Moran. Or Mark Paris, as you were. You did all of this. You were planning on killing your own wife today at that Wrap Party. But you missed. It proved dashed difficult in the event, didn't it? With your badly shaking hand? And the sluggishness caused by the opium still in your veins?'

Silvia had gone completely silent. Tom laughed amiably.

'My dear girl, you're quite wrong. Even if I was dallying

with the dresser – which I *wasn't*, for the record – surely it wasn't enough to want to kill my wonderful wife over? You're making a big mistake here.'

Posie shook her head. 'I'm not wrong. Unfortunately.'

Posie glanced over at the doorway to the landing. Feeling very alone, she continued:

'After you had heard Sheila's bombshell about the baby you were angry, desperately so. Rage drove you on to do what you did next, didn't it, Tom? Rage at having discovered what the two people you trusted most in the world had been doing behind your back in 1918.'

Posie was more certain of the puzzle pieces now.

She remembered Tom's words to her the day before when he had been telling her how wonderful Silvia was: '*she's made me what I am: I owe her all of this.*'

But at the time Posie hadn't realised he was being sarcastic.

Posie nodded to herself in the tremulous silence.

'But you had come to bitterly despise Silvia even before this shocking news about the baby, hadn't you? This whole thing has been a good deal about hate for you, hasn't it, Tom? You hated Silvia more and more over the last three months. You blamed her entirely for your current circumstances; your lack of standing, your measly pay packet each month which wasn't enough to feed your opium habit, your lack of any real possessions. Even the flat she had bought you was just a plaything for herself! She had brought you back to Worton Hall, and for what? And to make matters worse, she had gone on to become a movie star of epic proportions. Talk about a role reversal since those days in Flicker Alley! You had spent all of your own earnings on drugs in those pre-war days, I'm guessing. You felt it was all her fault. Even if things weren't going entirely her way now, and even if her star was shining a little dimmer.'

Posie walked about a little, tamping down her nerves.

She noticed that somehow Tom had managed to light up a Turkish cigarette, one handed. He inhaled deeply.

'This is crazy.'

'No, it's not really. You needed your wife dead and you'd been thinking about how to do it for a while. Hadn't you?'

'Of course not!'

'Why?' came the barely-audible whisper of Silvia, whose eyes were saucer-like in their fright, horribly reminiscent of the take which had been played again and again at the Wrap Party.

Posie waved the lawyers' note. 'This is the part of the puzzle which concerns *money*. It concerns the Hanro Family Trust.'

Silvia and Pamela both followed the note with their eyes. Posie continued:

'Another of the five key facts I realised was important today concerned Silvia Hanro's *age*. You're thirty next month, aren't you, Miss Hanro? Not too old, you protest, to be a star. But it *is* old to be unmarried and in receipt of a trust's income and capital, according to the fusty bunch of people who drew up the Hanro Family Trust years and years ago. You are the current beneficiary, but if you don't marry by age thirty, both income and capital pass immediately to your sister Pamela.'

Silvia stared. 'Is this important?'

'It is if you want the money. Or should I say, if a potential *husband* wants the money. Which he would receive, by the way, if you married him and then pre-deceased him. And Tom Moran wanted that money bigtime. He didn't want to be palmed off with a paltry little London flat in the Albany. He wanted serious money: the whole Hanro Trust.'

'This is all news to me,' said Silvia, her nerves holding.

'Your lawyers received letters asking for clarification on this point recently, apparently signed by you. I'm guessing that Elaine Dickinson, judging by the practice signatures up in her room, was a dab hand at imitating your writing.

She must have been in on this whole idea with Tom. She was very much part of the plan, and a good little actress in her own right: careful not to be seen around the place with Tom, careful to be seen visibly lusting after Robbie Fontaine.'

Posie then explained that answers had been sent to Silvia from the lawyers, but that these had simply disappeared *en route*, most likely ending up in other, interested hands. *Very* interested hands.

Posie looked directly at Tom.

'You had been meaning to convince Silvia to marry you in secret before her thirtieth birthday, anyhow, hadn't you? To break the rules Sunstar Films and the film industry in general had put in place about marriage. You had another month to go before her birthday. But anger at that revelation about the baby changed the whole plan. You had to act quickly now.'

'*What* plan?' whispered Silvia, audibly enough for them all to hear a sick fear in her voice.

Posie chewed at her lip. The whole truth was distinctly unpalatable.

'Initially, Tom here had been planning on marrying you, and then killing you, but much later, in private, after a good long while. He would have got the Hanro Trust money, and then married Elaine, I'm guessing. Or at least, that's what he told her, to judge by the clippings of wedding dresses up in her room. Her brother certainly thought she was going to marry.'

Silvia gasped.

'But the truth about the baby changed things. Tom saw a way not only to kill you and get your trust money, but a way to get revenge upon both you and Brian Langley in the most public, most humiliating of ways, with all the press watching. You'd be dead, and Brian Langley would be ruined, both as a man and as a Film Producer. And if Tom could plant enough evidence on Brian, he'd be had up for your murder. And Brian would hang. That was the most important thing. So time was of the essence: Tom had to act straight away. But you needed to be married first.'

Posie shook her head in quiet disbelief.

'I'm not sure quite how he did it, Miss Hanro, but I assume Tom forced you to agree to marry him on Sunday, despite your misgivings about going against film industry rules. I guess he told you he'd kill himself if you didn't marry him? Did he put a gun to his own head? Did you feel you had to go along with the marriage because you knew Tom might actually pull the trigger, based on his very recent mental health issues? And you felt guilty, of course. So you promised him you'd apply for the licence the very next day, the Monday, and get married on Wednesday. As quickly as the Registry Office would allow.'

Silvia stared at the floor in silence. Brian Langley nodded and tried to pull away from the man at his side, uselessly. 'That's right, Miss Parker. Spot on.'

He looked over at his leading lady with a mixture of scorn and choked emotion.

'Silvia came to tell me what was going on on Sunday afternoon and I advised her against it, of course. I knew Mark Paris of old, and while I felt sorry for him, what had happened to him in the war, I knew what he was capable of. He was always a man who sought his own satisfaction above all others. He had shown ruthlessness at every stage in his career and had lived the high life. You're right: I believe he spent all of his considerable film wages before the war. On drugs, I think. Silvia knew that, too: must have been terrified he'd become addicted again. I saw it again these last couple of weeks, the slide into drugs. I could smell it on him, see his apathy. At least in the hospital he couldn't touch those sorts of drugs. When I saw him there he was obviously in a bad way, but not as bad as this.'

'You visited him in the hospital?'

'Of course. As often as I could. His going to war had

been a huge publicity attraction for Sunstar Films: we had no idea what sort of war it would be. I knew Silvia couldn't bear to visit him, and he was alone: he had no other family that I knew of. He didn't tell you about my visits?'

'No.'

Brian Langley shrugged. 'It goes without saying that I didn't want Silvia to marry him. I assumed he might be after Silvia's film earnings, I didn't even know about a Trust Fund. I told her that the suicide threats were a load of old rot and to ignore them. Which she didn't, obviously.'

Posie nodded grimly. 'She *succumbed*. So with the secret wedding set for the Wednesday morning, Tom began, with the enthusiastic help of Elaine, to send death threats to his future wife, as a way of establishing a legitimate background if it was investigated later. You knew it was him, didn't you, Mr Langley? You wanted, in hiring me, to warn Tom off.'

'That's right. I knew he was dangerous. I wanted to nip it in the bud. I thought he'd get scared with you around, and stop.'

'I must have been a gift for you.' Posie smiled tightly, looking at Tom straight on. 'A lady detective, inefficient and bumbling, yet a credible witness to the situation, if needed, later on. It was indicative to you that Brian Langley was at least a bit rattled, wasn't it? And at least the police weren't brought in, sniffing around. For you were skating on thin ice, weren't you? Things were already going wrong for you yesterday. Badly wrong. Unravelling.'

Tom smoked reflectively, then ground out his stub on the floor. At his calm silence Posie continued:

'I mean with Elaine, of course.'

'Elaine?'

'Yes. While you and Silvia went out to get married on the Wednesday morning, Elaine had diverted from the agreed plan. She had been writing death threats to Silvia under your direct supervision. But yesterday she added a grisly memento for Silvia all of her own. It was a well-timed taunt, wasn't it, that finger with its tin-foil ring? What Silvia took to be a reference to her own marriage to you, was actually a jibe from Elaine, a reference to *her* eventual marriage to you. That the best woman would win the prize. *You.*'

Posie nodded, certain now.

'But she went too far, didn't she? You were furious when you discovered what she had done. How could you marry someone like that, even if it wasn't just yet? You said to me when I first met you: "*What sort of sick person sends a finger?*" And you meant that, literally.'

Posie frowned at the memory of the man telling her all of this, cool as a cucumber, out on the sun-drenched lawns, acting his part magnificently. She, for one, had been taken in.

'The spell you had been under for three months was broken. Elaine was now dangerous. I imagine you confronted Elaine about the finger early yesterday evening, and she probably threatened to reveal everything.'

Downstairs a door slammed, and then there was an intense hammering, but from far, far below.

Posie ignored it.

'I think that somehow you got Elaine to accompany you down to Silvia's dressing room after Silvia had left for the day having left you that horrid little note; so you knew the coast was clear. You gave Elaine a sweet drink, a Bees Knees, pretending to smooth things over between you. You had tipped in the water from the orchids, and then you held her down forcibly to drink it. You were good at setting up the scene afterwards, too: you made her death look like a suicide, while at the same time you managed to mock Elaine, even in death, with her own tin-foil ring and Silvia's clothes on, rather than her own. I imagine you then went back up to Elaine's room and ransacked the place, making sure to add pictures of Robbie Fontaine and Silvia

Hanro to the prized assortment of photos of *you* out on display.'

Posie thought about that wrecked room. She nodded.

'You threw about some cocaine, didn't you? To make people think the poor girl had been an addict. You didn't mind leaving the green ink and death-threat practice notes, in fact, you thought it might look like Elaine was a crazed fan, which was exactly how the police took it. It was a shame you didn't check to remove Elaine's attempts at Silvia's signature; otherwise I wouldn't have understood her role in all of this. Then you went straight off to Richmond to send the telegrams to the press, inviting them to the public murder of your wife the next day.'

'What led you to realise that Tom was behind all of this?' said Pamela in a very soft, quiet voice.

There was more hammering now from downstairs. Posie had a knot of fear in her stomach which kept tightening. *What on earth...*

But she turned to Pamela.

'It was today, this afternoon. Two other unconnected things. One was about a scent. Tom had said to me this morning, incongruously I thought, at the time, that "*the scent of death is with me even now.*" He said that strange phrase to me after Elaine's body had been discovered. At the time I thought he was talking about the smell of death in the trenches of the war. But this afternoon I realised he was being literal: he had indeed been talking about the awful smell in that small room last night; a corpse on a blisteringly hot evening, the terrible smell of death. He had probably gone back to the dressing room last night when he returned from Richmond, before taking his opium, just to check all was in order with his horrible suicide tableau.'

'What was the second thing?' whispered Silvia. The sound of banging was frantic now.

'Oh, *you* helped me with that.' Posie smiled, half her mind on the din downstairs.

'You told me that Mrs Thynne did pretty much anything for money. And I realised that what with the argument which must have taken place, and the ransacking of Elaine's room after her murder, someone must have seen or heard something. But what if that person, in a room next door, had been bought off? What if that person had been paid to say they had seen someone – Brian Langley – coming out of that room? When in fact nothing of the sort had happened. That was just part of the plan to implicate Brian, wasn't it?'

Posie paused and looked at Tom again.

'In fact, I think I overheard Mrs Thynne telling Sheila Fontaine, of all people, today, that you owed her money, and I expect it was for that. There was other stuff, too: you had gone the day before, in your boater hat, to bribe Brian Langley's gardener – who you knew through the opium connection, of course – into giving you his employer's gun, the Webley. To leave at the scene. You actually managed to throw it at Brian Langley in the darkness, which incriminated him as soon as the lights went up. What a shame for you that not all Webley's are the same: the police already know that the shot which killed Mr Fontaine came from *your* Webley, a Mark .455, and not Langley's, which was newer army issue.'

Tom Moran sat expressionlessly. 'Cleverly put, Miss Parker. You seem to have this all wrapped up, if you'll forgive the pun. Is there *anything* you don't understand?'

Posie thrust her chin out purposefully and tried to look like there was not much which got past her. But she *had* to ask. It was the only thing…

'*Why* are you two chained together? I don't understand that.'

Suddenly Tom Moran had risen to his feet, dragging Brian up with him, like a puppet, without resistance. The expression on Tom's shattered face had changed suddenly; he had stuck out his jaw in a determined way and a furious

375

light was dancing in his eye. Every nerve in his face and body was taut: he was a man possessed of a cool, steely resolve. Even now. Especially now.

'Oh!'

And it was almost a relief, for there it was, the sliver of a silver gun in his right hand; it must have been up his shirt-sleeve all along. His Webley. He trained it on Posie in an instant and she put her hands up.

Tom was aiming at Posie, but his right hand was anything but steady, and he was shaking all over the place: she could quite see how he had managed to miss shooting his own wife earlier, how he had got Robbie Fontaine instead.

Posie was curiously calm, despite Silvia starting to moan in a series of juddering whimpers.

'Now hang on a minute, old boy.' Brian Langley was sounding a little slurry still, trying not to add any additional jerkiness, but there was a definite touch of the hero of the trenches behind his words. 'There's no need for *that*.'

'Oh, I think you'll find there's *every* need for this, Brian,' snapped Tom, in a voice Posie didn't recognise. 'No-one here is getting out alive.'

Help.

Posie's mind was scrambling, trying to find a way out for all of them. But just then Posie's neck prickled suddenly and inconveniently. That old sign; someone was watching her from behind, from the doorway.

She spun around and gaped.

For the man in the doorway with a gun trained right on Tom Moran was no friend or saviour of hers. Quite the opposite, in fact.

It was Caspian della Rosa.

****

Thirty-Six

Posie gasped.

'You!'

Can this really get any worse?

There was no doubt. No doubt at all.

Small and stocky and incredibly well-dressed in an immaculate navy wool pin-striped suit and pink shirt, despite the sizzling heat, Count Caspian della Rosa stuck out like a sore thumb as he was the only person in the room not covered in white debris.

'Yes, my lovely. It is I.'

He smiled slowly, a peculiarly cat-like smile which split his bland, fleshy, unattractive face in two. Posie felt like running. For here was a much greater evil than Tom Moran.

Probably.

This was the man who had pursued her for more than two years, the international arch-criminal mastermind whose web of fortunes and contacts were spread, tentacle-like, all over the world. The man could, it seemed, disappear, Rumpelstiltskin-like, at the drop of a hat, and he had thus avoided police on every continent, despite heading every most-wanted list in the world. Count della Rosa was a chameleon, and loved disguises. But most importantly,

Caspian della Rosa was also a cold-blooded killer, who would stop at nothing to get what he wanted.

And he had made it clear, back in 1921, that what he wanted was Posie. At any cost. He had sent her cryptic clues and occasional hints that he was still alive, and still attentive. And for the most part Posie had tried to force these messages and clues from her mind, surrounding herself with lightness and pleasant thoughts, and the police, and Len.

And Alaric, of course.

'Good afternoon, Posie. How lovely to meet again after all this time. Nice hair, by the way, I can just about make it out beneath the dust. I was just dropping by. I see you are keeping really quite unusual company, these days. Is that not Miss Silvia Hanro over there, beneath the white paint?' He indicated towards the movie star casually, with a raise of an amused eyebrow. Silvia Hanro, cowering in a corner, looked as if she might scream.

The gun Caspian della Rosa held did not waver.

'Who, might I ask, is this?' spat Tom Moran, obviously a good deal put out. He nodded at Posie, who he still had in his gunsight.

'Some pal of yours? Is this the fella who was shooting rounds in here earlier? Some kind of lunatic, are you? You could have killed us all.'

Caspian della Rosa executed a mock half-bow and smiled again.

'That was indeed me,' he said in his perfect, only-just-foreign-accented English.

'But, you know, I, unlike you, from the looks of things, am a very good shot. I was aiming at the light fitting, with no intention of killing anyone. Unlike you, from what I have just overheard. You who have every intention of being the only one in this room to leave it alive.'

Posie couldn't resist asking. 'So why did you shoot in here then? Some strange fanfare to mark your arrival, was it?'

Caspian della Rosa smiled, a nerve in his cheek twitching. His eyes never left Tom's face, or his gun.

'Hardly to mark my arrival, my love,' he breathed softly. 'I've been here for what seems like hours. At least half an hour before you arrived, Posie.'

'*What?*'

Tom's gun continued to wobble, his gaze turning from Posie to Caspian, and back again.

'Quite. I've been out on the landing, in that adorable little bathroom of yours. It was a tight little squeeze actually, me, and my assistant, Roslington.' And here he indicated out onto the landing where a shadow made itself bend and twitch into the shape of a man.

And then a long, thin, very good-looking man in his late twenties came through the glass door. A military bearing marked his appearance.

'Good afternoon.' The immaculate young man smiled, taking his hat off briefly, his face registering neither surprise nor emotion at the scene he had walked into. *Another lackey, no doubt*, Posie thought to herself. *A man who will do whatever Caspian della Rosa wants…*

'And we were in there with your gentleman friend, too. He put up quite a protest, you'll be pleased to know. Even tied up in ropes and gagged…'

'*Len?*'

'That's the one. Bring him here, will you, Roslington? Gently does it, now.'

A scuffling sound could be heard outside on the landing.

It had been Len, a prisoner, that had been the kicking and moaning noise which had been heard earlier. He had been here all along, and he hadn't deserted Posie in her hour of need, at all. He had probably tried his best…

Posie felt like she was about to be sick.

Suddenly Len was pushed through the door by the scruff of his neck. His hands and ankles were bound tightly with string, and his face was almost obscured by a large cotton gag, which was dirty and damp. A smear of blood was high on Len's forehead beneath his tight dark curls. What could be seen of his green eyes registered panic and disbelief, and as they scanned the devastated interior of the office, and took in Tom with his gun trained on Posie, Len started to scream beneath his gag.

Posie's heart lurched. She balled her hands up into fists and willed herself not to move. She wanted to run to Len, to assure him all would be okay, even though she knew it wouldn't.

'Oh, do be quiet, my dear fellow,' said Caspian della Rosa calmly.

'He was most obliging, Posie. Let us in as if we were old friends; although I trust it was you whom he was expecting. You'd helpfully sent a telephone message to warn him to look out for you, and it was that which alerted us. I'd been monitoring your calls for quite some time, judging the best time and location to come and get you. I had a couple of false starts; like at Isleworth the other day. I was in a costumier's van, all ready to come and get you when Miss Hanro turned up, out of the blue. So I disappeared, pronto. Most disappointing. But here we are. All's well which ends well. Or maybe not.'

Caspian della Rosa twitched his gun at Tom.

'Who *are* you? And don't think you're about to steal my prize away from me now I've finally got her.'

Tom Moran laughed, and it was an eerie sound in the silent room. 'You mean Miss Parker? Call her a prize? You've got to be joking, right?'

Caspian della Rosa shook his head. 'Oh no, my dear sir,' he said, very softly. 'I never joke. About anything. And neither do you, if your recent acts are anything to go by.'

'What acts? I thought you didn't recognise this man?' asked Posie, quick as a pistol-shot.

Caspian della Rosa shrugged, but he had imperceptibly shifted position, had tightened his hold on the trigger of his gun.

'I *don't* know him. All I know is what I saw from the landing window while you were having a nice chat with your girlfriends in here, and I didn't like what I saw.'

'What was it?'

'Dirty tricks. Of the worst sort. This fellow here was sitting in a blue van. He got out and spoke to you on the entry phone, and then went and sat back in his van. A few minutes later he dragged this other angry-looking man out of the back of the vehicle. The second chap was in a bad way; unconscious by the looks of things, most likely drugged by your fellow here, who then rolled him up in black sacking and left him in the road, and then went and murdered a policeman.'

'*Sergeant Binny!*' gasped Posie in horror. 'Oh no! You're quite sure?'

'I'm certain. He shot him with the gun he's toting about here; couldn't fail to miss at that short-range, even with a jerky arm, and then he stole another gun from the dead policeman, and some handcuffs. He pushed the body of the policeman under the black car he had been stationed in, and then came back to your second man here. All I saw next on the street was him pushing the black sacking bundle through your doorway. I heard him coming up the stairs, though, dragging this man up with him, and then I watched him through the keyhole in the door of the bathroom.'

'Watched him?'

'On the landing. He quickly unwrapped his pal here, and then hit him about the head a bit, which seemed to wake him up a bit more. He hit himself, too, gave himself a bloodied nose and a cracked lens. He then clipped himself together to the second man using the policeman's cufflinks. He has the key, by the way,' Caspian della Rosa added. 'In his right-hand trouser pocket.'

The chain linking Tom to Brian was glinting in the still-strong sunshine, stretched to breaking-point as Tom continued to aim at Posie, and for some reason everyone's gaze swivelled to it.

'Not that anyone will be needing a key,' said Caspian della Rosa cheerfully. There was a whipping crack as he shot at the chain, breaking it apart in one easy motion and the bullet whizzed away, harmlessly.

'See?'

Brian Langley had collapsed on the floor, panting in relief. Down by Pamela, who had her arms about him within seconds.

Caspian della Rosa grinned but when he spoke, his voice was frighteningly free of any warmth:

'I don't know this man from Adam, but I heard you, Posie, asking why these two men were in chains. *I* can answer that pretty well, I'd say.'

He paused for effect. A consummate showman.

'When two men, both beaten up and both seemingly suffering from some sort of handy memory-loss-inducing agent, a drug, are chained together, it is impossible to say *who* chained the other up. I'd bet my life on the fact that your one-eyed friend here would have sworn blind, if caught by the police, that *he* had been the victim of this second man's actions. Who could disprove him? In taking a hostage, and drugging him, he was adding authenticity to whatever acts or crimes he had been guilty of, providing a useful suspect for when things got nasty. And, I'm sure he has planted other evidence upon the second man elsewhere. A sneaky move, even if I do say so myself.'

Posie found herself nodding in unlikely agreement. 'Why did you come in here and shoot around the place though? How did that help?'

'It didn't. But I knew this man was dangerous when I watched him out on the landing; the way he was carrying on with his two guns, dropping them and trying to conceal them about his person in jerky movements. I wanted to let him know there was someone else here, someone handy with a gun, someone *better* than him. To unnerve him. Your police cover had spectacularly failed you. It fails you still.'

'Where is the Inspector? Please don't say you've hurt him?'

Caspian della Rosa shook his head. 'Roslington here merely locked him out. He went down and shuttered up the door from the inside. Your Inspector must have found his Sergeant's body and then realised what he was dealing with. That's him down there hitting the door over and again.'

Posie drew a great shuddering breath of relief, but before she could register anything else, she turned to Tom.

He has two guns, she thought to herself. *He has Binny's gun, too.*

'What do you plan on doing now?' she found herself asking, hearing her own voice as if it were a stranger's in the room.

Tom stared at her.

'It's as your friend says,' he sneered. 'I'll shoot the lot of you. Including Silvia, of course. And no-one will ever know I was here. Your little foreign friend over there in the navy suit can go to hell. The whole thing will be blamed on Langley.'

'You'll never get away with this you know, Tom.'

Out of the corner of her eye Posie saw Silvia rising from her corner, moving towards her husband.

'Can't we work this out? Step away, my darling. Step away now. Put the gun down. No amount of money is worth all this fuss. Is it?'

And then the shooting started.

****

Thirty-Seven

It all happened very quickly.

Tom aimed at his wife, in a pelting stream of bullets, and she fell, and then he aimed at Brian Langley, who seemed to be lying dead already under the table.

But Caspian della Rosa was shooting, too, and with one expert move Tom's gun went arching smartly up into the air, and with a second shot Tom fell to the floor, writhing in pain, a bullet neatly in his leg.

Caspian della Rosa took in the scene in front of him, the bodies and the mess, and he moved around to where Posie was standing, stock-still behind Prudence's desk.

'We need to leave.'

She could barely register what was happening, barely heard his words, which came louder, more insistently:

'It's time to leave, my darling. And this time, I'm not taking "no" for an answer. Come with me.'

He pulled at Posie's white-dusted arms, manoeuvred her towards the front door, past Len, whose eyes were filled with disbelief, but whose tied limbs prevented him from doing anything. At the front door she turned, took in the carnage of her office, and resigned herself to her fate. It seemed a fate barely worth fighting for.

'I'm coming,' she heard herself say numbly.

And then there was another spray of bullets, and the swift, sickening thud of something falling, and a wet splash of something all over her back, and, turning, she saw that Caspian della Rosa had been shot, and was lying face-down in a pool of blood.

Tom Moran was shooting from the floor. With the second gun of Binny's which Caspian della Rosa had completely forgotten about in his hurry to get away.

Posie gasped, but not before Roslington had darted forwards, grabbed up the small body of his boss and heaved it like a sack of potatoes over his shoulder. He ran through the door and off down the stairs.

Posie slumped down by the door, almost regardless of her fate. She looked over at Tom, who was lying on the floor, losing blood from his leg wound, even now desperately trying to aim Sergeant Binny's gun in her direction. Out of the corner of her eye, Posie saw Pamela Hanro, alive and unhurt, dashing to and fro, trying to attend to both Brian Langley and her sister, both of whom appeared pretty lifeless.

Posie got up, anger coursing through her veins, and went over to where Tom was lying. She kicked the gun out of his hands, out of the way.

She stared down.

'Do you remember you told me yesterday how you're a walking reminder of the war? How people don't like being reminded about it? It seems to me that *if* you get out of here alive, you're going to be remembered for a whole lot more than your movie career, or your fake name, or your injuries. War turned a lot of us into ghosts and shadows, but you went that stage further, didn't you? War turned you into a monster. I have no pity for you. And I can't help you, although I expect help will come sooner or later.'

She spun around, aware of a small voice in the kitchen doorway.

'All right, Miss? Is it always this lively in here?'

Sidney seemed unfazed by the sights which met his eyes: the pools of blood and Tom writhing on the floor; the moans which seemed to be coming from Brian Langley.

'Was that Mr Roslington's voice I heard just now, Miss? You know, Mr Fontaine's old contact at the Burlington Arcade? Only, I couldn't be sure. And I thought I heard his Butler here, too? Mr Rose? The man seemed to be doing most of the talking. Why was that?'

Posie realised quite suddenly that Roslington, Robbie Fontaine's drug dealer, had been a puppet frontman for Caspian della Rosa and his unsavoury activities, of course.

But typically for Caspian della Rosa, he couldn't just keep himself in the background. He had probably relished the drama of placing himself in the role of a servant, loved being in disguise, keeping a watchful eye on things. Shockingly, it dawned on Posie that Caspian della Rosa had been here, in England, in the very heart of London, not ten minutes from her flat and her office, all along.

Right under Scotland Yard's noses. It was typical of the man, somehow. He had been watching and waiting for her.

Posie shivered.

Was he dead now? Did she care? He had probably saved her life, but only to better serve his own goals.

Her thoughts were interrupted by a terrible moaning noise over by the sash window. It was Len.

'I'll get some scissors,' said Sidney, sensibly, frowning over at Len curiously. He dashed into the kitchen, re-emerging with the scissors.

He trotted over to Len and began expertly cutting at the string and gag, Mr Minks at his heels.

At last the gag was off, and Len was desperately trying to stand, and almost falling over, and tottering to and fro, trying to rub life back into his numb hands and feet. Posie looked at him none too sympathetically.

You were supposed to help me, Posie felt like saying, but she bit her lip.

Len was just Len, after all.

How could he have fought off Caspian della Rosa and his lackey with their well-oiled plans and weapons?

But even so…

'Who's this?' Len said at last, staring at Sidney.

An idea came to Posie then. And it baffled her that it hadn't occurred to her before: it was so absolutely *right*.

'This is your new employee, Len. You were just telling us yesterday how you're going to be run off your feet again soon. Well, here's the solution. Sidney has all the makings of a very good shadower. He's an expert stringer already, aren't you, Sidney?'

Sidney beamed and nodded while Len just stared, unhelpfully, not much liking what he was hearing.

But just then there was a hurried step on the stairs, and what sounded like teams of hob-nailed boots bashing on the landings below.

It must be the police. At last!

Chief Inspector Lovelace darted through the glass door, followed by reams of men in uniform who went straight over to where Tom Moran was still twitching about.

'Posie!' Lovelace yelped. 'Thank Goodness! I didn't know what had become of you when that door was closed on me. I'd never have forgiven myself. But poor Binny…'

And then the Chief Inspector overcame anything like any professionalism and reached for Posie and took her into the shelter of his arms, oblivious to Len and Sidney and the stares of all of his men.

And Posie allowed herself to be wrapped inside his embrace, both of them covered in someone else's blood. It was warm and comforting and Lovelace was so very much not like a movie star or a monster or anything at all magical.

Not a hero, either. But no-one had been a hero today.

Posie closed her eyes and as she did so she was aware of men behind them tramping back and forwards, efficiently carrying stretchers.

'He'll live, guv!' she heard one of the men shout from the staircase. She assumed he was carrying Tom.

This was followed by another man, shouting:

'Say, ain't this that famous movie star, Silvia Hanro? Used to be quite the thing! She looks like she might live, too! Just about!'

But Chief Inspector Lovelace didn't reply. He didn't move.

Holding tight to Posie, it took her a moment to realise that he was crying.

****

(Two Weeks Later)
Epilogue

The hot weather had broken at last, and the dramatic thundery storms which had followed had given way to ominous pearly grey skies, and an August which already had a promise of autumn about it.

In fact, as Posie Parker stepped out of St Margaret's Church, in the grounds of Westminster Abbey, on the arm of her fiancé, Alaric Boynton-Dale, her black suede heels crunched down on dry, brown fallen leaves.

How depressing, she thought to herself.

Summer gone, already.

The sky overhead was the colour of pewter and it matched her mood.

'Smile, love! It might never happen!' shouted a cheery, irritating voice and a flashbulb went off. It was a newspaper journalist with his photographer in tow.

Several others started up. As Posie squinted into the lights she saw banks of photographers stood back behind several policemen, who had formed a guard between the press and the people coming out of the church.

'Alaric! Over here!'

'Miss Parker! This way! Smile!'

'Just grit your teeth and bear it,' muttered Alaric in Posie's ear. 'It will be over soon.'

'How can I smile? We've just come out of a funeral!'

Behind them a woman in black furs and sunglasses and a black mesh headscarf was stepping outside of the church and the press went mad, forgetting Posie and Alaric in an instant.

They had got what they had come for. The woman of the moment.

Silvia Hanro.

****

The church for Sergeant Binny's funeral had been packed to the rafters, despite the fact he had had no family. It turned out that he had lost his parents young and his two brothers had been killed in the first few months of the war.

Sergeant Rainbird had read out a surprisingly touching eulogy to his colleague, and had managed to make it through without crying. As had Chief Inspector Lovelace, although tears were obviously not far away.

A man who had served under Binny in the trenches had not fared quite so well; he had stepped down from the lectern after only a couple of short sentences, unable to go on.

The congregation were, for the most part, policemen, but Binny's old regiment, or what remained of it, had come along and were sat at the front right-hand side of the church; the wounded and those in wheelchairs nearest the aisle.

Behind the former regiment sat Silvia Hanro, in a row all by herself. She had, unbelievably, sustained virtually no injuries in the attack by her husband in the Grape Street

Bureau, and had apparently passed out in pure fear when he had started firing at her.

Behind her, frostily apart, sat Brian Langley, who had not fared so well. He was placed out in the aisle, in a wheelchair, and he shouldn't really have been released from hospital yet. It seemed unlikely he would ever walk again, having sustained several shots to his legs. He sat next to Pamela Hanro, who was attentive at his side, immaculate in an exquisite black dress and hat.

She had, apparently, been visiting Brian Langley daily in hospital, oftentimes bringing Hilda. At the Coroner's Inquest into Robbie Fontaine's death, Pamela had, like Posie, stood and given a Witness Statement. In this she had revealed that she had only attended the Wrap Party because Brian Langley had invited her months before, as a 'treat'. It was obvious she was deeply in love with the Film Producer, but less obvious was his return of that love. It seemed uncertain. It was also unclear to Posie whether Silvia had found out about Hilda, or whether she had even spoken to her sister since the shootings. But time, and circumstances, would, no doubt, tell. Posie thought again of that haunting Singer Sargent painting of the two little Hanro girls, clasped together forever in childhood, and marvelled at how far they had come. And how far apart from each other they had travelled. Even now, even though they were so physically close to each other.

The Grape Street contingent had sat in the pew behind, including Len and Prudence, who had wept far more than anyone expected – who knew that she had carried a candle for Sergeant Binny? – and also Dolly and Rufus.

Posie felt awful. As she did at all funerals. But this one was so shocking, so unreal. So uncalled for.

Poor Binny. Cut off in the prime of his life, with everything ahead of him and with everything going for him.

Poor studious Binny, who had survived the war, only

to end up dead now. Whose expertise and learning for the Inspector's exams would now never be called for. It was just awful.

Even now Posie's blood boiled at the unjustness of it all, the unfairness.

That monster.

Binny had been in the wrong place at the wrong time, as had Constable McCrae, whose funeral had already taken place already, up in Scotland.

Robbie Fontaine had been in the wrong place, too. His funeral was all set for the following week, and it sounded as if it would be comparable with a state funeral for a king or queen.

Posie sighed even now at the thought of attending, but vowed she would go, although it would be alone, as Alaric would have disappeared off to India by then.

Posie had sat quietly in the church, listening to the readings and hymns, and mulling things over, thinking about the public outcry which had greeted the news that Robbie Fontaine had been murdered.

The twisted, mangled version of the story which the press had put out was that Robbie Fontaine had been murdered on purpose by Tom Moran; who was actually Mark Paris, in a fit of jealousy over Silvia Hanro.

The press were suggesting there had been a duel.

While it was far from the truth, it had caught the public's imagination and the country were divided over who was the better man, Robbie Fontaine, or poor, injured Mark Paris, back from the dead.

The commercial effect of all of this was that Sunstar Films, directed by Brian Langley from his hospital bed, had released *Henry the King* much earlier than planned, and it was already on general release. It was a smash hit. Huge queues were reported at cinemas nationwide: there had never been such a rush to see a non-American film before, and Sunstar Films, and Silvia Hanro, were making hay while the sun shone.

Although it wasn't shining much for Mark Paris – or Tom Moran – as Posie had known him.

Some newspapers were running different reports; that Tom Moran was mentally unhinged, and they were relishing publishing grainy photographs which had been obtained just a couple of days after the attack at Grape Street, when Tom had been transferred from hospital to a secure cell at New Scotland Yard. His ruined face in photographs looked even worse than in real-life, and his re-emergence into public life was the talk of the town.

Chief Inspector Lovelace had told Posie that Tom's leg wound had been severe, but not life-threatening, and that he was being watched carefully in his police cell. He had been acting strangely in the last couple of weeks, and all items which he might harm himself with had been removed for his own safety.

Tom was being charged with double murder, and also for the manslaughter of Robbie Fontaine and Constable McCrae, but Lovelace had muttered darkly to Posie that he might not even stand trial, as he was perhaps going to be declared criminally insane.

As if, thought Posie, a trifle unsympathetically, perhaps. But then she looked at the small, plain wooden casket at the front of the church, with Binny's old constable's hat atop it, and the Blue Plume of Lovelace's, which he had insisted on placing there, dedicating it to Binny, and she felt the anger bubble up in her again...

The real story, with its Grape Street showdown, had been hushed up, as had the real reason why Robbie Fontaine had been murdered.

Elaine Dickinson's name, appropriately enough, had never even made the newspapers, despite her being listed as an official murder victim by the courts. At the end, she was as insipid and colourless in death as she had been in life. The death threats and the attempt to murder Silvia Hanro had never made the light of day either, amazingly.

Inspector Lovelace had told Posie that Silvia Hanro had already instructed Carver & Nicholas to draft up the necessary papers which would enable her marriage to Tom to be annulled. All traces of the events of 25th and 26th July were skilfully being erased.

But not for poor Binny.

****

An hour later, in the upstairs wooden-panelled cosiness of a private room of the Dog & Duck, the nearest pub to New Scotland Yard, and apparently Sergeant Binny's choice of watering-hole, people thronged to remember Binny and to toast his life.

Chief Inspector Lovelace was obviously very upset, and nodded simply at Posie from behind a glass of dark-coloured ale, not trusting himself to speak. His wife, Molly, was chatting with a bunch of other policemen's wives. Sidney, making himself useful despite being underage, was bobbing about collecting up old used plates and cups, wearing a black suit Posie had bought him specially for the occasion.

Posie lingered near one of the leaded windows, looking out across to the church they had just come from, and the green lawns in front of it. It had begun to rain again and the droplets pelted against the glass.

A small touch of a sleeve and Dolly was at Posie's side.

'You all right, lovey? You seem awful pale.'

Posie laughed. 'I should be asking you that. You're pregnant and probably needing a sit-down. How's everything going?'

'Oh, much the same, really. I'm pretty much under lock and key. But better than poor old Binny.' Dolly shook her bleached blonde head under its neat black skull-cap with twirls of netting and veils. There were twinkles of brand-new diamonds at her ears.

'I can't believe it. I'm sorry I egged you on into taking this case. You wouldn't have got into that car and gone to Worton Hall if I hadn't insisted on it, would you?'

Posie sighed. 'It's not your fault at all. I have the feeling I would have been dragged into it somehow or other.' She looked over at Silvia Hanro, who was sitting at a corner table, all alone and drinking brandy, being stared at from all sides. Posie hadn't spoken to her since the shoot-out, and she wasn't planning on talking now. There was something rotten about the girl. Even now, she was profiting from all this misery.

'I'll tell you one thing,' nodded Posie. 'I don't envy that woman there one jot. Not one bit. She can keep her furs and her jewels and her Trust Fund money, *if* she still gets it. Who knows? I hope to goodness her sister gets the lot; serves her right. Silvia Hanro has nothing I want. Nothing at all. That whole make-believe-world: it makes me sick. Sergeant Binny was worth one hundred of her.'

'Rightly said,' agreed Dolly. 'Although she *has* got beautiful hair, hasn't she? What a shame you went and had yours dyed back to brown. It looked quite fancy…'

Dolly winked at Posie, who almost managed a laugh. 'Now, are they anchovy paste sandwiches over there? I'll grab us some.'

Dolly wandered off, hungry. Posie stood at the window again. Alaric had been forever getting her a drink and she couldn't be bothered to chase him, or to look for him at the crowded little bar in the middle of the room. He had been very quiet these last two weeks, as had everybody. Needless to say, his big birthday party had been cancelled.

'I say, old girl. Bearing up, are we?' Turning, she saw Rufus, Lord Cardigeon, at her side. But today she barely acknowledged him and stared out of the window again angrily.

Rufus was drinking tea, and looking immaculate in a black suit and a Burberry summer cape. He was hatless and in the bright light Posie suddenly saw how he was losing his hair. He was broader than he used to be, too.

Sure as bread is bread he'll be turning into his father soon, Posie thought, without much amusement.

'How's your father?' she said curtly, without looking around.

'Oh, so-so. They say he won't make it until Christmas. I'd be surprised if he's still with us for Michaelmas, though. He'll be gone by the end of October.'

'I'm sorry.'

'Me too, surprisingly. I say, is everything quite okay?'

Posie turned at last. She checked Dolly was still in the distance, picking sandwiches from a serving tray with obvious enjoyment.

And then she lost her temper.

'I thought we were *friends*, Rufus.'

'What are you talking about?' Rufus scratched his head. 'We *are* friends.'

'Not any more,' Posie hissed. 'Tell me, is Dolly still in some sort of imaginary danger?'

Rufus stared. 'I don't know what you mean. I told you Dolly was in danger and she was. Still is. We have to be very careful. Nothing imaginary about that!'

'What's the danger? *What?* Tell me exactly.'

'I can't.' Rufus drew himself up to his full height. 'It's very confidential.'

Posie remembered Rufus's face from a couple of weeks before, outside in Grape Street. She had thought he looked shifty then, or angry, or nervous.

Now she realised he had looked embarrassed. *Guilty.*

Posie had thought then that something odd was going on.

'I thought all of this was strange from the start, this whole kidnapping plot: those fat nannies you employed, the requests to never let Dolly leave my side. You know I almost involved the police? But I gave you the benefit of the doubt, assuming you were acting in Dolly's best interests.'

'I was! I *am*!'

'No you're not! You're keeping her a virtual prisoner in the house, scared that she's going to run away from you. You've sent away the only person she had around whom she enjoyed to be with, who made the whole child-bearing and child-raising thing bearable, which, by the way, she hates. You're so scared of losing her and your unborn prince that you've brought in these awful women, and you even had me get in on the act! Getting *me* to keep Dolly "safe" at my side all the time, so she wouldn't leave. It stinks! You make me sick!'

'Come on, now,' muttered Rufus, but Posie could see that she was right: he was flushing a bright and unattractive shade of red.

'I'll tell you what to do, if you want to keep her,' hissed Posie, seeing Dolly begin to weave her way back through the room, bearing three plates like prizes. 'Find this French girl, Violette. Pay for her and for Dolly to spend one week in Paris, no expense spared. Pay for everything. Let her go.'

'Are you joking? Have you lost your mind? She won't come back to me!'

Posie nodded, staring at her friend. 'She will. She loves you, and your girls, even if she *is* fed up with the lot of you. You've got to let her have her own time, space, experiences. Otherwise, I promise you, she will leave you. And then she won't come back. She'll find a way. This can't go on, Rufus. It's terrible!'

Rufus had now gone very pale, and Dolly was upon them. She was already eating.

'Sorry, I'm starvin'. Anyone like one?'

Both Posie and Rufus shook their heads, bound together in secrecy and silence by their horrible conversation which would never be repeated.

397

'I say, look who Alaric's talkin' to!'

And Posie saw where Dolly was indicating. Further down at the end of the room Silvia Hanro had stripped out of her black furs and she was no longer alone at her table. She was whispering something to Alaric. Their heads were very close, and they seemed to be sharing a cigarette. Alaric was smiling.

It was the smile from the photograph.

Alaric seemed to sense Posie's stare, and he looked up at her quickly, waving easily.

Posie waved back. But there was a light in his green eyes which Posie had never seen there before, and which she didn't like. Not one little tiny bit.

The ominous feeling was back: that horrible dream sprung to mind again, wretchedly.

'Look, darling, there's something I need to tell you.'

Posie remembered her words to Dolly of not five minutes before when she had been talking about Silvia:

She has nothing I want. Nothing at all.

Posie swallowed, hoping they still rang true.

****

Thank you for joining Posie Parker

Enjoyed *Murder of a Movie Star* (A Posie Parker Mystery #5)? Here's what you can do next.

If you could take a moment to leave a short review on the platform where you purchased the book, it would be immensely helpful.

Your reviews play a significant role in spreading the word about the series and assisting new readers in discovering it.

In addition to "Murder of a Movie Star", Posie's other intriguing cases are available in various formats to suit your preference. You can find all the books, listed in chronological order here: https://www.amazon.com/author/lbhathaway

They are available in e-book and paperback formats, as well as in Audiobook format for those who prefer to listen.

Don't miss out! Take a moment to follow on Amazon and/or subscribe to the newsletter:

1. **Follow on Amazon:** Visit www.amazon.com/author/lbhathaway and click on "+Follow" button.

2. **Subscribe to the Newsletter:** Simply visit www.lbhathaway.com and enter your email address in the subscription box. By subscribing, you'll receive exclusive content, behind-the-scenes insights, and special offers straight to your inbox.

Historical Note

All of the characters in this book are fictional, unless specifically mentioned below. Timings, general political events, weather conditions and places (and descriptions of places) are all historically accurate to the best of my knowledge, save for the exceptions listed below.

For those interested in British silent films at this time, see the fuller note at the end of this book, but otherwise please note that I have simply tried to give the reader a *flavour* of the essence of British cinema in 1923 and of how I understand Worton Hall Studios might have been at the time (also see note 9, below, in bold).

However much research is undertaken, there are bound to be omissions or contradictions which creep in.

I am also aware that the term 'movie' and 'movie star' were slang terms in the early 1920s, and both were used interchangeably in Great Britain with the words 'film', 'film star' and 'moving pictures' (or more usually, 'the pictures'), as opposed to in America, where the term 'movies' and 'movie star' by this time were the more usual references.

As ever, both Posie's work address (Grape Street, Bloomsbury, WC1) and her home address round the corner (Museum Chambers, WC1) in London are both very real, although you might have to do a bit of imagining to find her there.

1. July 1923 was a scorching month in London, punctuated by huge storms; one of the hottest summers ever. The thunderstorm of the evening of 9th July 1923 was staggering in its force and is recorded even now as being a storm of rare intensity. By the end of the month, however, when this story is set, thunderstorms were on the wane.

2. The Zeppelin raid Dolly refers to in Chapter One did take place, on 8th September 1915. A bomb exploded just in front of the Dolphin pub in Bloomsbury, and then caught fire. Three men died in the bombing and many were injured. A clock still stands inside the Dolphin pub today, whose hands stopped forever at the time of the blast (10.40 pm).

3. The real-life film Dolly refers to, *Love, Life and Laughter* (starring the most famous British movie star of the day, Betty Balfour), was indeed the toast of British cinema in June 1923. It was produced by George Pearson, mainly at the Islington Studios, a rival to Worton Hall. Believed lost, a copy of the film was found in 2014 in a Dutch film archive and is now retained by the British Film Industry (http://www.bfi.org.uk).

4. The ice cream shop I have described in Chapter One, Caspari's, in Covent Garden, is fictional.

5. Nathan's Costumiers (properly entitled 'Berman's and Nathan's' but known by many in the trade simply as 'Nathan's') as first appear in Chapter Three were very real – the premium supplier of theatrical costumes in the trade for both stage and film work – but I have no idea what colour their vans were in real life. The blue-and-gold livery of the van is a flight of fancy of my own.

6. Sunstar Films as referred to throughout this story is my own invention, as is the film I describe being made at the Worton Hall Studios (*Henry the King*) during this time.

7. The character of Producer/Director Brian Langley is also fictional, although the reference made by Silvia Hanro (in Chapter Five) to film stars basically being 'owned' by their studios and being creatures of their Producers is taken from the (real-life) character of Producer Cecil Hepworth (1874–1953), who believed exactly this of his film stars in this period.

8. The 'marriage bar' I have included (meaning married women were automatically excluded from jobs in some professions in England, most notably the civil service) was already coming into place at the time of this novel but did not affect the film industry. This is a piece of convenient artistic licence I have taken.

9. **A Brief Note on Worton Hall Studios and G.B. ('Bertie') Samuelson.**
   Worton Hall Studios were based at Worton Hall in Isleworth, one hour from London. This lovely white-painted house (a former stately home) with its nine-acre estate was bought in 1914 by the maverick real-life (and larger than life) Film Producer George 'Bertie' Samuelson (who appears in this story as himself). It was retained by him until 1928.

   He famously created a cutting-edge film studio, mainly in the gardens, but also by utilising the whole house for dressing rooms, canteens, wardrobe departments etc. Many important and ground-breaking silent films were made at Worton Hall, especially in the period of the First World War. The studios were active right up until the 1950s.

   The landscape of the place as described (with its

background of farm and greenhouses) is correct, as are the descriptions of the internal rooms of the old house, including the location of the bedrooms for the actors and actresses to stay in, which were all situated on the top two floors of the house. However, I am uncertain of the exact layout with regard to the location of the ballroom, canteen, cutting rooms, viewing rooms and Mr Samuelson's office. Please be aware that the locations given and descriptions of such rooms are due in good part to my own imagination.

10. As mentioned by Silvia Hanro in Chapters Three and Six, Leichner stage make-up was a necessity on film sets during this time, and had to be applied all over the face and body to be effective. By 1923 (with the advances in more sophisticated set lighting) the make-up was an orange, or a skin-coloured tone (Leichner no 1). This is markedly in contrast with the early days of silent films when it was necessary for actors to use a dark red make-up (Leichner no 5) all over their faces and bodies so they would appear white under the blueish glare of the lights used (mercury vapour lamps, and then later Klieg lights).

11. The 'Klieg eye' effect caused by such early lamps (as referred to by Tom Moran in Chapter Seven) was, unfortunately, very real. For more on this see Matthew Sweet's *Shepperton Babylon: The Lost Worlds of British Cinema* where he quotes from Joan Morgan's novel, *Camera!* (1940) at page 19.

12. Silvia Hanro refers to 'extras' (a body or cast of actors making up crowd scenes) in Chapter Four. They are then referred to occasionally in the rest of the story in the same way. However, in 1923 'extras' were actually referred to as 'supers'. I have used the current term rather than the historically accurate one to make

things easier for the modern reader. Please note that the arrangement with the extras hanging around all day at Worton Hall is an invention of my own, although they *did* have to queue up at the end of the day for their wages to be paid out in petty cash.

13. The Royal Oak pub, where some of the extras eat their lunch in this story is real. The pub is still there, on the Worton Road at Isleworth. It was used by film extras and film labourers for lunch and snacks, and sometimes even by the film stars themselves, despite the in-house canteen at Worton Hall.

14. The hugely talented actress Meggie Albanesi (1899–1923) as referred to throughout this novel was very real, her life cut tragically short in December 1923 when she died aged twenty-four. She was the toast of the London stage and appeared in six silent movies, all of which are now lost. She is commemorated by a small stone plaque in the Foyer at St Martin's Theatre, London. The play *The Lilies of the Field* which is described in this book was indeed the hit show of summer 1923, playing to packed-out audiences at the Ambassadors Theatre throughout the continuing heatwave, including to the newly-married Duke and Duchess of York. She also frequented Ciro's, the café mentioned in this novel, night after night, apparently on the look-out for possible suitors.

Please note that as far as I am aware Meggie Albanesi did *not* have a stalker in her lifetime, and that Hector Mallow is an invention of my own. She was, however, the object of much adulation and adoration, both during and after her own lifetime, with the Producer Basil Dean obsessively (and rather creepily) scouring upcoming talent for a 'new' Meggie Albanesi lookalike after her death. This hunt for a new Meggie Albanesi was well known in theatre circles, and even Ivor Novello had his eyes peeled for just such a replacement. For more, see *Meggie Albanesi: A Life in the Theatre* by Frances Gray (Society for Theatre Research, London, 2010).

15. The Foundling Hospital in Bloomsbury Fields (as referred to in Chapter Nine and again in Chapters Twelve and Eighteen) existed and stood in central London from the eighteenth century until 1926, when poor air and a massive build-up of housing all around it made a move out to the Surrey countryside necessary.

16. At Chapter Nine we learn about Pamela Hanro's past as a suffragette. The arson attack described really did take place in February 1913, when a string of arson attacks were instigated by suffragettes across London, including at various recreational buildings at the public park of Kew Gardens. The arson attack on the Tea House/Pavilion at Kew was ultimately never directly attributed to the suffragettes, through lack of proof.

17. The description of Bute Street in South Kensington in Chapter Twelve (where Pamela Hanro lives) is accurate, albeit that the shop names are different (excepting the Zetland Arms). Now, as then, it was a small and useful commercial thoroughfare.

18. At Chapter Thirteen there is a reference to the real-life Cecil Court (next to Leicester Square in London) being called 'Flicker Alley' by those who frequented it, as it was so notoriously connected to those in the film industry. This was indeed the case in the 1920s, and I owe the historical reference to Matthew Sweet's *Shepperton Babylon: The Lost Worlds of British Cinema*.

19. At Chapter Thirteen Pamela Hanro plays 'The Teddy Bears' Picnic' on the gramophone. Please note that while the song could have been played on a gramophone at this point (it was composed and recorded by John Walter Bratton in New York in 1907) the lyrics as we know them were not 'added' until 1932.

20. While the marriage of the Duke of York and Lady Elizabeth Bowes-Lyon in April 1923 was indeed the society wedding of the year, and featured heavily in the press at the time (especially the wedding dress which was absolutely cutting-edge for its time, and served as a model which was much copied, up and down the land) the actual magazine cover I have described in Chapter Fourteen in *The Lady* is fictional.

21. The cocktail mentioned at Chapter Seventeen, the 'Bee's Knees,' is correct as far as its alcoholic content goes, but it was much more fashionable in America at this time, rather than in England.

22. The police medal awarded to Inspector Lovelace at Chapter Seventeen, 'the Blue Plume', is an invention of my own.

23. At Chapter Eighteen the Billie Carleton case of 1918 is mentioned and this is historically accurate; it was the media sensation of the time, highlighting the prevalence of (particularly) cocaine as the drug of choice for many actors and film stars and celebrities. In the same chapter the reference to the sensational film *Cocaine* (directed by Graham Cutts) which was released in Britain to both acclaim and horror in 1922, is also accurate. I owe both of these references to Matthew Sweet's *Shepperton Babylon: The Lost Worlds of British Cinema*.

24. The Middlesex Hospital on Mortimer Street as referred to at Chapters Nineteen and Twenty was indeed real: a teaching hospital from 1745, it closed in 2005.

25. Please note that the London telephone numbers and exchange numbers given here are completely fictional.

* * * *

A Short Note on British Silent Movies and Movie Stars in 1923*

This is a murky world which you enter at your own peril, a precarious make-believe world stuffed full of chancers, predators, pretty girls (and boys). All topped off with a good heavy sprinkling of drugs, sex and death.

From a historical research point of view, what can be agreed on is that the world of the British silent movies is largely now lost to us due to the fact that hardly any of these films actually survive. It is estimated that more than eighty per cent of the British films produced between the start of the twentieth century and the late 1920s have been lost. In fact, the British Film Institute keeps a 'most wanted' list.

I was frankly amazed at the lack of regard for what should have been an important archive; films which have disappeared due to careless loss, or, more frequently, large-scale destruction of the physical reels of film.

By the late 1920s there was a sense among many that silent movies had become worthless once the 'Talkies' had replaced them, and some films were lost that way. Other films were lost due to a financial need to melt down the nitrate stock to extract the silver contained therein (typically when a film studio had gone bust) or to aid the war effort (at the time of the Second World War).

1. The British Film Industry in 1923

The British movie world at the time this story takes place was doing its level best to produce first-class pictures, but the reality was that it couldn't compete with the glamour and high budgets of the increasingly popular American films (which the British movie-going public lapped up, although in 1923 we are still a few years away from the star attractions of Clara Bow or Louise Brookes).

By 1923 many British film studios were struggling to stay afloat, and many were not succeeding.

While British cinematic efforts had been pioneering and far-reaching from the start of the twentieth century, the race to stay level with the American market had already been lost by the time of the First World War in 1914 due to a combination of factors, listed below.

1. The Hollywood studios were backed by huge businesses, seeing an opportunity for investment, and the British Film Industry was rather led (and paid for) by one-off entrepreneurial individuals. They simply didn't have the same budgets. As a result, much of the British output was very reliant on the world of the theatre and quite unambitious in scope; stage-sets and scenery were often simply reworked from the stage for the big screen.

Much of the work off-camera was rather haphazard too, and it was often a case of 'all hands to the decks', with the Producer Cecil Hepworth expecting his leading stars to 'put in their hours in the developing and drying rooms if they were not required for filming' (Matthew Sweet's *Shepperton Babylon: The Lost Worlds of British Cinema*, Chapter One).

2. There was also a prohibitive system in place whereby British cinema companies took 'block bookings' of fashionable American films way in advance of their release dates, meaning that sometimes British films were not even given available showing space, even if they were good.

3. In addition, the British studios did not receive any financial impetus or encouragement from the British Government, who were tightening up in all areas of the economy, rather than trying to encourage the arts (this all changed in 1927, when the British Government introduced a requirement for British cinemas to show a particular quota of British films for ten years, the so-called 'Quota Quickies').

Please note that in 1923 we have not yet reached the days of the very established London studios at Isleworth, Ealing, Pinewood, Shepperton or the famous Gainsborough Studios at Islington (where Alfred Hitchcock plied his craft at the start of his career).

Instead, there were the Hepworth studios at Walton-on-Thames, Oswald Stoll's Cricklewood studios, and Bertie Samuelson's studios at Worton Hall. These studios produced films either using the money and expertise of their owners (such as Stoll or Hepworth), or else they would bring in professionals from outside, sometimes setting up whole new companies in order to fund ventures, which is what Bertie Samuelson did, frequently.

In the year 1923 several companies were shooting films at Worton Hall, either working with Samuelson, or renting the place from him (*British-Super Films*, the *Napoleon Film Company* and the *Samuelson Film Manufacturing Company*).

2. British Movie Stars in 1923

While there were 'famous' British actors and actresses, there was nothing like the star system of America in place.

Names which stick out from this time are: Betty Balfour, Lilian Hall-Davis, Chrissie White, Henry Edwards, Stewart Rome, Ivor Novello, Flora Le Breton, Gladys Cooper, Violet Hopson.

Please note that the impossibly handsome matinee idol Ivor Novello (who drifts into this story at the party scene in Chapter Twenty-Nine) had not yet come to the forefront of British cinema, with his first big picture being released in summer 1923 (although he was already well known for his musical contributions). It would not be until the mid-twenties that he would become the most pre-eminent actor of the period, an icon of cinema in films such as *The Rat* and *The Lodger* (1925 and 1927 respectively).

In 1923 while many of the movie stars were well-known actors drawn from the stage or music-hall, many were chancers and total unknowns who happened to be given a lucky break by a Producer or Director, with the occasional plucky aristocrat thrown in for good measure (for example Lady Diana Manners in *The Glorious Adventure* of 1922).

On the whole, in 1923 actors and actresses came and went with quite some regularity, and most of the names of the 'famous' film stars of the time have now long been forgotten.

Many actors (Violet Hopson and Ivy Duke are examples) were big stars for a while in the 1920s, only to lose their fame within a few short years, relegated to working as extras or taking bit-parts in the 'Talkies' in the 1930s, and it is not inconceivable that my character of Mark Paris could have been 'famous' at the time of the First World War, only to be relegated to working behind the scenes in the movie world less than a decade later.

What seems strange to us now is that movie stars in the 1920s were often chosen or 'discovered' because of their resemblance to another, more famous actor or actress; see for example the discovery of Chrissie White by Cecil Hepworth, and (later) Victoria Hopper by Basil Dean.

Stars were very often 're-named' for the movies by a Producer, even if they had enjoyed a successful stage career previously (Cecil Hepworth was famous for re-naming his stars, such as 'his' famous actor Stewart Rome, and would even chase his actors through the courts to protect these names).

While the characters in this story are fictional, the allusion throughout to the use of drugs (cocaine particularly) among film stars in the 1920s was a common theme.

****

(*This note is my own summary, and is not, of course, exhaustive nor meant to be a detailed guide).

Acknowledgements and Further Reading

This book is dedicated to my sister, Heidi. A real-life superstar.

My thanks go to the usual suspects: Marco and our small daughter, my parents and our wider family.

As part of the research for this story two books clearly stand out. These are:

1. Matthew Sweet's *Shepperton Babylon: The Lost Worlds of British Cinema* (Faber and Faber, London 2005); and

2. Ed Harris' *Britain's Forgotten Film Factory: The Story of Isleworth Studios* (Amberley Press, 2015).

Please note that this story is a work of fiction and does not in any way seek to replicate any of the scenarios listed in the books above or to draw details from them other than those specifically mentioned in the Historical Note. Needless to say, any mistakes remaining are my own.

* * * *

About the Author

Cambridge-educated, British-born L.B. Hathaway writes historical fiction. She worked as a lawyer at Lincoln's Inn in London for almost a decade before becoming a full-time writer. She is a lifelong fan of detective novels set in the Golden Age of Crime, and is an ardent Agatha Christie devotee.

Her other interests, in no particular order, are: very fast downhill skiing, theatre-going, drinking strong tea, Tudor history, exploring castles and generally trying to cram as much into life as possible.

The Posie Parker series of cosy crime novels span the 1920s. They each combine a core central mystery, an exploration of the reckless glamour of the age and a feisty protagonist who you would love to have as your best friend.

Get in touch with L.B. Hathaway or follow her on social media:

author@lbhathaway.com

Newsletter sign up:
https://www.lbhathaway.com

Goodreads:
https://www.goodreads.com/lbhathaway

Twitter:
https://twitter.com/LbHathaway

Facebook:
https://m.facebook.com/L-B-Hathaway-books-1423516601228019/

Made in the USA
Las Vegas, NV
26 September 2023

78160153R00246